A BROKEN HEART

"I want to go home." Impatiently, Elizabeth pulled her hands free, then swung her legs over the side of the chaise-longue. "I found out why Lord DeLacey asked to marry me, you see, and it won't do."

"Oh?" said Patsy. "What reason did *Harry* give you?"

"I'm the way the earl is repaying a debt he feels he owes my father," Elizabeth quavered miserably. "We saved his life at Waterloo, only I didn't recognize him because he looks so different now. I've never been so humiliated. If he'd told me the truth from the beginning, it wouldn't be so dreadful, for I remember him very clearly, and worried so about him and wondered what had become of him, but he didn't." She straightened her shoulders. "I will not be used in such a way, d'you understand? I will not!

"It was all a hum, just as Harry said in the beginning. I should've listened right then, but I didn't want to— not with Richard looking at me the way he was, his eyes all warm and smiling." She lay back with a little sob, staring at the ceiling. "Being in love isn't nice. It isn't nice at all. It's *dreadful.*"

*   *   *

ZEBRA'S REGENCY ROMANCES
DAZZLE AND DELIGHT

DeLacey's Angel

Monique Ellis

ZEBRA BOOKS
KENSINGTON PUBLISHING CORP.

ZEBRA BOOKS are published by

Kensington Publishing Corp.
850 Third Avenue
New York, NY 10022

First Printing: June, 1995

Printed in the United States of America

For those who kept me going
when the going was hardest:

Kate E., Kathy A., Helen P., and—of course—Jim,
who read, proofed, discussed, cooked, did dishes, and never
complained if I came to bed at five in the morning.

"She seemed a splendid angel, newly drest,
Save wings, for heaven . . ."
John Keats
"The Eve of St. Agnes"

Prologue

At first the colonel was aware only of the stench—rich farm soil soaked by the carnage of a desperate battle desperately fought, and the sharp tang of gunpowder mingling with the heavy smoke of combat. Sound came next—moans, pleas for water, squeals of maimed horses, persistent as the drip of summer rain, and rustlings and mutters as annoying as mosquitoes buzzing on a still summer night by the Thames.

Then came the cold, bone-deep, a shuddering thing with a life of its own, so sharp he thought he would never be warm again no matter if he lived or died.

Still his eyes remained closed, whether from lassitude or an inability to open he couldn't tell, but the world beyond his lids was dark. Night had fallen. It was over, at least 'til morning. But who had won the day, Wellington or the Corsican? Dear God—who had won?

The agonizing weight crushing one of his legs was all too clear, however. He blessed the pain for its reassurance, and assessed the rest of his body.

There was another leg throbbing just above the knee, its foot painfully cramped. They were no ghost-images, or he would have bled to death hours since. His thoughts crept upward. Flanks, hips, torso seemed well enough, considering. A hand *clutched something hard and cold. A saber hilt? Possible. At least there was a hand, and that meant an arm. And there seemed to be another, tangled in something rough. And a head. It was definitely there, blinding in its proclamation of existence.*

A moan echoed in his ears. He opened his eyes at last, searching for the source. He was alone, churned earth and an overturned gun carriage his first horizon. The moan was his then—another thing he owned.

Around him darkness stretched, just as he had pictured it, and above, here and there, a star. In that darkness figures scurried, clutching half-shuttered lanterns and crude sacks as they picked their way among the dying and the dead. Flashes of green and red and brilliant blue, gleams of gold and silver flickered on the periphery of his vision, and ghastly faces and contorted bodies like so much cordwood flung about by a careless giant. The gleaners of death were out, seeking their tawdry fortunes among the wrecked youth of a continent.

There was a stronger glow of light. The scrabbling noises approached, as clearly signifying he was the next victim of a conscienceless vulture as if it had been announced with the diction of a Kean. He lay very still, trying not to breathe, waiting. His wrist was seized.

"Hold the lantern higher, Jeremy," a voice floated. "I've found anoth—"

The colonel reared up with a roar and clouted the hidden face, sending the hovering figure to sprawl in a tangle of muddied petticoats and dark cape. Confused, he peered from the jumble of female garments to a boy of some fourteen years staring down the barrel of a cocked horse pistol, eyes wide with fear, a lantern clutched in his other hand.

"That was a bacon-brained thing to do," a distinctly English female voice protested. "Now the back of my togs're as damp as the front. I feel a positive dishrag! Jeremy, uncock the pistol. This muddle-witted Frog-bait is one of our own." Then, "You're like as peas in a pod," she chuckled, misinterpreting the colonel's croak. "Old Duro did it! A close run thing, I've heard, but

*Boney's well and truly rompéd at last. They say he's scuttling
for France like a crab to its hole. Now, sir, if I try to help you,
d'you promise not to dish up more of the home-brewed?"*

He tried again to speak, to apologize to this apparition that
could not exist in such a place at such a time. The best he
could manage was another harsh croak.

And then the figure was kneeling in the lantern light, wiping
his face with a cool water-soaked cloth, trickling a few precious
drops between his parched lips.

Dear God, he'd never seen anything so beautiful in his
life. A girl, perhaps seventeen, perhaps eighteen, dark hair
straggling in elf locks around her pale, mud-grimed face, brown
cape billowing behind her like an angel's wings, eyes great
pools of darkness into which one could sink forever. The gentle
fingers closed around his wrist again. Where had such a child
learned pulses existed, let alone how to take them?

"This one's not as bad as he looks. Get Papa," the soft voice
commanded. "No, take the lantern, Jeremy. We'll be perfectly
safe here in the dark. Bring Charles and Robert as well, and
Andrew if you can find him. That blasted contraption must
be shifted before Papa can see to this one's injuries, and it
looks heavy as Queen Charlotte's boots."

The light floated away like some fanciful Vauxhall artifice
as the colonel wrapped his fingers tightly around the girl's
wrist.

"Don't leave me," he managed. "For God's sake, don't stir
from this spot!"

He could hear the smile in her voice as she said, "Don't
worry—I shan't leave you to the scavengers. What they're doing
is reprehensible, of course, but one must sympathize, for they're
all quite poor, I fear. Papa will be here in a moment.

"He's a doctor, you see," the girl prattled on soothingly,
"and we're all here because he knew how terrible this battle
would be, and the army would never have enough doctors or
nurses to handle all the casualties. So we gathered supplies
and came to Dover from Devon—all except my brother John,

*who stayed behind to mind the practice, and Mama and the
little ones—and then Papa hired a boat to cross the Channel.*

"I'd best apologize for talking cant, which is most unladylike,
I know, but it's impossible not to with so many brothers—I've
seven, you see, and no sisters at all—besides being so much
more lively, but don't tell Papa or he'll scold, and there isn't time
for that because there are so many who require his assistance and
he mustn't think bringing me was a mistake because it's not
as if I haven't helped him for simply ages at home, but I've
tried him to the limit as I was to stay at our lodgings in Brussels
and roll bandages, only I snuck into the wagon and hid because
I knew he'd need me, and he went off like one of Whinyates's
rockets when he found me only there wasn't time to take me
back, thank goodness, for I'm most useful and not the least
afraid, and now he would—"

And then the muddy fields of La Haye Sainte close by the
little Walloon village of Waterloo faded from the colonel's sight,
and he sank into a welcoming darkness.

One

"How the devil many physicians with seven sons and but a single daughter can there be in Devonshire, Harry? It's not that big of a place."

"Still nothing?" Harry Beckenham, Viscount Marley-bourne leaned back in his chair beside the fire in his friend's study, red-gold hair glinting in the ruddy light, clear blue eyes staring into his brandy as he eased the stump of his left arm, lost at Salamanca in '12. The blasted thing still pained him when the weather turned uncooperative, for all it was fully healed at last. "Well, I can't say I'm surprised. It's a fool's mission."

Listening to DeLacey reminded the viscount all too clearly of himself a scant four years before, recently returned from the nightmare of the Peninsula, weak and in pain from his wounds and about to descend into an even worse nightmare. The man was obsessed, just as he had been. Leave it to the petticoats to destroy a man's sanity.

"How can you be so sure she really existed, Richard?" the tall former major now inquired with patient reasonableness. "The entire thing is patently unlikely. A young girl of gentle birth on a battlefield? Ridiculous! Besides which, if your paragon existed anywhere but in your imagination, you'd've found her by now.''

Richard DeLacey—Baron Monfort, Viscount Stanley, Viscount Rochemont, Earl of Rochedale—turned impatiently from the window where he stared blindly past dingy amber draperies. A dispirited drizzle had been turning the extensive grounds of his Palladian mansion on the outskirts of London into a glistening quagmire for the past sennight. Perforce housebound, he was sick of it.

His ebony cane struck impatiently on the dark oaken floor from which all carpets had been removed as his left leg awkwardly followed him around.

"Dammit man, if you'd been chained in hell and glimpsed a vision of heaven, don't you think you'd remember it rather clearly?" he demanded.

"Visions of heaven as observed from hell aren't necessarily reliable. In fact, they're most often competing visions of hell one can't recognize as such because of clouded vision. Heaven, if it exists at all, is more likely found where and when one least expects it, and wearing an improbable face."

"As on a battlefield."

Richard DeLacey limped to the matching burgundy wing chair beside the crackling hearth, his ebony cane tapping with a halting rhythm, his left leg dragging slightly.

The mild concussion was long over, of course. The bullet wound in his right thigh had healed well enough and, as with Beckenham's stump, now troubled him only when the weather was excessively cold or it rained—as on this day in the early fall of 1816, a year and more after the climactic battle of Waterloo. His left leg, broken in several places by a gun carriage's weight, was another matter. Shortened and slightly twisted, it alternated between the merely painful and the acutely agonizing. The surprise was that he still had it at all.

"She exists. I know she does," he insisted, golden hawk's eyes softening at the memory, "but she was off with the pistol-toting youngster before I had the wit to ask her name. Then her father started on me, and I lost interest in anything but oblivion. But, she was there, as real as you or I, and a damned sight more real than the baby-talking hothouse flowers my grandmother seems determined to thrust on my notice."

The thirty-five-year-old DeLacey slapped his ebony cane irritably into the rack at the side of his chair, grimacing as he eased his loose-limbed frame into the seat, left leg stiffly extended. "Giles found me in Brussels, propped against a pile of muskets in the Grand' Place and out of my head with fever, and took over, and that was that."

"Where is he?" Beckenham asked after a moment spent contemplating his friend—of medium height, too thin for all his powerful shoulders, his kindly face pale and far too deeply etched by lines of pain and fatigue for so young a man. Damn all Frogs to hell, and damn the curst diplomats who'd dillied and dallied and sent Boney to so insecure a place as Elba, and then hadn't the sense to keep proper guard over him. Waterloo, and its carnage, had been avoidable. "Upstairs sleeping off his travels on your behalf? Or, was he off at dawn to badger the Horse Guards for reactivation?"

"Giles? Neither. Still scouring Devon for my angel and her brothers, or possibly on the road home."

"How is the lad? I haven't seen him since—well, it's been a while."

"The same irrepressible scamp as ever, though he's no lad these days. What Quatre Bras didn't accomplish, Waterloo did. Forget his age. Giles Fortescue's a man grown. He earned his promotion to lieutenant. Remember how it was after our first battle?"

"Only too well," Beckenham admitted with a wry twist to his lips. "Was it you held my head, or I yours?"

"We took it in turns, hiding behind a supply wagon so no one would see us. They could hear us plain enough, though. What Johnny-Raws we were! Giles did well. Rather green about the gills is all, but I've told you that before. More bottom than sense, that's our Giles, and the devil's own luck. Came through with only his hair mussed and his lace tarnished. I remember that much from the Grand' Place—that, and his filthy grinning face when he found me."

Harry Beckenham nodded absently, staring into the leaping flames, imagining fortresses and redoubts among the glowing coals. Some memories never eased, no matter the distance or time. The flames fleetingly constructed a face for his consideration, its slight pout entrancing, then shifted to a gargoyle's mask. He shuddered.

Around them the shabby study loomed, oak-paneled, book-lined, graced with hunting prints and watercolors of sun-struck landscapes, a pair of pedestaled Roman busts hinting their presence in shadowed corners. The room was a comfortable and comforting haven on this somber day, well away from the cold elegance and overblown luxury that was the remainder of Rochedale House.

He detested the palatial monstrosity as much as he suspected DeLacey did. Why the man put up with his grandmother's constant vagaries of redecoration he couldn't fathom, but there it was: Richard DeLacey had a sweeter, more accommodating nature than was entirely good for him.

This time it was the entry and state reception rooms—a phantasmagoria to equal Prinny's Marine Pavilion at

Brighton, complete to a bloody domed ceiling set with colored glass chips, the whole so splashed with gold leaf and red Chinese lacquer it was as if a mad Midas and an eccentric Mandarin had been united in their dotage to touch where they would. What some men permitted the females who hung on their sleeves never ceased to amaze Beckenham. Even his brother-in-law showed evidence of the madness that infected DeLacey. Once, even he had.

"Good thing Giles found you," he threw in, "but, the rest of it? Well, perhaps it happened, but I doubt it was as you remember it."

DeLacey shoved an impatient hand through his thick, dark hair. "I know how it appears to all of you, even Giles," he admitted. "The maunderings of a disordered mind, and that's putting it kindly. It's not, though. I'd risk my last groat on that. I've *got* to find them. At the very least, I owe her father an immense debt. Without his intervention, I doubt I'd've lasted the night. Certainly I'd've lost my blasted leg."

Beckenham nodded his understanding, if not his agreement.

Almost of an age, the two men had been together at school, and later in the Peninsula. The friendship remained unbroken when the viscount was invalided out following Salamanca, leaving DeLacey to slog through the grizzly campaigns of 1812–1815 and their interruption of dancing at the Congress of Vienna during Napoleon's fleeting holiday on Elba. Now, with the Corsican Monster securely incarcerated on the island of Saint Helena and their army careers permanently ended by injury, the two former officers saw a great deal of each other.

"What'll you do if you find her?" Beckenham asked, not for the first time during the past eighteen months. "Limp up to her and say: 'I'm Rochedale, and richer

than Golden Ball. You saved my life at La Haye Sainte.
I offer you my lands, my title, my fortune, and my inestimable self in recompense. You won't notice the leg after
a bit, and in the interim you can make do with emptying
my coffers.' "

"Something along those lines, I suppose. I haven't
thought much beyond finding her, except if she's still
unspoken for—"

"A fiend from hell would've seemed an angel of mercy
on that battlefield! If you do find her, prepare yourself
for a shock. Daylight engenders clear vision. Your
'angel' is likely to prove a jade, like all the others of
her sex."

"I won't be in for any surprises," DeLacey smiled.
"In such a place and time, true character shines
through. It's not the same as Lady Sefton's where you
encountered—" He broke off with an embarrassed
clearing of his throat.

The girl's name had been Guinevere or Genevieve
or something equally medieval. Harry, along with a
horde of others, dangled after her just prior to their
departure for Portugal in April of '09. They'd had an
understanding of some sort, of that the earl was certain,
though Harry had maintained persistent silence on the
matter. Then, when Harry returned to England following the loss of his arm at Salamanca, nothing.

"I'm sorry," DeLacey now said hesitantly. "I know
how mention of that period pains you."

"Doesn't pain me in the least," Beckenham retorted,
blue eyes cold steel in the firelight, the faded saber scar
running from hairline to mouth barely visible. "I just
hate to see a grown man supposedly possessed of his
senses making a fool of himself over a female. They're
none of 'em worth it. At least those of the muslin company are honest in their requirements. It's not the matter of the sale or the goods offered, my friend," he

grumbled on, "but the matter of price and terms that distinguishes muslin from silk. If you're truly in the market for a wife, present yourself at Marlborough House tonight and offer for the first passable chit you see. You'll stand as much hope of happiness by that road as any other. Perhaps more. Fewer illusions."

"It's not always that way. Look at your sister and Rawdon, constantly in each other's pockets and as happy when they're at odds as when they're in agreement."

"You look at 'em! I've got to face their beaming phizes over the breakfast cups each morning unless I hide in my rooms."

"You're staying with Rawdon and Louisa this trip, then?"

"Opening the barn on Berkeley Square isn't worth it, and they do leave me pretty much to myself. Don't mistake me: I *like* Rawdon, and Louisa's well enough so long as she keeps her place, but they're unconscionably early risers, both of 'em. Sugary doses of marital bliss at seven in the morning don't suit my temperament."

A log collapsed on the grate, sending a shower of sparks over the fender and up the flue. Beckenham leapt to his feet, stomping the intricate tile work until the last winking dots subsided into sullen dark smudges. "Green wood," he scolded. "Ought to have at your supplier, or else change to coal. Safer."

"I'm my own supplier. Have it carted in from my place in Kent. I prefer a wood fire in here. Reminds me of my father. Why not stay with Lady Cheltenham, then," DeLacey inquired, changing the subject. The truth of the matter was, his grandmother detested wood fires. Maintaining one in his study was a small mark of independence. "She'd be glad to have you."

"Good Lord, man! I adore the old flibbertigibbet," Beckenham protested, returning to his chair, "but staying with Aunt Daffy would be like wading through an impenetrable murk every minute of the day, plus apprising the old dear each time I intend to take a breath—let alone do anything more daring. Aside from which, she lectures me constantly on my duty to beget an heir. Stay with Aunt Daffy? I thank you, no! Even the treacle dished up by Louisa and Rawdon is preferable."

"You could always stop by here."

"And subject myself to the equally importunate urgings of your grandmother? Don't be a fool. She and my aunt are bosom bows. I'd have the pair of 'em after me then. How about your descending on Aunt Daffy with me instead?"

"I'd be in the same spot," DeLacey acknowledged with a chuckle, "plus having Grandmama cutting me dead half the time for the insult I'd've handed her by not stopping here, and destroying my peace in every other manner she could invent the rest."

Beckenham grinned in response. "Dowager countess been badgering you to get leg-shackled, has she?"

"My grandmother? Badger? No, it's much more subtle than that. She sighs whenever she spots a child, any child, no matter how disreputably grubby and puling. Can you imagine what it's like to drive through the streets with her? At each urchin perceived, her bosom heaves with soul-wrenching sighs, and it's a considerable bosom! Then comes the sideward glance, infinitely calculating, infinitely reproachful. Am I properly cognizant of her distress? Adequately humbled? Sufficiently chastised? Will I be receptive *this* time?

"Then the furtive tear glistens. The trembling hand rises to sweep it away, so surreptitious it calls attention to itself as if it were the Colossus of Rhodes.

"Within moments, some tremulous comment concerning her advancing years and increasing decrepitude, her longing to hold her first great-grandchild in her arms. Decrepitude? She'll outlive us all, just to prove she can. No, a frontal attack would be preferable to Grandmama's subtleties.

"And then, there're the infernal morning callers. If I've had one mindless doll-faced miss of impeccable lineage and impressive dot trotted out for my approval, I've had dozens," the former colonel snorted. "What Grandmama considers suitable bride material is enough to make any red-blooded man run for his life—that, or take it in despair."

"Come to Marleybourne with me. I leave at the end of the week. There'll be no blasted females to tell either of us what to do, that I promise. Chased 'em off long ago."

"Even the squire's daughter? You know the one I mean. Little imp was forever following you about and getting into scrapes."

"Patsy Worth? An interfering prattle-box, like all her sex, gave up on me a few months after my return from the Peninsula. Won't even speak to me now. Patsy's become quite the local flirt, more fool they who pay her court! Boys mostly, barely out of short coats themselves or they'd know better. Her tongue's developed the sting of an asp."

"Do come with me, Richard. London's as bad a hell-hole as any battlefield. The wounds are equally mortal. Only the weapons differ."

"Can't, much as I'd like to," DeLacey sighed, shifting in the old leather chair until his well-shaped head rested against its soft back, warm amber eyes rueful. "Grandmama's holding a rout Thursday fortnight: my official reintroduction to the ton, you understand, as with this,"—he gestured at his stiff leg—"a ball's impossible. Rout'll be bad enough, what with all the standing about. The blasted thing still gives out on me if it's pressed too hard.

"But, she insists it's time my days of rustication and

bachelor pursuits were over, and she gives no more credence to the existence of my angel of La Haye Sainte than the rest of you. Hence all the workmen banging about, and the gargoyle's heaven she's created out there. Blasted place was bad enough before," he grumbled as he gestured vaguely toward the study door, "but Grandmama's never satisfied. Said it needed prinking up to match my position in the world.

"Giles's promised to be back in time, and Rawdon's assured me he and Louisa'll attend. Ned Connardsleigh may even tear himself away from his beloved mangel-wurzels and come up from Kent. Certainly he writes that Marianne wishes a trip to Town. Their eldest's to make her country come-out in the spring, and Marianne wants to see to her outfitting and have her try her wings a bit, discover something to converse about besides watercolors and horses and Greek statuary.

"I'd appreciate it if you'd stay 'til then, lend me your support. A few friendly faces'd be welcome. At least I've convinced Grandmama to have refreshments available, so it won't be quite as bad as such things generally are."

"To the slaughter," Harry Beckenham shouted with a bitter laugh. "Damn all females! Why can't they bloody well leave us in peace? Come back with me, Richard. I can cut short my visit. Louisa and Rawdon'll never notice. We'll leave today. Now, on the instant. It's your only hope of avoiding parson's mousetrap this Little Season."

"Grandmama won't get me to offer where I've no wish to," DeLacey countered firmly. "None of the rest of you may believe in my angel's reality, but I do. Did I tell you the little minx used cant? Claimed it was because of her brothers," he chuckled. "Seven of 'em! Quite out of the ordinary she was. Just a tiny slip of a thing, but with more bottom in her little finger than most of us have in our entire bodies. No boredom with that tidy package about to keep me on my toes. Insisted I was nothing more than a lump of bacon-brained, muddle-witted Frog-bait.''

"So you've told me before—perhaps a thousand times,'' Beckenham sighed. "Going to give the dowager countess a free hand in here one of these days?''

"Lord, no! She knows better than to ask.''

The two former officers fell into a companionable silence as the rain continued to slide down the slick window panes of DeLacey's *sanctum sanctorum* and the fire crackled on the grate, casting a warmth as much spiritual as physical over the book-lined walls and heavy chairs, the battered desk and tables, the old velvet settee bearing the imprint of years of use. Such was the friendship between these two experienced campaigners that Beckenham even reluctantly accepted DeLacey's *idée fixe*, praying only that if and when the man found his angel of La Haye Sainte she would not prove the bitter disappointment experience insisted she was bound to be. Enough there be one man without illusions in the world. Two would be one too many.

"*No*, Mama—*No!* I shall *not* permit it!''

Sybilla Wainwright stamped her foot pettishly for emphasis, towering over her petite, slender mother, eyes flashing like those of an avenging Fury.

Lady Wainwright shrank against her favorite *tête-à-tête*, sighed. She'd known Sybilla would be in a taking when informed the customary biannual invitation dispatched to Devonshire had been given an unprecedented positive response by her sister-in-law. But, this degree of vitriol? And, requesting Woodruff's assistance would do no good, no good at all. He was everything that made for a charming, loving husband. Unfortunately, those were the same traits that made for an overly indulgent father.

Now she watched apprehensively as Sybilla stormed across the morning parlor to glower past wine velvet draperies at the pocket-garden tucked behind their small townhouse on Portman Square. The girl's shoulder's were rigid, her fists clenched. Oh, *dear!*

And not only Sybilla presented a problem. It was unseasonably cool, Lady Wainwright protested to herself as she pulled her delicate shawl more closely around her shoulders. Fall ought not to be making its presence felt for another few weeks, and here it was already unless this miserable rain were an aberration. She prayed it was. An early autumn would be a dreadful inconvenience.

"This is your father's and my home, Sybilla, as well as yours," she insisted uneasily. "I believe we may invite whom we please when we please without seeking your approval."

"But, *Cousin Elizabeth?*" Sybilla spun to face her mother, her daringly cut gown and pert plump face artistically framed by the window's draperies. "*Here?* I can't abide the mealy-mouthed chit! She has no elegance of mind, no style—not the least thing to recommend her, and everything to displease. You intend me to appear among the ton with that dowdy rustic trailing me? Why, I'd become a laughingstock!"

"Elizabeth is your cousin," Lady Wainwright pressed, the copy of *La Belle Assemblée* she had been perusing moments before temporarily discarded, "besides being a charming girl and really quite lovely in an elfin fashion. She's just not in the common way, which is hardly to her detriment. Have you no family feeling whatsoever?"

"Not when it comes to enduring *darling*, bucolic Elizabeth. How can you—*My own mother!*—be so cruel and unfeeling?" Sybilla glared across the little room, her voice venomous. "The Earl of Rochedale is returned to Town at last. Are you aware of the size of his fortune? The number of his estates? They are in the dozens! The least of them would render any man the Season's greatest catch."

"I'm not an ignoramus," Lady Wainwright smiled in an effort to pacify. Then, at the self-satisfied smirk on her daughter's face, she added unthinkingly, "After all that's gone before, surely you don't intend to cast out lures in *that* direction?"

"Millicent Farquhar told me Lady Broughton-Saint James told her maid who told Lady Farquhar's abigail who told Lady Farquhar who told Millicent that Sally Jersey claims he's completely recovered from his wounds according to the Dowager Countess of Rochedale. It's quite the latest *on dit.* I'm only surprised *you* hadn't heard," Sybilla declared, casting her mother a withering look. "Do you want to spoil *all* my chances?"

"My! What a convoluted chain of informants. The news *must* be accurate."

"Millicent is quite useful," Sybilla agreed smugly, "for all it's a complete bore having her follow me about. Why, the child positively *worships* me. Spineless, Mama, and I do mean *totally.* Quite unlike Isobell, who at least had *some* opinions until she wed and discarded hers for those of her husband."

"I seem to remember another young officer whose disabilities you found unacceptable following his return from the Peninsula," Lady Wainwright commented dryly, taking up her collection of fashion plates and burying herself in it with determination. "This pelisse might do for Elizabeth if only she weren't so diminutive," she murmured.

"Dennis Killmartin? There's no comparison."

Sybilla tossed her head, sending her tight pomaded curls bouncing as she flounced across the room to seat herself in the elegant Sheraton chair next to the burgundy-and-lime striped *tête-à-tête*. She carefully settled the folds of her pink sprigged muslin gown, then leaned slightly forward with as much enthusiasm as she ever showed for anything, revealing a fair amount of pneumatic pulchritude.

"Killmartin had but a single title, and while his pockets were not precisely to let, he would never be considered *wealthy* by the discriminating," she explained as if to a child, grimacing as her mother kept her eyes determinedly averted. "And, but a single estate? *La*, Mama! Given the disfigurement of his features from that dreadful saber-cut, and," her voice dropped conspiratorially as she leaned farther forward, "I had it on the very *best* authority that his torso—well, suffice it to say the sight would have put *any* bride off, even one determined to do her duty. Nigel Farquhar saw him stripped at Jackson's Saloon, you see, and he told his valet who told Isobell's maid who told her, and she cautioned me. You can imagine my horror! It wouldn't have *done*, Mama."

"And who has there been of substance since?" Lady Wainwright sighed, glancing up from a plate showing a dinner gown of simple lines and simpler trim. "'Twas his pockets as much as his wounds, and we both know it. That, and the fact that he intended to retire to the country permanently once wed. What do you think of this for Elizabeth," she asked, turning the illustration towards her daughter.

Sybilla gave her mother a hard look, tore the collection from her hands and hurled it to the floor. "Bother, Elizabeth!" she spat. Then she shrugged at the long-suffering expression on her mother's gentle features, drew herself up.

"I realized immediately I accepted Killmartin's proposals that I'd made a calamitous error, whatever the

reason, and *that* was before his Peninsular madness,"
she insisted, eyes not quite meeting Lady Wainwright's.
"I was *much* too young to reach such a momentous
decision regarding my future. You should have prevented me. Why, even Isobell Farquhar looked on me
with pity, and she only nabbed a baronet."

"Prevented you? Oh, Sybilla—how short your memory is!"

"Well, what else is a mother for? As it was, I prayed
hourly for Killmartin's death. His disfiguring wounds
offered the perfect opportunity to extricate myself without being termed a thorough jilt," Sybilla retorted with
a demure fluttering of lashes from beneath which
peeped a pair of agate-hard eyes.

"I remember your intransigence at the time of your
betrothal quite clearly, my girl," her mother snapped,
driven beyond endurance. "Indeed, you rendered our
lives hideous by weeks of hysterics. What were we to
do?"

"Yes, well, be that as it may, how cheaply do you think
I should hold myself now? Surely you believe your only
child worthy of more than *Dennis Killmartin* could offer!
Don't be goose-ish, Mama."

"So—Rochedale's pockets compensate for any lingering disability?"

"Certainly, for they are excessively *deep* pockets," Sybilla laughed, confident she was making progress.
"Besides, once an heir was produced, we would go our
separate ways. Nothing else would be *civilized*," she
explained, clearly contemplating her delightful future
as Countess of Rochedale. "The cats have been hissing
for a year and more. By spring I'll be termed an ape-
leader. I'm determined to make a positively *brilliant*
match before then. Rochedale is the perfect solution.
Now d'you understand why it's impossible for that
scrawny antidote to join us for the Little Season?"

"You've never so much as been presented to Rochedale," Lady Wainwright objected, "and that's not for want of trying the one time he was home on leave. I recall both a twisted ankle at Hatchard's and a runaway horse in Hyde Park, for all the good either did you, as well as numerous other ploys of the most obvious sort. Your pursuit was both relentless and mortifying. When you speak of becoming a laughingstock—"

"Have done, Mama! I was barely more than a girl then, and besides, *you* refused me all assistance in capturing Rochedale. What was I to do? But, I know better how to go about these things now. If I decide he's acceptable, I need only lift my finger."

"Acceptable? *Rochedale?*"

"That, or lure him into a secluded corner at the next ball, tear my bodice, and cry rape," she added complacently. "How d'you think Isobell nabbed her baronet?"

"Your arrogance is beyond bounds! Besides, how d'you know you'd suit?"

"His pockets would suit me very nicely. What else is there to know of a man? Rescind the invitation, dearest, *sweetest* Mama," Sybilla wheedled, hand on her mother's arm. "Tell the vulgar little bore we are unexpectedly in black gloves. Tell her there is cholera in Town. Tell her what you wish, but fob her off. Dear heaven—even her *name* is off-putting. 'Elizabeth Driscoll,' indeed! Why not call her 'Betsy' at once, and set her to scrubbing pots? That's her future, you know—that, or hanging on her brothers' sleeves after Uncle Samuel dies. No man of discrimination would have her!"

"Sybilla," her mother sighed, "no."

"No? *No* to *what?*"

"Have done," she said, retrieving *La Belle Assemblée* and perusing its pages, voice purposefully abstracted. "Your cousin arrives in a week's time. You will keep a civil tongue in your head while she remains our guest, and you will refrain from proclaiming what you see as her faults to the skies when in company."

"I see reason is lost on you. I'm going to confer with Papa," Sybilla spat, surging to her feet. "*You* are fit only for Bedlam. I'll see he puts you there!"

"Your father joined his urgings to mine when I wrote your Aunt Suzanne. It's time and more for your cousin to make her bows."

"But, she'll ruin *everything*," Sybilla wailed. "Rochedale will take one look at her and hobble the other direction as fast as he can. No man of his stamp would willingly accept such a vile connection! How could you *do* this to me? *My* happiness and *my* future and *my* desires should be your first concern—not *hers.*"

With a choked sob Sybilla fled the room, slamming the door behind her and pelting up the stairs to her bedchamber.

She would do something! she stormed. She *had* to! No one could be held responsible for the less salubrious branches of one's family. Everyone was so cursed.

But, to have them in one's own home?

In one's own company?

At the insistence of one's own parents?

During the Season—even the *Little* Season?

It wasn't to be borne! Rochedale would spurn her. Every gentleman in the ton would spurn her. And, they would have justification.

"Evil days agin," the upstairs maid muttered, placing a stack of freshly ironed sheets interspersed with lavender sprigs in the linen press as Sybilla tore past her.

"May the saints preserve us all," mumbled Cook, sliding a tray of damson tarts into the baking oven and wiping her flour-speckled forehead with the back of her hand. "It's to begin again. The poor mistress and master."

"I take it things did not go well with Sybilla," portly Viscount Wainwright commented wryly as he entered the morning parlor after first ascertaining his daughter was well and truly gone. "That was quite an oratorio. I'm thinking of taking up residence at my club for the duration."

"You abandon me, Woodruff," his pretty gray-haired wife retorted, "and I shall see to it that you receive a command invitation from Great-Aunt Witherspoon."

The customarily good-humored viscount chuckled as he planted a kiss on his wife's smooth brow.

Delphinia Witherspoon was the terror of the family—an acid-tongued old harridan with no liking for anyone but Sybilla. Never wed, she set a cheese-paring table worthy of an indigent nonconformist preacher, expressed herself in a manner that would put a sailor to the blush, and lectured any family member so unfortunate as to be caught in her vicinity regarding his (or her) faults—real and imagined—with the force of a lion roaring in the jungle and the dogmatism of a Roundhead martyr. Besides which, she favored cats. *Hundreds* of cats.

"Send her Sybilla instead," he suggested, easing his bulk onto the striped *tête-à-tête*, "and spare us the approaching tempest."

"If only I could, my love," his wife returned regretfully, "but Sybilla would never go. *Now* she has her sights set on the Earl of Rochedale."

"What—*again*? He's so far above our touch it's laughable. I wondered how high her price might rise once she discarded Killmartin. Well, now we know. Naturally it would've been too much to hope she might learn from her past failures in that direction. But then, ambition springs eternal in her palpitating décolletage, along with a pair of pulchritudinous orbs purposefully displayed to the trout of the ton as lures."

"Woodruff! She is our daughter, after all!"

"By which you imply I must blind myself to her faults and foibles? Sorry, my dear—I've never held with this modern milksop attitude toward speaking the truth concerning a female. You might consider changing modistes, but I doubt it would serve. She's acquiring that brittle desperation which attaches to all unwed females over the age of twenty. I'm seriously considering a look about me for an eligible *parti*, and an end to the farce she plays us. We deserve some peace."

Cochrane, the staid, silver-haired butler, merely paused an instant in his meticulous polishing of the crystal decanters from his lordship's library. The altercation between mistress and mistress's daughter had been all too audible. It was not, after all, that large a house, and the walls were rather thin.

Troubled times? The Season had been distressing enough.

Lord Perrimble, a three-bottle-a-night sot, had not come up to snuff. A weak stomach discouraged by a fit of the vapors.

Heatherington of the explosive *harrumph* and the delicious bays had decamped with stiffened shoulders following a display of "delicacy."

Lord Pilkington of the mirrorlike Hessians' *Maman* had condescended to tea, sniffed, and whisked said green lord to the wilds of Yorkshire for a bit of bucolic release.

Even Collard Mardler, a cit well larded in more than his belly with nine in his nursery (All of the female persuasion after four—count 'em, *four*—wives!) and desirous of elevated connections to match his well-to-pass pockets and a lusty noble heir to grace his nursery, had retreated posthaste to his opulent mansion beyond Hans Town.

As for the basket-scramblers and half-pay officers his

lordship had sent to the right-about, the third and
fourth sons of mediocre parentage?

The current crop dancing attendance included the
Farquhar heir and one Aloysius Beckenham, a distant
connection by marriage of the Duke of Rawdon, both
striplings too purse-pinched and rackety to be taken
seriously. Even their attendance was sporadic at best.
The Little Season promised to be horrendous.

Then a furtive twinkle gleamed in the depth of his
eyes. If Miss Sybilla still despised the young Driscoll lady
so heartily, the girl probably remained a delight, fresh
and unspoiled and totally engaging. Certainly that was
how he remembered her from the time just after Waterloo: natural and friendly, always grateful for the smallest
service. Of course, the darkened eye and bruised cheek
would no longer be there permitting the occasional
restrained quizzing. But, her arrival would be welcome.

They were in for interesting times on Portman Square.
And, given Miss Sybilla, difficult ones.

Two

"Mama, don't be ridiculous!"

Elizabeth whirled across the sunny parlor of the Driscoll home in the village of Saint Mary-Grafton to kneel beside her mother's chair, slender hands gripping the arms, gamine face anxiously uplifted. The girl's gray-blue eyes flew from the disastrous letter in her mother's plump hand to her pleasant, cheerful face. There was a set to the lady's dimpled chin that didn't bode well for her only daughter.

"Please, Mama—don't insist on this. I don't mean to be disrespectful, but *I*? In *London*? For the *Little Season*? You and Papa are all about in your heads!" The girl sprang to her feet at the slight shake of Lady Driscoll's head, and backed away. "Look at me," she pleaded, gesturing from her shapeless gray stuff gown to the heavy mane of dark hair pulled back from her face in a severely practical braided chignon.

"I am, my dear," her mother responded with a slight smile.

Even the dowdy dress and governessy hair style could not detract from the child's bright, arresting allure.

Fashionable? Definitely not. Elizabeth probably never

would be—not with her impishly tilted little nose sporting its dusting of golden freckles and her glowing country complexion, her tough wiry frame, her forthright approach to all situations, her insistence clothes accommodate any position, permit any activity.

But, unforgettable?

She might be forced to concede a mother's prejudice, but she thought not. Sybilla Wainwright, who considered herself an Incomparable, would do well to look to her laurels once Elizabeth made her bows.

"I see you clearly enough," she twinkled. "There's no need to thrust yourself beneath my nose as if I required spectacles."

With a dispirited droop to her slender shoulders, Elizabeth retreated to the open window giving on the rear garden and the little tree-lined stream beyond it, pointed chin stubbornly set, eyes stormy, unconscious of the delightfully unaffected picture she presented haloed by mellow fall sunshine and framed by cheerful chintz curtains.

Two of the boys—scapegrace Steven and roly-poly William—were practicing their fly-casting under the ever-patient Andrew's tutelage, attempting to flick bright scraps of red flannel from the back of a dilapidated chair set in the dappled sunshine as target. Jeremy, at seventeen about to enter his last year at Winchester and desperate to present the appearance of an indolent town beau now he'd finally begun to sprout, lolled near the peach tree well out of the reach of flying lures and tangled lines, awkwardly wielding a quizzing glass of ridiculous proportions and ornate embellishment.

She remembered when John and Charles and Robert had been at the same uncomfortable stage, struggling to appear manly and knowing beyond their years, and not quite certain how to go about it. John was long past that now, and while lingering hints of dandyism were still to be found in the other two oldest boys' wardrobes, they rarely extended beyond the occasional preposterous waistcoat. Jeremy would survive.

Difficult to believe the would-be exquisite in the garden was the same lad who courageously threaded his way through the carnage at Waterloo, lighting their path with a flickering lantern while determinedly choking back his rising gorge at the unspeakable sights meeting his eyes. It had been difficult enough for her, and she had been assisting Papa at all manner of disasters for years. The super-abundance of fobs, the pot-metal snuff box and ludicrous quizzing glass purchased from an oily-tongued tinker would vanish eventually, the uncomfortably exaggerated shirt points shrink and the Jeremy of old re-emerge, wiser, matured, a man worthy of respect. There was time enough.

The younger boys waved and hallooed, begging her to watch and admire or, better yet, give them some pointers. Wiry, sandy-haired Andrew was an excellent instructor, but their sister was the acknowledged master of the trout stream. Leave all this for London? Not if she could help it. Elizabeth shook her head grimly as she answered their vigorous waves, then turned back to her mother.

"Do I look as if I belong among the ton, Mama?" she pleaded with a catch in her voice. "Aunt Mehitabelle is excessively kind to offer, for she must know attempting to bring me into fashion would be a thankless task, but the expense isn't to be thought of—not with John newly married and setting up his practice, and Charles and Robert at Cambridge, and Jeremy and Andrew at Winchester—besides which, I cannot *abide* dear Sybilla. To be forced to survive my sweet cousin's company for a month and more? We would begin at daggers drawn, and end with one of us swinging from the nubbing

cheat and the other in hell dancing to the devil's piping
for provoking the murder!''

"Must you use such cant terms," Lady Suzanne protested mildly. "I know they assault your ears daily, but
truly, my love, it isn't—"

"Sorry, Mama—I'll attempt to guard my tongue.
Besides which," the indignant girl concluded triumphantly even as a fierce blush stained her cheeks, "Tillie
cannot run this house single-handed—she's only an
upstairs maid, after all, and not a housekeeper—and
Papa needs me to keep his books and assist in his surgery, which Charles and Robert will be unable to do as
they will be returned to Cambridge, and Jeremy pre-
tends to faint at the sight of blood these days thinking
it tonnish for a gentleman to display heightened sensibilities as well as a lisp, and he and Andrew will be at
school in any case and *someone* must see to Willie and
Steven's lessons, and you shall be temporarily very much
unavailable for such duties at the exact time I should
be gone. You *know* the vicar said he'd never oversee the
boys' studies again—not after they let dozens of frogs
loose in the vicarage when the bishop was here last
spring. Not that I blame them, for he *is* excessively
pompous, and their description of his flapping about
the parlor like a beached whale *was* most humorous.

"So, you can see I am right. Next year, perhaps.
Charles will be down from Cambridge and able to assist
Papa, and even oversee the boys. Besides, if my luck is
in, by then Sybilla will be married at last."

"You're expected in London, my dear," her mother
protested gently, "and to London you shall go. As for
Sybilla's nuptials, there's nothing of the sort on the
horizon."

"I love Papa's sister dearly," Elizabeth pleaded, "and
Uncle Woodruff is *exactly* my idea of the perfect uncle,
but I simply could *not* survive in the same house as

Sybilla for more than a single day without running the risk of doing her a severe injury. You know we part brass rags if forced into each other's company for more than five minutes. She's the world's greatest cat, besides being vain and selfish and self-important and two-faced and spoiled and—well, I can't *abide* her, and she despises me with equal cordiality. If you've no sympathy for me, think of poor Aunt Mehitabelle and Uncle Woodruff. They don't deserve to live on the brink of a constantly erupting volcano."

"I have. They'll survive, and so shall you. The boys' returns to their schools will be delayed until our little addition has put in an appearance. Charles and Robert will assist your father, and Jeremy and Andrew will oversee the younger ones. As for Tillie, there's no problem. She's to accompany you for propriety's sake, then return as soon as may be. Her sister has agreed to lend a hand here, perhaps even stay on for the duration of your absence."

"You've thought of everything, haven't you."

"Well, at least we've made the attempt. Your father has ordered the traveling coach readied, and bespoken job horses and a driver from Old Thom at The Oaken Barrel. Alfie will handle the reins, with Young Thom riding guard."

"*No!*" Elizabeth wailed.

"You refused to make your come-out last year, begging exhaustion from the Brussels excursion and your father's need of you," her mother countered patiently. "There was some truth to your excuses, and the dear Lord knows Samuel was glad of your assistance when the entire neighborhood seemed to contract the grippe at once. Before that, you claimed to be continually throwing out spots, though to me they looked more like bits of raw dough stained with berry juice. They did have the lamentable characteristic of falling off at the most inopportune moments, dear, and you were never very adept at sweeping them out of sight. You should've tried dabs of gooseberry jam.

"And before that? I believe you claimed it was Sybilla's first season and you didn't want to endure her jealousy, when indeed it was her second, if not her third. My love, you're nineteen. The shelf is fast approaching. You've shown no preference for any of the young men in the neighborhood, nor they for you except as a hail-fellow-well-met companion on larks and sprees. What will be your excuse next year?"

"I'll find *something,*" Elizabeth muttered. "The entire concept is preposterous! I'm not hanging out for a husband. I'm perfectly content as I am."

"For how long?" Her mother placed the unwelcome letter on the small pie-crust table at her side and rose laboriously to her feet. "Yes, I know—right now everything appears perfect, the future a dim thing unworthy of a moment's thought and Saint Mary-Grafton the most wonderful place in the world. But, as your Aunt Mehitabelle says, the future may well pass you by if you persist in refusing a Season. It's not as if you were to be presented at Court. This is only the Little Season. Papa and I are determined: You leave in three days' time."

"But, the *expense,*" Elizabeth protested. "I won't take, you know, and it shall all be for nothing."

"You're perfectly aware your father long ago set aside funds for your come-out, and a portion of eight hundred pounds in addition—not generous by some standards, but generous enough by others. It won't be despised by one who loves you, but will never attract the Captain Sharps or basket-scramblers."

"And who's using cant now, Mama?" Elizabeth protested with a wistful, loving smile.

"In a household so dominated by men, what can one expect," her mother sighed. "I do so hope this little one will be a girl. With you gone, I shall need someone new with whom to conspire. Amelia Caroline would be a delightful name, don't you think?"

"*I* think you and Papa should give over this queer start *immediately.*"

The heavily *enceinte* Lady Driscoll turned ponderously to face her daughter, eyes serious.

"That will not happen, my dear," she cautioned. "Your Aunt Mehitabelle is quite right: It's time and more for you to make your come-out. And, you shall make it. We may live simply, but your father is nevertheless titled, for all the dear man refuses to use his title or move to the family seat, and I am in complete agreement."

Elizabeth's chin lifted as her heart sank at the beginning of the familiar lecture.

"Who ever heard of addressing a country doctor as 'my lord?'" Lady Driscoll continued, ignoring her daughter's rebellious stance. "Besides, the rental fees from the Hawls property are quite useful, what with your father never accepting payment of any sort from his poorer patients and constantly undertaking—and financing, which is more to the point—such projects as last year's dash to Belgium.

"No, we're quite happy as we are, but the fact remains that you are the great-granddaughter of an earl on the one side, and the daughter of a baron on the other. It's only for the Little Season," she concluded in a comforting tone. "After that? Well, if nothing interesting transpires, we'll see."

"You're trying to rid yourselves of me," Elizabeth quavered mutinously, glaring at her mother to hide the hurt. "Why?"

"No, dear child," she smiled, placing gentle hands on either side of her daughter's face, looking deeply and a little sadly into the girl's anguished eyes. "We only refuse to permit you to close doors before you know what may lie behind them. At the end of the Little Season you may return, if you truly wish it. We only ask that you pull in your prickles and enjoy London while you're there.''

With the assurance it was only a temporary purgatory, and not a permanent hell to which she was being banished, Elizabeth had to be content.

The three short days remaining she filled with country rambles, delighting in the verdant hedgerows and fecund fields, the bright clear skies, the hint of a nip in the air in shade and genial warmth of the golden sun. She darted into cool patches of woods to bid farewell to beloved haunts. She scaled favorite trees. She fished the trout stream. She caged apples from Squire Coyne's orchard. She took baskets of provisions to Granny Semple and sweet-faced Foolish June, promising a rapid return.

Elizabeth determinedly ignored her brothers' quizzing regarding her taking the ton by storm, along with the battered trunk that appeared in her tiny sleeping chamber on the morning after her mother's fateful announcement. When Tillie had carefully laid every stitch of clothing that might prove passable in London in the trunk, it was but a quarter full. The trunk vanished the next day, replaced by a portmanteau and a pair of bandboxes.

It was, her mother sighed, no great disaster Elizabeth had so little that appeared even marginally appropriate to the sartorial demands of a London Season. Even the little she was taking would probably be relegated to the dust bin the moment it was glimpsed by the always impeccably garbed Lady Wainwright.

Her taste was exquisite, Elizabeth's mother cautioned, for all that on the Wainwrights' rare visits the waspish Sybilla always appeared frivolously overdressed. London was vastly different from Saint Mary-Grafton. Elizabeth was not to protest when it came to the selection of her come-out clothes, nor plead an empty purse, nor insist on shapeless garments constructed of the sturdiest, darkest, longest-wearing fabrics. Aunt Mehitabelle's suggestions were to be treated as commands from above. When it came to *la mode*, even the angels of heaven would have bowed to her decrees if they wished to appear at the opera or the theater, or that holy of holies, Almack's, without being put to the blush.

Elizabeth crossed fingers behind her back and agreed.

A disgruntled Harry Beckenham returned to his brother-in-law's Grosvenor Square residence shortly before the dinner hour, stumbled over a trunk abandoned in the center of the spacious entry and let out an involuntary yelp as he nursed his barked shin, tall curly-brimmed beaver knocked awry. Behind him Mason, the footman on duty, closed the massive doors and snapped to attention.

It had been a miserable, frustrating week for Harry, today the worst of all. He detested meeting with his man of business. As for attempting to reason yet again with Richard DeLacey, he might as well have saved his breath for all the good it had done. The idiot was living within the marbled covers of a Minerva Press offering.

Now, *this*. What in blazes was going on? So far as he knew, no guests were expected. A pair of distinctly feminine bandboxes drew his brows into a furious scowl as he glowered at a second footman waiting to receive his forgotten hat. A gurgling laugh from the family parlor at the head of the stairs confirmed his growing suspicions.

"The devil!" he muttered. "I'll kill them all!"

His first thought was to slink quietly back to Rochedale

House, his second to take up residence at the Clarendon as had been his custom before Louisa's marriage to the Duke of Rawdon. His third was a precipitous departure for Marleybourne. The thing wasn't impossible. Thunderer, his great bay stallion, should still be on the pavement. He could send for his man and effects later. An inn along the way, *any* inn, even a hedgerow tavern, would be preferable to Rawdon House as things suddenly stood.

He dithered too long, undecided as to which perhaps cowardly solution would engender the least sniggering comment among his acquaintance, and so was lost. The parlor door flew open. His sister, his aunt, and his country neighbor's pert, acid-tongued daughter swept into the upstairs hall, laughing and chattering. He shrank into what few shadows there were in the bright entry, praying the women wouldn't notice him. Patsy Worth glanced down to see if her last trunk had been taken abovestairs.

With the feeling that his neckcloth was suddenly much too tight, Harry stepped out of the faint penumbra and sketched a silent, abbreviated bow in her general direction without bothering to erase the deep scowl from his face. His forgotten beaver tumbled to the floor. The rigid Mason swiftly retrieved the piece of offending headgear, features carefully blank. Patsy stared down at Harry Beckenham as the laughter faded from her eyes and her voice stilled. Then she gave him the slightest of curt nods in response to his cold *pro forma* salute and turned to Her Grace, Louisa Debenham, Duchess of Rawdon.

"I believe it's time I repair to my room for a short rest before dinner, and I do so want to see the twins as well," Patsy Worth proclaimed in a stiff, overly loud voice that carried clearly to Harry's ears, just as it was intended to do. "I've brought the most cunning doll for little Demetra. You can unbutton and button its clothes—teaches a child the rudiments of dressing itself, the toy shop owner claimed, unlike those dull *à-la-mode* things which one may only look at. How I detested those sorts of dolls when I was a child! I always wanted to exchange costumes between them, you see, and so totally ruined the things. What good is a toy one may only *look* at? The number of supperless nights I was accorded for that unreasonable opinion! As for Marcus—

"You *do* remember the joy he took from the Harry's old toy sloop last summer? Wait until you see what I've found for Marcus! He'll believe himself appointed Lord High Admiral. Harry's sailboat is nothing to it," she enthused, "but I suddenly find myself unutterably wearied. If I'm to see the children and have a few moments to gather my wits, I simply *must* go up now, besides which I *cannot* appear at dinner in all my dirt. You will excuse me, Louisa?"

Then suddenly she was the minxish Patsy Worth of old, tossing her abundant reddish-brown curls, kissing Louisa's and Lady Daphne's cheeks, gurgling with laughter, dashing up the stairs with a flutter of lace-edged petticoats peeking from beneath the hem of her elegant deep blue poplin traveling costume and a twinkle of tiny feet and slender ankles. Harry sagged against the heavy boule chest just behind him.

Damnation! Of all the coils his interfering sister could have engineered—

Worst of all, *he'd* forgotten to bring gifts for the twins when he departed Marleybourne two weeks ago. He should've remembered about the sailboat, and any clerk could have directed him to an appropriate doll, though he'd likely have presented Demetra with exactly the sort Patsy claimed children most despised. She'd shown him up as an uncaring boor, blast her. He'd have to rectify

that on the morrow. What in blazes was appropriate to
a pair of infants just above the age of two? Simple puzzles, he supposed, and soft things.

And then he straightened his shoulders, took a deep
breath, tossed his glove and cane to the patiently waiting
second footman and mounted the sweeping stairs with
the erect bearing of a soldier on parade.

"Aunt Daffy, I hope I find you well," he snapped.
Then without waiting for a response from the diminutive, silver-haired lady, "Louisa, I should like to see you
immediately in the drawing room, if that is convenient—which I suggest you make it. Or, any other room
where we may be private for a few moments."

"Oh, dear," Lady Cheltenham commented to the air
around them, "the lion roars once more in the glen.
Shall we tremble, Louisa, or merely slink away shamefaced? I do believe one or the other is expected of us
at this moment."

"But then, we never do the expected, do we, dear
Aunt," Louisa chuckled. "I'm sorry, Harry," she continued, turning to her brother, only laughing green eyes
in an otherwise bland face betraying her mood, "but
it's entirely impossible for me to accede to your so-
politely phrased request just now. Tomorrow, perhaps?
I must see to the flowers for the table and give François
some last-minute instructions concerning tonight's dinner. We sit down twenty—just a few special friends to
make Patsy's acquaintance—and I wish everything to
be perfect. As soon as I've seen to the table appoint-
ments and the flowers it will be time for me to make
my toilette. You do intend to dine here rather than at
your club, do you not? I'd appreciate it greatly, for if
you don't my numbers will be out. Besides, not staying
would offer the greatest insult to Patsy."

"Louisa," Harry countered, a dangerous edge to his
voice, "the drawing room. *Now!* Aunt Daffy, go torment

some other unsuspecting family, else I refuse to be responsible for what I may say or do.''

"I believe your poor brother is beginning to lose his hearing," Lady Cheltenham informed her niece. "Ah, well, it happens to the best of us as we age.''

"My hearing is perfect," Harry spat. "It's yours that's at fault, *my lady.*"

"Let's see to the flowers, shall we, and leave Harry to his own devices," their aunt suggested, placing a restraining hand on Louisa's arm. "Something festive without being overpowering is what we need. Something sweet and natural to match Patsy's best qualities. Such a dear girl, and so tolerant to acknowledge Harry's existence given the Turkish treatment he's accorded her these past three years. What the poor child has done to offend the beast I've yet to determine. Merely *exist,* perhaps? And perhaps *someday* he'll have the kindness to explain it to me, but until then—''

With a determined little tug she turned Louisa toward the formal dining room used for entertaining. When that pair brangled it was most wearying, and she had no intention of her enjoyment of the situation being spoiled.

"Rawdon is in his library if you're truly in need of company, Harry," she tossed over her shoulder.

Harry Beckenham watched his sister and aunt disappear into the dining room and snorted. Females! The older they became, the worse they got, damn them all for the interfering marplots they were. Why did everyone insist on cutting up his peace?

He'd come to terms with the female of the species years before.

Provide an heir for Marleybourne and the viscountcy? Not likely! He'd had enough of the conniving harpies for a lifetime, and to date he knew of no way to produce an heir without entering parson's mousetrap with one of the simpering two-faced golddiggers on his remaining arm. He'd rot in hell before he'd so burden himself. There was Cousin Oliver if Harry predeceased him, or the eldest of Oliver's starched-up boys—Aloysius of the jangling fobs and pouter-pigeon chest—to succeed to the title and estates. Not much of an heir, perhaps, but an heir all the same. The Beckenham line wouldn't die out just because he refused to become a martyr to progeniture and tradition.

With a barely suppressed oath Harry gave his neck-cloth a loosening twitch, settled his coat of deep green Bath superfine more comfortably across his broad shoulders, strode back down the stairs, tossed the surreptitiously grinning footmen a withering glance, stalked down the hall to Rawdon's library at the back of the house, and threw open the heavy oak door.

"What the deuce have you been permitting, blast you," he snarled. "I thought you had better control of those two conniving busybodies than this!"

"I beg your pardon, Harry?" His Grace of Rawdon raised deep gray eyes from the book he'd been reading, comfortably ensconced in a worn red leather chair by the fire. He took a second look at his brother-in-law, and smiled. "Ah—I understand. You've discovered little Patsy Worth has arrived at last. Louisa was becoming anxious. Most of the roads into London are thoroughly mired."

"You knew about this," Harry stormed illogically.

Of course the duke had known. Jamie and Louisa lived in each other's pockets. Most unaccountable for a married couple. They should've been at daggers drawn within days of their distinctly unconventional wedding, estranged within the month.

"Why the devil didn't you put a stop to it?"

"Louisa considers the girl a treasured part of the

family," the duke protested mildly, thrusting a finger between the pages of his book to keep the place. "You know that. Why, Patsy stood as godmother to Demetra along with Lady Daphne. I find the minx enchanting, and the twins would cheerfully lay down their lives for her—if they were old enough to know what the term means. More to the point, they insist she share their treacle tarts. No greater proof of devotion exists in the nursery world."

"Very touching."

"Come down from the boughs, Harry. You're making yourself ridiculous. I believe my wife is permitted to have a guest without seeking your permission. Why, I don't even insist she seek *mine,* not that it would do the least good if I did. Louisa's been begging Patsy to visit, and she finally agreed. Says," he grinned as he set his book aside as a temporarily lost cause, "that she needs to add a bit of à la modality to her wardrobe. Between the plethora of shopping expeditions she detailed the instant of her arrival and the avalanche of social engagements Louisa claims awaits her, I doubt you'll see Miss Worth one day in ten, and then only in passing. Lady Daphne has been mapping out a plan of campaign with the pair of them so all both desire can be accomplished."

"That's precisely what I'm afraid of—one of Aunt Daffy's campaigns," Harry grumbled, stalking to the fireplace as he glanced absently at the portrait of a young man in scarlet regimentals displayed above the mantel—Rawdon's younger brother, Charles Christopher Debenham, Viscount Lindley, killed in the confused retreat to Corunna in '09. He'd been only vaguely aware of who the boy was at the time. "I remember the last one only too well."

"As do I," the duke chuckled. "Since I was the

delighted beneficiary, I've no complaints with the old lady's machinations. She's quite astute when it comes to personalities, you know.''

"Well, *I've* no intention of falling victim to one of her schemes," Harry spat, turning to face his imperturbable brother-in-law.

"I don't think Lady Daphne's the least interested in you," Rawdon lied baldly. "Stop making a fool of yourself and take a seat. It won't be so bad—you'll see. How did things go with old Pennington? I'd've thought him rather past it."

"He is," Harry sighed. "I only consult him for form's sake these days. Nephew's taken over, and a sharper mind or tongue you'll never run across. It was the usual dull, detestable stuff, complete with columns of minuscule figures whose totals always seem smaller or bigger than they should be."

"Stop by DeLacey's?"

"I needed something to jostle me out of the doldrums after dealing with Pennington," Harry admitted with the trace of a smile. "It was that, or a gallop in Hyde Park—out of the question in this weather. Unpleasant enough jogging all the way out to Hammersmith. The roads are impossible, but DeLacey's so housebound in this weather it was worth the effort. His fortitude and lack of complaint make pikers of the rest of us. As for his willingness to live so out of the way for his grandmother's sake—well, the man's a saint, and there's an end to it."

"How's his quest progressing?"

"He persists," Harry grumbled. "No matter what anyone says, he persists. Richard's a fool!"

Upstairs a grim-faced Patsy Worth turned as Lady Louisa entered the airy yellow and green sitting room attached to her guest's bedchamber. Louisa paused,

gauging the girl's mood, then sped to give her friend
and former neighbor a garment-rumpling hug.

"I must apologize for Harry's rudeness," she said.
"There are times when I don't know how any of us puts
up with him."

"That's all right," Patsy dimpled as she returned the
hug enthusiastically. "He'll come round in the end—
you'll see."

Louisa shook her head, stepped back to survey the
slender, elegant young woman Patsy had transformed
herself into over the past two years. The chubby hoyden
of the Marleybourne trout stream and brambles and
apple trees was impossible to find unless one searched
the eyes. Even the miss just out of the schoolroom had
been altered beyond recognition. Patsy had truly grown
up at last, for all the good it might do her where Harry
was concerned.

"I don't know, my dear," Louisa sighed with a catch
in her voice. "I suspected his presence here might be
your motive for accepting our invitation at just this time,
but he remains as bitter and impossible as ever, no
matter how strongly he insists the contrary. He doesn't
trust himself, you see, and he remains terribly hurt,
battered even, by what happened."

"The devil take Gwendolyn Fortescue," Patsy muttered, apologizing for neither her temper nor her
choice of words. Then her brow cleared. "I went at
it all wrong when it first happened, you know," she
confessed forthrightly. "I thought it was his arm. Giles
confided the whole dreadful tale to me just after they
returned to Marleybourne. Poor Giles felt so guilty. He
just *had* to tell someone. And then Harry was treating
me like a leper, and Giles felt I deserved *some* sort of
explanation. I know Giles wasn't supposed to talk about
it to anyone, and I'm sworn to silence, but—" Patsy
broke off in horror, staring at her old neighbor and

mentress. "Oh, dear! You *did* already know about what happened, did you not? Otherwise I've done the most *dreadful* thing."

"Yes," Louisa admitted weakly, "I knew."

"I suspected you must," Patsy said wisely. "His grace would've told you, if no one else had. How anyone could be so conscienceless and cruel—"

She circled the delicately appointed room, straightening a bibelot here, a picture there, twitching at the golden draperies trimmed in white and green drawn against the inclement weather. The fire's warm glow gilded her hair, catching in its shining modish curls so that in her travel costume she seemed a deep blue iris set free to wander in a field of nodding daffodils. Louisa watched her silently, waiting. Patsy Worth was as transparent as the trout stream at home. The combination of pain and desperation in the girl's eyes would have touched a harder heart than Louisa's.

"I'm very grateful for your invitation," Patsy offered tentatively.

"It's not the first James and I have tendered you."

"I know." Then she whirled to face Louisa, eyes overbright. "Poor Harry! I ached so to help him, and I was too young and inexperienced to understand what he needed, and so I *argued* with him. Can you imagine anything so foolish? I told him his missing arm and scarred face didn't mean a thing to anyone but that dreadful hellcat, and he was well out of it. But, I suspect he was still half in love with her at that point, or at least with the paragon he believed her to be. He was furious when Giles told me what had happened—*furious.* Giles sported the most amazing blackened eye for days."

"Oh, *dear*," Louisa murmured.

"Oh, dear, indeed! I felt so guilty, for it was all my fault. Giles didn't speak to me for a week, which was most depressing to the spirits because Harry wasn't speaking to me either. Such megrims I had! Poor Mama and Papa—how they endured me I'll never know. Having children can't be easy. Have a care when Demetra and Marcus first give their hearts away."

"I shall," Louisa smiled softly, remembering when she'd finally given her own. "I'll try to be very understanding."

"I attempted to be Harry's friend and comforter, you see," Patsy tore on, "and prayed every day for more. I was a fool! Giles warned me of that, but I wouldn't listen. *He* said I was going about it all wrong. The angry loyalty of a child barely out of the schoolroom wasn't what Harry wanted, and of course that's all he saw—a child, just as he always had, while I thought I was all grown up. I made such a determined pest of myself that he finally threw me off the grounds and warned me never to come back on pain of a birching. And, he meant it.

"But, I'm older now, and, I hope, a good deal wiser. I shall go about things entirely differently this time."

"My dear, I don't think—that is, you—Harry is still so *dreadfully—*"

"Yes, he is, isn't he, and more," Patsy agreed. "But, just you watch! I'm far more determined to have him than he is not to have me. I love him so much," she choked as tears suddenly sparkled on her lashes. "I always have, I suppose, ever since I could trail after him when I was still in leading strings. There's never been anyone but Harry. There never will be."

"Never is a long time, Patsy."

"You truly believe there's no hope for me?"

"Quite frankly," Louisa returned bitterly, "the way he acts these days, I don't know why you even want to bother."

Patsy paused in her restless turns about the room, eyes glowing softly.

"D'you remember the time my dreadful Aunt Aurelia took up residence when Mama was so ill?" she asked. "She was *supposed* to be seeing to Papa and me and taking care of the household. All she ever did was complain we hadn't enough servants. She forced me to hold my spoon in my fist like a baby so I wouldn't spill my soup. If she'd let me hold it like a *person* the way I'd been doing for a year and more, I'd've *never* spilled. But no, *she* knew best. And then she *sneered* at me for being clumsy. She wouldn't believe me, drat her, and she *birched* me for spilling. Blast the dried-out old witch, she sent me to bed supperless!"

"It wasn't a happy time."

"What an understatement. Of course Harry learned what had occurred instantly," Patsy continued dreamily. "The servants probably, for nothing ever happened at one of our homes that it wasn't known instantly at the other. He climbed the tree outside my window and sneaked me a cold game pie. Pheasant it was, and very good, and I ate every scrap. He sneaked me a flagon of ale as well. What a head I had in the morning," she chuckled, "but Aunt Aurelia thought I was sulking and so I received another birching."

"Dear heaven—*ale?*"

"I've loved it ever since. And then there was the time Harry and I were playing in the winter garden. I wasn't supposed to be there because Aunt Aurelia considered the outdoors unhealthy, and I most definitely wasn't supposed to be with Harry. Boys were dangerous beasts, she said. I fell and skinned my knees and tore my stockings. Harry patched me up so Aunt Aurelia wouldn't find out. She never did either. Harry even managed to sweeten Cook up so she'd get me some clean stockings.

"Every single time Aunt'd do something dreadful, such as make me burn my hair ribbons because they encouraged vanity, Harry'd learn of it and find me somehow. He'd joke with me, and pull pennies from my ears and tell me Mama would be well soon. I don't know what I'd've done if it hadn't been between terms. Why, she even had my kitten drowned because she claimed loving a brute animal was unnatural.

"And then one day Mama was better, and Papa sent Aunt Aurelia away, and she never returned."

"It *was* a bad time," Louisa agreed numbly, remembering the vicious old harridan who insisted little girls sit silently in the schoolroom listening to improving sermons while pricking their fingers working samplers, even on the finest summer day. "But, you were so young, you don't quite remember properly. Miss Timmins didn't leave when your mother improved. Harry told me what she was doing to you. I told our mother, and she told Papa and they discussed it, and our father spoke with yours."

"So it *was* Harry," Patsy exclaimed, ignoring all other participants in the long-ago domestic drama. "It always has been. Did you know he gave me another kitten? And used his pocket money to buy me new hair ribbons? I still have them—every one.

"Harry's the sun and the moon and the stars. I don't think I can live without him—the *real* him," Patsy insisted. "He's still in there under all that bitterness. He's *got* to be. I know he's a viscount and I'm only the squire's daughter. He deserves so much more than me, and you've every right to be insulted by my presumption, but—"

"Oh, my dear," Louisa sighed, putting her arms around the girl once more. "What presumption? You're far more than Harry deserves. Were you to wed him today, no one would be more delighted than James and myself."

Patsy gave herself a shake, pulled away from Louisa's comforting arms, dashing the tears impatiently from her eyes. "That's all right, then, so long as you approve. I have a plan, you see," she said bravely. "I shall ignore him. He's not used to being ignored, at least by me, and he won't like it. Oh, at first he'll think it's heavenly, but then he'll begin to wonder. He'd better! And then? Then, you'll see.

"Remember all the times he pulled me from the brambles? Well, I'm going to force him to pull me from them again. Oh, the scrapes I'm going to get into! And, they won't be schoolgirl scrapes, either. They'll be very grown-up."

She peeped at Louisa from beneath long, sooty lashes.

"Are you truly certain you want me to stop with you and his grace? I may bring disgrace on my head before I'm done. Lady Daphne's offered to house me, which would be *much* better for you, but if I'm here it will be so much more convenient," she finished hopefully with a slight blush. "Harry will be readily accessible, you see: the breakfast table, passing on the stairs, that sort of thing. It's easier to ignore someone if he's there to ignore. I'd be dreadfully hampered by lack of propinquity at Lady Daphne's."

"My dear, you will have all our support, and any assistance you require. You need only ask," Louisa grinned at the younger woman, hope dawning in her eyes. "It will be provided on the instant. This is one of Aunt Daphne's famous plots, I gather?"

"Oh, no! The concept and method are entirely my own. Lady Daphne does approve the project, however, though she did caution me I may fail, and she insists Harry isn't worth the effort. I don't think she meant that, though. I believe she was putting me on my mettle. *Faint heart n'er won recalcitrant gentleman.*"

"I do hope you know what you're about," Louisa cautioned. "Harry may never return to the person he was."

"Oh, I'm *far* more determined he shall than he is that he shan't." Patsy turned away with a twinkle. "This isn't the first time I've come to Town, you see," she admitted impishly, ducking her head and clasping her hands behind her back like a child caught in a misdemeanor. "It's just the first one *you* know about."

"I've wondered. That ensemble is rather beyond the capabilities of any seamstress in the vicinity of Marleybourne."

"Most definitely! Look carefully, and you'll spot Holfers' fine Machiavellian hand in the choice of trim," Patsy agreed. "I've stayed with Lady Daphne several times while she and Holfers and Madame de Métrise between them brought me up to snuff. Lady Daphne says an elegant and properly provocative appearance is the first weapon of battle, along with ceasing to be such a sad romp, and she agrees whole-heartedly with my treating Harry with apparent indifference.

"I was, you know—a sad romp, I mean—with no more idea of what might suit me best in the way of clothes than a newborn infant.

"The dressmakers came to the house, and so did a dancing master and a voice teacher, and I don't know what all. I can even manage a tolerable watercolor now, though that's not really for Harry's benefit. It's merely so others will take notice of me, which Lady Daphne believes Harry will resent. That part *is* hers.

"Oh—and at the strategic moment he's to be permitted to glimpse a portrait of himself. I've *slaved* over it. Or, to be honest, I slaved over approximately ten dozen. Then we hired my drawing master—I simply *cannot* do faces, though pigs and sheep aren't too far beyond me so long as one doesn't insist on absolute anatomical accuracy—to produce a recognizable one. It's quite noble, and infinitely flattering, and I'm off in the distance, *also* quite recognizable, and positively *mooning* over him in the most maudlin fashion. That one *is* for him.''

''Dear Lord,'' Louisa chuckled, slightly aghast. Was there no end to Aunt Daphne's machinations? The vision of the extremely starchy Holfers, Aunt Daphne's dresser of so many years' standing she almost seemed part of the family, taking the irrepressible Patsy in hand as she once had Louisa, produced another slight chuckle. The battleground must have been strewn with cowering bolts of cloth and sobbing seamstresses. ''When did all this begin?''

''A year ago Christmas.'' Patsy plumped down on the comfortable cut velvet settee in front of the fire, patting the place next to her. ''Sit down, do. I've so much to tell you, and it can't be done in an instant.

''You were all at Marleybourne for the holidays, you see, since Harry refused to go to Rawdonmere for fear of being forced into female company,'' she continued as Louisa joined her by the glowing fire, ''and because you were there and wanted to see me, Harry was forced to put up with my occasional presence.

''You do remember my falling through the ice when we went skating, do you not?

''I'd snuck down in the middle of the night to saw through a special place in the lake—very difficult, as it had to appear natural—and then I was terrified someone else might fall through before I could. I wasn't even certain I'd sawed far enough. What an imbroglio! I had the grippe for the next three weeks, and for nothing. His grace pulled me out and gave me a dreadful scold and Harry didn't care in the least, blast him. Not even a basket of hothouse grapes or a note of inquiry as to how I did. He's impossible!

''But, Lady Daphne claimed while the plan was well enough in itself, I needed to be smoothed out first. Such a dressing-down she gave me! Freezing to death is apparently *not* the best way to capture a gentleman's interest.

"Now," Patsy proclaimed with immense satisfaction, springing to her feet and pirouetting, her exuberant reflection caught in the mirror over the graceful marble mantel, "I've been smoothed out, and the fun begins."

"I dearly hope so," Louisa said, caught between trepidation and laughter.

"It does," Patsy caroled. "Oh, it *does*. Trust dear Lady Daphne. We've all of us had enough of grim-and-grizzly. Now, we enjoy ourselves. Goodness, but I've been a prattlebox! Well, at least now you know everything, rather than merely suspecting bits and pieces. That's much more comfortable."

Then she spread her arms and became the Patsy of old, twirling until she collapsed on the pale green carpet, dizzy and giggling.

"Harry Beckenham, beware," she crowed. "Your doom is upon you!" And then more seriously as she caught her breath, "I shall succeed, you know, Louisa. I *must*."

Three

The rain was the worst, twenty-two-year-old Giles Fortescue decided as he turned Gorgon's head toward London once more—if one were willing to discount the gobbets of mud fouling his boots and encrusting his greatcoat. If one wasn't, the mud was its equal, but then without rain there'd've been no muck, so it all came down to the rain. The rain, and the ancient private coach that had just rattled past, baptizing him and his raw-boned dun mare with a liberal allotment of brown goo. He and Gorgon had been paragons of parade ground elegance after Waterloo by comparison with the appearance they currently presented.

The rain, the mud, the leaden skies promising more of the same for heaven knew how long were bad enough. The raw cold was their equal, and the wind transforming the steady downpour into stiletto points. There were moments when he swore if he ever found Richard DeLacey's "angel," he'd consign her straight to—well, he'd ignore her, go on his way. At least that was his current inclination, whatever he might do in actuality.

Mean-spirited of him? Spiteful? Perhaps, but a man had his limits.

No one and nothing was worth this, except the former colonel had been far more than his superior, even back in '14 and '15. Since that morning on the Grand' Place in Brussels the man had risen to a combination of friend, elder brother, even uncle. Giles had never felt entirely at ease with the Duke of Rawdon or Harry Beckenham, much as he liked and admired both men.

Of course, it hadn't been just the one coach. There'd been conveyances of all sorts along this boggy road to London, including the Mail speeding past with a shrill blast of the post horn. Wasn't much else one could expect if one were forced to walk along one of the major pikes leading to the capital.

Gorgon had done yeoman service during this latest foray into Devonshire. Then, with London only a day away, at least in clement weather, she'd thrown a shoe halfway between two tollgates. The next was still another mile down the mired road, the barrier and keeper's cottage squatting at the top of a long, slow rise. There he should find a lane leading to a village and a blacksmith and, if he was fortunate, an inn or tavern where he could warm himself by the fire, scrape off the mud and discuss a hot meal, however unimaginative or ill-prepared.

Impossible to tell the exact hour, he decided with a quick glance at the sky—which unthinking action netted him a brimful of water from his beaver cascading down his neck—but the light, never good on this dull day, was fading fast. Evening was coming on. He'd beg a room for the night if he could. If he couldn't, there would be stables and a bed of straw. Better yet, a bench by the fire.

It took the ginger-haired half-pay lieutenant the better part of an hour to reach the gate, beg directions from the surly keeper, and plod on to the unprepossessing hamlet of Badenton Major almost a league beyond the pike.

Despite its proud name, the village proved merely a handful of tumbled-down thatched cottages scattered in a hollow along the twisting country lane. Windows were shuttered, doors closed against the chilly night. No light gleamed through any chinks. No dogs roamed the lane. No pigs rooted beneath the trees. No fowl foraged in the garden patches. No villagers chattered on their stoops. No children played in the road or guided gentle-faced cows to their byres. A tiny Norman church with a squat tower and slitted windows hunkered at one end of the unwelcoming excrescence, a tavern whose weather-worn sign swung in the fitful wind at the other. At least there looked to be a blacksmith's shop, closed now for the night. The tollgate keeper had claimed he wasn't certain *what* amenities the village offered a weary traveler.

With a sigh, Giles splashed past the blacksmith's and through a series of puddles in the deeply rutted lane and turned in at the tavern, still leading his raw-boned mare. Gorgon gave a hopeful whicker. There were ramshackle stables to the rear, barely visible in the near-dark, and the scent of food in the air. A crook-backed ostler shuffled into the yard, cap pulled low over his eyes, collar turned up against the rain. The man held a pitchfork in one hand and a sputtering lantern in the other as he peered through the gloom at the sodden, disreputable Giles and his mud-spattered mount.

"Whatcher be wanting?" the man growled, and then hawked and spat on the ground.

"Stabling for my horse, a room for myself, and full bellies for us both," Giles returned with an effort at good cheer.

"This bein't a place fer the likes o' you, ye wall-eyed hedgebird. Get along with yer. Sides, we be full up." The ostler brandished his pitchfork at a smashed curri-

cle and an ancient begrimed coach. "And every one of
'em Quality-make, or so they says."

Giles's eyes narrowed, but his voice was milk-mild as
he said, "You're well off the mark. Natural enough, I
suppose. Normally you wouldn't have my custom," then,
after a look at the sour-faced man, tossed him a shilling.
"My horse threw a shoe a few miles back, needs a good
rub down and a dry stall, along with—"

"A likely tale," the ostler snarled, ignoring the coin
lying in the mud. "Get along with yer, else I'll be calling
the constable and *then* we'll see what tune ye sing!"

"In a place like this?" Giles snorted. "Give me credit
for *some* intelligence."

Two more shillings followed the first. Slowly the old
man lowered the pitchfork, still glaring doubtfully at
the young half-pay officer.

"There be a passel o' turned-off troopers taken to
the High Toby," he growled, "caging money and trin-
kets from h'onerst folk and raiding t'villages and t'country houses. Sartin ye bein't one on 'em?"

"I saw service with Wellington, if that's what you
mean," Giles returned coldly.

"Aye, that 'n' more."

"Which *doesn't* mean I'm not respectable. For God's
sake, man, do I *sound* like a hedgebird?"

"Not perticular, but then I've heard tell—"

"I don't care what you've heard," Giles spat, drawing
himself up to his full lanky six feet. "I'm Lord Giles
Fortescue, and I'll be *damned* if I'll let you turn me out
on a night like this. Now, take my horse, curse your
mangy hide, and see to it she's well cared for or you'll
wish you'd never been born!"

With that Giles unbuckled his sodden portmanteau
from behind the cantle, tossed the ostler the reins, then
stood glaring at him in the muddy stable yard. The

fiery glance that had worked with Wellington's troopers seemed to work here as well—that, or a certain tone of voice that offered no excuses, no explanations, and no room for discussion.

"No *lord* never rode no bone-setter like this 'un," the ostler grumbled dubiously.

"The old girl gets me where I want to go." There was a wealth of experience behind the icy words. "Don't malign her—she's sensitive. Now, hop to it!"

Slowly, reluctantly, with many a sidewards and backwards glance, the ostler set the pitchfork aside, retrieved the shillings and led the limping Gorgon into the dilapidated building as he shouted for the stableboy.

Giles let his shoulders droop, then turned toward the tavern. That had been a near one. Tired and miserable and discouraged, he wasn't certain what he'd've done had the blasted ostler continued to be recalcitrant. Taken him on right there in the mud and taught him a lesson or two, he supposed. And, given the troglodyte's sinewy arms and tree-stump fists, perhaps had his own cork drawn.

He depressed the latch with a grunt, ducked under the lintel and entered directly into the murky taproom.

A quick glance showed him the place was too small for private parlors, possibly didn't even offer sleeping accommodations. Well, what had he expected? White's famous club on Saint James Street, complete with befuddled old General Maitland sleeping off an overly copious dinner and two bottles of port in his customary corner?

At least a fire crackled on the filthy hearth, and the aroma of mutton stew mingled with the lingering stench of unwashed bodies, sour ale, stale smoke and rancid tallow. The unpleasant combination was all too familiar. DeLacey's insistence that somewhere in the wilds of Devon dwelt a girl with seven brothers, five of whom were named Jeremy, Andrew, John, Robert, and Charles, had meant a plethora of evenings spent under just such conditions. So far, he'd survived the experience.

He deposited his portmanteau on a scarred deal table well away from the door, pulled off his soggy gauntlets and dropped them and his hat beside the bag.

"What ho, the house," he bellowed toward the rear of the building, his words bouncing off the smoke-grimed walls and between the low rafters of the deserted taproom. Wherever the other guests were, it wasn't here.

He eased himself onto the crude bench beside the table, wriggling cramped toes in heavy, waterlogged topboots. Then, thinking better of it, he dragged the bench by the fire and settled there, taking off his single-caped greatcoat and draping it so it steamed and stank of wet wool from the fire's heat. If fortune smiled on him it might, just might, be dry by morning.

"House!" he shouted again.

Still no response. With a grunt of disgust he gained his feet and ducked behind the narrow bar, permitting himself the luxury of a two-footed limp now the day's journey was over.

The selection wasn't luxurious: local ale, rum, blue ruin, and a battered cask purporting to contain French brandy.

With a shrug he selected a tankard from the shelf behind the bar, poured himself a small measure of the black rum as the safest libation, downed it, coughed at its raw bite, poured a second measure and retreated to the fire, angling the bench so he could lean against the chimney breast. He sipped at the rum—which, given its flavor, was probably adulterated blue ruin—lulled by the welcome warmth and the steady drumming of the rain on the latched shutters. The tankard slipped from his fingers and rolled beneath the bench. A soft whuffling snore broke through his lips, then another, and another.

How long he slept, or precisely what awakened him, were puzzles at first. Groggy and disoriented, he squinted blearily into the murk, conscious only of a face that felt too warm and eyes that burned from exhaustion.

At first glance the place was still deserted despite the ostler's earlier assertions. Then, with a disbelieving scowl, he peered into a dusky nook well away from the chimney. A jumble of dark silhouettes resolved itself into three well-to-pass young fops with mayhem on their minds and rapine in their souls taunting a robust farmwife and her scrawny companion.

Giles let out an infuriated roar that brought mine host and his good wife scurrying from the back of the building.

Without waiting for assistance or approval, Giles bored in, fists flying, muddied boots lashing out to catch shins, buttocks, any portion of the leering louts' anatomies he could assault. The battle was vicious, brief, punctuated by insulted howls and aggrieved curses. That Gentleman Jackson would not have approved of his style mattered little, especially when considering the odds. Science was not at issue—only bottom, wind, and a punishing right.

In a matter of moments the three choice spirits measured their lengths upon the taproom floor, lips cut, teeth loosened, noses leaking, eyes shut. Giles rubbed his sore knuckles as he stared down at the unholy trio with no little degree of satisfaction. Then he turned to their victims with a boyish grin.

"You're all right?" he asked. "No damage done?"

"Nay, we be fine, young sir, thanking you kindly," the farmwife assured him with a relieved gasp as she pulled her coarse brown shawl more tightly about her shoulders, "though the dear Lord knows what them scalawags would've been doing hadn't you woked up. A plain mercy it was you come along while we was visiting the necessary and they was out to the stable. Gaming is what *I* think they was about. That, or trying to find theirselves a willing lass—which my guess is they didn't, being slime-worts as they are—and *that's* when our troubles begun.

"Slipped the landlord a crown, that 'un did," she explained indignantly, pointing to a pimply-faced youth with a slowly purpling eye and swelling jaw, "so's he and his woman'd stay away whilst they played their games, and us with Alfie and Young Thom sleeping out t'the stable, and no help a'tall. Drunk as lords the three of 'em were, and full o' the devil, besides which they wasn't best pleased to be trapped in a place like this by the mizzle," she prattled on, " 'cause they was for London when one of 'em goes and overturns 'em in a ditch and smashes up the fat one's curricle. They been here the whole day sousing, which tells the tale."

"It certainly does. You're positive you're unharmed," Giles prodded, turning to the child. "You must have been terrified."

"Right as trivets," she assured him, looking up at him with overly large blue-gray eyes in a too-thin, brown little face, "and *very* grateful for your interference."

The child, he realized as she rose from the bench, wasn't a child at all, but an undersized girl with a pert air and a pointed chin, and a neatly packaged set of delicately feminine curves almost hidden by a shapeless gray dress.

"Pleased I could be of assistance," Giles said with uncharacteristic pomposity, flustered by her glowing look of gratitude. Then he turned on the landlord with a deepening scowl. "So—you were paid to look the other way, were you," he said with slow menace. "What's the price for permitting rape these days?"

"T'weren't no such thing, your worship," the scrawny host protested. "Them lads just be young sprigs on a lark, don't you see, and enjoying the companionship. *She* were leading 'em on with her snooty ways, and not the vicey-versal."

"Asking for it, she was," his helpmate agreed, passing a furred tongue over thin lips, "with her come-hither looks, and her claiming t'be Quality when one look'll tell you she's naught but a serving wench giving herself airs, and a ugly one at that. Why, her master's sent her to Lun'un in a broke-down old coach no Quality'd set foot in! Go look, if'n you don't believe me. Fact of it is," she added slyly, "*that* one's an abbess or my name ain't Bessie Wogglum, and *this* one's a young piece she's bringing down from the country to—"

Giles's low growl sent the insalubrious pair scuttling backwards with uneasy sidelong glances at the girl and the farmwife and the three lumps of high-born flesh moaning on the filthy floor.

"I don't care who these ladies are, or what their business is, or where they came from, or where they're going, or what manner of conveyance is taking them there," Giles snapped, advancing on the owner and his wife. "Those who aspire to keep a public house have certain responsibilities. Don't take 'em very seriously, do you?"

"You're a fine one to talk," the landlord's wife spat, "using a h'onerst 'ouse for a milling ken like you been. I'm of a mind to send Dickie for the constable, I am."

"That's the *second* time I've been threatened with the law in this damnable backwater. The threat's meaningless to me, but if you think it's such a great one, I just wonder if it's as meaningless to you?"

Glare met unwavering glare. Finally, with a disgusted shrug, Giles turned to the two women.

"I'd suggest paying your shot immediately and spending the night in your coach with your companions standing watch," he said. "These young fools won't be in a cheerful frame of mind when they rejoin the world. Ugly cup-shot is uglier with a sore head the next morning. I'd leave soon as the sun's up, not meaning to borrow trouble, but I recognize two of 'em. Acquainted that one's sister—not *him*," he added at the sharp look thrown him by the farmwife as he pointed to the oldest. "She's a sweet little thing, but Nigel Farquhar? A craven milksop if you're the stronger, and a nasty-tongued viper if you're not. Can't be trusted, for all he flies high when he wants.

"That one," he continued with disgust, pointing to the pimply-faced youth with the rapidly swelling jaw, "is Aloysius Beckenham, some sort of cousin of an acquaintance of mine. The toad's a man-milliner, fuzzes the cards when he's got the chance, and fancies himself a nonpareil when he's naught but the merest whipster. He'd be the one overturned the curricle. Spends more time in ditches than on the road. Loose screws, both of 'em. Lardish one looks to be their equal. Just my luck to run across them here—the perfect ending to a perfect day."

The older woman nodded, grabbed a worn brown cloak and handed it to the girl, then tossed a few shillings on the table where Giles had deposited his portmanteau.

"We ain't eaten, nor yet we ain't seen a private room like we asked for *and* been promised, only the necessary, and you can imagine what *that* was like given the rest of this place," she said, "so that should ought to more'n make us square. Glad to offer you the coachman's seat for the night if you like, for all it wouldn't be total proper. Still, who's to know? Won't be too healthy for you here, not after the way you dispatched them lordlings, and we owe you thanks-and-amen.''

"I?" Giles chuckled. "Oh, I'll mount guard here in case these young asses get more improper ideas. Won't be the first night I've done without sleep for the sake of a higher goal." He glanced at the shillings lying on the table, then turned to the tavern owner's wife. "Bread, cheese, apples, hot soup—provide these ladies with some sort of meal they can eat in their carriage, and do it now," he ordered. "And I'll want that stew I smell, and whatever else you have to offer in this benighted place. Move your stumps!"

The scrawny farmgirl threw him a grateful glance, her mouth opening. The woman at her side gave her a minatory frown, tied the cloak at her neck, pulled the hood over her head and thrust her further into the shadows.

"Hush," she hissed repressively. "Keep your words to yourself, Miss Lizzie. Them four's Quality, every last one of 'em, and you might be seeing of 'em again. Least any remembers of this, the best for all."

Then she smiled at Giles.

"Thank you kindly, young sir, and we'll be glad of the victuals for we're that hungry, having spent the day on the road with nary a hot meal, and a pure misery it was—so long as you think *they'll* not poison us," with a contemptuous glance at the innkeeper and his wife. "Me, I don't think that besom could boil water without burning the pot."

"Sometimes, when one is on bivouac," Giles chuckled, "one must simply run the risk if one is hungry enough. Good night, ladies. Sleep well."

The woman and the scrawny girl slipped out into the rainy night, the girl throwing a grateful little smile over her shoulder. Giles turned on the innkeeper and his wife.

"I'll trouble you to busy yourselves, unaccustomed though the exercise may be," he said gently. "See to the ladies first. And get me some lengths of rope. I've no desire to be attacked from behind, and those bounders are just the sort to try it. Cowards, every last one of 'em."

Lady Lavinia DeLacey, Dowager Countess of Rochedale, was holding court.

In more simple terms, this was the afternoon she was at home to callers, but if one considered where she was at home—in the cavernous state drawing room of the great Palladian mansion of the Earls of Rochedale close by Hammersmith—holding court was by far the more appropriate term.

Strapping footmen attired in the subtle Rochedale livery of gray and silver, their powdered wigs stiff miniature clouds, attended to the comfort and refreshment of elegant ladies and simpering misses swirling like shattered rainbows. Well-bred chatter filled the great space. Delicate laughter rang like chiming silver bells. Pouts drew rosy lips into provocative moues inviting stolen kisses. Thin muslins revealed nubile charms. With this bevy of buds spreading sweet fragrance, the rain that greased its way down the soaring silk and velvet-draped windows might not have existed.

The dowager countess was in her element, as close to glowing as that lady ever came.

That so many were in attendance on such an inclement day, and so far from the infinitely more fashionable environs of Mayfair, was undisputed proof of her power within the ton, the respect and fear and even reverence in which she was held. This acknowledgment of her primacy was everything she could have wished. An air of self-satisfied complaisance suffused her strong features with something very akin to warmth.

Well-placed hints in the proper places had brought every lady related to a tonnish young miss of impeccable birth and breeding and generous dot calling, potential bride in tow, in anticipation of the earl's presence, for the earl, Lady Lavinia had intimated to a select few—knowing the tale would travel—was in search of a suitable wife. That the facts were other, that, indeed, *she* was in search of a suitable wife *for* him, was an immaterial detail. That he had never, and would never put in an appearance at one of her at-homes was another detail none of these sheep need know.

Silver coiffure shining in contrast to the elegant black gown she sported, famous Rochedale rubies glowing on chest and ears and wrists, the famous betrothal emerald of the Rochedales glittering on her hand like the all-seeing orb of an Eastern dragon, Lady Lavinia portrayed the very essence of regal unapproachability. With the exceptions of Lady Sally Jersey (too useful a tool to offend), Lady Daphne Cheltenham (a spineless cipher, but also a tractable friend of such long standing that she must always be permitted a certain latitude) and Lady Serena Duchesne (eldest daughter of the Duke of Hampton, and possessed of a social power that, Lady Lavinia reluctantly conceded, might almost equal her own), none would have dreamed of approaching the thronelike chair from which the dowager surveyed the lambs on the block unless invited.

Now her eyes again darted over the young misses presented for her inspection. She raised an imperious hand to summon a petite blonde with cornflower eyes and rose-petal cheeks.

This would be the sixteenth she had interviewed.

Of the preceding fifteen a third had proved idiots, another third pert and far too coming, all but one insufficiently deferential, and all ten affected beyond what was bearable. That did of course leave the final third, but of those one had a squint, one butterteeth, one flaming red tresses—a sure sign of an intractable nature and uncertain ancestry, no matter how stubbornly the foolish miss and her pandering mother pretended otherwise—and another freckles. That left but one chit of sufficient looks, breeding, and consciousness of the honor being accorded her to be worthy of consideration, and *she* was barely sixteen. Far too young for someone of Rochedale's experience. She'd bore him in an instant, and Lady Lavinia had no desire to render her grandson actively miserable if it could be avoided.

Indeed, she had wanted to present him with a choice. Men preferred it that way. Of course, she could always merely *appear* to be presenting him with a choice while having already made the decision herself. It worked out that way more often than not. Men never understood what was in their best interests.

She looked the girl over at close range, gimlet eye intended to cow. It succeeded.

"I've forgotten your name, my dear," she said graciously.

"Millicent Farquhar, if you please, your ladyship," the child whispered, ducking a graceful curtsey.

"*Millicent?* Outlandish name!" the dowager countess snapped, graciousness forgotten. This one might do. Looked like butter wouldn't melt in her mouth, and the figure was well enough. Plenty there to keep a man occupied, at least for a time. Farquhar? Not an impossible family, though the father drank too much, the brother was a wasp-waisted fop with more hair than wit, the elder sister wed to a mere baronet, and the mother a nonentity who dressed like a guy for all she had the sense to see her daughter properly garbed. "What's wrong with 'Mary' or 'Sarah' or 'Jane'?"

"I don't know, your ladyship," Millicent responded after a dubious glance at her hovering mother when the silence stretched to such an uncomfortable length that it was clear the dowager countess expected some form of answer to her unanswerable question. "Is anything wrong with them?"

"Don't be pert, Miss!"

"Why, I'd no intention of—"

"And don't contradict your elders and betters! Haven't you taught the chit *any* manners?" Lady Lavinia snapped at the horrified Lady Farquhar.

"Apologize to Lady DeLacey," the girl's mother hissed frantically under the guise of adjusting her sash. *"Now. Immediately!"*

"For my name?" the girl whispered in a quake, cheeks flaming, well aware she would be plunged into irretrievable disaster did she not say precisely the correct thing.

Lady Lavinia's voice carried far indeed when she wished. The drawing room had fallen silent, the guests turning in their direction. Even Lady Serena Duchesne's laugh was stilled, her ill-coifed head craning awkwardly on its storklike neck as she absently stroked the head of the pug tucked beneath her arm.

Lady Jersey sidled up, eyes gleaming. This was one young lady who'd not be receiving vouchers for Almack's when the time came, the powerful patroness of those exclusive assembly rooms decided. Not that she cared particularly for Lavinia DeLacey, or would ever consider deferring to her, but there were those who did. It paid to trim one's sails to the social breezes and keep a wary eye out for the shoals if one wished to be credited with omniscient omnipotence within the ton.

"For existing. For your name. For being rude," Lady Farquhar hissed. *"For anything and everything! Do you want
to be ruined?"*

"I—I'm most deeply sorry, Lady DeLacey," Millicent
quavered, ready to sink. "I'd no intention of offending.
I beg you to forgive my lapse in decorum. I'm certain
had Mama known my name would prove unacceptable
to you, she'd've selected one more to your taste."

"Toadying ninny," Lady DeLacey muttered too low
for the girl to hear, regarding her as if she were a scrap
of spoiled meat.

"Please feel free to call me anything you wish, your
ladyship," Millicent concluded, sweeping a curtsy worthy of a Royal Drawing Room after throwing anxious
glances at her mother and the formidable dowager
countess to ascertain her success in the art of self-abase-
ment.

"Then I'll call you *idiot,*" Lady DeLacey snapped with
no small satisfaction as Lady Farquhar blanched, "for
that is precisely what you are. Off with you! I've no time
for lack-wits and maw-worms."

She turned her back on the child, eyes sparkling with
delight. And so another social career had been ruined
before it was fairly begun. The chit was only recently
out of the schoolroom. They might as well send her
back to it, or pack her off to the country. How delightful
such power was. How positively *lovely.* How gratifying.

Gradually the chatter resumed, now on a slightly more
frenetic pitch, as the multitude feigned turning from
the interesting little tableau while still watching avidly
from the corners of their eyes should something more
of note occur. Tonight's entertainments would be all
the more entertaining for this little incident. One thing
was certain: the ill-gowned Lady Farquhar and her vacuous daughter would be remaining closeted at home,

the one in spasms, the other in tears. Indeed, it was to be doubted if even the foppish Nigel or his father would have the effrontery to show their faces in their clubs.

"Was that truly necessary, Lavinia?" a soft voice inquired at the dowager countess's elbow. "If the child demonstrated lack of breeding, your conduct was worse."

"Oh, Daphne—*there* you are."

Lady DeLacey turned with what might have passed for a tiny smile and looked her old friend up and down. Really! Daphne Cheltenham should learn to dress more in accordance with her age. Such determined girlishness was idiotish in the extreme, besides being hardly in keeping with her station. Today's fashions were hardly suited to any woman worthy to be called such.

"Yes, it was necessary, a small test if you wish, which the ninnyhammer failed utterly. I will *not* have Rochedale wed to someone unacceptable, and his Devonshire miss, if she exists at all, would prove totally unacceptable. A sawbone's daughter? Deliver me! I *must* find a suitable substitute, but this fall's crop"—her gesture took in the roomful of delicate misses—"is hopeless. The Farquhar chit is typical. If they're not idiots, they're platter-faced. If they're not platter-faced, they're pert. If they're not pert, they're idiots. The modern generation is nothing to what we were. How can one expect elegance of manner or figure when they trip about in little more than nightrails," she snapped, throwing a disparaging glance at Lady Daphne's very modish afternoon ensemble, "and lisp like the veriest infantile mawk-minds?"

"Oh, I think you're being a trifle harsh, don't you?"

"I don't see your precious Harry dancing attendance on any of 'em!"

"Why, no," Lady Daphne returned soothingly, "but then he's not particularly in the petticoat line and never has been."

"Still wearing the willow for the Fortescue chit, is he? Men're fools!"

"You've ruined that child for sheer amusement," Lady Daphne protested, accepting the small gilt chair offered her by a hovering footman as her eyes flew to where Millicent Farquhar (in tears) and her distrait mother (in the first throes of frenzied vapors) were departing through towering doors held open by a pair of supercilious footmen. "And, you *have* ruined her, at least for the moment. That was not well done of you, for she'd said nothing deserving such treatment."

"She has the temerity to exist. That's offense enough."

"This isn't like you. Surely you remember the misery such ostracism causes, especially when it is undeserved."

"You know nothing whatsoever of what is like or *unlike* me, and never have." Then, at her friend's look of reproach, Lady Lavinia capitulated ungraciously, "Oh, very well, I'll do something to rectify the matter. Take her up in my carriage, perhaps, on the next fine day. *You* say something appropriate to The Jersey. She'll spread it about, never fear. Now, have done, do! I've no desire to come to cuffs with you."

"Thank you, my dear; I know it was merely irritation of nerves caused you to act so cruelly. Most out of character."

"Oh, let it be. I wonder," Lady Lavinia said thoughtfully, glancing across the room to where the Duke of Hampton's daughter hovered at the edge of a group of young misses, avidly absorbing their chatter, "precisely how many years Serena Duchesne might have in her basket. Substantial dot there, that I *do* know. And impeccable breeding, for all she has the face and voice of a mule."

"You're not considering—"

"She's no fool, at least," Lady Lavinia said with a look

of heightened interest as she peered at the angular
thirtyish spinster, "for all her pugs and her good works.
A skilled manteau-maker could work wonders there,
and a decent coiffeur. She merely requires some expert
guidance."

"Why, Serena Duchesne's older than Richard by at
least two years, and has been on the shelf since I don't
know when," Lady Daphne protested, well aware of her
friend's determination to see her grandson wed by the
end of the Little Season.

"No daughter of a duke is *ever* on the shelf, my dear,
not *irremediably*—even the Lady Serena. It might serve.
Yes, it just might serve."

"You'll come home by weeping cross if you attempt
it," Lady Daphne chuckled with considerable lack of
tact. "The ton will laugh you out of London if Richard
doesn't send you packing first, mark my words. Elderly
grandmothers and aged aunts, no matter *how* devoted
and well-meaning, have only so much power."

"We'll see," Lady Lavinia returned with an enigmatic
smile. "At least she's preferable to all these Millicents
and Melisandes and Mirandas."

Harry Beckenham watched as the two toughs scuttled
around the corner, rubbing absently at his jaw, then
wiggling it, blood-stained swordstick tucked beneath his
stump. Three, it had been this time. The other one lay
stretched at his feet, gurgling and fouling the pavement,
never to trouble any man again, honest or otherwise.

The former major glanced up and down Curzon
Street.

No sign of the Watch, which was just as well. They
were less than useless, the Charlies a joke. There was
nothing he wanted less at the moment than to stand
before a magistrate and explain himself. Someone was

sure to stumble across the lump of filth lying on the cobbles and see it was properly disposed of before morning. And, if they didn't, the matter wasn't serious. Some maid would come out at dawn to scrub the stoop, have hysterics, and become a heroine-for-a-day belowstairs.

A good thing he'd thought to provide himself with a weapon, though he'd almost laughed at the foolishness when he placed the order for a special stick designed with a spring release suitable to a man with but a single arm. Still, old habits and old precautions died hard. There'd been a prickling at the back of his neck for a week now, and since he hadn't been able to explain it at first—and still couldn't, for that matter—he'd thought to placate his uneasy sense that something was most definitely not as it should be. Instead, he'd most likely saved his life.

It had been sheer common sense to vary his route to White's after the first incident. He'd done it almost without thinking, but that apparently hadn't been enough—unless "enough" were to confirm the old business just after his return from the Peninsula had begun again. Only, it wasn't the old business, he'd swear to that. This was different in some way he couldn't identify, and it terrified him. The unknown and inexplicable always did, no matter how well he managed to hide it from others.

Of course, there was always the possibility he was seeing goblins where none existed. London was a dangerous place these days, a man with only one arm easy prey. Attacks on prosperous-appearing citizens were constant, even in full daylight. There might be nothing more to it than that.

He retrieved the sheath from where he'd aimed it so it wouldn't trip him, and sank onto a convenient step with a grunt.

He was shivering, by damn, and his heart still

pounded, and it wasn't from exertion. He'd dispatched the trio with ease. But then, he'd seen them coming. What if he were distracted, and so didn't notice the next time?

Because there would be a next time. Once was chance. Twice wasn't, not even in London, not even at this hour of the night.

Someone wanted him dead.

He set sheath and slim sword beside him with a snarl of disgust, pulled out his handkerchief and, trapping it beneath his Hessian, managed to wipe the blade fairly clean. Being one-handed was a damned inconvenience, and that was all there was to it.

Oh, he'd adjusted, but it hadn't been easy and it hadn't been quick.

For a miracle Louisa had the grace to understand when assistance would be appreciated during those first hard weeks after he'd arrived fresh from the Peninsula, and in more pain than he cared to admit. And, she'd known when to leave him alone, and never—*never*—had she avoided looking him directly in the face. At that point he hadn't been certain which bothered him more: the scar or the missing arm.

Now he knew. It was the arm.

The face had mattered only because of Gwendolyn, for he wasn't always conscious of it if there weren't mirrors about. There was no way one could be unconscious of a missing arm, especially if it were one's own.

He sheathed the stick and stood, studying the refuse on the cobbles, now very still and cooling. He'd never seen it before. He'd never seen any of them before.

Strange to think it had been a babe once, suckling innocently at its mother's breast—though probably unwanted and unloved, and innocence was something that would have vanished early in the stews from which such vermin sprang.

With a sigh at the bitterness and futility of life, and feeling faintly foolish, Harry Beckenham closed the staring eyes and weighted them with a pair of coins from his purse, not for the tough's sake, but for the sake of the babe it had once been. Then he set off once more for Grosvesnor Square and his brother-in-law's residence. The trick would be to let himself in and sneak up to his rooms with no one the wiser. Still, it was very late—or very early, depending on one's definition and position in life—and he had a key. The thing shouldn't be impossible. Even the porter would be abed by now.

He wanted no questions. Most especially, he wanted no questions from his astute and overly observant brother-in-law. Rawdon had a way of cutting to the nub of matters that could be decidedly uncomfortable on occasion. Whatever happened, happened. His life wasn't worth much anyway, and he didn't want Louisa fretting. Or Aunt Daffy, for all her interfering ways.

South Audley Street was quiet, only the occasional elegant town carriage returning a sodden pleasure-seeker to his home in the small hours, senses sated and purse depleted. He crossed Mount Street, tipping his hat to the passing Watch with a certain delight in the ironies of the situation. On this night he had become, if one wanted to be technical about it, a murderer. The strange thing was, he felt nothing at the taking of this particular human life. He'd felt more, in fact, when he'd skinned and spitted a young hare he'd just killed while near by Badajoz, and held it over the crackling fire. One moment it had been running wild and free, grace in its every movement, and the next it had been dead merely to fill his belly. That had seemed by far the greater shame, for the hare had been a thing of beauty.

With a sigh he turned into Grosvenor Square.

It was so quiet, so very peaceful. A trace of mist—

one couldn't call it fog, so tenuous it was—snagged
on railing and leaf, the occasional condensed droplet
falling to the ground, the trees standing silent sentinel
duty in the park, the lights of the great houses extinguished, their fires banked, their inhabitants deep in
slumber. He climbed the steps leading to Rawdon
House, silently turned his key in the well-oiled lock, let
himself in, closed the door, and eased the well-greased
bolts home.

There was no one about, thank the Lord. He'd done
it.

He sat on the slanting footman's chair, removed his
boots, then made his way to the library at the back of
the house. A glass of brandy was the only thing he
wanted at the moment, or perhaps two or three, and
then his bed.

He eased one of the tall oak doors open, slipped
inside, shut it softly behind him. No light leaked through
the tall windows, their green velvet draperies drawn
against the night. A good thing he'd come to know the
room as well as the back of his hand.

Moving slowly so as not to stumble over some dis-
placed chair or table, he made his way to the fireplace,
fingered the mantel for a spill, finally located one and
shoved it among the banked coals. A single flame flared.
He lit a brace of candles, blew out the spill, went over
to the heavy table where decanters of brandy and port
and madeira were invariably kept, poured himself a
brim-full glass, downed it in three massive gulps,
coughed, and refilled it.

"What're you doing, Harry?"

He froze, then whirled in disbelief, staring at the slight
sleepy figure curled in one of the red leather chairs
beside the fireplace, reddish-brown curls in disarray,
provocative satin dressing gown dripping lace and rib-

bons tucked around her knees just as if she were still a child. A discarded book lay in her lap. A guttered candle stood on the table beside the chair. They offered explanation enough of her presence there, dammit. He should've remembered Patsy Worth's habit of reading whenever she couldn't sleep, and spending half the night napping in the squire's bookroom. He should've checked the moment the spill was alight. He should've *thought*, but then perhaps he was beyond thinking at the moment. It wouldn't surprise him.

"Damn," he muttered.

Patsy Worth yawned, regarding him disapprovingly. "Haven't you had enough of that already?" she asked. "You appear to have whipped the cat 'til it went yowling home." Then she took a more careful look, scrubbed her eyes and looked again. "Dear God, Harry—what have you been about? You look as if someone tried to murder you."

She was on her feet, book tumbling unheeded to the floor as she flew over to him, hand coming up to gently touch his jaw as she stood on tiptoe.

"It's swollen," she said. "I'll get some ice from the kitchens. François insists there always be a supply," and was through the doors before he could stop her.

"Damn," he muttered again, considered locking her out and decided against it.

Patsy Worth in an inquisitorial mood was a force to be reckoned with. Locked doors might easily inspire her to call out the house. Better to deal with her alone than with Rawdon and Louisa and the Lord knew who else as well. He'd always managed to get the chit to agree to anything he said, even if it took a bit. Louisa and Rawdon were another matter.

She was back in what seemed an instant, bare toes twinkling on the old Persian carpets. "Sit," she ordered, pointing to the other chair flanking the fireplace and closing the door behind her. "Have you no sense at all? You look all done in."

Then he was in the chair, against his jaw he held a small towel containing ice she'd crushed. It was infinitely soothing, even if it made him shiver again.

"*You* sit," he said, eyes carefully avoiding curves more than hinted at through the satin and lace as he flushed furiously. "Over there," pointing to the chair across from him. "And keep that blasted gown in place. Have you no sense of propriety?"

"Very little, I'm afraid. Besides, when was I ever miss-ish around you? You've probably seen most everything of me there is to see at one time or another. Louisa tells me you even changed my nappies once."

"Hussy!" he said. If only he could keep her distracted.

"She said you made an excellent job of it, too. Where have you been, Harry?"

And so it was to begin again, just as when she was a child. *Where have you been, Harry? What have you been doing, Harry? What's an opera-dancer, Harry? Why's your face all red, Harry?* Damn!

"None of your business, brat," he blustered.

"Perhaps you'd prefer to explain your appearance and your return at this hour to Louisa," she suggested sweetly with a look he remembered only too well. "Where have you been, Harry," she insisted.

"You presumptuous, interfering little—"

"*Where*, Harry?"

"All right, blast you—I was at White's."

"That may explain the hour. It doesn't explain your appearance," she countered. "You're battered, not cup-shot, now that I look at you more carefully."

He glared at her, but it did no more good than it had when she was a member of the infantry.

"I had a disagreement with a gentleman over the turn of a card," he ground out.

"That calls for pistols at dawn, or possibly swords, but *not* fisticuffs or blood on your cloak, and *not* in the middle of the night. D'you take me for a flat?"

"We decided to settle matters immediately."

"If it's done in such a manner, it's all very formal, and it's done at Gentleman Jackson's with scads of others looking on to make sure all's right and tight, and with the Gentleman himself officiating. And again, it's not in the middle of the night. I *am* more than seven, you know."

"Oh, stubble it, will you?"

"Cut line, Harry. Something's wrong. I can see it in your eyes."

"Nothing's wrong that couldn't be cured by the absence of a certain interfering little marplot who's always been more trouble than she was worth," he snarled. "It's none of your affair, and there's an end to it."

She stared at him wide-eyed, sudden tears sparkling in her lashes.

"Not even *then*, Harry?" she whispered in a tremulous little voice.

"No, not even when you were in plaits," he retorted, understanding precisely what she meant, just as he always had.

Then, at the sight of her crestfallen face and the tears trickling slowly down her cheeks, he swore again. He didn't mind if she cried so long as she made a noisy, attention-getting business of it. It was the silence, the despair, the fact that she didn't even seem to realize she was crying that turned his heart over in his breast like a leaden lump.

"Yes, *then*," he said, started to toss her his handker-

chief, took one horrified look at the grimy thing, stuffed
it back in his pocket hoping she hadn't noticed all the
blood, unwound his neckcloth and tossed that to her
instead. "Of course, then. Now, too, I suppose. Here,
wipe your face, brat. I'm not worth your tears."

She obeyed him, hardly seeming to notice what she
was doing, her eyes never leaving his face. Then she
stood, handing him the neckcloth.

"Thank you," she said, "for saying once upon a time
I wasn't such a burden, even if I am now." She watched
him another moment, such a jumble of emotions on
her face he couldn't read them. Then, with a sigh, she
went and planted a soft sisterly kiss on his hair. "Harry,
something's dreadfully wrong," she said. "I just know
it is. I've *always* known when something was wrong. I
won't go bearing tales to Louisa or his grace, or even
to Giles, but you must promise me something in return:
If there's anything I can do to help—*anything, ever*—
you'll tell me. Will you promise me that?"

"It was just a disagreement between two gentlemen
who were slightly well-to-pass," he said dully, folding
the neckcloth with extreme care. "You were right in
the beginning. We didn't know what we were doing.
Could've caused quite a scandal. One does not employ
White's for a mill."

"Nevertheless," she said gently, "anything and ever.
Promise me."

"All right—anything and ever," he agreed, repeating
a phrase that had been part of her childhood, and part
of his youth. "Now, will you get yourself to bed? You're
too old to be wandering about the house garbed in that
thing. It's totally indecent."

Blast it, why did the pernicious chit have to be so
gallant, so loyal, so completely un-missish? So damnably
alluring, with her tousled curls and gentle feminine
curves?

Little Patsy Worth had grown up while he wasn't watching. He wasn't sure if he liked it, and he wasn't in the least sure what he should or could do about it. He no more needed another complication in his life than he needed to lose his remaining arm.

Why couldn't she have stayed a child, the way she was supposed to?

"Good night, Harry," she whispered huskily as he glared at her. "You'd best seek your bed soon. It's very late."

Then the door closed and she was gone, forgotten book still lying on the floor. Harry dropped his head against the chair's back, stared at the dark ceiling, cursing softly and steadily, ice once more held to his jaw.

Four

London was a nightmare.

Elizabeth Driscoll had known it would be, of course. Having her opinion confirmed within moments of her arrival on the Wainwright doorstep—wet, bedraggled, battling a fierce headache and exhausted by what felt like a lifetime spent in the ancient family traveling coach and then a farmer's gig—was perhaps a bit much, however.

The journey from Saint Mary-Grafton had been disagreeable in the extreme. Once beyond Devon, mired roads and constant drizzle interspersed with downpours so heavy the cumbersome and ill-sprung Driscoll coach was forced to pull in at any available inn to wait them out conspired to extend what should have taken four easy days into six interminable ones.

Job horses threw shoes and came up lame with discouraging regularity despite Alfie Throssel's best efforts.

Accommodations at respectable posting houses arranged for by her father evaporated as soon as she stepped through the door. Two nights were spent curled under cloaks and rugs in the coach as Alfie and Young Thom took turns mounting guard, Tillie sniffling as she battled a fierce head cold. Another was passed in the taproom of what proved little better than a hedgerow tavern. Insults, leers, even demands for service given Elizabeth's worn cloak, plain dress, and lack of suitable duenna (for poor Tillie did not qualify as a proper personal maid), were continual even in the best of places.

In the worst?

She did *not* want to think about that, she decided with a shudder. Thank heavens for the mud-spattered stranger at the disreputable tavern where they spent the next-to-last night. Only his timely intervention averted a horror of such proportions it didn't bear contemplation.

She'd begged for a return home that night—to no avail, of course. Alfie stubbornly and correctly insisted London, and the safety of her uncle's house, was closer. Tillie concurred, and given her years of service in the Driscoll household, her word was as close to law as they were likely to come. Tillie sneezed and snuffled her way through that icy, miserable night, cold worsening in the drafty coach.

Then, only miles from the outskirts of town, disaster compounded with disaster, its first indication a yard of tin braying in the distance. A common stage barreled down on them, ricocheting across ruts and slewing through boggy low spots. Atop swaggered the three sprigs from two nights before, faces battered, eyes nicely decorated. Pimply-faced Aloysius Beckenham was again in his cups, gripping the reins of the runaway team in one hand, a dark bottle definitely not containing tea in the other. The equally inebriated coachman brandished the broken brake handle as the would-be driver's two cronies entertained the other shivering outside passengers with a highly improper version of *Scarborough Fair.* Shrieks of terror soared above the horses' pounding hooves.

Alfie Throssel sawed at his team's hard mouths, aiming for a lane which came upon them too swiftly to offer safe haven. The swaying stage forced the old Driscoll coach from the road as it racketed past on a northerly curve, holding to the crown. The coach groaned mightily at the indignity, tilted and slithered into the ditch, upper wheels spitting splintered spokes, not quite a turtle on its back, but no longer a viable (or repairable) mode of transportation.

"Damnation," Elizabeth had muttered, disentangling herself from a heavy carriage robe and righting herself as she rubbed an abused elbow. "Well, the poor old arc was only held together by lacquer and prayers anyway. Hush, Tillie. You've nothing broken, do you? It's just the surprise of traveling up and down and sideways rather than along?"

Tillie nodded, gulping as she gripped her shoulder.

Shaken, her ears ringing with the squeals of terrified horses, Alfie and Young Thom's curses and Tillie's quieting sobs, Elizabeth struggled to force the heavy door, gave it up, wrestled the window down and scrambled up to teeter on the coach's side. Alfie was pressing one arm to his side as he and Young Thom struggled with the maddened team, dodging lashing hooves and snapping teeth. The stage was already far down the road, topping a sweeping rise as it lurched like a toper staggering his way home after a particularly convivial evening. With a final blast of the horn it disappeared over the crest.

There were no other vehicles in sight, not even a farmer's cart, and just when she needed the pike to be as crowded as it had been through six unendurable days. Fate was proving distinctly uncooperative.

"Are you both in one piece?" Elizabeth called to Alfie as she slid from her precarious perch into the muddy ditch, landing up to her ankles in standing water. Then, with a practiced look at the gingerly way Alfie held his arm and the whiteness around his lips, "Let me, blast you, Alfie! There's no need to make bad worse. Here," seizing the reins from him, "Young Thom and I can manage."

And, manage she and Young Thom had, years of handling her father's ancient gelding and an instinctive understanding of brute animals' fears coming into play as Alfie called instructions and nursed his cracked ribs and broken arm. At last three of the floundering team were quieted, disentangled from the traces, unhitched, led a bit down the road and tethered to a hedgerow. The fourth, its eyes rolling, its right fore shattered, was then dispatched with a single shot from the pistol Young Thom carried as protection, Elizabeth rather than the blanching Thom performing the merciful act, then leaning weakly over the ditch to cast up her accounts as unaccustomed tears scalded her eyes. The poor dobbin had known what was to come—she could swear it.

An hour later the hapless quartet was grouped around the fire in a Samaritan-spirited farmer's cottage, partaking of peppermint tea and downing thick sandwiches of homemade cheese and locally cured ham. Alfie's ribs had been bound and his arm splinted. A cool compress eased the ache of Tillie's bruised shoulder, and her feet were soaking in a basin of hot water in which floated slices of lemon and crushed mustard seed. The shattered coach had been hauled away, the surviving horses bedded in the farmer's barn, the dead nag dragged out of the ditch to await the knacker.

Elizabeth argued forcefully with her three companions for an instant return to Devon by whatever means possible, including shank's mare.

"It's a sign from above," she insisted, fingers crossed, having sized up her new acquaintance within moments. "God doesn't intend me to reach London. He tried to tell us with all that rain, don't you see? When the rain didn't convince us, He took more direct action."

"God may work in mysterious ways," the farmer's wife

took up the argument with a touch of reproof, her chapel leanings clear, "but I never heard tell He used drunken rapscallions to do His work for Him, nor yet that He'd cause a poor beast what never done anybody harm to die like that, let alone risk your lives and those of all those poor souls on that coach into the bargain."

"Rather more like you been slogging through the Slough of Despond to reach the Celestial City," her husband rumbled in agreement, referencing Bunyan's *Pilgrim's Progress* with the air of one well-acquainted with the work.

"Sides which," Alfie threw in, "what'm I to say to the doctor if'n I takes you back? Bad enough the coach be in splinters. Have my hide, he would, and yours too, Miss Elizabeth. Not that I ain't that grateful you took care o' my arm so quicklike, and for your nursing when Old Thom was took so hard with the flux last winter, but all o' Saint Mary's knows as how they been planning your come-out, and you wriggling like a Mayfly to keep from going."

"You've the right of it, Alfie," Tillie agreed between bouts of sneezing. "We'd all be chased frob the village, a'd rightly so! A'd, I'b not wanding do leave Saind Bary-Graftond, dod eved for Bizz Lizzie."

"Honor thy father and thy mother, that thy days may be long in the land the Lord thy God giveth thee," the farmer quoted sternly, handing Tillie a large square of dingy gray cotton as his wife tossed a handful of pungent crushed juniper berries in the basin and added more hot water.

"Nothing, absolutely *nothing* will convince me God intends to give me London," Elizabeth protested. "I don't *want* it."

"The Lord works in mysterious ways, His wonders to perform," the farmer's wife countered, placing a comforting arm around Elizabeth's shoulders. "It's not for you to

be saying what He intends and what He don't, miss. If Azrael here hadn't been moved to climb the hill back o' the house to hunt out Sukie's calf—which is a Sign in itself, being so Biblical, though not quite so much as it'd've been if he searched for a lamb, mind—he'd never've caught sight of you down on the road, and you'd still be in that ditch.''

"But, look at me," Elizabeth wailed, indicating her muddied skirts and sodden boots. "I belong at home. I even belong *here*. I could be useful, you know," she interjected hopefully, glancing from the stalwart reformist farmwife to her chapel-going husband. "I'm *very* good with animals, and I'm not afraid of hard work, and my muffins're almost as good as Cook's. We could say I've gone to London, and then at the end of the Little Season—"

"Fide clothes is as fide clothes does," Tillie retorted and sneezed.

"Never heard tell mud made the difference 'twixt a lady and those who ain't," the farmer's wife agreed. "Mud washes off. Sins don't."

"*Exactly* my point," Elizabeth crowed, changing tactics and keeping her fingers tightly crossed. "I'm who God intends me to be just as I am."

"And just as you are, so shall you bear witness to His wonders among the fleshpots," the farmer lectured sternly. "If it's to London your good parents sent you, then it's to London you must go, for neither Sodom nor Gomorrah could turn the righteous from His path, and neither will London turn you."

"But Alfie and Young Thom and Tillie are—"

"No need to be worriting yourself. We'll shelter and feed 'em, and we'll see 'em on their way as soon as may be. You put me in mind of our youngest," the farmer chuckled. "More excuses for not doing something she must than a nettle has prickles, though she always docs

it in the end. Keep telling her she'd save a mort of time
if she'd just get on with it and stop nattering like a jay
defending its nest. Married now, she is, and lives over
Hampstead way."

Then with a nod to her three companions and a slight
smile for his wife, he took matters into his own hands
and loaded Elizabeth's portmanteau and bandboxes
into his gig, wrapped his wife's cloak and a quilt around
the protesting girl, draped their shoulders with a tarpau-
lin to keep off the worst of the wet and set off under
lowering skies for the nearby city.

Night was already falling when the reluctant Elizabeth
and her kindly escort reached Portman Square.

The confusion of that arrival, the mortification of
being refused the door by a new footman and sent
round to the tradesmen's entrance, then of being
refused admission *there* because she'd nothing to deliver
and so the door was closed in her face before she could
be recognized, had come close to reducing her to the
tears that would have overcome most young ladies long
before. Jaws clenched, eyes blazing, head pounding,
she returned to hammer on the polished lion's head
knocker just as Cochrane—summoned from overseeing
the setting of covers for the evening's meal by the confused footman on duty—opened the narrow black front
door.

After one amazed glance at the unfashionable conveyance and its even less prepossessing driver, and another
at the shivering and bedraggled Elizabeth, Cochrane
took efficient charge.

A hastily summoned Lady Wainwright, dressing gown
thrown over her déshabille, had come gliding down the
stairs to spout tearfully dismayed apologies and warm
welcomes. Portly Lord Wainwright appeared from his

library at the sounds of arrival, face wreathed in smiles, to add his mite. Sybilla, fortunately for everyone's equanimity, remained in her room beautifying herself for that evening's entertainments—a comedy at the Theater Royal, Lady Wainwright explained, followed by supper at Grillon's (a hotel noted for its elegance and excellent chef) as the guest of Lord and Lady Farquhar. Neither she nor her husband were to be of the party, thank goodness, so there was no need to send their excuses. Sybilla, of course, would go as planned.

The confusion sorted itself out with amazing rapidity. The kindly farmer was rewarded for his assistance and taken to the servants' hall for a hot meal, nag and gig sent round to the mews. Elizabeth, divested of sodden cloak and bonnet, was whisked abovestairs by her distressed aunt, a maid summoned to attend her, portmanteau and bandboxes toted to her room by the mortified and anxious-to-please footman. A fire was lit, bowls of flowers and bath salts and scented soaps brought in, dressing gown and towels set to warm, hot bricks placed between the bed sheets.

Tea and a bath in a deep copper tub proved highly restorative. A supper tray loaded with tempting dishes appeared in Elizabeth's cozy bedchamber as at the wave of a conjurer's wand just as she completed her bath and slipped on a warm woolen robe.

Half an hour later, replete with *fricandeau de veau*, pigeon pie, mushroom fritters, mashed peas in cream sauce, stewed salsify and turnips, glazed sole garnished with crab and mussels and dressed with wine and lemon and parsley, the luxurious repast completed by a dainty confection of hothouse raspberries and spun sugar encased in a delicate pastry basket, the world of London had begun to look a trifle less dismal to the exhausted Elizabeth. Even her aunt's dismay when the contents of her portmanteau and bandboxes were revealed couldn't

touch the young girl's sense of well-being as she lay
nestled in the warm bed, its curtains drawn back to
permit the glowing sea coal fire to add its share of cheer,
a handkerchief soaked in lavender water across her tem-
ples, her hair dry at last and spread about her in a dusky
cloud.

"The matter is easily rectified," Lady Wainwright dimpled after her first horrified gasp. "Your dear mother
did warn me I most likely wouldn't permit a scullery
maid to appear in your best finery, let alone a young lady
of grace and breeding. As for the rest," she shrugged, "it
didn't matter in Devonshire, I suppose, though these
are a bit much," indicating three coarse, mended shifts
and a gray dress that was little more than a sturdy,
commodious tube, "but here it *does.*"

"Mama did insist I was to follow your recommenda-
tions," Elizabeth smiled back sleepily. "I suppose I *shall*
have to have a dress or two, though it does seem a
dreadful waste," she conceded grudgingly. "Nothing
suitable here is likely to be of the least use when I return
to Saint Mary-Grafton, and I'll only be in London such
a very short time."

"*A dress or two?* My dearest child, you haven't the
slightest notion," her aunt laughed. "As to your
returning home so very soon, well, we shall see. You
may find London to your liking after all."

With that she had kissed her niece good night and
slipped from the room.

The next morning dawned as drearily gray and sodden as most of the other mornings since Elizabeth left
Devonshire. That would have been grimly doom enough
for an active young miss anxious to be out and about
and see the sights. It proved only the beginning.

The few things she would truly have liked to do—

visit the British Museum (if that were possible) and the Tower and the Roman Wall and Saint Paul's and Westminster Abbey, attend a performance at Astley's Amphitheater, peep in at the Royal Exchange and Ackerman's Repository and Madame Tussaud's, witness the displays at Vauxhall, explore the botanical gardens at Kew—were denied her.

Lady Wainwright firmly explained such excursions were suitable only for bluestockings—Heaven forfend!—or schoolroom misses. Elizabeth was in Town to make her come-out. Her father was a baron, for all he had come into his title oddly and late, her mother the granddaughter of an earl. They were not country nobodies, no matter where or how they lived.

"Certainly the provision for your outfitting is generous, though not excessively so," Lady Wainwright concluded triumphantly, "and you do have a dowry of eight hundred pounds."

Sybilla snorted delicately at this evidence of well-lined pockets.

Eight hundred pounds might attract a country squire's cloddish youngest son, she informed her mother tartly, or possibly an impecunious curate who sought nothing better than an impoverished country parish. It would certainly buy Elizabeth nothing better in the way of a husband. The current rate for a baronet was as high as two thousand pounds, depending on his breeding and prospects.

To Elizabeth's protest that she had not come to London to purchase a husband, Sybilla returned an irrefutable, "Then what are you here for, pray tell? You won't be snapped up for your beauty or wit, as you lack either. The only other option is purchase, and you'd find your eight hundred pounds stretching much further in the country. I tell you only as a favor, so you won't be disappointed."

Lady Wainwright instructed Sybilla to still her waspish tongue and whisked the girls off on a preliminary round of shopping for Elizabeth's all-important come-out wardrobe. They never reached the carriage.

It had been raining since before Elizabeth's arrival, a dismal draining of the skies that left streets slick and spirits sodden. Steps, too, were slick. Lady Wainwright tangled her foot in her hem. Sybilla leapt to steady her mother. Instead of regaining her balance, the luckless Lady Wainwright plunged to the pavement below, almost as if purposefully propelled.

"Oh, Mama—*No!*" Sybilla shrieked. "You *are* all right, are you not?"

But Lady Wainwright was far from all right. Not only had she suffered numerous painful bruises. She had broken her leg.

Confusion reigned for two days, the viscount distraught and hovering, Sybilla sulking at the sudden curtailment of her social rounds, Elizabeth sharing nursing duties with her aunt's abigail.

Then, to pacify the sullen Sybilla, Miss Imogene Pugh, her former governess, was summoned from retirement to serve as the cousins' chaperon. From her bed Lady Wainwright instructed Sybilla to search her wardrobe for ensembles suitable for Elizabeth's temporary use. Sybilla grudgingly handed over a few castoffs intended for the charity box, ignoring her mother's instructions to summon a seamstress to perform needed alterations. Lady Wainwright sent out a flurry of notes to her acquaintance, and the social round resumed.

To Elizabeth's pleas that she be permitted to return home—which pleas were given a strong seconding by Sybilla—or else devote herself to nursing her aunt until such time as she was recovered, Lady Wainwright gave a determined refusal. Elizabeth was not in London to spend her days in a sickroom. They would, Lady Wainwright insisted, contrive. The situation was not beyond remedy.

"But, I've not the slightest desire to go about in company," Elizabeth protested. "Without you to introduce me and show me how to go on I shall be most unwelcome, and likely make a perfect cake of myself into the bargain."

"Nonsense, child," her aunt smiled, well aware Elizabeth would use any excuse to delay her entry into society. "You will accompany Sybilla when she pays morning calls, and you will be present whenever she receives callers.

"As for more formal occasions, your hostesses will be particular friends of mine. They will see to it you have an agreeable time, and meet those you ought. Of course," she frowned, "there's the Rochedale rout. The dowager countess *is* an exception, for we hardly move in such exalted circles as a usual thing, but I'm sure even she will prove most accommodating. I never shall understand how we came to receive *that* invitation, for we are not on such terms—though slightly acquainted, naturally—and of course Sybilla will insist on attending without me, no matter how inappropriate that may be, and if she goes, *you* go also. I've made that perfectly clear to her."

And that had been that for the past week.

Receiving callers, each more mindless and insulting than the one before, had been bad enough. The gentlemen postured and pontificated on the merits of champagne in boot blacking and how many fobs constituted the correct number, and gossiped concerning those not present. The ladies and girls simpered and compared their gowns and their beaux, and gossiped concerning those not present. Having no interest in the topics discussed and the individuals anatomized, Elizabeth never troubled to hide her boredom. As for Sybilla, she ignored her cousin unless it was to order her about like a servant. After a single mortifying experience, Elizabeth learned to dress for callers, present herself for her aunt's inspection, descend the stairs, then slip quietly away.

Paying morning calls proved even more excruciating for the miserable, ill-clad, tongue-tied country girl, for Sybilla stressed Elizabeth's father's profession to all auditors at the first opportunity. Faces froze. Noses lifted. Backs turned. Suddenly she was invisible or transparent, Elizabeth was not sure which. No way then to hide in corners, pretending she heard and saw nothing. No way to slip from the room and join her uncle in his library or sneak off to her bedchamber.

She and Sybilla reached an accommodation after one miserable round: Elizabeth amused herself reading in the carriage while Sybilla swept into the tonnish homes trailed by the sniffling, vapid Miss Pugh to make her devoirs and share gossip. The girl gave shallow excuses for Elizabeth's absence, implying lack of breeding on her country cousin's part on the one hand, while hinting to her hostesses they should be grateful she had single-handedly arranged the little mushroom's absence on the other. Both young women assured the colorless, prune-faced Miss Pugh this was how they preferred it. With no desire to return to the monotonous penury which was her retirement, Imogene Pugh held her peace.

Evening parties posed more of a problem. Each time Lady Wainwright reviewed her niece's toilette, she bemoaned the current impossibility of shopping. To the despairing suggestion that her favorite dressmaker be summoned to the house, Elizabeth had given a determined refusal.

"My funds are extremely limited," she reminded her aunt. "A seamstress such as we have in the village is the best I can afford. I left half the ready Papa gave me with Charles and Robert as pin money for when they return to Cambridge, and some with Jeremy and Andrew as well so they can afford a few treats at school, and I'm determined the majority of the sum for my wardrobe be held back for John and his bride. Setting up a practice is deuced hard going at first. Physicians don't exactly roll in lard, you know, and Clarissa is already increasing.''

"At least your 'ready' won't be wasted trying to fashion a silk purse from a sow's ear,'' Sybilla had muttered, to which Elizabeth blithely agreed.

After all, the Little Season was merely to pacify Mama and Papa. It didn't matter *what* she wore, even ill-fitting castoffs of Sybilla's. At the end of it she would return to Saint Mary-Grafton, delicate muslins and spangled gauzes useless, and resume assisting her father with his practice and keeping his books and teaching the little ones. Squandering money on an elegant wardrobe would be unforgivably wasteful.

But, worst of all, in the evenings it proved impossible for her to remain for hours in a dark carriage with only coachmen and grooms and footmen for company. On this point Miss Pugh had been startlingly firm despite her adored Miss Sybilla's insistence to the contrary, mandating with much sniffling and many incomplete sentences that Elizabeth must at least accompany them within doors. Thus it was Elizabeth had found herself sent belowstairs like an abigail as soon as their party entered each elegant residence, which was not necessarily unpleasant when compared with the strain of surviving in polite company.

Then, someone narked.

Servants probably, Elizabeth decided, since they appeared even more given to gossip than their masters and mistresses. Or, perhaps one of her supposed hostesses had sent a note inquiring as to the reason for her absence. It didn't matter who was responsible. What mattered was disaster struck.

Lady Wainwright threatened to dismiss the tearfully incoherent Miss Pugh.

She threatened to send Sybilla on a prolonged visit to Great-Aunt Witherspoon.

She threatened to have a special sedan chair constructed so she could attend the various entertainments with her daughter and niece.

She threatened Lord Wainwright—who despised the stultifying social rounds as much as any other gentleman of retiring disposition, scholarly inclination, and sedentary habits—with enforced escort duty.

Elizabeth pleaded their cases and agreed from that day on she would submit to her aunt's dictates.

She would spend her evenings abovestairs (where she very much did not want to be) rather than belowstairs (where things were so very much more jolly).

She would permit her hair to be dressed becomingly.

She would set aside her comfortable boots and wear the slippers loaned her by Sybilla.

She would respond with propriety if spoken to.

She would not venture an opinion on anything except the weather, and that opinion would be in accord with everyone else's. Above all, she would state no opinion on such topics as were the province of gentlemen.

And, she would do her very best not to appear bored and she absolutely would not yawn, even if a gentleman took it in mind to prose on forever about his purchase of a snuff box, or the clever new way he had found to tie his neckcloth.

She would, in other words, behave in a conformable manner.

That this disaster occurred on the very morning of the Rochedale rout seemed to poor Elizabeth the culmination of all the misery and mortification her London visit had brought down on her helpless head.

At least the other evening do's had been relatively

modest: card parties, an informal dance, a brace of dinners followed by young ladies displaying their talents on pianoforte and harp as the sole entertainment. If she had been forced to be present, it wouldn't have been too terrible.

A rout was another matter entirely.

The house would be a blaze of lights. The company would be multitudinous and exalted. Only the wealthy held true routs and balls, for only the wealthy had the space to accommodate hundreds of guests. There would probably be no refreshments. There would probably be no music or dancing. The sole purpose of a rout was to cram as many guests as possible into one house, then let them see and be seen. Such affairs were called "dreadful squeezes" if they were successful. If they weren't, they were called nothing and those in attendance pretended they had not been so foolish as to go.

Elizabeth dragged through the day, exhibiting false cheer when in her aunt's room for that distraught lady's sake while cringing at the thought of the evening ahead.

She composed yet another letter to her parents, stating her case for a rapid return home with all the logic and force she could muster.

She accepted the bedraggled gown Sybilla was ordered to unearth from the back of an attic armoire with the best grace she could, stood patiently for the interminable alterations insisted upon by her aunt and overseen by Bartlet, Lady Wainwright's abigail. She dressed for the evening's festivities with a reluctance only those about to mount the scaffold can know. She even permitted Bartlet to dress her hair in a softer style with a few curls loosened to frame her face.

And, when the dreaded hour arrived, she departed for the Rochedale mansion with all the eagerness of a reluctant martyr about to enter the Roman coliseum.

London was indeed a nightmare.

Five

The crush of carriages inching its way toward the soaring portico of Rochedale House was enervating enough. Merely to travel past the gates and up the drive took more than an hour, Sybilla carping all the way. Worse were the haughty footmen, opposing pairs on each step of the great entrance staircase. Worse yet was darting through the rain to the sheltering green canopy with what felt like thousands of disapproving eyes boring into her.

Elizabeth Driscoll shivered as her cousin Sybilla indicated the twin marble staircases leading to the state apartments with a flick of her spangled fan.

Those, too, were lined with footmen. A grinning marble Eros shot his mischievous darts at arriving and departing guests from an arched alcove between the flights, tunic fluttering in a breeze none but he could sense. How many servants did this earl have? Enough to staff Carlton House and the Marine Pavilion and a dozen other royal residences? Well, at least he provided employment, Elizabeth sighed.

"Since Mama insists you actually be in attendance," Sybilla snapped, "and not merely on the premises, find a spot from which you may watch without putting yourself forward in an unbecoming manner." The older girl glanced at her country cousin's démodé white sarcenet gown overlaid with spangled spider gauze and gave a moue of distaste. The thing had been impossible, even when new. Now? A rag on a broomstick. "You'll do well enough if you stay in the shadows, but I do *not* want you going through the receiving line," she added waspishly. "Were the dowager countess to realize we are connected, it would spoil *all* my chances. Mama is so *unreasonable.*"

"I didn't want to come, you know," Elizabeth said for what must have been the dozenth time, blue-gray eyes darkening like storm clouds.

"Then why didn't you acquire a migraine, or throw out spots? My rouge pot is always available to you. Aren't you the least creative?"

"Apparently not," Elizabeth shrugged, glancing surreptitiously at the daringly sophisticated lines of Sybilla's new olive green gown, its amber tissue overlay heavily embroidered in gold, as she twitched uncomfortably at her own borrowed finery.

If only Sybilla's cast-off didn't gape so dreadfully, nor present quite so many knots and streamers, so many ruffles and silken flowers to the disdainful eyes of the guests thronging the entrance rotunda. Aunt Mehitabelle's abigail had done her best, but there was only so much altered seams, strategic tucks and raised hem could accomplish. Sybilla was proportioned on far more generous lines.

"I dislike this as much as you do," Elizabeth protested tiredly.

"Pray permit me to differ with you on that point, sweet Cuz," Sybilla hissed as she scanned the latest arrivals. "There is no way you can dislike it *half* so much. That you should be the beneficiary of all my efforts—!"

Not that they had been particularly arduous. Elizabeth was well aware gaining admission to this highly select soirée uninvited had merely required browbeating the ever-spineless Millicent Farquhar. Within Sybilla's reticule reposed the Farquhars' gilt-edged invitation, their names and direction so water-stained as to be illegible.

Sybilla's eyes lit up as she spotted her initial prey of the evening. She swept to a sweet-faced young girl accompanying a much older woman sporting a plumed and jeweled turban and a young man tightly encased in foppish evening dress.

Elizabeth froze, then shrank back, ducking her head. Dear heaven, it was one of the Badenton curs. She'd sworn Tillie and Alfie and Young Thom to secrecy, but if *he* recognized her . . .

"Millicent, *chérie*," Sybilla caroled. "It's been an *age*, I swear. *La*— how *delicious* you look. Why, you *quite* put me in the shade. Nigel," roguishly tapping the young man's arm with her fan, "you are *so-o-o* elegant, as always. Nugee—*do* tell me I'm right," naming a London tailor famous for extreme cut and *farouche* style. "It *is* Nugee, is it not?" now gently smoothing a hand across the heavily buckrammed shoulder of the wasp-waisted peacock satin coat, and according the flushing Nigel a moment's coy fluttering of lashes. "Do tell me I'm *au courant!*"

Then she turned to more crucial prey. "Lady Farquhar," performing a curtsy so deep it verged on the impertinent, "the *most* important for last, *naturellement*. What a *ravishing* shade of puce. Your sense of style is so *particulier*, so *à point*."

"Sweet child," Lady Farquhar murmured absently, presenting her delicately powdered cheek to be airkissed. "I cannot think *what* became of Rochedale's card. It was on the mantel only days ago, I know it was.

Why, we almost weren't granted admission! And how does you dear mother do?"

"Still sadly pulled by her recent accident. *Chère Maman!* Such a *misère* to her not to be here. I am *accompagnée* of course, but *she*—" Sybilla gestured at the nervously sniffling Miss Pugh, "is *precisely* the sort one *doesn't* desire at one's side. It would save me a *deal* of mortification if you would permit me to join you," she pleaded winsomely. "Nigel is *such* a thoughtful escort, and in your *compagnie distinguée*, I should be *so* comforted for *chère Maman's* absence that I would *hardly* notice it."

"Why, you poor child," Lady Farquhar exclaimed, glancing at Pugh (who was sufficiently dowdy to be respectable). After a moment's careful survey of Sybilla's toilette, she nodded.

"Naturally you may join us, my dear. You present a most *interesting* contrast to dearest Millicent. The invitation *was* there, I swear it," she grumbled on. "The servants are so careless. I've a good mind to dismiss the girl charged with dusting the front parlor, and *without* a character." Then, "What *is* that thing huddling behind your companion?" she inquired, lifting her jeweled quizzing glass for a closer inspection.

"I've no notion," Sybilla returned airily, staring straight through her cousin. "So mortifying to be caught in its *voisinage*. Someone's stray country relation, I suppose."

Nigel glanced idly at Elizabeth, then frowned in puzzlement. Elizabeth hunched her shoulders, ducking further behind Pugh. Nigel shrugged, turned back to the gushing Sybilla with what he considered lordly grace. Footmen had already relieved the ladies of their wraps and Nigel of his hat and cane and cape. Now they crowded to the foot of the ascending staircase, the Farquhar ladies on Nigel's either arm, Lady Farquhar still fussing about her inexplicably missing invitation.

The faded Miss Pugh cast an apologetic glance at Elizabeth and trailed after the more important of her charges, a faint aroma of peppermint and musty trunks clinging to the gray silk mourning gown provided her for the occasion. At the foot of the stairs Sybilla executed what appeared to be a small dance step, replacing Millicent on Nigel's arm. The younger girl was thrust to the rear to make her way as best she could in the company of Miss Pugh.

Elizabeth sighed. Then, determined to garner something amusing to include in her next letter home, she straightened her shoulders, handed her cousin's tenth-best evening wrap to a smirking footman and trudged up the stairs, slipping past her cousin, the Farquhars and the unfortunate Miss Pugh.

If the marbled entry was a jewel box of shimmering colors and spangled reflections, the great open area at the top of the stairs was a fairyland. And she had thought what she glimpsed of society at the other soirées fashionable? They were to this as a May fête in Saint Mary-Grafton was to them. As for the surroundings!

The domed ceiling, soaring fully two stories above, was glazed with stained glass, lights cunningly hidden at its periphery so that rather than looming dark and mysterious, it glowed with rich reds and blues and greens and golds. A massive chandelier dripping crystals depended from the vault, hundreds of candles casting a midday brilliance. Flowers were everywhere, and palms—forests of them. And more candles, reflected by the gleaming rosy marble columns and mirrorlike black marble floor.

And gold. Gold *everywhere*. And brilliant red. And niches holding statues that appeared to have been sculpted for some Roman emperor's villa.

And people. Hordes of them, sporting enough jewels

and silks and satins to have financed Wellington's army for a decade, providing food, surgeons, uniforms, munitions, pay—all that army had needed to ensure success, achieving success through sheer courage and determination in spite of the lack. It was a disgrace!

"Dear Lord," she whispered, shrinking from the crowd as she edged her way along the wall, "I shall never accustom myself to such useless ostentation—*never.*"

The earl sank another notch in her estimation. Of course, again it could be said he provided employment, but such *meaningless* employment. One would have thought a gentleman accustomed to the privations of military life would have more sense.

The Farquhar party appeared at the head of the stairs, Sybilla gliding to the fore, hands extended, plunging décolletage luminous. Through a break in the group Elizabeth caught a glimpse of silver hair, sparkling rubies, and the stiff black brocades and embroidered taffetas of another era.

"*Such* an honor," Sybilla gushed, her voice reaching Elizabeth through a lull. "I have *longed* to tell his lordship—We are old friends, you know, for Lord DeLacey has rescued me on more than one occasion from the unfortunate results of my own impetuosity," she interjected archly. "So wonderful to see him again, and in such fine trim, for he has been sadly missed! You are to be commended for restoring him to us!—of the *profound* esteem in which I hold him." Her angle shifted, her coy words purportedly for the dowager countess, all her attentions on the earl. "The reports of his bravery have had me positively *quivering* with admiration! Such *courage.* Such *sang-froid.* One of our *greatest* heroes. With *him* to guard our shores, is it any wonder the *parvenu* little Corsican was defeated?"

Though the brave hero in question remained hidden, Elizabeth had a sudden unimpeded view of the dowager countess's rigidly erect, black-clad figure.

"An acquaintance of yours, Richard? I do not believe," her voice floated as she glanced to where her grandson remained hidden, "I have previously had the pleasure—"

Then, as if storm-driven, waves of superbly elegant humanity closed over the amusing little scene and sound was lost. Elizabeth tucked herself behind a palm where she could observe the beau monde greeting itself and congratulating itself on its infinite superiority to the general run of humanity, swirling in only to swirl out again, bent on being seen at as many fashionable rendezvous as possible in the course of the evening. Suddenly her view was blocked. Sybilla had planted herself before the sheltering palm, reaching behind to give Elizabeth's arm a sharp pinch.

"They're very taken with me," she hissed triumphantly. "I could tell. How Rochedale's eyes warmed! The leg isn't *too* off-putting—merely a bit awkward, and there's no law says I must appear with him in public once the vows are spoken. Of course, his features are *impossible*. Too harsh by half for true male beauty. But then, when the candles are extinguished—which I shall insist upon—I won't have to see them, will I? I'll be a countess by Christmas, just see if I'm not!"

"Congratulations," Elizabeth muttered.

"One doesn't congratulate a bride-to-be, you ninny! That's reserved for the groom. One wishes *her* happiness and health."

"My apologies. Happiness and health."

"Thank you. Such a *perfect* setting for me! Of course, the old witch will have to be packed off. I will *not* have her about meddling, and she appears *just* the sort to do so. Stay out of sight. If you ruin things now, I'll kill you where you lie in your bed.''

She was gone, sweeping past the Farquhars, Nigel's excellence as an escort forgotten. Elizabeth sighed, rubbing her assaulted arm. Again there was a hiatus, and a dark-haired man leaning on an ebony cane was revealed standing beside the dowager countess. This would be the current earl, Elizabeth decided. Wounded the year before at Waterloo, yes—and the more fool he, for putting himself in harm's way, Sybilla had sneered, which sentiment had caused Elizabeth to bite her tongue—but rich as the Golden Ball and a great matrimonial prize. Clearly Sybilla was willing to overlook any lingering disability after viewing his palatial London residence.

Now Elizabeth studied the man curiously.

Of slightly above medium height and with a whipcord frame, the earl presented a figure of strength rather than effete elegance. Not handsome, definitely not in the current fashion of male prettiness, his craggy features were far more forthright and candid than either. Interestingly, his severe black evening attire and snowy linen were anachronistic in the setting of his home, almost as if he did not belong there.

She hoped Sybilla wouldn't manage to sink her talons in him. He appeared far too kind and trusting to deserve such a fate. She hoped he was also too intelligent.

Then her eyes narrowed.

The man was pale far beyond what was fashionable. Deep lines slashed between nose and mouth. Etched by pain? Probably. Residual pain now, and a great deal of pain before. A faint sheen of sweat glistened on his brow. Dear heaven, how long had he been standing there forced to mouth polite nothings? He appeared exhausted.

A woman swept up to him, laughing as she tapped him flirtatiously on the arm with her fan, turning first to the dowager countess, then to the earl. Through a lull in the incessant chatter Elizabeth caught pleasant tenor tones.

"Delighted to see you again, Lady Jersey. You grow younger and more beautiful with each day."

"Naughty! Shall we be seeing you at the Princesse de Lieven's ball tomorrow?"

"Unless today's young ladies prefer sitting to dancing," came the rich, self-deprecating chuckle, "I rather think balls are a pleasure I'll forgo for the present."

"With *you?* Their preference would be anything you might suggest," Lady Jersey countered with a roguish wink. "*Anything* at *all.* The fall crop has some true beauties in it. High time you were setting up your nursery, as I'm sure your grandmama has told you. Come look the girls over. That's what balls are for, you know."

"Too kind," the man muttered, no longer quite so pallid—did men actually *blush?*—as Lady Jersey moved off and an anxious mother with two nubile daughters in tow swam into her place. The earl did the pretty, and they were replaced by a tall blond man with a missing arm followed by what appeared to be a family party.

"Harry! So, you decided to brave this deplorable crush after all," the earl chuckled warmly.

Goodness, but she liked that slight rough edge to his voice. Gave it character.

Now he was making a fuss over the sparkling girl at the one-armed man's side. The dowager countess was turning to a petite silver-haired lady with the minxish look of a girl in her first season, then to a tall, dark, distinguished-looking man and an elegant willowy blonde with melting eyes. A rangy young man with fierce side whiskers and ginger hair strode up, heels beating a sharp tattoo on the marble floor.

Dear heaven! She could be mistaken, but was that the traveler who rescued her at the inn? He had the same air about him, and the hair and whiskers were most distinctive. Tillie had been right. And, if she had encountered him and that Farquhar person, perhaps there *was* a chance the other two would appear as well. One of them was *bound* to recognize her. Oh Lord, but she wanted to go home!

She shrank further into her hiding place, shuddering.

"Twins—imps—veritable scamps," floated across the room, along with much laughter and some incoherent military cant.

Lady Jersey turned to watch the new arrivals, a smirk twisting her lips. What an *unpleasant* woman. There was a sly look about her that didn't bode well for any who crossed her.

Then the group moved on, granting Elizabeth a clearer view of the earl. He was trembling with the effort to hold himself erect, cane bowed, face livid in the candlelight. No one seemed to notice his trouble— not his grandmother, not the nearby footmen, not the family party now making its way to where refreshments were being served, not the dainty silver-haired lady pausing to speak with the avidly curious, ever-watchful woman named Jersey. Were they all blind? The poor earl was about to suffer the ignominy of fainting in his own receiving line! He didn't deserve that, no matter how overbearing his home.

Without conscious thought the incensed Elizabeth dashed across the marble floor, careened into the woman called Jersey, pretending to twist her ankle as she seized the earl's arm, forcing him erect while giving the appearance she was the one receiving assistance.

"Please help me, sir," she gasped as the earl's cane clattered to the floor. "My ankle's broken, I know it is. Over there—that's a bookroom, isn't it? Oh, *please!*

People are staring so, I can't *bear* it," she ended on a slightly hysterical note as she realized every eye was indeed turned in her direction. *"Quickly, now."*

"Of all the unmitigated—" the dowager countess spat, drawing herself up.

With grim determination, Elizabeth propelled the earl across the floor and into his study, hissing to a footman to retrieve the cane and follow them as the dowager countess stared after her with a look of disgust and Sally Jersey burst into laughter.

"Hussy!" the dowager countess snapped. "She's not even limping!"

"Well, now I've seen *everything*," Lady Jersey chuckled. "The most originally executed variation on an ancient ploy in many a Season. What a complete hoyden! I wonder who she might be?"

"Dear God—what d'you think you're doing?" Richard DeLacey muttered past clenched teeth as he stumbled through the doorway.

"Getting you out of harm's way," Elizabeth said, guiding him to a small settee. The room was so dark after the brilliantly lit reception area—only a single candle on the desk and the remains of a fire glowing on the hearth—she could hardly see where she was going. "Come on, now. Just a few steps more."

"You'll be utterly *ruined*, child."

"As if I cared for that! Besides, I'm not *entirely* bacon-brained. No one knows me here, so we're neither of us in the briars." She almost laughed at his sudden sharp look. "Don't be chuckle-headed, my lord. I've no designs on you whatsoever. It's just that I couldn't bear to see you humiliated. Sit. *Sit*, drat you! Head between your legs. If you won't do it for yourself, I'll do it for you. You were about to measure your length. Don't try to deny it. I know the signs. You may berate me for unseemly behavior later, not that it matters in the least."

She spun to the visibly shaken footman, the earl's cane still dangling awkwardly from his hand.

"His lordship has a man, I presume? Good. Get him. Tell him to bring whatever preparation the earl uses for pain. Laudanum, I presume. There's not much else available in the standard pharmacopoeia. *Hurry*, blast you! Stop laundering the air with your tongue like an addle-pated spaniel. And, for heaven's sake, close that door behind you or some importunate fool will come in before his lordship is himself again. That we don't want, for it would cause all *sorts* of talk. In fact, I think I'd best lock it after you. Set that silly cane down and move your stumps, man!"

"I was all right, you know," the earl's voice came weakly from between his knees, tinged with amusement, as the cowed footman sped away, "or, I would've been. These fits pass as quickly as they come upon me."

"Be that as it may, it will pass much more quickly with your head down," Elizabeth countered sternly from the door, snapping it shut behind the footman and turning the key, "and there's not the least assurance it would've passed at all."

"Suppose you're right," the earl mumbled. "Also suppose I must thank you. Deuced embarrassing situation to be caught in. Don't like to admit it, but—"

"Hush! Don't try to speak. Just keep your head down. It really helps. A faint is caused by the sudden interruption of the smooth flow of blood to the brain. Lowering your head below your heart brings it back."

"What—no burnt feathers? No hartshorn? No *sal volatile*?"

"Totally unnecessary. Besides, I despise them all, don't you? So unpleasant! Fainting's bad enough without that, not that I ever *have*, but I have it on the best authority that it is *excessively* nasty—almost as bad as casting up one's accounts. Keep your head *down*, blast you!" Elizabeth darted back to the settee, shoved the dark, curly head down. "Do I have to hold you there," she demanded in exasperation, "or will you behave?"

"Dear God, but we needed you at Waterloo," he gasped. "Wellington would've made you a general on the spot."

"A female? Don't be a gapeseed. *Keep your head down.* Besides, I was there, and it didn't do you much good."

The earl froze, then reluctantly obeyed her. "Where were you?" he asked softly.

"Waterloo, and nobody offered me a brevet. *Please* keep your head down. You're as bad as Willie when it comes to following instructions."

"Who's Willie?"

"One of my brothers. Head *down!*"

He reluctantly obeyed once more. Then, very quietly, very gently, very slowly, in wondering disbelief, he said, "You've got quite a tongue in your head, young lady."

"Shocking, isn't it? Not at all the thing, of course, but you would too, if you had nothing but brothers. I'll apologize later, if you insist."

He gripped her wrist then, long powerful fingers like a vise despite his temporary infirmity. "Don't leave me," he pleaded. "*Please* don't vanish into thin air. I don't think I could bear it."

Almost as if he did not dare, he raised his head to study her in the soft light.

It had been a year and a half. She was older. She was garbed in some overtrimmed flimsy thing with a gaping neckline, obviously the discard of a more generously endowed young woman with no sense of style. Her hair was neatly, if severely, dressed, her face clean. Gone were the dark cloak, the lantern, the mud.

The heavy dark hair. The delicate elfin features. The

slight frame. The eyes, so filled with life and warmth and humor and guileless innocence.

There was no question. It was his angel of La Haye Sainte.

"I'm all right," he said in a carefully controlled voice. Then, unable to contain himself, "Dear God," he whispered, the words almost a prayer. "My own house! Unlikely indeed." He took a steadying breath. Then, in a more natural tone, "I truly am, you know. All right, I mean. You may take my pulse or check my pupils if you wish, like a good little nurse."

"How d'you know I can do those things?" Elizabeth asked, pulling her hand away and bustling about the room to light more candles.

"I just know," he responded with a small smile. "Trust me."

"Well, naturally, your lordship."

"None of that! You've saved me from a most embarrassing *faux pas*. My debt to you is incalculable, and my name is Richard DeLacey."

"So I have been informed," she returned uneasily, placing a flaming candelabra on the scarred Jacobean table by his side. "There, now we shan't go blind. You *do* look slightly better."

"The polite thing would be to give me your name in return."

"I'm not certain I should do that, your lordship. No one knows me here, you see," she threw over her shoulder as she scurried about inspecting the room for exits. "Well, *almost* no one, and so our rather unconventional position . . .

"Under the circumstances, ignorance is your best safeguard. As things stand, you can later claim I was an abigail dressed in her mistress's cast-off finery acting on a dare, and suddenly realized both your need and my duty. But, as you are a gentleman, if you knew my name, well, that would be totally totty-headed, don't you see?"

"Are you afraid of compromising me? Oh, my dear girl!"

"Well, that is—"

Elizabeth ducked her head, blushing furiously. "I didn't think ahead," she confessed, shamefaced. "Papa claims that's my worst fault, that I leap in without thinking. I've a *very* bad habit that way. I never realized—" She gestured toward the locked door. "But you were so unwell, and there was that dreadful Jersey woman hanging all over you making *quite* improper innuendoes, and you *blushed*— I liked that, for I've a mortifying tendency in that direction myself, and so I simply *couldn't* abandon you, being a fellow sufferer—and then your grandmother called me a hussy, and that Jersey woman laughed and said more dreadful things, but it was too late to stop and besides you required assistance, and no one else seemed to be paying you the least attention, you see."

"They weren't," he said, cutting to the essentials.

Dear Lord, but she did run on. Of course she was probably nervous at the moment, backing away from him the way she was, which might account for it. So, for that matter, was he. Nervous? His guts were cramping as if he were once more about to lead that last advance at Waterloo.

"If you decide to wallow in guilt," DeLacey said with an attempt at humor, "I'll give you a severe birching. Someday I may even explain how grateful I am for your impetuous flights—unlike your father, *I* consider them your greatest virtue—but for now simply accept my humble thanks, as well as my assurances that I consider you a veritable Angel of Mercy."

She was, he decided as she stood there twisting a tattered silk flower between her fingers and watching him warily, somehow totally and miraculously unchanged. He hadn't expected that.

He'd expected to have to deal with false memories, and he had none.

He'd expected a less open, less candid face, and it was precisely the same.

He'd expected the impish grin to have been superseded by something more studied, and yet it had beamed at him moments before just as he remembered it.

And her character? Her personality?

He'd had only minutes on that bloody battlefield to construct an entire being from a few hints, and yet here she was, perfect in every essential, beloved detail.

He leaned back, resting his head against the sofa, stretched out his legs, regarding her from beneath slightly lowered lids, drinking her in, a foolish grin quirking his mouth.

Impetuous? Impulsive? A prattlebox?

He'd learn over the years, for he was damned if he'd let any other man near her, here or in the future, now he'd finally found her.

He'd been right. By God, he'd known in an instant, surrounded by hell and half crazed with pain, and now heaven's portals were opening to him. There was no way he would permit them to slam shut until he passed through, dragging her with him if he had to, preferably escorting her decorously on his arm. His decision was instantaneous. This ridiculous situation, with all its overtones of social disaster, was perfectly tailored to his only goal. By damn, she *said* she was impetuous. Well, so was he when the occasion demanded. And, impatient. After almost eighteen months, that was his right.

A lazy, relaxed smile played around his lips as he watched her tugging at the impossible dress.

"Well, your man should be here in a moment," she

said hesitantly. "You'll be all right now. There's another way out, isn't there? One where I wouldn't be noticed? Even a balcony'd do, for I can climb trees so that's no problem in the least, and if I tear this dreadful thing, why, that's no more than it deserves. I'll just sneak away before my presence causes you serious inconvenience, and return to—"

"Not quite," he interrupted her smoothly. Would that be the pattern of their days? She prattling on interminably, he interrupting? "How d'you know Banks won't forget me, too? You're the only one who hasn't," he added wryly, glancing at the door from beyond which came sounds of considerable dithering, "so I'm your responsibility 'til your replacement arrives. Military custom. D'you like London?" he asked as the silence caused by her unease began to build.

"Like London?" she whooped, startled by such an improbably fatuous question. The man hadn't *seemed* given to banality, but then one never knew. "I despise it! Dirty, noisy, smelly, unhealthy—how *could* a reasonable person like it? Especially when one isn't permitted to do anything truly interesting."

"Such as?"

"You'd laugh at me."

"No—truly. Tell me. Perhaps one day I might be able to arrange something you'd enjoy. I do owe you a debt, after all."

"Well, Vauxhall, for one. They say it's beautiful at night."

"Getting a bit chilly for that. Have to wait 'til spring. What else?"

"The Tower?" she proffered. For a miracle, he neither sneered nor laughed. Well, in for a penny, in for a pound. "Saint Paul's and Westminster Abbey. Kew. The Royal Exchange."

"A perfectly reasonable itinerary," he smiled, "but

you still don't sound very enthusiastic. Where would you *really* like to go?"

"Home," she returned wistfully. "Saint Mary-Grafton. The country."

"Saint Mary-Grafton? Where is that?"

"Nowhere. Devon, off by itself where most people only stumble across it by accident. There's nothing of any consequence nearby, and no one's ever heard of it, but it's the most beautiful place in the world."

"I believe you. Only the most beautiful place in the world could produce the most beautiful girl in the world."

"Spanish coin! I'm plain, always have been, and know it. Stop bamming me."

"I'm not. You know, I despise London, too. This house is over-blown, just like your London dress: perfectly suited to my grandmother and her set, but totally unsuited to me. I despise senseless opulence and self-important bores with nothing but their pedigrees to recommend them. Don't you?"

"Of course. But then, why stay here? You're a man. You can do precisely as you wish. *Your* parents didn't tell *you* you had to come to London for the Little Season did they? And order you to squander all *sorts* of money unnecessarily."

"You think so? Think again, my dear, though not precisely my parents—my grandmother. Well," he conceded with a grin, "perhaps I *can* do precisely as I wish at that. Especially with your help. We'll see. D'you like me?"

"What an improper question. Have your wits gone begging?"

"Hardly. Besides, we're not *entirely* proper, either of us, are we? In addition to which, propriety is a highly over-rated virtue, don't you think? Boring! D'you like me?" he persisted.

"I don't know you well enough to like you," she frowned, cocking her head and considering the matter. He did deserve *some* sort of recompense for not laughing at her. "You do have a kind face," she admitted, "even if you have a way about you that says you're accustomed to ruling the roost."

"Then, at least you do not *dislike* me, or find me objectionable?"

"Goodness, no! On such short acquaintance? How could I?"

"Does my leg disgust you?"

"Why ever should it? It's a shame, of course, for it must be most inconvenient and very painful, but it's nothing *you* can help."

"Spoken like a true physician's daughter."

"How d'you know my father's a doctor?" she demanded suspiciously, once more edging around the room in search of an auxiliary exit. "Did Sybilla point me out and say something cattish about Papa? I suppose that would account for your current behavior."

"I've no idea. Who's Sybilla?"

Elizabeth whirled in her tracks, giving a shout of delighted laughter. "*You*, my lord, have just become my *favorite* person in the entire world," she crowed. "*Like* you? I *adore* you! Sybilla is my cousin—a despicable, two-faced spoiled cat, and selfish as she can stare, and— Well, I shouldn't say such things about her, so don't encourage me for it isn't ladylike, even if they're true. Besides, Aunt Mehitabelle and Uncle Woodruff are the sweetest dears in the world—aside from Mama and Papa and my brothers, of course. And, Clarissa. She's part of the family now, too."

"Ah, yes: your famous brothers. How many d'you have, I wonder," he said thoughtfully, a gleam in his eye. "I'll bet you I can guess."

"I doubt it," she laughed.

"But I must try. You *do* see that?"

"No, not particularly."

"I must," he insisted. "In the nature of things, if one encounters a beautiful mysterious unknown lady who refuses to give her name, one *must* wager with her."

"Another military tradition, I suppose?"

"Precisely. If I am wrong, I shall give you . . . shall we say a dress to replace that damnable rag on your back? One you must *not* climb trees in. Something that fits, in a clear deep blue or rich forest green, or perhaps a wonderful dark red. Red would become you, I think. To keep things proper, we'll have Grandmama present it."

"I know this is ugly and doesn't fit," she protested, "but it's all I have because Aunt Mehitabelle fell and broke her leg. It used to be Sybilla's. You *truly* don't know who she is? You're sure you're not roasting me?"

"I've already told you: I haven't the slightest notion who Sybilla is, nor do I care."

"How perfectly wonderful! D'you know," Elizabeth confided trustingly, "just after she made her curtsy to you and your grandmama, she came to where I was hiding behind a palm tree because I look so dreadful and know no one at all, and she said she could tell you were taken with her. *Very* taken. She intends to marry you before Christmas, so be forewarned."

"Oh, I am," he chuckled. "Not to worry: she'll catch cold if she attempts such a thing. Now, about our little wager concerning how many brothers you have?"

"All right," she twinkled. "I owe you *something* for not knowing who Sybilla is. She thinks she's a diamond of the first water, you see, and that I'm a country dowd, which I suppose I am, though it's not nice of her to say so, but then it isn't nice of me to call her a cat even if she is one. Guess away."

"How many may I have?"

"Guesses?" she inquired, head cocking once more. He nodded.

"Why, only one. Otherwise, it wouldn't be much of a wager. You'll never win, you know, not in a million years, so this is *most* unfair, but just in case you do, well, what is to be my forfeit? My pockets aren't precisely to let, but I'm not rolling in lard, either. I won't be able to afford anything *too* dear."

"Don't worry—your forfeit shall cost you nothing."

"My name?"

"No, not your name. Well, perhaps in a manner of speaking," he grinned, "if you insist on being absolutely technical about it, though actually something else entirely."

"And it won't be improper?"

"This from a young lady who's locked herself in a room with a man unrelated to her? A man she never met before tonight, but whom she rescued with the intrepidity of a Nelson? Whom, if we are to be absolutely honest about it, she has still to have presented to her in the socially accepted manner? Where is your sense of adventure!"

"You're right, I suppose," she conceded. "Andrew would say I've no bottom, and I *am* in your debt. Jeremy would've said that a year ago, but he's risen above such idioms as 'bottom.' He claims they're uncouth, while I think they're descriptive. It's his age, you know. They *all* go through it. I'll wager even you did, once upon a time. Jeremy's seventeen, you see.

"All right, guess away. If you win, I'll pay my forfeit, no matter what it is, though I'd be much more comfortable if you'd tell me in advance, if you please, my lord."

"That's my angel," he said approvingly, carefully watching her face. "Game as a pebble, as Andrew would say, still being given to colorful turns of phrase, though *never* Jeremy at the moment, albeit he might have a year ago.

"Now, let me see: Would it be ten," he teased. "No, that's too many. I know you've at least two. You told me that yourself. No, *three*, for there's Willie as well. Five, then? No, I don't think so. That's *still* too few. Shall we say—aha! The gamester's lucky number. You have," he announced in sepulchral tones, *"seven brothers."*

"My luck is out!" Elizabeth whirled toward the door, from which was coming discreet, if insistent, taps and scratches. "Oh, dear—your man. I'd best let him in."

"Leave it," he barked in a parade-ground voice, easing forward. "Let them wait, I said. And, *my* luck is in? I guessed aright, I gather?"

"Unless Mama has been confined, and it's Augustus George instead of Amelia Caroline," she admitted, glancing nervously at the door, "but we're hoping for Amelia Caroline. Eight sons and but a single daughter would be a bit much, don't you agree? Besides, Mama's tired of the nursery being painted blue."

The surreptitious taps had become more determined knocks.

"Seven it is! Can't count any that haven't been born yet or you don't know about," he laughed. "Twouldn't be fair."

"I suppose not. Then you won fair and square. What is my forfeit? I prefer to pay my debts as quickly as may be. John says it's the only way to go on. He's another of my brothers—the eldest."

"Will you trust me?" he asked gently, golden eyes suddenly earnest, boring into hers. "No matter how strange things may seem at first, or how uncomfortable or unaccountable? I promise you won't suffer for it."

"Trust you? I suppose so. Wellington did, I gather. That's a pretty high recommendation."

"Very high. Do exactly as I tell you, and ask no questions. First, tiptoe to the door and unlock it. Is it unlocked? Good. The next part goes very quickly. Come sit here beside me. Closer. Very good." He gazed down into her questioning eyes. Dear Lord, another brother! He'd never even considered the possibility. "You see, your forfeit is to permit me to compromise you."

"Whatever are you—"

"Hush! I require rescuing—from my grandmama, who wants me in London, and from all the Sybillas who want to be countesses by Christmas. You are about to rescue me. *That* is your forfeit." He closed his eyes, jerked at the offending neckline. It gave way at the shoulder with a dry crack. "Slap me."

"You're mad," she choked, caught between laughter and puzzlement as she tugged at her dress. The neckline torn wasn't much more indecent than the neckline whole.

"I've never been saner in my life. Are you about to deny a debt of honor? I thought not. Slap me. Hard. Harder," he insisted under cover of the pounding on the door. "My face must bear the clear imprint of your hand. Better. At least that stung a bit. Now, scream. Top of your lungs."

That, at least, was easier than striking this defenseless madman with determinedly clenched eyes and deep pain lines marring his craggy, care-worn face. She gave a full-throated whoop that was instantly stifled as he pulled her into his arms and slammed his mouth against the place he assumed hers to be, first missing the target, then swiftly and expertly adjusting. She stiffened, trying to wrench away.

Then something definitely odd happened as the initial harsh assault became gentle, infinitely sweet and longing and coaxing and tender. She was only vaguely aware of the door crashing open behind them, of voices, of shrieks that rivaled hers of moments before. Unconsciously her arms crept around the former colonel's neck as she melted against him with a soft sigh.

"You see," he whispered beneath the brouhaha, "I told you to trust me. Everything will be perfect. We've just a few rough spots to get over first. The real forfeit is, you must marry me. The other was only a ruse to make it instantly possible."

"*Richard!*" came a scandalized, disbelieving male voice. "Are you gone *mad*?"

The earl lifted his head, surveyed the individuals—his grandmother, Lady Daphne, Harry Beckenham, Sally Jersey, the Duke of Rawdon and his duchess, Lady Farquhar and the foppish Nigel trailed by the vacuous and delicate Millicent, pretty Patsy Worth clinging to ginger-haired Giles's arm, and naturally his man, Banks, along with a footman whose name he could never remember—crowding into the small room. Behind them loomed a solid mass of guests, necks craning, eyes darting, as they attempted to see what was happening.

"Never saner in my life," he proclaimed triumphantly. "Ladies, gentlemen, permit me to present the future Countess of Rochedale."

From beyond the door rose a horrendous screech.

"Oh, dear," Elizabeth whispered into DeLacey's neckcloth, "*that's* Sybilla. Don't be surprised if I am murdered in my bed. 'Future Countess of Rochedale,' indeed!"

"What is the young person's name?" his grandmother's voice broke icily through the amazed pandemonium greeting his announcement. "If you can spare a moment to inform us, that is?"

"Why, ah, ah—"

"Cat got your tongue, Rochedale?" Lady Jersey inquired sweetly. "Or, is it you have forgotten the identity of your lady in the—ah—*heat* of the moment?"

"Help me," the former colonel implored in a soft whisper. "I can't get us through this without your coop- eration."

"Elizabeth," Elizabeth hissed.

"Elizabeth!" DeLacey proclaimed loudly. "This is Elizabeth. A lovely name, don't you all agree? Eliza- beth—ah—ah—" Then, "Elizabeth *what?*" he pleaded desperately in her ear. "You've *got* to help me."

"Driscoll," she giggled, slightly hysterical.

"Elizabeth Driscoll," he stated firmly. "Miss Elizabeth Driscoll, daughter of Doctor Driscoll of Saint Mary- Grafton," he threw a disparaging glance in Giles's direc- tion, grinning at the young man's stunned expression, "in Devonshire and his delightful wife, and the sister of seven amazing brothers, or perhaps eight, or perhaps seven and a sister, in which case the name shall be 'Amelia Caroline,' which is what we are all hoping for as eight sons and but a single daughter *is* a bit much, as my fiancée has kindly informed me. Otherwise it shall be 'Augustus George.' We're not entirely certain at the moment. Not even John or Andrew or Jeremy are cer- tain, and while one can't be surprised at Andrew or John's lack of knowledge, Jeremy's is astonishing, as he believes he knows everything, having reached the startling age of seventeen intact, which none of us thought he would do. Miss Driscoll's mother awaits a blessed event, you see, which is why the rest of the family could not be here for our announcement, though naturally they share in our joy—even Willie, who's the youngest."

"He's foxed," came a low mutter, "foxed beyond coherence."

"You're babbling," Elizabeth cautioned.

"No, I'm not," he returned softly. "I'm confusing them. Elementary military strategy, my dearest Eliza- beth. *Always* confuse the enemy."

Still hiding her flaming face in his neckcloth, she whispered indignantly, "I'm *not* your dearest *anything*. We need to have a talk. A *serious* talk. Immediately, my lord!"

"Later. When we've our privacy again."

"*Now*. I'm in no way suited to be a countess."

"Oh yes you are, minx. You're perfectly suited—but only to be *my* countess."

"You *are* mad!"

"No, my love, merely a very happy, very determined man."

Then he looked up at Harry Beckenham, who was leaning over him, hand outstretched to wrest Elizabeth from his arms. *I've found her!* Richard DeLacey, Earl of Rochedale mouthed. *Wish me happy!* under cover of the confusion.

Harry stiffened, backed away, staring at the rumpled girl nestling bemusedly against DeLacey, her face still hidden from view. Harry's eyes widened. Then he spun to face the others, expression grim, as Giles stared from him to the couple on the settee in dawning comprehension.

"It's his old head wound," Harry baldly informed the stupefied witnesses to the outré betrothal announcement. "This happens sometimes, unfortunately—even years later." Giles pulled Lady Daphne aside, whispering and gesturing urgently. "Nothing to be seriously concerned about, and certainly nothing for which the poor man can be blamed, though precautions must be taken."

"What the *devil* d'you think you're about, Harry?" DeLacey sputtered. "I'm as sane as any man here. Saner!"

Harry Beckenham's smile was pitying as he seized Elizabeth's arm, clearly intending to encourage her from DeLacey's grasp.

"You must not let the earl distress or frighten you, Miss Driscoll," he cajoled, tugging. DeLacey held onto her for dear life. "Come now, Miss Driscoll. His lordship is not accountable for his actions. This is all a hum. However, while I do not believe him to be in any way dangerous except to himself, nevertheless it is not wise in you to—"

"Damn you, Harry—"

Beckenham dropped Elizabeth's arm, turned to the dowager countess. "The earl should be escorted to his rooms and his physician summoned," he insisted desperately. "A strong sedative must be administered, followed by a period of total seclusion and quiet, preferably far from Town excitements. These flights from reality and responsible behavior will become less frequent over time. In the interim, I suggest—"

"Stubble it, Harry!"

Beckenham whirled on his aunt in fury. Lady Daphne Cheltenham swept forward from where she had been lingering by the door, Giles Fortescue and Patsy Worth in her wake.

"This announcement's been pending for over a year to my certain knowledge," she informed her fascinated audience. "My dear Elizabeth, let me be the first to wish you happy," she proclaimed, kissing the top of Elizabeth's head as her cheek remained unavailable. Then she looked DeLacey straight in the eye. "It's taken long enough. Congratulations, young man. You appear to have done well for yourself. Patsy, give Miss Driscoll your shawl. Her gown is in a slight state of disrepair."

In the stunned silence following Lady Daphne's firm seizure of the reins, Imogene Pugh's high-pitched, faintly apologetic voice could be heard from beyond the door, pleading for someone to provide burnt feathers. *Sal volatile* was having no affect at all upon poor, dear, sweet, abused, betrayed Miss Wainwright.

Six

"Dear heaven," gasped Lady Wainwright from her bed, clutching her husband's arm with one hand as she delicately fanned herself with a lace-edged handkerchief with the other. "There's no question?"

"About my being compromised? I'm not so certain about that," Elizabeth returned thoughtfully, voice rising over the commotion in the hall as she pulled Patsy Worth's shawl more tightly around her thin shoulders. "The precise circumstances which constitute compromise among the ton are beyond my knowledge. But, about my being betrothed? No, I don't believe so. The earl was most insistent, both in public and in private. We are to be wed by special license in three days' time. I presume that means I'm currently betrothed."

From the door came a shriek of rage.

Sybilla paused there, head flung back, lips drawn in a snarl, then stormed across her ladyship's pretty bedchamber—all restful pale silvers and grayed blues and lavenders, the heavily fringed draperies drawn against the night—trailed by the hapless Miss Pugh.

"I *told* you she'd spoil everything!" the girl shrieked. She whirled on Elizabeth. *"Hussy! Harlot! Haymarket-ware!"*

Her stinging backhanded slap cracked in the sudden silence. Then she was spinning back and forth, addressing first her parents, then her trembling cousin.

"I want her *gone!* I want her gone on the *instant.* She *entrapped* him. *Hell-cat! Viper!* The drab *stole* him from me because she knew *I* wanted him. And, I *had* him. A week, and he'd've offered. A countess! Do you comprehend? Your daughter would've been a *countess,* and rich as Croesus, and now it's all come to nothing because of that country jade. *Fish-wife! Strumpet!* She should be *transported.*

"*And I permitted the baggage to wear my favorite gown from my come-out year!*"

Her father, face inscrutable except for the steadying glance he threw his niece, leaned forward, eyes cold.

"Sybilla, a trace of decorum, if you please," he said as the tirade wore thin. His voice was low and level as he gave his wife's hand a reassuring squeeze.

"*Decorum?* You dare preach to *me* of *decorum?* What about *her,*" pointing scornfully at Elizabeth. "Do you know what she *did?*"

At this he stood, customarily sunny cherubic face stern, portly figure imposing despite his lack of height, and slowly walked to the foot of his wife's bed. There was something vaguely menacing in his movements. Sybilla shrank back, head still defiantly high.

"We've enough to consider without contending with your flights of fancy and viper's tongue, Sybilla," he said. "You've no more chance of attaching the Earl of Rochedale than an aboriginal from the Antipodes. Less, perhaps. If you cannot contain yourself, you will leave the room. Your rantings are of absolutely no interest."

"They had best be of interest! Your sweet little *bumpkin* has *ruined* us. She *locked herself in his study with him.* He was ill, and she *trapped him* when he was *defenseless,* and so I shall inform *everyone.* She'll gain nothing by her duplicity—I'll see to that. A countess? *Ha!* She'll be received *nowhere*. What have you to say to *that?*"

"Sybilla," he snapped, voice the lash of a whip, "my patience has run out. You will be still. If you cannot be still, you will leave this room, either of your own volition, or escorted by as many footmen as it takes to remove you. If that proves necessary, you will be locked in your room until I decide what to do with you, probably an extended visit to Aunt Witherspoon. Is this clear?"

"You wouldn't *dare.*"

"Try me."

She clenched her fists, tossed her head and threw her father a sneer. Wainwright turned slightly, gray eyes studying Miss Pugh.

The former governess hovered just behind Sybilla, twisting a furry rag in her hands, mouth opening and closing like that of a beached fish. Her cheeks bore the imprint of a multitude of vicious slaps. Her faded brown hair fell about her face in pathetic wisps, short and thin and lank. The viscount's eyes twinkled in surprise: the tattered thing was a postiche—a hairpiece designed to supply what Nature withheld. Vanity from Pugh, of all unlikely things! What next?

"I believe we owe you an apology, Miss Pugh," he said kindly. "As this is a family matter, and you have already performed your duty in returning the girls to us more or less intact, I suggest you retire to your room. You appear completely done in. Ring for hot milk, a restorative, a bath, supper, whatever you wish."

"My fault," the hapless Miss Pugh babbled. "Couldn't help it. Can't watch two at once. Not *such* a two! Did my best, *truly*. Wasn't good enough. But, Miss Driscoll vanished. *Vanished!* And then," she paused dramatically, "she *reappeared*. In *such* a way! Sorry, *so* sorry. Poor Miss Sybilla! Such a shock to delicate sensibilities. Overpowering. Positively *overpowering*. *Viper* nourished in our *bosoms*."

"Think nothing of it. I doubt even her ladyship could've controlled the situation. Scoot, now. Off you go."

"Not Miss Sybilla's fault," Pugh persisted with an anxious glance at her former pupil as she edged toward the door, still tormenting her hairpiece. "Innocent victim. Such *delicate* sensibility. Strong reaction to be anticipated. *Total* betrayal. Young love blighted," she quavered, then whirled, dashing for safety.

"Can't that woman speak in full sentences?" demanded his lordship of his wife. "Has she always been this way?"

"More or less," Lady Wainwright sighed. "She was the last of several gross—I never realized the whole of England contained so many governesses!—and the only one who would stay, I think because she knew no one else would have her. Rather a pathetic creature and I took pity on her. And, I was tired of the constant departures in high dudgeon. You do recall the situation?"

"Oh, I remember," he returned grimly. "I remember very well indeed. Some lasted but a single day, some less than that." His eyes flicked to his wife's abigail, hovering anxiously at the dressing room door while making valiant attempts to appear invisible. "Everything will be fine, Bartlet," he said. "No one will assault your mistress, and she isn't about to have the vapors. I won't let her, aside from which it isn't her style. She waits until *after* a crisis to indulge herself, and then it's usually only a grumble or two, as you are well aware. So, take yourself off. Close the doors behind you, if you would. I'll see to anything her ladyship requires once this matter is resolved."

He waited, the charming but rather self-effacing figure generally ignored by all but his wife now a suddenly commanding presence in his lady's delicate bedchamber. His daughter began to rethink the opinion she had always given out—that he was a nonentity suitable only to be overlooked.

After Bartlet reluctantly vanished with a curtsy, he looked steadily first at his wife, then at each of the girls.

"Sybilla, this is really no concern of yours," he said, raising his hand in caution as she flew forward, mouth opening to protest. "No concern whatsoever," he insisted, then waited for her mouth to close. It did at last. "If you nonetheless wish to be present, I have no material objections if your cousin does not." Here he glanced at Elizabeth, who shook her head. He smiled slightly, turned back to his daughter. "Very well. You will take the chair by your mother's fire. And," he speared her with eyes that brooked no argument, "you will remain absolutely still unless spoken to. Now, go sit down."

Wills clashed in the cozy bedchamber as Elizabeth held her breath. Then, clearly puzzled by her own unaccustomed obedience, Sybilla grudgingly retreated to the prescribed chair by the fire. The viscount nodded his satisfaction, glanced quickly at his wife who rolled her eyes to heaven, then turned to his niece.

"Have a seat, my dear," he instructed, pointing to the comfortable armchair in which he had been keeping his wife company before the girls' return. "You must be somewhat fatigued. A glass of ratafia, perhaps? Or, something stronger? I feel the need of some brandy, myself. In moderate amounts it clears the head and encourages clear thought—quite the opposite of what it does when overindulgence is the goal. Clear and relaxed thinking appears to be what we're most in need of at the moment. How about you, my dear," gazing fondly at his wife. "Can I convince you—?"

"Port," she smiled, "but *please* don't inform Bartlet. She'd be horrified."

"And you, my dear," he repeated, glance shifting to Elizabeth, now perched on the edge of the chair at his wife's bedside. "I do think a drop of brandy is in order. You appear as done in as Pugh, and we may be at this for some time. Family conferences aren't known for short-windedness, any more than are Parliamentary debates."

He went to the tray placed on the dressing table for his convenience earlier that evening, poured a glass of port, a generous dollop of brandy, another more restrained one, distributed the prescribed restoratives, and shifted a chair to a point that blocked his daughter's view of her cousin, but from which he could keep a wary eye on Sybilla if necessary. He sat, crossing his legs and leaning back comfortably.

"Now, Elizabeth," he said, "I want you to tell us everything that occurred. *Everything.* Begin with the moment you left this house, and do not stop until you are back in it, sitting in this room. Omit nothing, gloss over nothing, forget nothing. It's very important, my dear."

"What about *me?*" Sybilla burst out from her corner by the fire. "Will you offer *me* no restorative? *I'm* the one who's been abused, betrayed, and deceived. And now my own *father* chooses to *insult* me!"

"If you want something, help yourself," Wainwright returned indifferently, eyes smiling at his wife. This ignoring of Sybilla was infinitely soul-satisfying. It also appeared to produce desirable results. Why had they never thought to try it before? "Otherwise, be still. Now, Elizabeth—"

He paused as Sybilla made a great show of flouncing across the room, rattling decanters, clattering glasses.

"There's nothing here fit to drink," she complained. "Ratafia is swill, port for the lower orders, and brandy gives me a head."

"Then go without." Indifference to his daughter's vagaries was turning this bizarre situation into a pure delight. "Return to your place."

He didn't bother to watch, but he listened carefully. For a miracle, Sybilla, after a moment's hesitation, actually regained her seat by the fire.

The viscount suddenly had no doubt that his niece was truly, and in some strange manner honorably—one could imagine nothing less in her case—betrothed to the Earl of Rochedale, as improbable as that might seem on first hearing. This was a night of miracles, and the miracle of such a betrothal was far less unlikely than the miracle of obedience, even reluctant obedience, from his daughter. A slow, wondering smile spread over his pleasant features.

"Tell us all about it, Elizabeth," he coaxed. "I know we're not Samuel or Suzanne, but try to pretend we are if you can, my dear, just to help you along."

"While here I *do* think of you as my parents," Elizabeth protested, "for I've been nothing but a bother, and you've been *so* kind and welcoming."

"Sybilla, as well?"

"Oh, no—we've ever parted brass rags. You know that, Uncle Woodruff. Sybilla no more cares for me than I care for—oh, my *wretched* tongue," she blurted as her uncle gave a shout of laughter. "We're such *different* people," she apologized weakly.

"You are indeed, my dear," he twinkled. "If you want the truth with no bark on it, I don't particularly care for the wasp-tongued termagant myself. Far too avaricious and self-centered. I don't see who could," then chuckled at the indignant gasp from beside the fireplace. "It's no wonder she remains unspoken for.

"Someday Sybilla may change," he continued, "but I doubt it. She hasn't the intelligence or the capacity or the strength of character or the desire, from all I've observed, but I do have a lingering hope that one day she may come to the realization that she causes the sun neither to rise nor to set. I am, after all, her father, and partially responsible for her presence in this vale of tears.''

A furious mumble came from behind him.

"You spoke?" he inquired, head turning slightly.

"No-no, nothing, Papa," Sybilla proclaimed in arctic tones.

"I thought not. You have, after all, been instructed to hold your tongue." Then Wainwright glanced at his wife. Her eyes were round with disbelief, her lips slightly parted to reveal still-perfect small white teeth. He beamed at her bracingly. Her mouth snapped shut. "Well, Elizabeth?"

"It's all quite prosaic, believe it or not, if slightly odd, but first I'd best give you these."

She rose, still clutching the shawl around her shoulders, and handed her uncle a pair of notes. He looked at her inquiringly.

"One's from Lord DeLacey," she explained, "and merely states his intention to call upon you at nine o'clock this morning as you stand in place of a father to me here. He begs your indulgence for the early hour, but says he is anxious to put matters in hand. The other, and I don't understand this at all but she insisted I bring it to you, is from an old lady named Daphne Cheltenham. I *think* she's a countess, and I don't believe she's even a connection of Lord DeLacey's, but I'm not entirely certain. She says we are to do absolutely nothing until she has spoken with you, no matter what his lordship demands."

"I'll read them later," he said, tucking the missives in his waistcoat pocket. "Now, on with your story. Lord knows, we've been waiting long enough to hear it."

Elizabeth gave a brief account of the evening, reluctantly admitting to Sybilla's instructions in the rotunda under her uncle's pointed questioning, detailing the earl's sudden weakness, stumbling over events in his private study as she blushed furiously. More probing from her uncle brought out details, some of which, such as the contretemps concerning her name, had the viscount roaring with laughter, others, such as Harry Beckenham's attempted interference, frowning in puzzlement.

"There's more here than meets the eye," he commented thoughtfully when finally the story had been told in enough detail to satisfy him, "though I'm blessed if I know what it is. You've obviously accepted him, a man known to you for less than an hour. You're not mercenary, so it can't be for his fortune. And, you've no desire to put yourself forward among the ton, so neither his title nor his Peninsular and Waterloo fame can be much of an attraction. Why then, Elizabeth?"

"I don't know. It just somehow seemed I *must*, if you can understand that. As if it were the only thing I *could* do."

From her place by the fire Sybilla emitted a delicate snort. She received not so much as a glance in response, a fact most galling to that young lady. Instead, her father continued to peer narrowly at Elizabeth.

"There must be more," he said.

"Well, I suppose there is, though it's not very logical. In a way he reminds me of Papa, though they're not in the least alike so far as I can tell, except they're both very determined. I felt *safe* with him, almost as if I'd come home, which is, of course, perfectly preposterous. As if I'd known him forever."

"You don't claim to love the man."

"How can I? I've barely met him. But, I suspect I will come to. Certainly I like him. I like him *very* much. There's something about him—I can't explain it. I just know it's there. Being with him felt *right*, d'you see? As if I'd known him forever. No? Well, I don't quite see myself, so that's no surprise, but he's *comfortable*.

"I've never felt that way with any of the London beaux. They've all been bores of one sort or another. His lordship's certainly no bore. He's kind and generous and clever, and he has as keen a sense of the ridiculous as you and Papa do, and he despises London and the ton as much as *I* do, and for all he's several years my senior there's nothing the least stodgy about him, but he's not like the boys in Saint Mary-Grafton, either. They're silly as they can stare, most times. Not an idea in their brainboxes beyond hunting and fishing. Hunting and fishing are all very well, but there's more to life than foxes and trout—or tying neckcloths and selecting snuff boxes.

"Of course," she admitted after slight hesitation as her uncle continued to watch her steadily, brows rising, "Lord DeLacey does appear rather accustomed to having his own way about things, but then I've only known him a few hours.

"You see," she sighed, "I'm wise enough to realize Mama and Papa hope I'll return to Saint Mary-Grafton betrothed. *This* takes care of the matter in the simplest manner possible, for I shall return wed, and to a man I think they will admire and respect, and who, more importantly, will admire and respect my father and all the rest of my family. In fact, I rather imagine the boys will follow his lordship about like Tantony pigs, hanging on his every word and coming to him with all their troubles, and generally making him far too full of himself. I shall become totally superfluous," she chuckled.

"Rochedale isn't known for insanity," her uncle said, frowning. "I know him by reputation only—the air in his vicinity is far too rarefied for our humbler status— but he's always had a level head on his shoulders, even as a green lad first on the Town. Typical military type. I'll be interested in what he has to say for himself in the morning."

"Well, I won't," Sybilla snapped, surging to her feet. "He's fit for Bedlam—it's that simple, and your trollop of a niece's taken him in. I'll put a stop to it, see if I don't! And, if I fail, there's always the dowager countess. She's known to be a very high stickler. Do you truly believe she'd want *that*," indicating the bedraggled Elizabeth with disdain, "for a granddaughter-in-law?

"Don't worry, Papa, I'm relieving you of my presence. I just wanted to see how far the vixen would go in twisting events. If you desire to learn what *truly* transpired, I will enlighten you on the morrow—beginning with how she tore her own corsage so it would appear he'd compromised her. And *that* is only the start. You will be *mortified*. In the interim, I shall seek my bed. I'm unutterably wearied by all this moonshine."

After hastily retrieving the ensembles she had been forced to loan her cousin from Elizabeth's sparsely populated armoire, Sybilla returned to her bedchamber, set herself down at the escritoire and composed a letter to her aunt and uncle in Devonshire. She made several false beginnings, attempting to achieve just the right distraught tone, and then things went better.

The instant she was satisfied with what she had contrived she rang her bell, had her maid summon a footman, instructed the footman to summon a groom, paced the floor until the groom made his appearance. She handed him her sealed message along with a heavy purse, and instructed him to take the best horse in the stables and ride posthaste for Saint Mary-Grafton sparing neither nag nor shillings, making as many changes of mount as required and taking no rest. A dire family emergency had arisen.

Then, ever aware of what best ensured silence, she

distributed generous vails all around and, quite pleased with herself, sought her pillow at last.

Elizabeth Driscoll, a countess? Not while *she* breathed.

In Saint Mary-Grafton the stars wheeled decorously across the midnight sky, tiny points of glittering light that cast a glow over fields and furrows, picking out the roads and country lanes with silver and throwing the hedgerows into soft relief. The barest whisper of a breeze rustled the leaves of the peach tree in the Driscoll garden and ruffled the petals of late-blooming roses. The little stream at the base of the lawn burbled to itself, a peaceful lullaby whose threnody filtered to the open windows of the ivy-clad house from which came the sound of subdued young male voices below, and the impatient tap of anxious young male footsteps pacing, turning, pacing once more.

A wisp of smoke, white in the starlight, threaded its way from the kitchen chimney, rapidly dissipating in the night sky. Warm light streaming through the windows cast golden squares and rectangles across the lawns and over the hedges.

. Not a curtain had been drawn, not a drapery, so that all the world of Saint Mary-Grafton knew there were doings this night at the doctor's house, and waited to hear whether the new arrival would be Augustus George—as the men of the village insisted, conservatively seeing no reason for the *status quo* to alter—or Amelia Caroline, whose advent was prophesied by the ladies of the tiny community and its outlying farms after many a surreptitious glance at the level at which the child had ridden.

In the gracious old master chamber at the head of the stairs Samuel Driscoll beamed at his exhausted wife, a boyish grin on his face, a squirming red-faced bundle squalling in his arms.

"Well?" Lady Suzanne demanded as Tillie scurried around the room collecting soiled linens. His lordship— for all that he wasn't to be *called* that, which didn't change in the least what he was, however much he might think it did—insisted on a rule of cleanliness that kept the household in a constant dither of scrubbing and boiling.

"Ten fingers, ten toes, a dusting of red-gold down atop, and everything perfect between," the new father announced proudly, "just as always," a teasing glint in his warm hazel eyes.

"The same as always, Samuel?" Lady Suzanne sighed. "I should've expected it, I suppose, but this one did feel so different, more like Elizabeth. Ah, well—welcome home, Augustus," she smiled wearily, extending her arms. "You've plenty of playmates waiting downstairs, but I insist we paint the nursery yellow this time."

The good doctor backed away from his wife, the mischievous look on his face clearly the pattern from which William and Steven had drawn theirs. "Now, my dear," he cautioned, retaining the new infant securely, "I merely meant the child was perfect."

"Have done, Samuel," she protested. "I'm not disappointed, truly I'm not. Whatever would I do with a little girl? Why, I've no more memory of how to sew miniature dresses after all the shirts and waistcoats than the man in the moon. Give me Augustus, do. The poor mite is upset enough at being torn so rudely from his warm, soft nest, and sounds hungry into the bargain. No need to compound the insult."

"Amelia Caroline," he corrected smugly, then grinned more broadly at the look of stupefaction on his wife's face. "I'll just clean my new daughter up a bit, and then you may have her all to yourself."

"At last," she breathed in disbelief. "It's not that I don't love the boys, you know, but I really *have* become quite tired of a nursery all decorated in blue. It's been that way for eighteen years. And, I've the strangest feeling about Elizabeth's Season, as if she were lost to us even before she departed for London. Indeed, I've felt that way since your return from Brussels, which makes no sense at all."

"Sense or not," her husband chuckled, "I've come to trust these unaccountable feelings of yours. It's a good thing Amelia Caroline has come to join us."

"You'd best inform the boys," she murmured in sleepy response. "If I know them, they're wearing holes in the carpets this very instant."

It was some time later, with his wife properly settled for what remained of the night, their diminutive new daughter cozily tucked in the crook of her arm, that Samuel Driscoll descended the stairs. Tillie, sworn to secrecy on the newest sibling's gender, had found it easier to scurry down the back way than face the six anxious young faces awaiting news, and was by then back above with the boys none the wiser, the master's cot made up in the dressing room, and herself drowsily regarding her sleeping mistress with awed pride. Not a peep the dear lady had made—not a one! Just some very loud singing, as was her wont.

Cook, up the long night like the rest of the household, had indulged in a frenzy of baking to fill the anxious hours. Tarts cooled on kitchen sills. Cakes reposed on dressers. The aromas of coffee fresh-brewed, sizzling gammon, grilling kidneys and cinnamon-laced muffins just pulled from the hearth wafted into the hall and up the stairs. Driscoll poked his head through the door. The rotund woman's head snapped up.

"T'mistress?" she inquired.

"A trifle tired is all, and sleeping from it like a babe,"

he grinned, "and Amelia Caroline with her. Give me five minutes with the boys, and then bring on breakfast. I could eat my way to London and back."

"It be a girl, then?"

"It is indeed: a dainty, winsome lass to gladden all our hearts."

"You be a'minding of Willie, then," Cook cautioned with the familiarity of long country service. "Him's wanting a lad, no matter what t'rest of us be thinking."

Driscoll nodded. Willie hadn't said much, but the little he *had* said had been quite definite.

Then he was down the hall and into the main part of the house, still grinning foolishly, the miracle of their ninth child every bit as great as their first. He paused in the parlor doorway, surveying the six of his sons still at home—bleary-eyed, the lot of them, with collars rumpled and hair mussed by repeated distracted finger-combings, their eyes over-bright from lack of rest.

"Well, lads," he boomed, but softly so as not to waken those sleeping above, "why haven't you sought your beds? It's already tomorrow."

They spun, regarding him narrowly, excitement as well as a touch of anxiety on their immature faces.

"Mama?" they chorused.

"In fine fettle, as always."

"And—" Charles, the eldest remaining at home, questioned reluctantly after taking a deep, relieved breath.

"And? And *what?*" their father teased.

"Papa!"

"Well, let's put it this way," he grinned after a moment's anticipatory pause, "if she ends up missish, it won't be because of you lads."

"Six shillings!" Robert crowed, whirling on Jeremy with hand extended as Andrew caroled—"I *knew* Mama'd do it! Bully!"

"Mama's all right? *Truly?*" Jeremy demanded, indolent dandyism forgotten as he reached for his purse.

"Truly," his father assured him, then glanced at his youngest. Willie stood slightly apart from the others, lower lip thrust out in a furious pout. "What's the matter, lad?" Driscoll inquired, putting an arm around the boy and pulling him aside as the others indulged in hand-shaking and back-slapping. "Not particularly liking the idea of a wee mite of a sister to keep you hopping?"

"Girls're sissies," Willie mumbled defensively. "Don't need none of *them.*"

"Elizabeth isn't."

"Oh, Lizbeth," Willie sighed disparagingly. *"She's* not a *girl.* 'Sides, it's *drefful* being the youngest. And, I still *am.*"

"Amelia'll need you to teach her to walk, you know," Driscoll reminded him, "and to catch frogs and go fishing, and how to toss a ball. And, she'll need your protection from bullies. That's a brother's job, protecting his sister. The others'll be gone, and we'll all be depending on you to see her over the rough spots."

"Don't know *nuffin* 'bout girls," Willie protested. "Don't *want* to. Gustus, now—I could've taught *him* stuff, but not a *girl.* Girls don't listen. 'Sides, if it *was* Gustus, I wouldn't be the youngest anymore. Girls don't count when it comes to being youngest," he explained. "Only boys. That's what Stevie said." Then he glanced hopefully at his father. "Can we send her back, please? It *should've* been Gustus, you know. *Somebody* made a mistake. None of us'll know what to do with a girl— not even Mama."

"No, no exchanges and no refunds," his father smiled. "And, no guarantees. That's the way the good Lord intended it, and *He* knows a lot more about these things than we do. Trust Him. We were hoping for a girl, though—your Mama and I."

"But what does Mama want with a girl when she's got *us*," the boy demanded, gesturing at his brothers. "I should think *we'd* be enough."

"Well, Willie, your mama wanted to paint the nursery pink, you see," Dr. Driscoll explained with the hint of a smile, "because she's so very tired of blue. She couldn't do that with a boy, now could she?"

"Country upstarts. Nobodies," Lady Lavinia DeLacey, Dowager Countess of Rochedale spat, and so the dispute—they were ladies of the highest ton, so it couldn't be termed a tavern brawl, especially as there was nothing the least physical about it—continued. "Why, even the Wainwright woman and her husband are nobodies! As for that *impossible* daughter of theirs—"

They had retreated to the sitting room comprising a minuscule part of the official head of the family's west wing suite, she and Lady Daphne Cheltenham, once they managed to rid Rochedale House of the curious, the importunate, and the impertinent. Richard had been packed off to Rawdon House along with Harry Beckenham and Giles Fortescue, the servants set loose to clean, straighten, and restore.

And then? Then they had looked each other in the eye, heads held high. They knew each other well, these gallant survivors. Silently, because there was no need for words between them, they drew the lines of battle.

Then they climbed the stairs to Lady Lavinia's apartments, rang for tea and biscuits, had the fire rebuilt, glared at each other, and set to it.

They had been at it for hours, unrelenting in attack, unyielding in defense. Chins set, rigidly erect in thronelike ebony chairs whose backs were formed by hideous jeweled dragon's heads, they slogged grimly on, hammering at each other, seeking chinks in armored defenses, breaches in bastions of logic and social *savoir-faire.*

"A *sawbones*' daughter?" Lady Lavinia concluded once more with what she considered eminent good sense and unassailable logic. "He's *mad.* I'll have him locked up for his own sake—see if I don't."

"And cause an even greater scandal? *You're* the one who's mad."

Lady Daphne gazed wearily at her old friend.

A dear woman, Lavinia. Loyal and supportive in times of affliction beyond anything common among the ton. First encountered as a bride at a Royal Drawing Room, abandoned by her husband and mama-in-law, feathers drooping and paniers sadly crushed and yet determinedly smiling, gay, vivacious—an object worthy of admiration rather than pity, Archibald had said, and so over they had gone, he charming, and she? Lady Daphne wasn't certain what she'd been, other than taken aback that her handsome young husband should be so determined upon his course of rescue. Whatever it was, it had gained her this friend who was always there, no matter how many the months or years between meetings, and no matter what the temporary disagreements between them.

And, because Lavinia had cold-bloodedly married far above herself on the strength of an impressive dot, she was now determined never to see the act repeated no matter what the size of the dowry or the sentiments of the individuals.

Fool! But, because she'd realized at the wedding breakfast that she'd sacrificed everything to gain an illustrious title, Lavinia protected that title with a deter-

mination bordering on the manic. Pedigree was everything. And, character? Nothing.

They'd been through the wars together, the figurative
and the literal. They'd buried their husbands, one with
great relief, the other in deepest shared sorrow, within
a year of each other. They'd buried parents, brothers,
sisters, and children. They'd each, very quietly and with
only the other in attendance, buried a beloved *cher ami*,
Lady DeLacey while still trapped in her disastrous
arranged marriage, Lady Cheltenham just the year
before, an affaire that began only many years after her
tragic early widowhood, and would have continued to
her death had his not preceded it.

They were tired, both of them, exhausted not just by
this chaotic evening, but by all the evenings, the days
and weeks and months and years preceding it.

Though there was a new generation coming along,
that was precisely the rub: It was a *new* generation, with
new ideas and new standards. In a very real sense they
had only each other, these two old champions of the
lists of the ton, and the few others of their age and
memories who still clung to their faculties. The young
were so very sure of themselves, so very determined the
world be ordered to their conceptions. Unfortunately,
those conceptions were often at odds with realities only
time and experience and misfortune could teach. Still,
some things *did* need changing, among them Lavinia
DeLacey's clinging to the rigid caste standards of an
earlier time.

"Don't be mutton-headed," Lady Daphne now
cajoled for what felt like the hundredth time. "The
girl appeared to be thoroughly presentable once we
emptied the place of the curious."

"Presentable? A milkmaid with the stench of the barn-
yard about her? Pert and gauche, lacking beauty, lacking

style, lacking grace, lacking even countenance? A dowd
of the most banal sort? Come, now! Were it young Harry
were speaking of, would you still consider her presentable?"

"Highly."

"Then *you're* the fool," Lady Lavinia snorted. Then,
patiently, reasonably, she explained as if to a babe in
arms, "She'd be cut left and right, and correctly so.
While the mortification she might suffer does not concern me in the least—She would have earned it ten
times over!—I *will not* have such an insult tendered the
Countess of Rochedale.

"Worse, Richard would be ostracized—with cause.

"One *does not* wed beneath one's station—or above
it—without suffering the penalties such lack of consideration for one's position, and the position of others,
engenders. As for any whelps produced by such an intolerable *mésalliance*, being neither trade nor servant nor
ton, there would be no place for them anywhere—
unless one considers transportation to the colonies
where *anything* appears acceptable."

"The child needs some polish, granted, but the family
is eminently respectable. Your sponsorship would render her position unassailable." How many times had
she said this, patience and intractability colliding with
patience and intractability, neither yielding an inch?
"Her father may be a country sawbones, but he's also
Baron Hawls of Hawlsey Manor, for pity's sake. Perfectly
good ton. The Suffolk Hawls—you've heard of them.
Very old title, and her mother is the granddaughter
of—"

"I haven't the *slightest* interest in her mother's antecedents or her father's purported honors and style.
Trumpery, all of it."

Lady Lavinia did not precisely lean back in her chair,

but there was a slight relaxing of muscles as she surveyed the purple silk hangings, the gilded and frescoed ceiling *à l'Italien*, the priceless jades and porcelains and paintings and furniture she had purloined from various Rochedale residences to furnish these rooms she'd grimly clung to after Wharton's death. Why should she have relinquished this elegance upon her husband's death? She had the best of everything, which was only as it should be.

"The man accepts payment for services rendered, 'for pity's sake,'" she snorted, "which makes him no better than a servant. No better? He's worse! No sense of the proprieties of position, or the duties he owes his title and class. As for the chit, she is *impossible*. No, it won't do—not for *my* grandson. Can you imagine her in these?"

Lavinia DeLacey's fingers delicately stroked the famous ruby parure of the Countesses of Rochedale which she had refused to relinquish when her son finally married, rubies, she claimed, not being suitable to a blond ingénue of seventeen. She had buried three daughters-in-law, the rubies firmly clasped about her own neck, dangling from her ears, surrounding her wrists, sparkling in her hair. She had buried Mowbray, her feckless indolent son, in the same manner two years before. The rubies were *hers*, for until the day of her death *she* would be the only Countess of Rochedale who mattered.

"Do not make yourself ridiculous, Daphne," she concluded tartly. "There is nothing to recommend the girl for the most menial position in Richard's kitchens, let alone as his wife."

"Her father saved his life!"

"Problematic. Richard might very well have survived unassisted. He is young, strong, and *very* determined."

"A fact you might be well advised to consider in your opposition to the course of action he has decided upon."

"Pooh! If I can't out maneuver a callow boy—"

"Callow he is not, nor is he a boy. At the very least, you must admit Baron Hawls saved Richard's leg."

"And botched the job. I should be grateful for that?"

"Lavinia!"

"He shall be paid like any other servant, but he'd best not expect too much."

"So *that's* what you intend," Lady Daphne said, eyes narrowing. Here, at last, they were breaking into new territory. "You'll attempt to buy them off."

"If necessary. I've a few other notions on how to handle this lamentable situation, however. Money need not necessarily change hands. Richard will thank me on bended knee one day for rescuing him from such an unsuitable entanglement. You're perfectly aware I've a delightful girl in mind for him—Lady Serena Duchesne, the Duke of Hampton's eldest. Style, elegance, dot, pedigree: all are flawless."

"A moldy plowhorse of a female several years his senior? Butter-toothed and platter-faced? Not an ounce of femininity to her, and she sleeps with her dogs, all hundred-odd of 'em. You're the one who's mad, not Richard. I've already told you, *that* won't wash."

"He's *my* grandson, not yours."

"For which he will curse heaven should you persist in such a course. If you're wise, you'll accept the situation gracefully, and hand over the rubies into the bargain. You've held onto 'em, girl and woman, long enough."

"I cannot believe he would marry with me on my deathbed," Lady Lavinia countered with a slight smile.

"I've no intentions of being unsubtle. It's only that first one thing shall go wrong, then another, delay piling on delay, until Richard sees the folly of his ways. As for the rubies, I shall be buried in 'em. Not a one of these modern chits has the presence to carry 'em off, certainly not a milkmaid from Devon.''

"And the Rochedale betrothal ring?"

"I've lost it until he comes to his senses."

"Where? In your reticule? Your jewel casket? Beneath your pillow?"

"Grant me *some* intelligence. No, it's better provided for than that. Polluted by gracing such a base hand it shall never be. I've no intention of being forced to have the thing melted down."

"It won't work, you know—attempting to buy them off. Neither will any of the rest of it. One look at that innocent's eyes should have told you that."

"You think not? The only question is price, if I'm forced to it."

"As for Richard, he won't be so easily manipulated."

"Perhaps not, but the chit will. No match for me, that one. None of 'em are. None of 'em ever have been. None of 'em ever will be. *I* shall decide when and where Richard casts his handkerchief, and no one else."

Seven

"Don't be ridiculous!" Lady Daphne's smile took any sting from her words. "That is precisely *not* the way to go about things unless you wish to court disaster."

She, Richard DeLacey, and the senior Wainwrights—the viscountess had been carried downstairs for the occasion—were closeted in the viscount's library, the ladies looking slightly out of place in the severely masculine, if decidedly comfortable room. A heavy silver tray holding pots of coffee, tea, and chocolate in addition to plates of buttery triangular wigs paid homage to the early hour.

The aroma of cigarillos clung to the dark green draperies, floated up from the priceless oriental carpets scattered across the scuffed oaken floor. Stacks of books and papers littered every available surface. The fine overlay of dust bespoke a man who forbade the cleaning of his *sanctum* on penalty of stormy scenes. Last winter's ashes still clogged the grate, sloping high against the chimney's blackened brick walls. Unless Lady Daphne missed her guess, not only removal of ashes was needed, but the services of a sweep as well, and the sooner the better as fall was coming on.

And not a flower in the place! She'd have to caution

Lady Wainwright about that eventually. Too much of a good thing was too much of a good thing, even male sanctuary. A woman's touch was required. It was incumbent on the lady of the house to provide it, even in this male bastion and over severe male protest.

"It's a good thing I insisted upon being present," she continued amiably, "for were I not here I do believe, between you, you'd've made a *dreadful* mull of matters. Do you *truly* wish to ruin Miss Driscoll?" she demanded, rounding on the earl with a speed that caused him to draw back uneasily in his chair. "*Totally* ruin her, Richard? *Forever*? Because I cannot imagine a better way to go about it, if that is your goal."

"I only want to wed her," DeLacey protested, "and that as soon as possible. Of course I've no desire to ruin her. I *love* the girl."

"Which is *another* matter you have yet to explain," Lady Daphne retorted. "I believe in many things, but 'love at first sight' is *not* one of 'em."

"Believe it or not as you wish, but it's true. I *will not* release her, and I *will not* brook interference from you or Grandmama or anyone else, including your blasted nephew."

"*There* we're in complete agreement," Lady Daphne chuckled unexpectedly as Lord and Lady Wainwrights' eyes flew from one to the other, expressions of deep unease clouding their features. "Harry's little enough use to himself at the moment. Squirrels in his cockloft, and it'll get worse. Oh, this is going to be a *delightful* Little Season. As for your grandmama, she loves you dearly, Richard, even if her love has rather more of controlling than giving to it."

"I'm not playing games, nor will I permit them," the earl scowled. "If it becomes necessary, I'll whisk Miss Driscoll to Gretna Green."

"Now *there's* a brilliant concept," Lady Daphne

exclaimed, throwing Lord Wainwright a cautionary glance that caused him to subside in his chair behind the desk, lips firmly clamped, scowl deepening. "Calamity upon calamity! And I always thought you'd inherited your grandfather's fine mind, Richard—and a fine mind he *did* have, for all his many deplorable characteristics. I can see I was deluded. It must have been the uniform and exaggerated reports of your level-headed behavior on the Continent. Wake up, my boy! What do you wish to accomplish? What is your target, your objective? What heights do you wish to storm?"

"I want to marry Elizabeth," he said simply. "I want her at my side for the rest of my life."

"That's generally what marriage entails," Lady Daphne retorted, "however much the miserable actuality may vary from the anticipated bliss. Deliver me, dear Lord, from the idiotishness of all men with but single ideas in what passes for their brainboxes! You say you love her? Then *prove* it."

She sighed in her turn, glancing at the others. "He has blinders on," she said rather flatly for one given to the swoops and swirls of animated diction. "I think the rest of you do, as well. After last night, what's called for is *not* an instant ceremony followed by a precipitous retreat to the country. How tongues would wag! What better way to give the appearance of discreditable doings?

"It matters not in the least if you both despise London, or that Miss Driscoll is amenable to your plans," she continued, rounding on the earl once more. "The country? If that's what you both prefer, excellent, after a bit. Marriage by special license? I can even understand that, but *not* in three days' time. And *not* with only yourself and the girl, and a witness or two dragged off the streets, in attendance."

"I really didn't like that part of the project myself,"

Lady Wainwright interjected in support of her new acquaintance as Lord Wainwright heaved a heavy sigh of relief. "We may not move in the highest circles, but such hasty doings are *not* our style."

"Precisely," Lady Daphne beamed at her. "I was positive *you'd* understand, even if none of the rest of these loonies did. As for Scotland, it's not to be considered."

"I'll consider anything I bloody well please, madam," the earl growled, courtesy forgotten.

The entire situation was getting out of hand. Lord— it had been out of hand since the moment some interfering idiot opened his study door the night before. No, it had been out of hand since the moment he had registered that gentle voice spouting cant, stared up in disbelief, and recognized his angel of La Haye Sainte. He must've been foxed to go about things in such a havey-cavey fashion, or else delirious with fever, but there was little he could do to rectify the matter now.

"I despise the prattleboxes as much as you do, Richard," Lady Daphne returned with every semblance of calm reasonableness, "but there are times when it pays to listen to what others are saying, and circumvent careless cruelty to the best of one's ability. Do you *truly* wish Miss Driscoll to be cut at every turn? Refused admission *everywhere*? When old comrades and schoolfellows stare right through you, you'll understand well enough, but it'll be too late."

"Don't be ridiculous," DeLacey sputtered. "No one would—"

"Try walking into White's tonight, if you don't believe me. The petticoats will have been busy. Half your friends won't dare speak to you, and the other half won't *want* to. Maitland, over in his corner, might because he'd be too fuddled by drink to know what he's doing, but he's the only one."

"Then they'd not be my friends, confound it!"

"And, when the day comes, do you truly desire to see your children ostracized as well, not for their faults, but for yours?" she continued, ignoring his outburst. "I know it says in the Bible that the sins of the fathers shall be visited upon their sons, which means daughters and wives as well, unto I don't know *how* many generations, though it's definitely excessive. But *nowhere* does it say fathers or husbands are *required* to commit sins for the precise purpose of their hapless wives and children inheriting them. *And,* what you propose is a sin, at least among the ton."

Then, eyes twinkling she glanced from Lady Wainwright to Richard DeLacey, then pointedly at the tray before her. "If you would not think me presumptuous," she said, "may I pour out for you, Lady Wainwright? I believe part of Lord DeLacey's problem may be insufficient breaking of his fast."

Lady Wainwright beamed her approval. DeLacey watched in silent impatience as the two ladies conferred over the social amenities, reluctantly accepted coffee unadulterated by cream or sugar, and at Lady Daphne's insistence, three wigs, the scowl on his face giving ample evidence of his opinion of the entire time-consuming ritual.

For a few moments there was only the sound of cups rattling as eyes flew uneasily about the room, met and dropped. Then, true to form, Lady Daphne calculated the time and pounced, setting her tea aside with a loud sigh.

"Perfectly delicious wigs," she complimented Lady Wainwright. "You must give me the receipt," then whirled on DeLacey. "No, like it or not, Richard— which you clearly *do not* at this moment, as it interferes with your short-sighted inclination for speed at all costs—you are a member of the ton. There is no other society of which you have ever formed a part, or ever could. And before you tout your military years, let me inform you they do *not* count.

"It's all well and good to consider the world well lost for love, but that lost world has a habit of returning to haunt one if one's not careful, and that can blunt the most enthusiastic love. Difficult enough to build a successful marriage without *that* set of chains to drag about."

"What do you believe advisable at this juncture, Lady Cheltenham?" the viscount broke in easily from behind his desk. "I can't help but agree with you that Lord DeLacey's projected schedule of events appears unnecessarily precipitous. Perhaps a compromise can be reached."

"No compromises," Richard DeLacey snapped. "There cannot be the slightest objection to my suit. My character is known to be forthright and honest, and Lord knows I can support Elizabeth in a style any woman would envy." Then, uneasy at the silence that met his words, he turned to the viscount. "There isn't any objection to me, is there, my lord? My leg—"

"None in the least," Wainwright returned soothingly. "At least, *I've* none as of the moment. You have none, do you, my dear?" he inquired, turning to his wife. She shook her head. "I didn't think so, and I'm positive my sister and her husband will be delighted to welcome you to the family. There are Elizabeth's brothers, but if this is what she wants, they will want it also, though you may face rather pointed inquiries from them on matters you might consider none of their business, given their ages. Humor them, should that happen, or you'll find yourself in the suds. That leaves my daughter on our side of the affair, and while she is totally opposed to the match, I think we can dispense with her opinion as immaterial."

"So, there are no objections."

"I didn't say that. There does remain the dowager countess on your side. Has she stated an opinion on the matter?"

"Her opinions are of no more consequence than your daughter's."

"Of slightly more importance than that, Richard," Lady Daphne threw in. "She could make Miss Driscoll's life a misery if it pleased her. No, marriage without Lavinia's nod isn't to be considered. You and your Miss Driscoll would come to detest each other in a matter of weeks, for she would do everything she could to foster ill-will and misunderstandings between you, and she is decidedly clever at such exercises when it suits her. Don't worry about Lavinia, however. I shall see to *that* matter."

"Which is to say she has strong opinions and they are negative," Wainwright concluded with a troubled look.

"Negative in the extreme," Lady Daphne chuckled. "More tea, Lady Wainwright, Lord Wainwright?"

She rose gracefully, skirts swirling around her elegant ankles as she seized upon the correct pot, swiftly refilled their cups, winking surreptitiously at the viscount and his wife, then giving them the slightest shake of her head.

"And, Richard, I insist on your having more coffee. You haven't eaten your wigs! How d'you intend to keep up your strength?" she reproved, piling three more on his already overburdened plate. "As to Lavinia DeLacey," she said, replacing the coffee pot with a clatter of irritation, "she's an unpardonably foolish old woman on occasion, and this is one of 'em. She insists the Earl of Rochedale make a splendid match, and doesn't give a fig what happens to Richard in the process. Ever hear of Serena Duchesne, the Duke of Hampton's eldest? Then you understand."

She dimpled at the Wainwrights, regained her seat,

glanced at DeLacey's forbidding scowl, gave the tiniest of shrugs.

"Now, as to the wedding," she said. "Yes, *wedding*, and not the hole-in-the-wall travesty you intend, Richard. A *real* wedding. Perhaps you'd be so good as to take notes, Lady Wainwright? Now that we're making progress, we need to organize ourselves."

She waited patiently, a secret smile lighting her eyes as the viscount fussily extracted paper and one of the modern wood-encased lead pencils from a tray on the desk, sharpened it, swept away the shavings, then provided his wife with a lap desk and the required writing materials. The Wainwrights were rather like a brace of plump graying partridge, she decided, fluttering, inoffensive, mildly interesting, totally devoted. Soft, like down pillows. A pleasant pair, with nothing to their detriment other than an impossible daughter who was welcome almost nowhere.

"Saint George's on Hanover Square," Lady Daphne continued briskly as Lady Wainwright's hand flew across the page, "bride clothes, wedding breakfast, champagne flowing, lobster patties in abundance, white soup by the gallon, ices from Gunter's, and unidentifiable wedding gifts displayed on every available surface. I imagine you'll want Harry to stand up for you?" she asked, whirling on DeLacey.

He admitted he'd been planning on requesting the favor of his old friend as Lady Wainwright glanced up interestedly from her labors.

"Good, though he'll make it seem like a wake if he can. I'll press Patsy Worth into Miss Driscoll's service as *her* attendant, then," Lady Daphne continued, eyes flying to the viscountess, whose pencil had resumed its frantic scurrying. "The girls must become acquainted immediately, for everything must appear as commonplace as possible since *you,*" whirling once more on

DeLacey, "foolishly began in such an outré manner. *And*, Miss Driscoll's family present in force, with her father to give her away.

"Three weeks' time," she insisted as she retrieved her own cup and served herself, then selected one of the two remaining wigs. "You can wait that long, can't you? You've been waiting a year and a half, after all. What's another three weeks compared to that, or to the rest of your lives? Six would be *much* better for reasons we all comprehend, but I shall accept three. Miss Driscoll won't disappear on you again if you agree to this minor delay, my boy."

"No." DeLacey's voice was cold, his eyes dangerously level. "Three days, and I don't care where the church is or if we eat bread and cheese afterwards. As for bride clothes, I'll buy her anything she needs later. Lord knows, I don't want the idiot responsible for that rag she was wearing last night to have the dressing of her."

"You're being unreasonable, my lord," Lady Wainwright broke in gently, pencil poised as she ignored the slur on her taste. "A girl weds but once in her life. It's a very special day. She'll want her parents present if at all possible, with Samuel to give her away and Suzanne to turn watering pot for one of the few times in her life so long as she hasn't been confined yet. And all of her brothers, or as many as may come. They're a very close family. Wed Elizabeth in their absence? You couldn't be so cruel or selfish."

"Elizabeth wants anything I want," DeLacey returned stubbornly. "Her uncle can give her away. Three days. That should be long enough for her to acquire a decent gown and bonnet. If it isn't, we'll dispense with the decent gown and bonnet."

"If your presence weren't essential to carry this off," Lady Daphne proclaimed tartly, "I'd have you locked up until it was time for you to meet Miss Driscoll at the

altar. I could do it, too, you know. I've a *very* good friend
at the Horse Guards—a Major Jason Ventriss, though
I do believe he's a colonel now—who owes me a favor
or two. Have you heard of him, Richard?''

The beleaguered earl gave a reluctant shrug which
admitted more than a passing acquaintance with the
extraordinary colonel's existence and reputation.

''I suspected you might, so you know I'm not whistling
air. Colonel Ventriss would clap you behind bars in an
instant at my request on any charge I wished to invent,
or no charge at all. If I *must*, I will make the request. Is
that clear?''

''You've no conscience whatsoever, have you,'' DeLacey responded bitterly.

''More than you'll ever appreciate,'' Lady Daphne
smiled. Then her face sobered. ''I sympathize with you
in every particular, Richard. Miss Driscoll, what little
I've seen of her, is *utterly* delightful. I can't imagine
anyone more suited to you, and I believe you're truly
suited to her. Otherwise, I'd be joining forces with your
grandmother instead of with you. And I *am* joining
forces with you, no matter what you may think. But,
while impetuosity may be delightfully romantic, it's not
a sound foundation for a lifetime of happiness. *This* is
the manner in which we shall proceed, and you *will*
cooperate in every particular, Richard. If you won't protect your future wife and children, I shall. Given your
head, you'd make mice-feet of everything.''

DeLacey squirmed in his chair, not quite meeting
Lady Daphne's militantly flashing eyes. Then, resigned,
he shrugged. She nodded her satisfaction. He had as
good as given his word, which was fortunate. She wasn't
sure just how far Ventriss's friendship might truly have
stretched, nor how great he would consider the debt
he owed her.

''First, you'll squire Miss Driscoll everywhere,'' she

instructed the recalcitrant earl with an airy wave of her hand. "Morning calls—oh, yes, I know you despise 'em. So do I. So do most people of sense. A waste of time if ever there were one. That's of no importance. You'll do it.

"Next: Hyde Park. Every afternoon at five unless it's pouring buckets. I've seen your curricle. It'll do nicely. Tiger up behind, mind you, playing gooseberry.

"Evenings? There, with your permission," she said, turning to the viscountess with a smile, "I shall offer my services as you are currently prevented from undertaking the nonsense. My niece and I shall chaperon the young couple. Excellent way for Patsy and Miss Driscoll to become acquainted. Having the Duchess of Rawdon sponsor your niece should confound the gabble-mongers and cut Lavinia off, no matter *what* she plans.

"Betrothal party at Rochedale House, naturally— same purpose," she continued, overriding Lady Wainwright's profusion of babbled gratitude. "It *is* Richard's home, after all, and Lavinia will be unable to refuse him the use of it. Three days? No, too soon. Even *I* cannot manage that. One week, then."

"This is all totally unnecessary," the earl grumbled. "What use is it, being Rochedale, if I can't proceed as I wish?"

"It's precisely *because* you're Rochedale that you can't, Richard," Lady Daphne explained with what patience she could muster, then, at DeLacey's forbidding expression straightened her shoulders as she leaned forward. "Did you storm Ciudad Rodrigo without first laying siege to it? Or Badajoz? Indeed, as I remember it, Badajoz resisted more than one siege, and a bloody business it was in the end. We must lay siege to the ton for your Miss Driscoll's sake just as you did to Ciudad Rodrigo, or her rout will be far more disastrous than any you would have suffered had Wellington not proceeded with reasonable caution in the Peninsula, Richard.''

DeLacey slowly raised rebellious eyes to meet her flashing ones, chin thrust out. Lady Daphne's eyes remained as uncompromising as her posture. At last the starch melted as a grudging smile toyed with the corners of his mouth.

"How Old Duro could've used you," he chuckled suddenly. "All right—a wedding. A real one. Just don't ask me to pretend to enjoy it!"

Lady Daphne nodded, tossed a triumphant smile at the relieved Wainwrights.

"Now, bride clothes," she said as Lady Wainwright's pencil continued to fly. "And, current wardrobe, of course. I shall take Miss Driscoll to my home and put Holfers and the inestimable Madame de Métrise to work the moment this conference is over and our battle plan"—she threw a meaningful glance at DeLacey—"understood *and accepted* by all.

"I wouldn't select a cap, let alone a gown, without first consulting Holfers. My dresser, you understand," she specified at Lady Wainwright's puzzled look. "Pours over *La Belle Assemblée* as if it were the Bible. And, I'll send a note to Patsy Worth to join us. Time the girls got to know each other. The goal is to bring Miss Driscoll into instant fashion, transform her into an Original. If we set the malicious to gabbling about *that*, they'll have no time for anything else. That's called 'distraction of the enemy,'" she said, glancing at DeLacey. "I believe you employed similar methods when you desired to confound the Frogs? And, if I'm not mistaken, we were treated to a touch of it yesterday evening as well. Head to toe, inside and out, Miss Driscoll will become the latest stare."

"I like her as she is," DeLacey protested. "Don't

make her into a simpering mannequin, by heaven, or
I'll—"

"Credit me with a *little* sense. But, you won't see her
until it's time for you to take her driving, Richard, and
when you do you won't recognize her. I'll have Monsieur
Jacques do her hair, I think. It's going to be a *very*
busy day. Don't worry about the bills. I'll have 'em sent
'round, and you can hold 'em for Richard," she said,
turning to the viscount. "The boy wants speed, and
speed costs. No reason for Lord Driscoll to foot the bill,
aside from which, I doubt if Richard would permit it."

"Damn right, I wouldn't!" the latter fumed.

"Didn't think so," Lady Daphne agreed as she turned
back to the earl, ticking items off on her fingers. "Jewels.
The Rochedale betrothal ring: Have it sized to fit Miss
Driscoll if you can pry it loose from Lavinia. If she won't
hand it over, have a copy made. If you don't remember
precisely what it looks like, I'll make you a sketch. *Hideous* thing, but that can't be helped. We need all the
panoply of tradition we can muster.

"Select some jewels suitable to a young girl of excellent family and comfortable—but *not* inordinate—
means, Richard. Nothing suitable to a married woman,
mind, and everything in the latest mode. I'll give you
a list. How old is Miss Driscoll? Eighteen? Nineteen?
Then no diamonds, mind you. Not until the betrothal
party, and *then* it should be the Rochedale rubies. We
don't need those for a week, and then she should only
wear 'em that one night until after the wedding. Have
'em cleaned, and the settings checked. I want the rest
here by the time we're done with my modiste."

"Modiste, curricle, petticoats, Saint George's, lobster
patties, rubies," Lady Wainwright murmured rather
breathlessly. "There—I think I have it all." Her eyes
flew uncertainly to her husband, who gave her a swift
amused nod.

"If you've forgotten something," he whispered, "we'll confer later."

"Now, what else?" Lady Daphne continued as if there had been no interruption. "Oh, yes, notices. Send 'em to all the appropriate journals, Richard. Get the family details from Lord Wainwright. Make it a betrothal revealed rather than announced, with the wedding to follow in three weeks' time at St. George's. A hint dropped here and there about your wanting to be fully recovered from your wounds prior to undertaking the wedded state should silence the tattlers. Start with White's. Then pass by Tattersall's, ostensibly to consider a mount for your betrothed. That should do it, but I'll put Rawdon and Giles on the trail as well. No reason for them to lollygag when the rest of us will be working ourselves to the bone."

DeLacey muttered something beneath his breath. Lady Daphne watched him for a moment. Reluctantly his eyes rose to meet hers once more.

"You really deem all this necessary?" he protested.

"Very necessary. I'll see to the ladies myself, starting with Sally Jersey. Something very close to the truth, I think: that you encountered Miss Driscoll when wounded and fell in love on the instant. Sally will gobble it up and spread it about with all the speed of which she is capable. She's not known as 'Silence' for nothing. Most useful she can be on occasion, if only she knew it. *Totally* dependable. And," throwing an apologetic glance at Lord and Lady Wainwright, "she rather despises your daughter, I'm afraid, and will be delighted to make the girl seem foolish after her histrionics of yesterday evening. That was *quite* a performance.

"Now, is there anything more? Of course! *Invitations.* I'll have Patsy and Louisa see to those," she smiled as Lady Wainwright continued to scribble. "They can begin arrangements for the wedding breakfast, as well.

I suggest it be held in *your* home, Richard—more space, and we need Lavinia visibly present if not actually involved. Make lists, Lady Wainwright,'' she said as that lady raised her head with a weary sigh, ''lists of everything you can think of. We'll need every scrap of assistance you can render.

"*There*. That should be all for the moment. Oh—a letter to Miss Driscoll's parents explaining the situation, and requesting their presence at the wedding. You *will* see to that on the instant, will you not, Lord Wainwright?''

"Naturally,'' the viscount returned with a twinkle.

"You're enjoying yourself inordinately, aren't you, Lady Daphne?'' DeLacey commented wryly.

"Never more in my life,'' she returned, ''unless it was that marvelous Christmas I spent in Kent watching Ned Connardsleigh make a cake of himself. That was amusing, and *quite* rewarding. I believe I'll send off a note to Ned and his wife. Their Lucinda would make a *most* attractive bridesmaid. She's just old enough, and I think both Miss Driscoll and Patsy would enjoy her company. *Two* attendants would be *far* better than one.

"I'll save your neck in spite of you, young man. Now, shall we disperse? We've all a great deal to accomplish before five o'clock.''

"I'm sorry,'' the earl murmured apologetically in Elizabeth's ear some minutes later as Lady Daphne was about to whisk her out the door. ''This is not my choice, but I do see the sense of it. My own preferences *were* rather ramshackle. The only thing that surprises me is she hasn't told us where we are to go once the ceremony is over.''

"I'd wager that's only because she hasn't thought that far yet,'' Elizabeth giggled. ''Lady Cheltenham'll be sure to have suggestions once it occurs to her—she has suggestions for everything else—but she *is* rather a dear in spite of her overpowering ways." Then, more seriously, "I dread the unnecessary expense all this will entail."

"The expense is nothing. Besides," he said with a disparaging glance at the shapeless gray gown and old cloak she sported, "you do stand in need of a few decent things. *Those* wouldn't do, not even in the country. There's a deal of difference between being a carefree girl in Devon and a married lady in Kent, unfortunately. No, it's the boredom I dread. You've no conception what a London betrothal and wedding are like."

"*Well!* Just look at the turtledoves!"

Elizabeth spun, coloring. DeLacey turned more slowly, favoring his throbbing leg, free hand coming to rest protectively on Elizabeth's shoulder, cane tapping against the entry floor.

Sybilla stood poised at the head of the stairs, brilliant peacock gown dripping golden ribbons, shawl draped perfectly at her elbows, gazing down at them with a sardonic glint in her eye. Elizabeth, garbed in a worn gray round gown and threadbare brown cloak, appeared to worse effect than usual. Perfect! Retrieving her own cast-offs had been an excellent notion.

"How touching," Sybilla cooed. "His lordship's prop and support. How do you fare today, Lord DeLacey? Quite recovered from last evening's contretemps? A costly time *that* was for you, but I'm sure the chit has seen reason."

"Costly?" he inquired carefully. "I don't grasp your meaning, young woman."

"Yes, you do," Elizabeth returned, glaring at her cousin. "She means you're saddled with *me*."

"You *must* have been completely foxed, my lord, to permit yourself to be so easily entrapped. Nothing else explains it," Sybilla commiserated as she sauntered down the steps, hips swaying, reddened lips pouting. "But, Elizabeth's a good little thing in her countrified way, and knows her place. I'm certain she'll release you from vows you had no intention of making if she hasn't done so already, and leave you free to pursue other more suitable interests."

"The question is not whether Miss Driscoll would release me, which she has repeatedly attempted to do, but whether I would release her," Richard DeLacey countered, sweeping Sybilla with a gaze as insulting as he could render it. "The answer is no, I will not."

"Oh, come now, my lord! I was there. You have no need to put a better face on this farce than it deserves for *my* benefit," Sybilla smiled archly. "Pay her off. That's what you're here for, isn't it? I happen to know our little bumpkin is most concerned regarding her eldest brother's new medical practice. An hundred pounds should settle the matter, if indeed *that* much is required."

DeLacey pulled the trembling Elizabeth firmly against his side, squeezing her shoulder in caution. "You fail to comprehend the matter, young woman," he returned flatly, "whoever you may be. I count myself infinitely fortunate that I've been able to browbeat Miss Driscoll into accepting my suit."

"That's Sybilla," Elizabeth hissed. "Be careful. She'll repeat anything you say, and twist it until it becomes something else altogether."

"Of course," he returned clearly, "who else could it be? Miss Wainwright fits your description exactly," eyeing the malevolent young woman with distaste.

"Well, no one else's going to consider you fortunate," Sybilla spat, any pretense at flirtation or good humor vanished. "The Dowager Countess of Rochedale has all my sympathy! How she'll hold her head up in public I've no idea, for this drab is so far beneath you as to be laughable. No one's going to believe she's anything but a little golddigger. Cream-pot love, it's called," Sybilla proclaimed, tossing her curls. "I would've thought you'd hold yourself in higher regard, my lord. It would appear what they said of Wellington's best was erroneous—that, or you were not among them. Of course, your leg proves that, doesn't it? Had you the least ability or wit, you'd've avoided injury."

Lady Daphne, whose ears were rather more acute than Sybilla bargained for, swept over, eyes flashing. "That's *not* the way to go about it," she informed the posturing girl with contempt, "not that you'd succeed even if you did know how to go on. Now," she demanded, turning to DeLacey, "d'you see what I meant?"

"Clearly. I bow to your superior knowledge of the breed *Tonisca viciosa*. We do indeed have something of a siege on our hands." Then, disgust and anger overcoming good manners, he gestured contemptuously at Sybilla. "D'you mean to tell me so many brave lads fought and died for that?"

"Hardly," Lady Daphne twinkled, intent on defusing what boded to become, from the sour expression on Sybilla Wainwright's face, a heated exchange of incivilities. "You fought for this," indicating Elizabeth. "Am I right?"

"As always," he sighed, then turned to Elizabeth, chucking her under the chin. "I'll see you at five. Don't keep me waiting, sweet. The rain may've ceased, but horses shouldn't be left standing in the chill."

"Yes, sir," she grinned determinedly, snapping to what she assumed was attention and attempting a salute, refusing to permit Sybilla to destroy the morning. "At your orders, Colonel DeLacey. Will there be anything further, sir, or am I dismissed?"

"Minx!" he chuckled. "Behave yourself."

"A futile request, my lord," Sybilla's voice stabbed sibilantly between them. "She's a hoyden incapable of the least decorum, as you shall learn to your sorrow."

"Good," DeLacey said clearly. "She's perfect just as she is." He stooped, placing a gentle kiss on Elizabeth's cheek. "Don't let the vixen upset you," he murmured for her ears alone. "She's jealous, that's all. How you've endured her—"

"Enough of that for now, Richard," Lady Daphne laughed, placing a firm hand beneath Elizabeth's elbow. "We've siege engines to bring up, baggage trains to command, and sappers to set to their tasks."

"Lay on, Lady McDaphne," he paraphrased, smiling slightly in response, a possessive knuckle gently stroking Elizabeth's furiously blushing cheek, "and damn'd be he—or she—who first cries 'Hold, enough!' Doesn't rhyme, but—"

"But, it suits well enough," she chuckled. "Come, child—we've miles to go before this afternoon."

"Lord DeLacey," came her uncle's voice as Elizabeth followed Lady Daphne from the house, "I'd like to see you privately for a moment, if you don't mind. There are a few matters I'd like to clear up before attempting a letter to my sister and her husband, and then there's the business of the notices. We'd best make that a cooperative effort."

"It's fairly simple and straightforward," Richard DeLacey protested moments later, glancing at the library's dark paneling and book-lined walls as he leaned heavily on his cane. The place reminded him of his own retreat, but that didn't help. The time he'd spent here so far had left him feeling little more than a grubby schoolboy caught pilfering tarts intended for Sunday's dinner, rather than the wealthy titled suitor he knew himself to be. "She doesn't remember me," he continued, "and I doubt her father will, but I didn't encounter your niece for the first time last night."

"I suspected as much." Wainwright gesturing for sherry to be poured and then dismissed the curious hovering footman. Once the door had silently closed, he seated himself in a worn leather armchair beside of the cold fireplace and leaned back comfortably, crossing his legs. His appearance of ease would be unsettling to the former officer, he knew, especially if he neglected to show the man the slightest courtesy now the ladies were gone, and he wanted this young noble lord as ill at ease as possible until he was satisfied Elizabeth was not being made a May Game of. Too much did not ring true. "Lady Cheltenham's comments were not as obscure as you might've wished, though I doubt my wife understood. Waterloo?"

"La Haye Sainte, actually," DeLacey specified, still standing, shoulders proudly squared, "if you want to be technical about it."

"Same thing. My brother-in-law saved your life?"

"Without any doubt."

"And your leg as well, I suppose?"

"I've been told he performed miracles."

"And now you intend to wed Elizabeth in recompense." The viscount put as much insult into the words as he could as he studied the man in front of him. It wasn't that he disliked what he saw, precisely. It was just that he distrusted it. The Earl of Rochedale moved in circles for which the Samuel and Suzanne Driscolls of the world existed only as faceless conveniences. That the dowager countess viewed the proposed alliance with distaste didn't bode well for Elizabeth's future happiness or peace of mind either. "Rather arrogant, don't you think? We're long past the days of such rewards, if indeed they ever existed beyond some poet's overly imaginative scribblings.''

"Reward? Good God! If I wanted to reward the man, I'd give him a hospital, or a few thousand pounds, or something of that nature.''

Wainwright shrugged, still dissatisfied. ''Something's missing here,'' he said flatly, ignoring the twinge of guilt he felt at leaving the young man standing on a leg that could barely support him.

The earl's face was pale and drawn, his cane quivering under the pressure he exerted on it. But if DeLacey hadn't the humility to request the seat of which he was clearly in need, then he wasn't ''requesting'' the honor of marrying Elizabeth either. He was merely ordering things as he wished them, with no thought for the needs or desires of others. Marriage to a man of that stamp would be the shortest road to misery for his niece that he could imagine. It was a cruel test, but a necessary one.

''You tell me what that missing something is with no round-aboutation,'' Wainwright insisted sharply, ''or I'll recommend to my brother-in-law that he forbid the banns and whisk Elizabeth back to Saint Mary-Grafton instantly. In fact, I won't bother writing him. I'll take her there myself and explain the matter when we arrive. Do I make myself clear, Lord DeLacey? Better the girl suffer a little confusion and mortification now than profound humiliation later. I'm rather fond of her, you see.''

DeLacey shrugged and nodded. The cherubic viscount had a bite of acid to his tongue. All that morning's grudging concessions were only the beginning unless he agreed to whatever this uncle of the woman he was determined to marry proposed. It was galling, but there was nothing he could do but explain himself or else show himself the door and forget Elizabeth, and *that* he was completely unwilling to do.

"May I?" he requested, pointing to the matching chair across the fireplace from his unexpectedly forbidding host. "I'm afraid this blasted leg is about to give out on me, and I don't think I'd bear up very well under the humiliation of falling at your feet."

Wainwright nodded cold permission. Then—this playing the heavy-handed villain did not suit him at all—he quickly replaced the sherry on the table beside the obviously exhausted earl with a generous portion of brandy.

"Drink up," he recommended in a slightly warmer tone. "If you've need of laudanum, I'll ring for my wife's abigail. I know there's some about the place."

"No, this will suffice," DeLacey muttered through thinned lips, downing the brandy as if he were a shipwrecked sailor and it the first potable water he'd seen in a month. "Thank you."

"My pleasure," Wainwright returned, regaining his place by the cold grate. "Now, my niece is an exceptional young woman. Worth a hundred of that harpy I'm cursed with for a daughter. I won't see the girl hurt. She deserves more than a marriage of convenience and an absentee husband."

"You believe that's what I have in mind?" DeLacey bristled.

"The situation gives every indication of it, but Elizabeth's too green to recognize the signs. I'm not. An instant proposal to a country miss of fecund family history, but little dowry and no social graces? Rapid incarceration in the country—precisely what you intend, from what you said earlier. Nine months later, an heir. And then, *whoosh*, back to your gentlemanly 'amusements' in Town while she languishes abandoned on some distant estate? She wouldn't be the first to suffer such a fate. What sort of fool d'you take me for! Go ahead," he concluded, somehow managing not to smile at the mixture of disgust and fury on the earl's face, "prove me wrong. I'll listen."

DeLacey glared at his host.

The viscount's face remained imperturbably bland, but his eyes were unflinching. From the street came the clatter of hooves, the rattle of wheels against cobblestones. Lady Daphne and Elizabeth were safely embarked on their quest for an instant tonnish trousseau. From the stairs Sybilla's sharp accents came to them, demanding the carriage be brought round so she could pay a promised call on little Millicent Farquhar.

The earl shuddered, eyes flat, no longer seeing the room around him, the worn books, the clutter.

"Have you ever been in hell?" he asked softly. "Well, I have. Can you conceive what it's like when an angel appears in hell? I doubt it, but let me tell you, it's not something you forget. And, afterwards, you search for that angel. You search for weeks, and then for months. You ignore the contempt of those few who know what you're about, the titters, the laughter. The months stretch into a year and more, and they call you mad, and still you search. You can't live without that angel, you see, once you've encountered her. And, when you find her at last—"

"Elizabeth's no angel," her uncle countered, embarrassed by the raw emotion in the man's voice. "She's a flesh-and-blood girl, with all the faults and foibles flesh and blood are heir to."

"She's an imp with a rare grasp of schoolboy cant. She's impudent, impetuous, heedless of her own best interests and safety, giving beyond—

"She was *in* that hell. Her father—damn him forever for not better protecting her innocence, and bless him eternally, for I'd never've encountered her otherwise—

permitted it. I knocked her almost senseless because I believed her a corpse-robber. I'm sure she carried the mark of my fist for weeks. I was weak, but I wasn't dead yet and I was damned if anyone was going to rob me until I was. D'you know what she said when I struck her? She said I wasn't very gentlemanly! And then she was on her knees beside me in the mud, moistening my lips and chattering about her brothers, and—

"I knew everything she was in that instant," he insisted raggedly. "Courage? Fortitude? It was *dangerous* on that battlefield. When I think of the risks she ran without a thought for herself! She's *mine*, and to hell with any prosing fool who claims differently, yourself and my revered grandmother included."

Wainwright nodded, the hint of a smile lurking at the back of his eyes.

When Samuel and the children stopped by London on their return from Brussels, Elizabeth had sported traces of what must originally have been a blackened eye of magnificent proportions. She'd spoken of a man with a crushed leg, dwelling on his uncertain chances with heartbroken anxiety, concerned even her father's assistance might not have been enough. There'd been something special about that particular officer, she'd insisted wistfully. According to Suzanne, she still spoke of him on occasion, wondering where he was, how he did. Best the young earl not learn of *that* any time soon, or he'd render all their lives impossible with his demands for speed.

"You've told Elizabeth, of course?"

"No, not yet. I don't want her to think me mad, and I don't want her to think I'm marrying her as payment for services rendered. Once she accepts I love her above life itself, maybe then it'll be safe. The tale sounds preposterous—even I realize that. She likes and trusts me enough to marry me. That's all I care about for now."

He glanced up, eyes still haunted. "I'll make her love me, that you can believe.

"I didn't realize who she was at first, you know," he continued almost conversationally. "My blasted leg was acting up, and I think I had a touch of fever. She swept me out of the damned receiving area, and began to berate me for not keeping my head lowered. One thing led to another, and then I knew. She hasn't changed a bit, you understand. I thought I'd have to adjust to a reality at considerable variance with my memories. I don't. She's not less—she's *more*."

The viscount sighed, leaning back, steepling his fingers over his considerable girth, elbows propped on thickly padded chair arms.

This was more or less the coil he'd anticipated: an impetuous former officer accustomed to making instant life-or-death decisions and having things his own way, and further cursed with an ancient title and more wealth and position than he knew what to do with, and a total disregard for convention. The man might protest all he wished, but it was clear he considered himself a prime catch, shattered leg or not. It was as he'd said—the father to be rewarded through the daughter.

"You're not being fair to Elizabeth," Wainwright protested finally. "Besides, what if she or her father recognizes you? What then?"

"Recognize me? As the tattered half-corpse they succored in Brabant? In the dead of night, with only a pair of lanterns for light and not the slightest interest in my face once they'd determined I'd no serious head injuries? It's clear you've never seen wounded left on a battlefield. They don't resemble themselves very much."

"Still, something could give you away. A turn of phrase, a reference, anything."

"And pigs will fly over Saint Paul's next Michaelmas!

God alone knows how many of us they assisted. I was one of dozens at the very least. A begrimed soldier half crazed with pain, bloody, smoke-stained and smeared with mud and worse isn't particularly memorable, you know. Just odorous and often foul-mouthed.''

"Samuel frequently remembers chance patients, and certainly he would recognize his own work. What if he insists on examining your leg with the best of intentions?"

"In the unlikely event he does, I'll take him aside and tell him the truth immediately and swear him to secrecy."

"Why? Why not admit you've seen the girl before, and where and when, and court her openly and honestly?"

"I've waited over a blasted year and a half," the former colonel growled. "I'll be damned if I'll wait any longer."

"Petticoats?" the viscount inquired after an uneasy pause.

"Since La Haye Sainte? None. Before that? It's none of your business. I may be no monk, but I'm no lecher either."

"You claim to love Elizabeth."

"I can't live without her. Isn't that enough? I've had men tearing Devonshire apart searching for her ever since my return."

"Perhaps you weren't supposed to find her."

"And perhaps I was. She turned up in my own home at a social event to which neither she nor any of your family was invited, and which I had been vigorously delaying for months. She rescued me—again. Lord Wainwright, I'm no basket-scrambler, and I'm no gamester. I don't drink to excess, my leg is marginally functional, and there are those who will attest to my sterling character, beginning with His Grace of Wellington if you wish. I'm not offering your niece a slip on the shoulder. I'm demanding marriage and she's agreed. State your objections, and they'd best be valid ones, or hold your peace.''

"Suppose it were your and Elizabeth's daughter, and an impudent young pup arrived on your doorstep spouting the tale you've regaled me with? What would you do?"

"I'd—I'd—" DeLacey's shoulders sagged. "Oh, hell-fire and damnation! I'd show him the door, and plant my boot on his posterior to ensure alacrity in the process."

"Or perhaps have the impertinence to question him rather closely?"

"That, too. *Thoroughly.*"

"Then you perceive my problem. Good. See you do it when your turn comes. See to it you're reasonable, as well."

Sudden silence hung between them, no longer uncomfortable or accusatory. DeLacey's eyes glinted with appreciation of the older man as the viscount refilled their glasses.

"It's quite clear you worship Elizabeth," Wainwright commented. "I'll be a great deal happier about all this when you can tell me you simply love her. An unpopular and unfashionable sentiment among the ton, but I hold to it from personal experience of the married state. Pedestals have a tendency to wobble.

"I'll write Samuel today, and I'll hold my peace about La Haye Sainte. I recommend you inform Elizabeth immediately however. Were my niece to learn of it from another, the results could be disastrous. She has a crotchet concerning honesty—comes from having all those brothers. Arrow-straight, every last one of them. And then, there's the bit about marriage as a reward for saving your life. The slightest hint of such a thing, and she'd break with you on the instant.''

"No, not now. Not yet. I daren't. There's too much at stake."

"You're a fool," Wainwright shrugged, "but it *is* your business, I suppose. You'd best understand: Samuel will want to examine that leg as soon as he meets you. Unless you want a very irate father and seven combative bothers breathing fire on your doorstep, he *must* be informed of those little details you see fit to hide from your intended bride. Otherwise he'll believe you either utterly mad or in search of a complaisant wife—not a good recommendation as future husband to his only daughter."

"Yes, I can understand that. About settlements—"

"Oh, an *angel* is worthy of the best you can offer," the viscount chuckled, good humor restored, "and then a bit more. A woman who is cherished for herself alone will accept considerably less. By all means, arrange the settlements while you still view Elizabeth as one of the heavenly host. She'll profit considerably, and so will her family."

Eight

In her gilded bedchamber, surrounded by her favorite *objets d'art*, face paled by a dusting of the finest white flour, eyes and cheeks hollowed by strategically applied lampblack, Lady Lavinia DeLacey reposed against a tumbled mountain of lace-edged pillows. The draperies were drawn. A single green-shaded candle burned at her bedside, casting a sickly hue over her forceful features.

The stage was perfectly set, but where was the audience? To be forced to go to such lengths, and for so many hours, was outside of enough. Richard deserved to be horsewhipped!

She daren't leave her bed. She daren't read. She hardly dared breathe.

Richard had returned. According to Thatcher, he and his abominable personal servant were tearing the bookroom apart. The safe behind the fireplace had been gutted. Now the desk was being ransacked. Much good it would do them. In a matter of minutes the boy would come scratching at the door, demanding that which he could not find where it was customarily kept.

In the meantime, her own summons of him went

unanswered. It was degrading, positively *degrading*. The little milkmaid had much to answer for.

Lady Lavinia had sent her morning chocolate away untouched. Her breakfast tray had been meager upon special instructions to the kitchen—four dry toast fingers and a single cup of pallid lukewarm tea—and equally untouched. She had waved away the light nuncheon recommended by Josiah Burrows, her current Harley Street specialist, when he responded to her demand for his presence regarding a putative sudden weakness and malaise. Now, famished and bored, she glanced at the little gilt clock on the table beside her bed.

Dear Lord! It was barely half past the hour of one.

At least she had a loyal ally, so all was not loneliness and desperation. Thatcher, her dresser of thirty years' standing, was an avid participant in the plan to save Richard from himself.

Superior servants were always supremely conscious of what was due their employers' consequence, and guarded that consequence jealously. Upon it depended their status within their own ranks. Should Richard be permitted to persist in his folly, every one of the servants would leave her employ—well, *Richard's* employ, if one were to insist upon technicalities—because *none* of them would serve a country nobody. It had taken her years, positively *years*, to assemble a passable staff.

Even Thatcher would abandon her, and *that* wasn't to be thought of. They were both too old to change.

Yes, when all else failed, one could always depend upon self-interest to aid and abet one.

Thatcher would inform Richard how debilitated his beloved grandmother was, how fragile her hold upon life despite her apparent robust health. It was all courage, Thatcher would explain, the determination of a great lady not to inflict her troubles on others. Thatcher would mention the physician's visit, list the rejected sustenance. Thatcher would tearfully inform him that celebrations and entertainments of any sort weren't to be considered during the present crisis. As for a wedding . . .

And, Thatcher would be completely convincing because it was the truth as far as it went. An alliance between a country nobody and the Earl of Rochedale *was* impossible. Generations of earls and countesses would spin in their graves, or at least rotate decorously, should such a *mésalliance* be contracted.

After the rest of the house was abed, Thatcher would manage to sneak her a substantial supper tray, but that wouldn't be for hours. She was hungry *now*, and it was all Richard's fault—Richard's and that little *parvenue's*. And Daphne, traitor that she was, had been of absolutely no assistance whatsoever. In fact, quite the contrary, if her information was correct.

Lady Lavinia shuddered, turning her mind from food—rich frothy chocolate, muffins dripping butter, coddled eggs steaming in a Wedgewood cup, paper-thin slices of gammon gilded by a quick stir in sizzling butter, plump stewed apricots, tart damson preserves—with the force of character of a great general before a major battle. Something could be learned from the little Corsican, if one were only willing. She doubted most sincerely if Wellington had spent the night before Waterloo stuffing himself with overly rich, tainted food. Bread and cheese, more like, and water.

Oh, *dear*—even they would be welcome at this moment.

What she needed was something else to occupy her mind while she waited for Richard.

Waited for Richard. Now *there* was a phrase to ponder. Being forced to dance attendance on a stripling in his thirties went beyond the permissible. Unfortunately, the fury that customarily roiled at the thought of her quiet, stubborn grandson refused to erupt quite so easily as usual.

And, Richard *was* impossible: insisting on purchasing himself a pair of colors, then insisting he would go to the Peninsula, heir to title and estates notwithstanding. Reason, tears, the arrival of a delicious little opera dancer in his rooms at the Albany had availed nothing. He'd handed his sobbing grandmother a handkerchief, sent the expensive Paphian on her way and set sail for Lisbon just as planned, the ungrateful, selfish boy.

Of course, his father was alive then, and in the best of health. That had been his excuse—that, and the fact that if men of conscience didn't bestir themselves there might be no titles, no estates, no England left.

Mowbray. Now *there* had been a dutiful, attentive son. So unlike his father. So unlike Richard. So malleable. So very, very spineless.

She gave a contemptuous smile at the memory of her tall, rather portly son. Then her smile faded. Not so very malleable after all. Yes, Mowbray married where and when he was told. Repeatedly. He never protested her retention of Wharton's rooms, knowing he was far from his father's equal and didn't deserve them. He never insisted she repair to the Dower House at Lacebrough, nor that she abdicate her position as first lady of the family. He never demanded the rubies or the great emerald ring for his various brides. But, there had been the study, and the matter of the servants.

She had weeded out the last lax, insufferably independent-minded egalitarians employed by Wharton in his "The American colonists have the correct idea" madness immediately after Mowbray's death. Richard was still off playing with Wellington then. To the boy's protests over the absence of certain familiar faces when he finally returned, she had responded with an unequivocal: "They were past it, doddering. I've done them a kindness. They're provided for." Meagerly, perhaps— Why be generous to those who had never given one proper service?—but provided for nevertheless.

The London staff was now the best to be had in all of England with one unfortunate exception: Richard's former batman and current valet, Banks. The rest bowed to the current earl, but understood hers was the hand upon the helm and hers the instructions which mattered. But Banks? He took orders from no one but Richard.

She'd *tried* to get rid of Banks.

A scullery maid no better than she should be had been convinced to claim the disrespectful lackey was father to her unborn child. A few guineas saw to that. Of course Banks denied the charge. That was to be expected. He was no more the father than *she* was. But, Richard believed him no matter what *she* said, and no matter how many convincing details concerning Banks' anatomy the slut choked out under questioning thanks to the coaching of a cooperative footman. That she had not anticipated.

Sending the impertinent Irishman a note in Richard's hand informing him his services were no longer required, carefully phrased to raise his dander, proved equally futile. Apparently the lout couldn't read, for all he'd been a sergeant in Wellington's army. The scoundrel had gone directly to Richard complaining he should know better than send written instructions. Naturally she denied any knowledge of the matter, claimed Richard must have penned the thing while under the affect of laudanum and then forgotten it, which perfectly explained the irregularities in his hand. The fracas had been demeaning, her suggestion that if he penned such a note he must have meant it ignored. The only result was Banks became more firmly entrenched than ever.

She'd arranged a brawl between the vermin and an

accommodating groom. Her subsequent insistence that
Banks be summarily dismissed, or banished to the country where his coarse pug-nosed features and deplorable
character would no longer assault her sensibilities or
cause disruptions among an otherwise exemplary staff,
had met with intransigence. The groom, truly a magnificent specimen, was the one Richard dismissed.

She'd interviewed five very superior gentlemen's gentlemen, offered Richard his choice of the lot. He'd
refused to so much as speak with even one of them. If
the rest of the staff couldn't get along with Banks, Richard had the gall to inform her, then the rest of the staff
would be replaced.

That was how things now stood. The situation was
intolerable.

With a sigh she considered the matter of the country
sawbones' chit. No one might believe her, but she was
acting in the girl's best interests as well as Richard's and
her own. Perrault's *Cendrillon* was a pretty tale, and most
engaging, but life, and the living of it, began precisely
where Perrault had chosen to stop. She ought to know.
She had wed far above her station. The groom had been
everything girls dream of: well-built, incredibly handsome, of distinguished bearing, and with such an *air*,
graceful in his compliments, deferential in his attentions—at least until the vows were spoken. And, an
earl—a belted earl.

Of his birds of paradise, his *cocottes*, his gaming and
drinking, his dissolute character and immoral intellec-
tual maunderings and repulsive carnal appetites she
had suspected nothing until their wedding night. He
might have posed for every one of Hogarth's viciously
accurate paintings of which she had heard such scandalous whispers.

Those discoveries had been bad enough. But, they
hadn't been all.

She did not *fit*, he informed her hours after the ceremony, for all her father's heavy coffers. She had no notion how to dress to advantage, how to comport herself, wear jewels without seeming ridiculous. She was not even capable of opening her mouth without rendering herself contemptible in the eyes of all who counted and repulsive to her new family and their acquaintance.

Treated with disdain, her coppers welcome but herself rejected, she had struggled on, producing the required heir, tending the old dowager in her last illness, ignoring her profligate husband and ignored by him. No one should have to survive such torment. At least, that was how *she* remembered those early days. Wharton and his overbearing dragon of a mother might remember them differently, she supposed, but then they had ever been masters of self-delusion.

Then, Daphne Cheltenham had appeared out of a crowd of posturing macaronis and supercilious *grandes dames*, Archie at her side. After that it was better, but not much, until Wharton finally succumbed to his excesses, mad, blind, and drooling.

No, she was doing the chit a favor. While Richard was no Wharton, the girl would never adjust to his world, never be accepted by it—she would see to that. Permitting the foolishness to continue would only doom Richard to ridicule and the girl to the ultimate humiliation of existing as a despised interloper under her noble husband's roof. Clean and quick was best under the circumstances. One need only be possessed of sufficient determination and courage to achieve the necessary end, and those she had in plenty.

Besides, the chit was a nobody, and that counted for more than anything else. If she were hurt in the process, she had no one but herself to blame. *Like to like* was a valid rule, one she was not about to see broken.

There was a peremptory knock at her door. Lady Lavinia started, then draped herself artistically among the pillows, closed her eyes, and signaled Thatcher.

The door creaked. Thatcher whispered urgently, indecipherable syllables rising and falling in a melancholic tone.

"Sorry to hear it, but I must see her." Richard's loud voice was firm.

Drat! She could hear his one strong footstep, the tap of his cane, then the other with that dreadful dragging scuffle. He really should make *some* attempt to use the leg instead of pandering to his deformity so shamelessly. No pride. None of this benighted generation had the least pride. Of course, she already knew that. No man with an ounce of pride would contemplate the course he intended. The scrawny little country sparrow wasn't even worthy of a slip on the shoulder, let alone a wedding band.

"Good afternoon, Grandmama. Sorry you're feeling not quite the thing." A swish, then sudden blinding light. Dear God, he'd opened the draperies. "You'll be glad to know all is satisfactorily concluded, and the notices have been sent. Wish me happy."

"Richard, moderate your voice," Lady Lavinia pleaded in fainting accents. She opened her eyes, squinting in the glare as she raised a trembling hand to her forehead. "I am much too unwell—"

"You're in a snit, Grandmama, that's all," he returned evenly. "Nothing else ails you, unless it's foolishly refusing to eat in order to cow me. I've sent Thatcher to order something, for you must be truly gut-foundered after fasting to this late hour."

"I will not permit such language—"

The earl's hand swept across her forehead, leaving it rosy-complexioned. "Flour? At your age? A paltry nursery trick. Really, Grandmama, I'd've thought you more creative. And is that lampblack beneath your eyes? Have a care. I'm told it stains. Now, where is the ring?"

"Ring?" Her bewilderment was, she thought, masterful. "What ring?"

He stood silently, face impassive, waiting.

"I don't know what you're talking about," she snapped petulantly when the silence became too long for her liking.

Still he waited, saying nothing, expression blandly expectant.

She glared. He smiled slightly.

She gave him the back of her head. He blew out the candle, removed the tray of colorful tonics and cordials from her bedside, and tossed it out the window he had opened.

"You'll feel a deal better if you cease quacking yourself," he overrode her indignant protests. "Now, where's the ring?"

They became two statues, given life only by their clashing eyes. Seconds stretched to minutes, Lady Lavinia's chin high, the earl's firm. Thatcher bustled in followed by a maid toting a heavily laden tray. DeLacey watched as a table was dragged over, a collation of cold chicken, watercress soup, fresh crusty bread, and a selection of jellies laid out. He inspected it, and nodded his satisfaction. Once the little maid had bobbed herself from the room, he turned to his grandmother.

"Something to sustain you," he informed her politely. "Eat sparingly. I've accepted an invitation for us to dine at the home of my betrothed's aunt and uncle this evening. We'll be proceeding to several do's afterwards. See you're recovered in time to join us. Your absence would both give insult and occasion comment. That's something I will not permit."

"You *dare* issue me orders?" Lady Lavinia fumed.

"Perhaps not. Consider my words a suggestion, then. A very *strong* suggestion. I suggest you be prepared to accompany me at eight o'clock this evening. If you find you are so enfeebled by the rigors of town life that such an excursion is beyond your strength, I suggest you repair to Kent for the sake of your health. The Dower House is always ready to receive you. I have infinite concern for your well-being, and equal respect for your crotchets. A spell in the country should put the roses back in your cheeks, and perhaps encourage you to see the world, and your place in it, a bit more clearly."

"I have not spent one second in Kent since your grandfather died!"

"No? Perhaps now is the time to reacquaint yourself with the place. If you are not below at the appointed hour, I shall order the old traveling coach you favor be ready for you in the morning. Have a pleasant afternoon."

He smiled, turned slowly to regard Thatcher with calm, steady eyes.

"I suggest you assist your mistress in selecting her toilette for the evening with care," he said. "And, see to it her ladyship eats sufficiently to recoup her strength and regain her perspective. Otherwise you'll both be departing on a repairing lease of indefinite duration."

Then, still with a slight smile, he gave his grandmother a courteous bow and departed, closing the door softly behind him.

Harry Beckenham strode briskly up Bond Street swinging his swordstick, curly-brimmed beaver angled jauntily on his shining red-gold locks. It was a superlative day, warm and gilded by the mellow fall sunshine. Elegant équipages passed him, high-stepping horses tossing their heads and almost prancing with delight at the release from sodden gray drabness as they jangled harness and bridle. He nodded with the regularity of a marionette as he passed acquaintances: ladies trailed by parcel-laden footmen and scurrying abigails, young blades on the strut, older gentlemen out to take the air and replenish supplies of snuff and books and gossip.

There was a festive air to Bond Street, a swirling of colors that held the ebullience of spring, or that last desperate gaiety before the snows of winter descend. Some of summer's leaves still clung to the trees, whispering like silk petticoats in the brisk breeze. The interminable rain had ceased at last. London was at its best, smoke blown away, the sky so piercing a blue it almost hurt the eyes, and with nary a cloud to be seen.

The change had come in the night. By morning the world, which had appeared so grim in Richard's study the evening before, had turned itself around. Oh yes, there were lingering puddles in the streets and patches of damp on the pavements, but the sun would see to those. Everything was different now, entirely different, and all it had taken was a change in the weather and a quick trip to White's.

Admirable place, White's. If the club hadn't existed, it would've had to be invented merely to provide the conveniences necessary to a gentleman of the ton bent on the rescue of a very dear friend. He'd just left the place, "just" being the amount of time it had taken to make his way from Saint James to Piccadilly and up Bond Street, continuing steadily north as the street widened and newer buildings appeared.

He glanced in the bowed shop windows as he passed, admiring the displays of bonnets, of shawls and reticules and feathers and other female fripperies, considered purchasing some nonsense or other for Louisa. She was really a decent sort most of the time, and she and Rawdon had been most welcoming, after all. Of course, a gift for Louisa would mean some trifle must be purchased for Patsy Worth, given she was a guest of the house. That wouldn't do at all. Patsy had the lamentable habit of endowing events with meanings that existed only in her fertile little mind.

Something for the twins might be best: a bag of sweets, perhaps, or matching silver mugs with their names engraved on the faces.

Engraved mugs would take time though, and he didn't want to wait. He wanted to give someone something in celebration of the day, of the sunshine, of Richard's impending rescue, and he wanted to do it immediately, while the mood was still on him. This feeling of exuberance didn't come on him often these days. Sweets, however, didn't seem festive enough, and he couldn't think of anything else suitable to a pair of infants who drooled on their bibs and fouled their nappies and generally made loud, sloppy pests of themselves—when they weren't being disgustingly endearing, that is.

He passed a small jewelers, a new bootery, a shop selling delicate china and crystal bibelots. He restrained himself from breaking into a boyish whistle with the greatest of difficulty.

Yes indeed, it was the most marvelous of days. The very best.

And, he'd had to do precisely nothing to bring it about. That, perhaps, was the most wonderful of all.

He flicked his swordstick at a cheeky sparrow bathing in a puddle, bowed to Tabitha Brassthwaite, a particular friend of his aunt's. Then, filled with goodwill, he paused briefly to ask how she and her gouty husband did.

Beautifully, the plump little lady enthused, delighted by the handsome one-armed viscount's attentions. Edmund could walk without assistance now. Lord Beckenham must stop by for tea one afternoon, or a drop of madeira. Edmund would be glad of the company now he was once more in sorts. And what was this she'd heard concerning a brouhaha at the Rochedale rout the evening before? He'd been in attendance, had he not, being such a good friend of the earl's? The shops were simply full of tales, most of them quite incredible.

"A tempest in a teapot," Harry grinned at the bright-eyed, inquisitive little lady. "DeLacey was taken ill briefly is all. His old wounds, you understand. The rest is moon-shine, if it's the same tales I've been hearing."

"But, a country miss no better than she should be? And the earl entrapped, so foxed he didn't even know his own name," she protested.

"It was the girl's he didn't know," Harry chuckled. "Neither did anyone else. How could we? A complete stranger who sought shelter from the storm, I'm told, and just happened to've been put in DeLacey's study at the worst possible moment by a soft-hearted lackey with no more sense than a peacock. The earl recovered and the girl was sent down to the kitchens where she belonged, and that was the end of it. A trifle unusual, perhaps, but nothing that out of the way."

"Oh," said Mrs. Brassthwaite, much deflated and infinitely disappointed. "How dull. As your aunt was there, I made sure something more interesting had hap-pened. She seems to attract drama wherever she goes."

"Not this time. I know she'd appreciate it if you help scotch the tales. Most embarrassing for DeLacey and dowager countess. Done nothing to bring such scandal down on their heads. *She* is a dear friend of my aunt's and quite overset by yesterday's events. Unconscionable, how people're spreading rumors. DeLacey betrothed to a farmgirl? Not likely. You'd be doing an immense favor."

"But who told you all this?" she protested. "I have

it on the very best authority DeLacey affianced himself on the spot, and declared he'd wed a fishwife if he wished."

"And I have it on the best authority it was nothing of the sort. You know how it is when the weather turns foul. People are bored, and amuse themselves in any way they can," he shrugged. "Tales are invented and they mushroom without regard to truth. It's as simple as that."

"There must be a grain of truth to it somewhere," she insisted. "There always is, if one but searches deep enough. Who has been telling you such things?"

"It's in all the clubs," he smiled airily. "One just hears, you know. Where and from whom doesn't particularly matter, nor is one likely to remember, for it's all so unmemorable. The girl was a little nobody, and is receiving far more attention than she or the regrettable incident deserve."

"Oh, dear—how positively depressing."

He bowed, quite pleased with the confusion he had raised in the bustling little lady's mind, and sauntered on. She'd spread those tales, just as young Farquhar was spreading his, and confusion would compound on confusion.

It was Nigel Farquhar, pernicious weasel though he might be, who had unconsciously shown Harry how to proceed. Soon no one would know what to think. Then the ton would invent something discreditable it could accept, spread that tale, subscribe to it, defend it, and that would be the end of the matter. In the process they'd ruin the Driscoll girl. One always ruined country nobodies if enough were at stake. Better they should suffer than those who really mattered. She'd slink back to Devonshire where she belonged, thoroughly chastened, and Richard would be freed of his entanglement. That was all that counted—not how it was done, or who was hurt in the process—but that the world be firmly placed upon its axis once more.

For Nigel Farquhar had been at White's when Harry deposited his hat and swordstick and glove with a lackey and wandered up to the reading room to see what he could learn, still was there for all Harry knew. As one of the elect present at the rout, the young fop had been holding court, an unusual triumph for a loose screw ignored by the other members more often than not. The reading room had buzzed with conversation, a most unaccustomed occurrence in that customarily tomblike place.

Harry had wandered from group to group, standing on the fringes, listening.

The talk had all been of the contretemps at DeLacey's, and so muddled it was impossible to separate fact from fiction. And that had been the clue, for one thing stood out from the plethora of rumors: the brazen hussy who locked herself in DeLacey's study was beneath contempt. That single detail persisted from group to group. All else differed in content and emphasis. As for Farquhar, his tale altered according to what seemed to most intrigue or titillate his auditors of the moment, details reversing themselves like leaves on a windy day.

Harry had slipped away unnoticed. There had been no need for him to do the slightest thing, prepared though he had been. Of course, if presented with another such superb opportunity as the Brassthwaite woman, he'd again add his mite to the confusion. Not to do so would be foolish and hardly serve Richard's interests.

Not that he particularly disliked the little Driscoll girl, but she had one major failing: she was a female. From that followed an entire pantheon of faults from which she could no more escape than she could change her sex, and he was damned if Richard would fall prey to the disillusion and despair those faults invariably caused.

A week or less, that's all it would take, and Richard would be free again.

Harry paused in front of a toy shop, a pleased grin on his mobile features. His grin broadened. In the window stood a miniature coach and six, complete to passengers and whip-cracking coachman. Marcus would love it. And, over there—wasn't that a cottage, its front wall detachable so a little girl could play farmwife at will? Thatched roof, no less, and cunningly wrought tables and stools and a Dutch cupboard-bed, and shining copper pans and pewter mugs and plates, and chickens and cows and kittens and dogs, and minuscule children playing in the dust before the fire. There was even a donkey and cart and a well, and a tree to shade the whole.

Ships of the line and dolls one could dress and undress? He'd just see how the tots reacted to *these*, and watch Miss Patsy Worth's nose spring decidedly out of joint. What a day! What a glorious, wonderful, triumphant day.

Moments later he was back on the pavement, two cumbersome parcels tied together with string dangling from his hand, swordstick tucked high beneath his stump, his purse considerably lightened. Yes, he could have had the gifts delivered, but that would hardly be so amusing as arriving toting the things himself. The distance wasn't far.

He strode on down the pavement, garnering disbelieving stares on his way. A gentleman *never* so burdened himself—not as a usual thing. The occasion, passersby concluded after glances at his beaming face and sparkling blue eyes, must be special indeed. Hearts lifted at the sight of this delightful young man who would permit no disability to stop him on his determined course. Empathetic smiles followed him, the bright day brightened even more by his passage.

So it was, encumbered as no self-respecting member of the ton should be, that Harry, with a start of displeased surprise, almost ran down a pouter-pigeon-chested young man garbed all in lemon yellow and white emerging from a tobacconist's.

"Aloysius?" he said in disbelief. "Good God—what brings *you* to London?"

"Cousin Marleybourne? Oh, my! This is a surprise," the exquisite exclaimed, cochinealed hand rising to carmined lips as he turned a most unbecoming shade of pink beneath his heavy paint. The tone clashed hideously with his golden togs and carefully curled thin yellow locks. "How are you keeping yourself?"

"Tolerably," Harry responded curtly. "Yourself?"

"Oh, toddling along, you know, just as I always do."

The slight accusatory tone set Harry's teeth on edge. He made the boy's father a generous allowance—incumbent on him, as the man was his heir—but the sum never seemed adequate. A dunning letter had arrived only the week before, forwarded from Marleybourne by the punctilious Bedloe. As for this sprig, his hand was ever out.

"Come to see the sights?" Harry inquired with an effort at bonhomie.

"Well, you see, it's like this," Aloysius explained, eyes darting from the parcels dangling from Harry's hand to his empty sleeve with morbid fascination as shoppers swirled around them, "Papa thinks it's time I acquire some Town bronze. I'm *his* heir, after all, just as he's yours. Must be able to hold up appearances, what? So, here I am. Meant to call on you soon's I got the chance," he concluded hopefully. "Been *awfully* busy. Fact of it is, hoped you'd put me up. Everything's so dreadfully dear in Town! Bronze *costs*. I've quite outrun the constable, don't you know? Can't even offer you a pinch of snuff. Haven't any."

"Learn to trim your sails to the wind," Harry almost snarled in exasperation.

"Oh, I shall, I shall! But, I do stand in need of assistance," Aloysius persisted. "Not shillings, of course. Wouldn't dream of presuming. But a bed, and a meal now and then, that's a different matter. Wouldn't even know I was there."

"Sorry," Harry said, not in the least sorry, "but I'm the guest of others myself. Out of the question."

"Just a bed? I *am* your heir, after all, in a manner of speaking. Not the thing to turn me away."

"Impossible."

"Harry? My heavens, whatever are you doing so lumbered?"

The two men spun. Patsy Worth stood before them, twirling a pagoda-shaped sunshade in her little gloved hand, a fetching bonnet framing her pert face. Harry turned the color of a perfectly steamed lobster.

"Whatever *are* those?" she demanded, pointing to the parcels Harry had just set down beside him with an exasperated grunt. Then she smiled archly, throwing a fluttering glance at the gawping Aloysius. "Well, what are they?"

"Never you mind," Harry snapped.

"Oh, but I *do* mind. It must be something magnificently important for you to present such an appearance on Bond Street."

"If you must know, it's a little something for Marcus and Demetra."

"How thoughtful of you! Whatever it is, I'm sure they'll adore it. But, *little?* You appear to have all of

Windsor Castle there! Aren't you going to present your companion to me?'' she inquired, throwing another flirtatious glance at the bowled-over Aloysius.

There was nothing for it. Scowling blackly, Harry made the introductions.

"Charmed," Aloysius gleamed. "Absolutely *charmed.*"

"But, I know you," Patsy gurgled as she coyly extended her hand for his salute—not at all the thing to do on the street, but she didn't care. Harry was scowling, just as he was used to do when he found her dabbling her toes in the trout stream at home. "Don't you recall? We played together as children when you and your parents came visiting at Marleybourne. I pushed you in the pond when you broke the mast of Harry's toy sailboat. You came up all waterlilies and mud."

"Oh, dear," Aloysius exclaimed, taking a step back, hands rising to protect his lacquered curls from a sudden gust of wind.

"A lamentable incident," Patsy twinkled. "I was *such* a hoyden, but I'm not the least dangerous now, believe me. I hope you'll forgive me, even if the apology has taken simply years."

"I'd forgive such a lovely lady anything," Aloysius proclaimed with a deep bow.

"How *sweet* of you. Such a gentleman, to forgive a lady so readily," she enthused, throwing a minxish look at Harry. Both fools were eating it up. How delightful! "But where are you both off to? Or," with a surreptitious wink at the fulminating Harry, "is it possible that you're not together, but merely chance-met?" She remembered only too clearly how deeply Harry detested his distant cousins, this one the most of all.

"Chance-met," Harry agreed curtly. "More to the point, Miss Worth, what are you doing here unaccompanied?"

"Oh, Hortense is somewhere about," Patsy smiled

with an airy wave at the shop windows behind her. "I wouldn't dream of going anywhere without my abigail. Give me credit for *some* conduct, Lord Beckenham. Goodness, how formal we're being! As childhood playmates, don't you think we might dispense with titles and such?"

"Delighted to do so, Patsy," Aloysius beamed.

"Being a tad forward, aren't you?" Harry protested, still scowling.

"Oh, I don't think so," Patsy laughed. "We are old acquaintances, after all. Pushing someone in a pond— or being pushed—does permit some liberties. It's *quite* an intimate connection," with another arch look at the posturing exquisite at Harry's side. "Well, I must be off, if you'll forgive me. I'm expected."

"And just where're you going?" Harry demanded.

"Why, to Lady Daphne's. She sent round a note requesting my presence, and it was such a lovely day I couldn't bear the thought of summoning a carriage. Of course, a distinguished escort would make the stroll all the more delightful," with another arch look at Aloysius.

"Pleased to be of service," the latter beamed, mincing forward and extending his arm with a flourish.

"Blast it, Patsy," Harry muttered, "I'd accompany you myself, but with these parcels—"

"Yes?"

He clenched his jaw, eyes hard.

Patsy dimpled at him as she roguishly accepted Aloysius' arm. "I'll see you this evening, Harry," she said. "Don't do yourself an injury. Those parcels appear *dreadfully* heavy. You should've had them sent round. I'm sure Demetra and Marcus could've waited, for they're much too young to expect gifts as yet."

Then she was trotting down the street on the fop's arm, skirts swaying to reveal a hint of neatly turned ankle, Hortense striding close behind. Harry stared after her, cursing inventively. Then, with a final muttered oath, he took the parcels by their string handle and set off once more for Grosvenor Square.

The glow had gone from the day. And his gifts? They were ridiculous, far too complicated for infants barely beyond the age of two. Damn Patsy Worth and her unending flirtations!

"He's nothing but a worthless man-milliner, and a loose fish into the bargain!" Harry roared. "And that die-away air is as contrived as his curls! Didn't have either when he was younger, you'll remember. You *will not* go walking in the Park with that prissed-up lump of turtle dung tomorrow. Giles'll be glad to substitute."

Patsy Worth stared across the bright, yellow-and-blue drawing room at the front of the Duke of Rawdon's town home in feigned surprise.

She'd timed her return from Lady Daphne's perfectly. Harry had been about to go abovestairs to change for dinner when she swept through the door. He'd seen her—she'd made sure of that—snarled something incoherent, grabbed her by the arm and dragged her across the entry into this little-used reception room, overriding her protests with the force of a cannonade as he'd slammed the door.

They'd both be late now, not that *that* mattered in the least. Louisa had seen and understood. The delighted grin she'd quickly hidden had been message enough.

"I *always* go walking with Giles," Patsy protested with the force of truth as she watched Harry storming from window to chimney to door and back. "A lady likes some variety in her escorts, you know. To be seen with the same beau too often presents a most *peculiar* appearance. People begin whispering of impending announcements, and that wouldn't do at all. Besides, I thought Mr. Beckenham *most* gentlemanlike," she countered innocently. "And *so* elegant. Did you know his hair is dressed *à la chérubin?*"

"Don't be a wet-goose! Why, even my father couldn't stand him, and he tolerated most everyone, even Cousin Oliver and his whining wife."

"But, Harry, he'd dressed all in yellow on account of the sunshine! He told me so himself. Wasn't that a clever conceit? And he said *I* added to the sunshine, even if my dress was blue. He said together we were the sun and the sky. Of course, he said if my dress'd been gray then I would've been a storm cloud, and he a ray of hopeful sun peeping about my edge. He showed me just how he'd peep, too."

"Twaddle!"

"No one's ever paid me quite such an elegant compliment before," she countered dreamily. "The entire sky—just think of it! That's even better than being likened to a violet or a bluebell."

"Is that what you're after? Meaningless fustian?" he growled. "I never took you for a peahen, no matter what else you may be."

"Well, ladies do like to know they're appreciated," Patsy conceded from the striped Sheraton chair where she sat with her hands demurely folded. "It makes all our efforts to present an attractive appearance worth it, you see."

Then, at the look of disgust on Harry's face, she broke into helpless laughter.

"He is rather much, isn't he," she gasped. "Did you see his boots? *Yellow,* with gold and silver tassels and heels a mile high. He staggered about like a babe just learning to walk. I was in a panic lest he twist an ankle and propel us both into a kennel! D'you know he creams his face?"

"Good God!"

"*And* recommended I join him in the exercise because of the deleterious affects of the sun, even offered me a receipt of his own devising: equal parts of mashed cucumbers, curdled cream and egg yolk strained through a silk stocking, then boiled to a thick paste over a spirit lamp. It must be applied warm," she giggled. "He hasn't changed a bit!"

"Then what in blazes did you mean by going off with the bounder?"

"It does a young lady's consequence good to be seen on a gentleman's arm."

"Not on his! What the devil d'you think you're about?"

"Well, I *am* here for the Little Season."

"Husband-hunting?" Harry exploded. "You're still as green as a spring meadow!"

"Now that," Patsy dimpled, "was a very lovely compliment, even if it wasn't intended to be."

"Baggage!"

"I'm sorry, Harry—I didn't quite catch what you said?"

"Nothing. See here," he rounded on her, "I won't have you going about with Cousin Aloysius. He's a toadying little monster with his pockets forever to let, just as he was when you were children. D'you happen to remember why you shoved him in the pond? It had nothing to do with my sailboat."

"Then why d'you think I did it?"

"He'd kicked your shins because you wouldn't share your bag of sweets."

"No, Harry, he kicked *your* shins because you told him they were *my* sweets, and that you'd bought them specially for me and he was to stop badgering me and pulling my hair. That's why I pushed him in the pond."

"Amounts to the same thing," Harry retorted gruffly.

"Not quite."

Harry stared at her uncomfortably for a moment, then flushed and turned away. "What were you doing at Aunt Daffy's?" he asked.

"Having a delightful time. You know, Miss Driscoll's quite charming."

"*She* was there?" he growled in disbelief, whirling on her. "What the devil business had she with my aunt?"

"Lady Cheltenham is seeing to her wardrobe because Lady Wainwright—she's Miss Driscoll's aunt—is incapacitated and there's not much time."

"Busy as ever! I'll have her roasting on a spit one day, see if I don't. That still doesn't explain your presence. I'll not have you mucking about in that mess."

"Why, Harry—there's so much you won't have me doing. First, it's accepting the escort of a perfectly respectable young man, and your own relation, too. Now it's befriending your best friend's fiancée. Next you'll be telling me how to dress my hair and which gown to wear to dinner and deciding whether I may waltz and with whom. I never realized you'd appointed yourself my guardian."

"Someone needs to see to you," he spat, "for you've no more notion of how to go on than the old king!"

"Careful, Harry—those are treasonous words. I'd hate to see you in the Tower."

"Damn your impertinence!"

"But I would, Harry," she protested, calling up a tear. "Why, you'd positively wither away. I couldn't *bear* it."

"Not much chance of that," he snapped, "unless *you* play informant. I'll know whom to look to should the guard come pounding on the door in the small hours. Oh, the devil!" he grimaced at the genuine tears suddenly coursing down Patsy's cheeks. "Here," tossing her a handkerchief, "I didn't mean it. You know that. My bark's always been worse than my bite. Mop up, you little ninny."

"That's what you always said when I was a child," Patsy hiccoughed, "to 'mop up, little ninny.' Oh, dear— I'm not generally a watering pot, truly I'm not, but I was so frightened it might happen all those years you were in the Peninsula, you see," she explained after scrubbing her eyes and giving her nose a good blow, "only it would've been the French chaining you, for I *knew* you'd never give your parole if you were captured, and for you to think such a thing of me—for I was *so* relieved when you were invalided home! The arm didn't matter in the least so long as you were safe," she trailed off helplessly at his sudden scowl.

"I won't have you consorting with the Driscoll girl," he repeated, returning to the essential because it was easier than confronting the reason for Patsy's tears. "I mean that, so don't try me."

"That will be rather difficult, Harry," she said, giving her nose a final blow and tucking the sodden handkerchief in her reticule. "You see, I've agreed to play bridesmaid, and *you're* to stand up for Lord DeLacey. He plans to ask you tonight."

"Oh, Lord," he groaned. "You will make your excuses, understand me? You'll make your excuses, or I'll write the squire and tell him you're playing the flirt with every half-pay officer and basket-scrambler in Town. We'll see just how long your Season lasts then, my girl."

"No, you won't. I've already accepted, Harry, and there's not a thing you can do about it."

"Patsy, you don't understand what's going on," the former major protested with an attempt at a calm voice. "Richard's dug himself into a hole, and someone's *got* to pull him out."

"I understand Miss Driscoll is a very sweet, unaffected young lady with more common sense in her little finger than you have in your entire being—that's what I understand! The earl stopped by while I was there. It's clear as glass he's top-over-tail. The glow in his eyes when he looks at her gives *me* shivers, and I'm not in the least involved. As for his voice when he speaks to her—"

"To hell with his voice! The man's fit for Bedlam."

"I don't comprehend how it happened so quickly, and neither does she, but it *did*, and there's an end to it. You will *not* interfere, Harry—with them, or with me. If you do, I'll hate you forever! And watch your tongue. You curse entirely too much in front of the ladies, and I *am* a lady, no matter what you may think."

Patsy sprang from her chair, glaring murderously into Harry's eyes, stamped her foot, then whirled and dashed through the door, slamming it behind her.

"Damn," Harry muttered, pounding the graceful Adam mantel with his fist. *"Damn, damn, damn!"*

Nine

The two days following Lady Daphne's firm seizure
of the reins passed in a blur for the bemused Elizabeth.
Severe braided chignon softened and raised, garbed in
glowing gowns of highest fashion and greatest simplicity,
the young country girl met her reflection with a bewil-
dered—if secretly delighted—gaze. Lady Daphne had
been true to her promise. She was still herself, just as
Lord DeLacey decreed, but a self such as she'd never
believed possible. If she hadn't realized it unaided, Sybilla's sneering barbs concerning her new appearance
were ample proof of Lady Daphne's success. As for his
lordship's reaction, it would have been enough to turn
any girl's head.

Now, with a last glance at herself and an impish giggle
and grin tossed to Bartlet, she slung a beaded reticule
over her wrist, tugged on her gloves, slipped from her
bedchamber and sped down the stairs, tying the wide
moiréd silk bow of her new blue velvet bonnet perkily
beneath her ear as she went. Lord DeLacey was already
there, leaning on his cane as he watched her descend
to the entry, a definite twinkle in his eyes.

"I'm so sorry, my lord," she panted as she reached

the last step. "I'm late—again! I'm not generally such a tortoise, I promise you, but togs like these?" Her impatient gesture took in the elegant royal blue pelisse and the neat jean halfboots peaking beneath the hem. "Well, they take ever so much more time than my usual, you see, and I haven't learned to plan properly, and it seems I'm *forever* behind time. As for my hair—heavens! It won't happen again, I swear it."

"Very fetching, Elizabeth," he approved, ignoring Cochrane's paternal hovering as he placed a proprietary kiss on her flushed cheek, "particularly the bonnet. I'm always glad to wait for such delightful results."

"I'll start sooner next time, my lord," she blushed. "Really I will."

"What happened," he inquired indulgently as Cochrane swept the door open upon another sunny afternoon, "bury yourself in a book again and lose track of the hour?"

"Well, I had a few minutes to spare when I returned from Lady Daphne's, and this one was most excellent," she burbled. "I deserved some sort of recompense for permitting them to stick pins in me for hours, don't you agree? I thought I did! Have you read Ricardo's treatise on the price of corn? Fascinating—if a bit challenging. I finally finished it.

"And then, there was a new romance—well, new to me at least. I believe it was published last year. Have you heard of *Mansfield Park?* Utterly delightful! Poor little Fanny is such a mouse, and her aunt and uncle so puffed up and uncaring—not at all like dear Aunt Mehitabelle and Uncle Woodruff. I snuck just a peek and then quite lost myself in her troubles, while thanking heaven and earth I wasn't faced with such a coil! If Aunt Mehitabelle hadn't sent Bartlet to remind me—"

DeLacey admitted to being acquainted with the popular novel as he handed Elizabeth into the sleek low-slung curricle, then, slipping his cane along the floorboards, grasped the sides and propelled himself onto the seat beside her with a strong heave of his shoulders. His tiger passed him the reins, leapt up behind, and they were off.

"So," he said with a definite glint in his eye as he negotiated the corner leading off Portman Square, "Fanny and Edmund are more interesting than I?"

"Oh, no, my lord," she stammered. "*P-please* don't think that. It's only once I open a book, I just can't seem to put it down—not if it's in the least interesting—and I never think to look at a clock, which Papa says is one of my besetting sins. Why, he says I'm almost as bad as Robert, and if you could see *him*—Well, you will, won't you!—then you'd understand what a setdown *that* is. Only—"

"My dear," DeLacey interrupted swiftly, as he turned onto the road leading to the Park, "how many times must I remind you that my name is Richard?"

"I try, really I do," she said, glancing into his suddenly stern face, "but—"

"But?" he encouraged.

"It doesn't seem quite right, somehow," she said contritely in a small voice. "It sounds so disrespectful."

"My love, you'll be my wife in under three weeks' time," he reproved, "and I don't hold with the cold formality common among the ton. I want a *wife*, not a cipher or a statue. Most determined on that point, as a matter of fact."

"Well, I'm not that, at least, my—*Richard*."

"No, my love, that you're not," he agreed, grinning swiftly at her, then twined the curricle between a coach and a drayer's cart with only a whisker to spare. "Not to put too fine a point on it, I find you a constant surprise and delight in *all* ways except the use of my name. Prepared to beard the lionesses of the Park?"

His question met with uncharacteristic silence. They rode on for some distance, he scowling, she with a lost expression marring her piquant features. Finally, shifting the reins to one hand, he gripped both hers, gave them a reassuring squeeze.

"Yesterday was unpleasant," he said under cover of the street noises, "but I doubt there'll be a repetition. And, perhaps we'll have time to go by Saint Paul's afterwards. That's next on your list, isn't it?"

"I do so hate people *staring* at me as if I were a prize pig," she mumbled.

"I warned you there'd be some difficult parts at first. Are you regretting our wager and your forfeit already?"

"Oh, no!" she breathed, glowing eyes meeting his shyly. "I don't think I ever could!"

"That's all right, then," he smiled with relief as he turned into the Park, entering the elegant parade with skill if not a little impatience. "Any news from home?"

"Only the one letter, which must've been written the moment I departed," she sighed, "but then I've been gone but a fortnight. I do so worry about Mama, and Willie *doesn't* want another sister, which could prove most troublesome, and then I wonder how Papa's getting on without my assistance, for none of the boys is the least use in the surgery no matter what Mama may think, and—"

"I suspect," the earl broke in with a definite grin, "that your father has plans to do without your services well in hand. He sounds a most organized gentleman. There's Lady Jersey, my love. A smile and a gracious nod, now."

Elizabeth's diffident greeting was met by an arctic inclination of the head sent exclusively in the earl's direction, herself ignored.

"Oh, dear," she whispered at DeLacey's scowl, "did I do it wrong?"

"No, my love—you could never do anything wrong. The lack of courtesy is all on Lady Jersey's side."

'They despise me," she said, cheerful smile pasted across her face belied by the torment in her eyes. "This is *impossible*, Richard. The more I'm thrust beneath their noses, the worse it becomes. I *told* you how it would be. One doesn't set a scrawny duckling among the swans without—"

"It was a cygnet among the ducks, my dear, in case you don't remember. They're naught but foolish fat mallards, all of 'em," he insisted, a jerk of his head indicating the carriages and pedestrians thronging the Park at this elegant hour of taking the air.

"Your grandmama—"

"Will come round, you'll see. So will the rest of 'em. If Lady Daphne could convince you to put aside that old gray rag of yours and don something as becoming as this bonnet and pelisse, she's *certainly* up to handling the ton. You were most intransigent at first, I believe?"

"Yes, I was, but it didn't do much good," Elizabeth giggled unexpectedly. "Lady Cheltenham is a *most* determined lady. And then, Miss Worth kept prodding me, and insisting this or that was ever so much better than my usual style, and what with one thing and another—"

"You see? Besides, whose opinion is of account— Grandmama's or mine? And *I* think you the most charming, the most intelligent, the most desirable, the most beautiful young lady in all of England. It's me you're marrying, after all, not her."

"One doesn't just marry an individual," Elizabeth protested wisely, "no matter what you may think. One marries every connection, every friend, every acquaintance. Most especially, one marries those who form part of the household. For me, that's your grandmama. And then, there's Lord Beckenham. He's your very best friend, and he positively despises me. That's bound to cause trouble."

"Don't concern yourself over Harry," he chuckled. "He'd despise you if you were the Queen herself, though he might be a bit less pointed in letting you know about it. It has nothing to do with Devonshire or your family. Leave Harry to me. He'll come round in five or ten years. That, or he'll keep himself away. Can't stand sugary doses of marital bliss," DeLacey grinned at her, "and that's all he'll find wherever we are."

"I wish I were as certain as you are," she sighed. "Oh, dear—there's Mrs. Drummond-Burrell. I suppose I must bow to her?"

"Indeed you must, and smile as well, there's my angel. And Lady Sefton and the Princess de Lieven just beyond."

Mrs. Drummond-Burrell's barouche swept past at a steady slow trot, Mrs. Drummond-Burrell's eyes fixed on her coachman's back. Lady Sefton's glance passed over them, came back as she smiled slightly, then turned for a moment at her companion's sharp comment. Slowly her brows rose. Then her eyes slid back, cool, more curious than genuinely condemning, as she examined Elizabeth minutely.

"Unprepossessing, but not as impossible as I'd been led to believe. At least she's properly garbed, which I did not expect!"

The words floated to them clearly. The earl cursed beneath his breath.

"*Please*, Richard, may we leave now," Elizabeth pleaded.

"We can't," he muttered. "No way to turn about in this press. Chin up, my love. Not a one of 'em counts for anything."

* * *

"Damnation!"

Samuel Driscoll glared at the patchouli-scented missive he had just flattened, and began making his way laboriously through its garbled lines for the third time.

He didn't consider himself a choleric man, and he definitely wasn't given to attacking inanimate objects, but the blasted thing was damn near illegible through all of its two miserable gilt-edged pages. What little was legible was damn near incoherent. Of course, crumpling the blasted thing and flinging it out the window the first time he'd attempted to read it hadn't helped much. Or, crumpling it repeatedly since.

Dearest, Dearest <u>Darling</u> Uncle Samuel and Aunt Suzanne, the thing began, which was in itself a farce.

If there was one thing Mehitabelle's vain and self-important daughter had made clear from the first, it was that her country cousins were beneath contempt. John was disrespectful and hateful (he had wisely ignored her), Charles disgusting (he had unwisely attempted to present her with his pet frog to end a fit of the sullens), and Elizabeth not a girl at all, but a dirty crude boy in petticoats (Elizabeth had offered to take her fishing). As for her aunt and uncle, *they* were irremediably vulgar—all this in an affected little lisp accompanied by affected little waves of her dainty little hands.

The nursery party, after the first round of spats, ignored her as best they could. It had been more difficult for Suzanne, watching toys smashed in fits of pique, food thrown at walls and floor, tantrums staged at every turn that instantly gained the vixen whatever she demanded from her cowed Mama and doting Papa. That Sybilla must never be overset was the eleventh commandment.

As for Samuel's comment that the little changeling

deserved nothing so much as a swift paddling and
sequestration each time she played her tricks, his sister
had replied in shocked accents that the poor dear beautiful mite had such pretty ways *most* of the time that
such a course wasn't to be considered.

Samuel remembered clearly the sweets on which the
child gorged herself, the wholesome food she rejected,
the chaos she caused.

The projected month-long visit (intended to put roses
in Sybilla's cheeks following a bout of the measles), had
shrunk to a single week of which each day seemed a
year. Subsequent visits passed in much the same manner, each more swiftly curtailed, until the last had to
be endured but a single night. That had been two years
ago.

It didn't appear Sybilla had changed much.

*It is in desperation, my life in ruins, my heart broken,
with scalding tears blinding dulled eyes which shall never
look with joy and innocence upon the world again,*

the ludicrous, melodramatic thing went on,

*that I undertake the wretched task of apprising you of
the unconscionable actions of my Cousin Elizabeth (whom
I have ever held in greatest affection no matter what she
may have said about the matter in the past, for she has
ever been a lying, unprincipled tale-bearer) among the
ton. Did I not most sincerely fear for her welfare, her
virtue, the very salvation of her soul, were I not convinced
your horror will be as great as mine, nothing would
induce me to share with you the unbearable burdens she
has placed upon my frail shoulders and those of my
dearest parents.*

*Even then, family loyalty might give me pause, were
it not that I am not the only sufferer. There is Another*

whose agonies exceed even mine own, and as <u>*mine*</u> *are
like to kill me, you can imagine* <u>*his*</u>*.*

    *Therefore, it is with not only deepest reluctant sorrow,
but also with the certainty that you will comprehend the
legitimacy of my distressed appeal for your assistance,
not for my poor innocent and betrayed sake, but for that
of she who has so greatly wronged me and abused the
generous hospitality of my home and my love and my
trust, and for* <u>*his*</u> *whom she has even more tragically
wronged—*

And there what little coherence existed ran out. The
first lines were blotched, more resembling a page upon
which water had been artfully sprinkled than one upon
which tears had fallen. Of the rest, only tantalizing
phrases remained decipherable, marred by massive and
clearly intentional smears.

What sort of bumble-broth had Elizabeth tumbled
into? At the very least, it appeared she and his sister
and Wainwright were in dire need of rescue. And, possibly some young buck with more hair than wit who'd
fallen into Sybilla's clutches. Sybilla on a rampage—
he'd witnessed them often enough, unfortunately—was
as unprincipled and ungovernable a baggage as he'd
ever encountered.

He sighed, staring out the window at the last leaves
clinging to the peach tree.

He had no desire to leave Saint Mary-Grafton. The
easiest would be to give Elizabeth permission to return
home. Sybilla at her best was impossible. Sybilla in a
passion was beyond bearing. Poor Elizabeth had
pleaded not to be sent to London for the Little Season.
Whatever had happened, it was not her fault. It was his—
his and Suzanne's—for insisting she go. Spinsterhood
wasn't that terrible a fate. When the time came, one or
another of the boys would willingly offer her a home,

and she would become every niece and nephew's favorite Aunt Lizzie.

"Papa?" Chubby William poked his tousled head around the door of his father's surgery at the side of the simple, pleasant house. "What did that dirty man on the horse want? You waked up Melia Caroline roaring. You wouldn't do *that*, Mama says, 'less it was something *important*, and she says p'rhaps you should go upstairs so she c'n help."

"Ah—Willie! Heard me all the way upstairs, did you?"

"I think they heard you all the way to the *rectory*."

"Dear me." The doctor leaned back in his chair, smiled at his youngest son. "I suppose they just might have," he agreed.

"Well, you did sound *ferocious*."

"I shall take care not to do so in the future."

An anxious Andrew appeared at the door, lanky fifteen-year-old frame encased in the most disreputable clothing he owned, fishing poles and sack in hand, closely shadowed by eleven-year-old Steven. The older boy glanced from Willie to his father, dropped the sack and propped the poles by the door.

"I don't believe we'll be going fishing just yet, Stevie," he apologized, ruffling the younger boy's hair with a large, gentle hand. "It seems the clan is about to gather," as a bored-appearing Jeremy craned his long neck behind them, attempting to see into the surgery. The troubled frown marring his father's normally open and pleasant countenance told its own story.

"What's to do?" Jeremy demanded, affected lisp and mincing saunter forgotten. "I heard the commotion all the way from my dressing room."

"A letter from your Cousin Sybilla," Driscoll sighed, not even tempted to chuckle at the grandiose name Jeremy had recently bestowed on an unused attic cubby. "It seems there are big doings in London. Trouble is, the curst thing is so blotched I can't make out most of it, but it does appear Elizabeth has gotten herself into some sort of predicament."

"Oh, *Billa!*" Willie said with disgust. "Whatever *she* says, you c'n count on it being *'xactly* the opposite."

Robert, eighteen, scholarly and myopic and a future vicar—or military historian or journalist, or perhaps classicist or antiquarian, he had yet to decide which—eased his way past the younger boys.

"May I see, Papa," he requested diffidently, "or is it too personal? I've no desire to intrude where I'm not wanted, but I might be able to decipher the thing if you wish." At his father's soaring brows and doubtful expression, he explained, "I was experimenting with encryption and decryption last term, believing an understanding of the techniques might enable me to think more logically, and perhaps I might have a go at some of the hieroglyphs from Thebes, and, well, I became fairly good at it even if I couldn't make head nor tail of the glyphs, and if Lizzie's in trouble—?"

Dr. Driscoll shrugged and gestured at the blotched piece of correspondence.

"Have at it, my boy," he said, abandoning his chair. "Whatever concerns one of us, concerns us all. I'd prefer to have something intelligible to say to your mother beyond the fact that as usual your cousin is—well, we'll leave that be."

Robert slipped behind the cluttered desk, peering near-sightedly at the muddied sheets as he sank into his father's battered, over-sized chair. Then he seized pen and paper, gripped his lower lip between strong white teeth, and slowly began to transcribe. Charles, at twenty-one the oldest still at home, peeked in, then entered as the others found perches on chairs rimming the room and their father restlessly paced to and fro, throwing anxious glances at the boy behind the desk.

The waiting seemed interminable. Robert was meticulous, precise, no matter what task he undertook, no matter how disheveled his customary appearance. Now his hand raked through thick brown hair, sending it into a halo as he struggled on, occasionally holding one sheet or the other against the light streaming through the windows. It took half an hour of muttering and low whistles and held breath, but in the end he looked up at his pacing father and grinned.

"Lizzie, in a scrape? That just might be, given Lizzie." He paused dramatically, then as his brothers started to rise menacingly from their seats, quickly appended, "Our sister, Miss Elizabeth Mary Driscoll, appears to be the future Countess of Rochedale!"

"What?" six voices chorused.

"At least, I *think* she is. And, Sybbie's ready to cut her down where she stands, for all her prattle about love and devotion and duty and all the rest of that tommyrot. Must've had her sights set on the same man. Come see."

Robert went over to the windows, holding a page against the light and pointing as the others crowded around.

"Sybbie blotched it pretty thoroughly at this point," he explained, using a pocket knife as a pointer, "but the nib dug right into the paper. See this and this, where it's a bit darker? She must've been in a whale of a taking. The words're almost perfectly clear. Only the occasional letter missing. I think it's 'The Earl of Rochedale' here. Of course, it might be Koehdate or Rodudale or Koekefale, or something of that sort. Her penmanship's atrocious, besides being littered with so many curlicues and squiggles it's a botch even where it's clear.

"Anyway," he said seriously as he turned to face them, "I've never heard of a Koehdate or a Rodudale or a Koekefale, but there *is* a Rochedale who's an earl. Family

name's DeLacey. Came into the title while still in the army, wounded at Waterloo, named in dispatches after Salamanca and Talavera and Ciudad Rodrigo and I don't know what all. Took a bullet intended for one of his troopers during the Corunna retreat, got 'em all through, wouldn't even accept treatment until they were embarked. Quite the hero. Outstanding officer. His units *always* distinguished themselves.

"Yes, I know," he enthused, "I sound like a dispatch myself, but he's really *quite* extraordinary. If Lizzie *is* betrothed to him, she couldn't do better, at least from my point of view. The very *thought* of meeting Colonel DeLacey—why, it'd be like meeting Caesar or Horatio, or Oliver and Roland! Sold out now, unfortunately."

"And our Lizzie's to wed *him*?" Jeremy questioned, visions of London and Weston and Hoby dancing before his eyes.

"Unless she plans to jilt him, or unless he's making a May Game of her, which is what Sybbie implies in one elevated garble—You can't call 'em sentences!—while claiming Lizzie stole him from her in the next.

"See here? *'It pains me to inform you that Elizabeth is too green to comprehend the ways of men of fashion and the advantages they callously take of country rustics, nor does the self-seeking little fool condescend to understand that such an elevated personage as the Earl of Rochedale's only possible interest in such a bumpkin would be to offer a Carte Blanche, but persists rather in her folly, and indeed will likely be forced to accept such an arrangement given the way she is going on.'* Lizzie, become a Cyprian? Any man of sense would know 'twas impossible after one look at her!

"And now, just listen to this: *'I am loath to believe it, but spiteful jealousy alone can have prompted her to entrap poor Rochedale in such a conscienceless manner, for the earl and I have been unofficially betrothed for years—a fact of which she was totally aware when she ripped her own corsage in her successful effort to entrap my poor, darling Richard into an enforced offer of marriage.'*

"Colonel DeLacey ain't the sort to be entrapped into *anything*. Besides, if anyone's doing some trapping, I'll wager it's dear Sybbie. Rather addlepated, our sweet cuz. Can't seem to get her stories straight."

"She ain't ours," Willie protested in disgust. "She b'longs to Aunt Hitabelle and Uncle Woodruff. 'Sides, what's Billa mean 'bout Lizbeth ripping her dress so's he'd make her an offer? I can't see how tearing your clothes means you got to get married. I do it all the time, and *I'm* not getting married. And 'sides *that,* our Lizbeth, a *countess?* D'you think she'd like it, Papa—having to wear diamonds and fancy dresses and act snooty and high-in-the-instep like Billa all the time, and never go fishing or climb trees anymore? Leastways, I don't *think* countesses climb trees."

"I don't know *what* to think. It's barely two weeks since she left," Samuel Driscoll sighed. "None of this sounds the least like Elizabeth. I suppose the only thing for it is to go there and clear up the muddle. I *despise* London."

"I'll go with you, Papa," Willie offered, sticking his hand in his father's, "and if he *is* making a May Game of Lizbeth, I'll call 'im out."

"We'll *all* go," the younger ones chorused as Charles quietly offered to delay his return to Cambridge once more and act as locum, and Robert, Jeremy, and Andrew insisted Elizabeth was more important than Latin or isosceles triangles or the Punic Wars, and Steven promised if he were permitted to go there'd be no more frogs in the vicar's parlor ever.

"And the morning dress of Nile green muslin trimmed with deep green satin ribbons and *écru* lace, *and* the claret carriage ensemble and matching bonnet and sunshade—Holfers says *that* one is best of all—and I don't know what all," Elizabeth laughed as she and Patsy Worth tripped merrily down the stairs of the Rawdon town residence heading for the family parlor. "And *that's* only what was delivered this morning. Why, soon I'll have more costumes than hairs on my head! Oh, yes—and the gown for Saturday."

"You tried that on immediately, of course," Patsy dimpled. "It would seem you're accustoming yourself to being a lady. And in less than a week's time! Quite a change, isn't it? I thought I'd *never* adjust, but Lady Daphne can be quite determined when she's certain she's right."

"She can, can't she! And transform the most *dreary* drudgery into fun, which is quite an art. Of course, Holfers takes it all so seriously that she tends to make it seem a matter of life and death—which it is, I suppose, to a dresser. You know," Elizabeth confided, placing a trusting hand on Patsy's arm, "I *never* thought I could look like that. Why, I must've stared at myself in the glass for an hour, turning this way and that like the veriest *ninny* while Lady Cheltenham and my aunt chuckled fit to beat the band. And I was grinning like a prissy little fool with nothing but clothes on her mind," she confessed, "which I'm really not at all. Only, the dress one will wear to the rout given to celebrate one's betrothal *is* just a *little* bit important, isn't it? Richard assured me it is. Ice-blue underdress, overdress of sheerest spider gauze shot with silver and embroidered with tiny deepest blue pansies—it's *magnificent*, and actually succeeds in making me appear elegant, which is nothing short of a miracle."

"I remember the fabric. It's lovely."

"Isn't it? I felt just like a fairy princess. What a vain looby *that* makes me sound, for I shall never be more

than just short of plain, you know, being so small and
thin and brown, even if Richard says I do have pretty
hair! And I don't care how foolish they thought me
because I thought myself foolish as well, but I couldn't
stop and I do *so* want to make Richard proud of me
and convince his friends he's done well for himself in
spite of the fact that I'm a nobody and he's *quite* clearly
a somebody, and I think he will be—*pleased*, I mean—
when he sees me in it because it's the absolute *antithesis*
of that dreadful rag I was sporting when we met, besides
being trimmed in deep blue which is a color he says he
favors for me—though it won't do to wear those dreadful rubies he's forever speaking of. Pearls would be just
the thing, or possibly sapphires. Oh dear—I *am* being
foolish! To even *consider* wearing jewels—a little brown
sparrow such as I.''

"You aren't in the least foolish," Patsy chuckled,
glancing at her companion. The rosy morning dress
with its touch of burgundy sprigs and high ruched collar
had been the first addition to the girl's scant wardrobe—a very minor sacrifice on Patsy's part. Best of all,
it had required almost no alteration, just the taking in
of a seam here and there, for they were much of a size,
though Patsy's figure was slightly fuller. "Indeed, you
are precisely what every young girl in love should be."

"Is *that* what it is? I'm in love?" Elizabeth said wonder-
ingly, pausing on the stairs. "Is *that* why everything
seems so much more fun and vivid, and why I'm willing
to consider things I've *never* considered before?"

"I suspect so," Patsy grinned broadly.

"Goodness! So quickly? And I thought *Richard* mad."

"Falling in love isn't like growing a tree," Patsy
returned wisely. "I rather imagine it can happen in an
instant, or it can take a lifetime. It all depends on the
persons involved. From what I've observed of you and
Lord DeLacey, an instant is all it took. You're both

infinitely fortunate, you know. For others it isn't so easy or simple."

"The course of true love never did run smooth," Elizabeth quoted with a slight frown. "I don't see why it shouldn't, if there's to be love at all. I never *did* approve of that sentiment of Shakespeare's. *Much* too gloomy."

"But accurate for some of us," Patsy rejoined, still smiling slightly. "Come—they're expecting us below. Miss Connardsleigh and her mother have just arrived, and Lady Daphne is anxious for you to meet them. Entertaining the twins is all fine and well, and I know how much you miss your brothers, but you *do* have obligations.

"I think you'll like them both, by the bye. *She's* sweet, and quite striking—rather like an ice princess with all that flaxen hair and those pale blue eyes—but lively and funny and *totally* unaffected, and her mother's lovely."

"I'm sure I shall, if *you* do," Elizabeth returned with a twinkle. "We seem in accord on so much."

Trailing slowly after Patsy as they finished descending the stairs, she thought over her new friend's words.

She? In love? Was it probable? Was it even possible?

It was unarguable that, against all logic and all odds, she had been at the Rochedale rout, which was precisely the sort of place she did *not* want to be. How *that* had happened Elizabeth would never understand, for Aunt Mehitabelle had known she had no desire to attend, and she *had* to have realized there was something definitely havey-cavey about the invitation, and *still* she had insisted. And so there she had been, and there *he* had been.

But, *love?*

Well, perhaps it was.

She supposed it could happen to anyone—even to her. Certainly there was no one in the world quite so wonderful, so kind, so intelligent, so distinguished, so understanding, so dear and courageous and thoughtful, so handsome as Richard. Or, so comfortable. Or, quite so amusing to be with. And, when he so much as took her arm, or smiled at her in that special way he had, she positively *melted*—a most unaccustomed sensation, and really rather pleasant.

Was *that* what love was? Preferring to be with one person above all others, and feeling lovely little shivers run up and down one's spine when he looked at one in just *that* way?

If it was, then she'd gone top-over-tail before she'd even known she'd begun. *That* was a lowering thought. One ought to have been able to enjoy every instant, and instead she'd just tumbled in pell-mell like Stevie falling into the trout stream at home, quite by accident and totally unaware of what was happening until it was all over.

Logic said such things didn't happen beyond the pages of a book, but it had, just like a fairy tale.

A footman opened the entry door as Elizabeth and Patsy reached the top of the stairs leading to the main floor. Patsy paused, watching, as Harry Beckenham stormed in, deep scowl marring his handsome features. He flung his hat, glove, and walking stick at the hovering footman, whirled to ascend up the stairs, froze at the sight of the two girls.

"Damn," he muttered.

"Good morning, Lord Beckenham," Patsy said in dulcet tones, sweeping a regal curtsy, spun on her heel. "Come, Elizabeth—we are expected."

"Good m-morning, your lordship," Elizabeth quavered. Why did the man so unnerve her! Well, he *was* a special friend of Richard's, and he *was* the Duchess of Rawdon's brother, and he *clearly* detested her, but that wasn't sufficient reason to be transformed into a quivering blancmange each time he appeared. "I h-hope you are k-keeping well?"

"Miss Driscoll," he snarled, then "Miss Worth," to Patsy's retreating back, not bothering to bow.

Elizabeth glanced from Patsy's set features to the scowling viscount. Really! He was the rudest, most callous boor she'd ever encountered. And he and Patsy were to stand up for them in barely two and a half weeks' time? Why, the church might well become an open battleground. *That* would never do.

Squaring her shoulders, pasting a scowl across her elfin features to match the irascible Beckenham's, Elizabeth impulsively darted down the stairs, head high.

"I believe we need to speak privately, my lord," she blurted before she lost her nerve, indicating the reception room in cold blues and hard yellows just off the imposing entry. "In here, if you will be so kind? Don't worry," at the venomous look he threw her, "we shall leave the door open. I've already entrapped one fiancé—That's what you believe, isn't it?—so you're *perfectly* safe. I've no need of another."

Harry threw her a furious look, eyes flicking to the avid footman. Then, with a shrug, he opened the door to the small drawing room and gestured for her to precede him. On the floor above, Patsy Worth returned to the head of the stairs, watching in surprise as the unlikely pair disappeared from sight. Then, seriously concerned and ignoring propriety, she settled herself on the top step to wait.

Inwardly quaking, hands trembling, and knees like water, Elizabeth led the way determinedly. Once in the coldly formal room, she gestured toward a pair of stiff Sheraton chairs upholstered in a brocaded silk of blue and yellow stripes, then sank into the nearer.

"We will be in plain sight here, my lord," she

informed him, "but unable to be heard unless you take it into your mind to roar, which I understand is your customary mode of expression. *I* shall keep my voice lowered in any case, so our business will be as private or public as *you* desire."

"You unprincipled, impertinent little baggage," Beckenham muttered under his breath, refusing the proffered chair. "I've a good mind to—"

"Indulging in personalities will serve neither of us, my lord," Elizabeth fumed, now so thoroughly angered fear was forgotten, "and your caddish threats concern me not in the least. I suggest you govern your tongue with a little more care."

He towered over her, unconsciously menacing, single arm thrust behind him as if to keep from striking her. "Well," he growled, "what d'you want?"

"You don't like me," she explained without prevarication, "and you don't like Miss Worth. You don't appear to care for your sister. I don't believe you even like your aunt, who is everything that is charming, so there is only one thing I can conclude: You don't like women on general principles, which is fairly ridiculous and shows a distinct lack of discrimination and intelligence. I also suspect you don't like yourself very much, which is not the least surprising as you are not, after all, very likable, but that is your problem, and not mine. However, your contemptible rudeness to Miss Worth and myself *is*. In just over two weeks' time I am to wed a man you consider a close personal friend. You *do* consider yourself Richard's friend, do you not?"

"Yes," Harry ground out.

"Then *act* like one!" she snapped. "You distress him with your continual boorish behavior. Indeed, I don't know why he puts up with you."

"So—you intend we should part ways," he snarled.

"Not in the least. If Richard wants a friend who is

churlish, self-absorbed, and makes himself totally ridiculous most of the time, that is *Richard's* concern, not mine. However, when you distress Richard, you infuriate *me*, and I could prove a rather formidable enemy if you make it necessary."

"You," he snorted, "a formidable anything? Don't be presumptuous!"

"You fear me," she returned calmly, "almost as much as I fear you. Why?"

"I don't fear you. I *despise* you—you, and every other two-faced, conscienceless, grasping jade."

"How am I two-faced?"

"You're a female."

"Positively brilliant! Of course I am. Even an idiot could see that. Why else?"

"Isn't that reason enough?" he blustered, heedless of the open door leading to the entry hall and the curious footman hovering as close as he dared.

"Hardly. Just because *you're* a boor doesn't mean I consider every man in England a boor. Some are, and some aren't. Individuals should be judged by their merits, not by the faults, real or imagined, of others."

"What a sanctimonious little brat you are! You'll drive Richard mad within a week. All right, consider the facts with no treacle on 'em: You, a penniless nobody, to wed one of the greatest fortunes and oldest titles in England? You'd known the man less than an hour when you accepted him. And why? To feather your barren little nest, that's why! There's no other possible interpretation."

"What an *abominable* thing to suggest. Why, you're calling your own friend a blind idiot, aside from what you're implying about me. You're *despicable."*

"I'm not implying it, I'm *saying* it," Beckenham exploded. "It won't do! It simply won't do!"

"Richard thinks it will, and it's his opinion that matters." She took a deep breath, looked at him consideringly, head cocked to one side like a small bird's. "Grasping," she said thoughtfully, "and conscienceless and two-faced." Her eyes narrowed. Then, certain of her ground, she planted him a facer. "Who was she?" Elizabeth inquired demurely. "Did she make a total fool of you? Is that why you dislike women so much? Is that why you dislike *me*?"

Harry Beckenham froze, shaking. "Why, you—"

"Tut-tut," she broke in. "No name-calling and no roaring. It's not an applicable response to a simple statement of obvious fact. Besides, this is supposed to be a *private* conversation. Was it Patsy? I *can't* believe it of her."

"No," he admitted grudgingly, "it wasn't Miss Worth."

"Then stop behaving as if she bore sole responsibility for your embarrassment, and all the rest of us assisted her. That's all it was, wasn't it—simple embarrassment? You were played for a fool, and you didn't like it. Well, all of us are fools at one time or another. That doesn't mean one must *persist* in playing the fool."

Harry stared at her, nonplussed.

No one had *ever* spoken of that time in his presence. No one had *dared*. Well, Patsy had, but she'd learned better. And now this country nobody was calling him ridiculous. Little did she know! But, she'd shown her colors. Vicious, that's what she was. Vicious and unprincipled, like all the others. He was *damned* if he'd permit her to ruin Richard's life, and nothing seemed to be working, *nothing*. But, there was one thing that might: the truth. *All* of it. The man would thank him one day. As for Patsy, she could go hang.

"Then perhaps *you* should stop playing the fool," he snapped, eyes narrowed, "as you recommend it so highly. You *are* aware of why Richard's marrying you, aren't you? The *real* reason, and not the clap-trap he's been spouting?"

"Lord DeLacey *says* he loves me. He's given me no reason to doubt his word."

"Love you? Hardly." Harry's smile was all that was condescending, all that was insincere. "How could he? Look at yourself! You've *nothing* to recommend you. No—he's using you to pay a debt."

"What?"

Her upturned face was puzzled, vulnerable, the eyes wide with the first wary hint of pain. He ignored the vulnerability, steeled himself. She'd no business in any of their lives. The sooner she scurried back where she belonged, the better.

"He's using you," Harry repeated, separating each word as one would when attempting to converse with an idiot, "to pay a debt. A very considerable one. I can't make it plainer."

Elizabeth paled, hands twisting in her lap. So ended the fairy tale.

"What debt," she asked, "and to whom does he owe it? Was it one of those silly wagers at White's over which drop of rain will reach the bottom of the pane first?"

Harry considered lying, decided the bald truth would be damaging enough.

"To your father," he said flatly. "The lot of you apparently saved Richard's life after Waterloo. Now, he's recompensing you in the only way he knows."

"I don't believe it!"

"The man with the crushed leg who knocked you down," Harry persisted. "Don't tell me you've forgotten, for that would be the final irony."

"That was *Richard?"*

"In the flesh," Harry affirmed, experiencing a slight twinge of conscience at the stricken look on her face. *"Now* d'you see why it won't do? He doesn't love you.

He doesn't even *like* you. How could he? No, he's merely rewarding your father by taking a gawky, unmannerly, unmarriageable brat off his hands. As I said, it won't do."

Tears welled in Elizabeth's eyes. She dashed them away even as her lips quivered. Harry snorted, tossed his handkerchief contemptuously in her lap. Between this chit and Patsy, he was going to have to order a fresh supply.

"What won't do?"

The adversaries whirled at the sound of the familiar voice coming from the open door, Elizabeth's hand flying to her wet cheek. The Earl of Rochedale stood there leaning on his cane, Giles Fortescue at his side.

"Damn!" Harry muttered.

"Well, what won't do?" From the doorway, Richard DeLacey surveyed the pair, Harry's face at once guilty and thunderous, Elizabeth's despairing. "What in *blazes* have you been up to, Harry?" he demanded.

"It's all right, truly it is," Elizabeth sniffled. "I've just been treated to a salutary dose of reality, that's all. I—I release you from our betrothal, my lord," she quavered, rising from her chair and sweeping a dignified curtsy. "If you will please see to sending the proper notices to the journals, I would appreciate it greatly, and I wish you a very happy and successful future. Unfortunately, I find I can play no part in it. Now, if you gentlemen will be so good as to excuse me—"

She dashed across the room and through the door and pelted up the stairs.

"Stop her, Giles!" DeLacey roared. "Harry, if you've done what I think you've done, I'll murder you with my own two hands!"

Giles tore after Elizabeth, coattails flying, as the helplessly sobbing girl careened blindly into Patsy's waiting arms. Patsy gathered her close, glaring over her tumbled dark curls at Harry, now standing uncertainly in the doorway of the little drawing room.

"You despicable monster," she spat. "I *never* want to see you again!"

Then Giles was beside them, his arm protectively around Patsy's shoulders, as he pushed a distracted hand through his short ginger hair.

"Can you manage things?" he asked Patsy urgently. "I'm afraid if I don't get right back down there, Richard'll call Harry out."

"Let him!"

"You don't mean that," Giles insisted, "you know you don't. I'll give him a set of fives myself, and have done with it. *That'll* satisfy the proprieties. Then Richard'll give him a bear-garden jaw, and Rawdon'll cut him down to size, and maybe Harry'll start seeing sense for the first time in dunamany years. You *can* manage, can't you? Richard'll be wanting to speak with her as soon as may be."

"Of *course* I can manage."

"That's the ticket!" Giles gave her an encouraging pat on the shoulder, tore back down the stairs, squared off in front of Harry. "Sorry about this," he said, ignoring the footman by the door, hauled back and gave Harry a taste of the home-brewed. Harry slumped to the floor. "Demmed idiot," Giles muttered. "That's the *second* time I've had to draw his cork."

He leaned over, grasped Harry's boots, and unceremoniously dragged him down the hall toward Rawdon's library. After a moment's indecision, DeLacey followed.

"Come," Patsy Worth whispered after waiting a few moments for the sobs to calm.

Thank heavens neither Louisa nor Lady Daphne had heard the fracas. And with little Lucinda Connardsleigh and her mother there as well, and heaven alone knew who else! She suspected the fewer aware of this contretemps, the better for everyone's sake.

Well, perhaps most especially for Harry's. What he appeared to have attempted was unpardonable. They were all rather tired of continually being forced to forgive Harry his queer starts. This latest vagary might place him so deeply in everyone's black books he'd never extricate himself. Little Miss Driscoll had become an instant favorite among all the family.

"We'll go upstairs to my room, and you can repair the ravages and tell me what this is all about," she said, rubbing a comforting hand on the girl's heaving shoulders. "*Nothing* is ever so bad as it first seems."

Elizabeth shook her head. "I want to go home," she whispered, shuddering violently. "Please, Patsy—have my aunt's carriage called."

"Not if you promised me a royal crown. Upstairs," Patsy insisted, turning the girl around and propelling her across the spacious landing to the foot of the next flight. She wasn't about to let Elizabeth out of the house until things were again as they should be. Once at her aunt and uncle's she could hide forever, or slink back to Devon with her departure undetected, and then there'd be nothing *anyone* could do, at least for a considerable time. "Now!"

"I want to go home to Saint Mary-Grafton," Elizabeth hiccoughed dully.

"And leave Harry victorious on the field of battle, rubbing his hands in glee? Well, his *hand.* Don't be such an idiot!"

"That's what *he* said—that I've been an idiot. I suppose I have."

"The only idiot in this house is Harry Beckenham. Now, up you go."

It took considerable cajoling and not a few threats,

but at last Patsy Worth had Elizabeth comfortably
ensconced in a chaise-longue by the large windows of
her sitting room, a soft furry coverlet draped across the
distraught girl's legs, a handkerchief soaked in lavender
water across her aching brow, cucumber slices hastily
ordered from the kitchens on her burning eyes.

"Now," she said, seating herself by the country girl's
side and chafing her hands, "what's to do?"

"I want to go home," Elizabeth repeated listlessly.

"Utter foolishness! If you won't tell me, Giles will, for
you may be sure the earl will get the truth out of Harry,
and if he doesn't, the duke will. Now, what sort of
Banbury tale did Harry Beckenham regale you with?"

"It wasn't a Banbury tale. It was the truth."

"Haven't you encountered darling Harry often
enough in the past few days to realize he's an embittered
fool and not to be trusted?"

"No, it was the truth." Impatiently Elizabeth pulled
her hands free, took the cucumber slices from her eyes
and tossed them on the waiting plate, then swung her
legs over the side of the chaise-longue. "There's no way
he could've known otherwise. I found out why Lord
DeLacey asked me to marry him, you see, and it won't
do."

"Oh? What reason did *Harry* give you?"

"I'm the way the earl is repaying a debt he feels he
owes my father," Elizabeth quavered miserably, hunch-
ing into herself. "We saved his life after Waterloo, only
I didn't recognize him because he looks so different
now. Lord Beckenham knew. *You* knew. Everyone seems
to have known but me."

"Not everyone. Only his grandmother and Giles, and
a very few others."

"I've never been so humiliated. If he'd told me the
truth in the beginning, it wouldn't be so dreadful, for

I remember him very clearly, and worried so about him and wondered what had become of him, but he didn't." Then she straightened her shoulders. "I *will not* be used in such a way, d'you understand? I will not!"

"Of course you won't," Patsy soothed, "but don't you think Lord DeLacey's explanation might differ a bit from Harry's?"

"I never want to see that man again!"

"I don't blame you. Harry *is* impossible."

"I don't mean Lord Beckenham. He's done me a favor, cruel as it may seem. I mean Richard."

"Oh? Well, there you're being unpardonably foolish, if you'll forgive my saying so. Maybe I should tell you Giles's been combing Devon for the last year and a half—at Lord DeLacey's expense. He's been searching for a slip of a girl with seven brothers whose father just happens to be a physician."

"What difference does that make?"

"You're going to be stubborn, aren't you. And, no matter what anyone says, you're going to refuse to believe Lord DeLacey loves you, and has since Waterloo, and you're going to throw away your best chance of happiness just because Harry decided you should. You *are* a fool."

"Look at me," Elizabeth protested. "I'm nothing, nobody! Well, at home I am, but not *here*. *This* makes sense. The other didn't."

"Sometimes love doesn't make sense," Patsy returned bitterly. "Look at *me!*" She sighed at Elizabeth's questioning glance, shrugged. "I've been in love with Harry Beckenham since I was in leading strings," she admitted ruefully. "Hadn't you wondered why he and I always come to cuffs? Oh, we may go on fairly well for a bit— we did just the other day—but then one of us says something out of turn and it's all ruined. I'm beginning to believe it always will be. You see, something rather dreadful happened to him just after he lost his arm, and he can't forget it."

"A two-faced, conscienceless, grasping jade," Elizabeth quoted, brows rising.

"How did *you* come to know? It's supposed to be a secret."

"He more or less told me himself, though he didn't realize it."

"I see. Well, I despise Harry for what he's tried to do to you and the earl, but I still love him anyway. I suppose I always will. Can you forgive me?"

"Of course." Elizabeth gave a tentative, watery smile. "I think I understand, you see," she blushed, "for if I *did* love his lordship *before* I found out why he wanted to marry me, then I still love him now—and I shouldn't, for he's used me most callously."

"He hasn't at all. He's merely tried to assure himself of the woman he loves with the least fuss possible. That's typical of men, you know, if they're given half a chance, and he *did* search for you for eighteen months. That proves something, don't you think?"

"He paid others to search for me," Elizabeth countered. "That's not quite the same thing."

"You expect him to have jounced over rutted roads with that leg of his? Why, he can't even mount a horse yet! Don't be idiotish. It would've been the cruelest sort of torture."

"I know," she whispered. "Oh, dear—I know, and I wouldn't cause him pain for the world. But it was all a hum, just as Lord Beckenham said in the beginning. I should've listened right then, but, well, I didn't want to—not with Richard looking at me the way he was, his eyes all warm and smiling. I never *dreamed* eyes like that could lie.

"It *hurts*, Patsy. I never dreamed *anything* could hurt

so terribly, like I have nothing but a huge hole inside me. Being in love isn't nice. It isn't nice at all. It's *dreadful.*"

She lay back with a little sob, staring at the ceiling.

Richard had been everything she secretly dreamed of while claiming she'd no desire to be wed *ever:* humorous, generous, intelligent, and gentle and kind—constantly cheerful despite the terrible pain of his leg, and with an innate strength upon which one could rely totally, just like Papa and John and Charles. Better yet, he hadn't seemed to consider her preference for the country the least outrageous.

Best of all, when they'd conversed, it hadn't been prattle. They'd spoken of real things: family, and books, and the current problems in the Midlands, and the Corn Laws. He'd really listened to her opinions, too, just as Papa listened to Mama's, and hadn't insisted his were correct just because he was a man.

And, he was the officer at La Haye Sainte whose eyes had gazed up at her with such wondering warmth before he lost consciousness, and who had gripped her wrist so tightly, insisting she stay with him!

And it had all meant nothing.

She turned on her side, sighing once more, tucked her legs up beneath her skirts and pulled the coverlet over her shoulders as Patsy tiptoed from the room.

It had been only a dream, nothing more—a very short, very beautiful dream—but its ending hurt more than anything had ever hurt before. No wonder the ladies in the Park had looked on her with such contempt! They had known. Everyone must have known—everyone but she.

Tomorrow, she'd return to Saint Mary-Grafton, and if occasionally her thoughts turned longingly to a certain dark-haired peer with a painful limp, no one would ever know but herself.

Ten

Patsy paused by her dressing table, swept a brush through her short reddish-brown curls and retied the bandeau that held them off her forehead, pulling a few tendrils down to soften the effect. Then she considered her appearance critically. *Soignée?* Definitely. She always presented a sleek, sophisticated woman to the ton's ever-censorious eyes these days. Gone was the hoyden of the bramble patches and trout streams. But, was that quite enough on this particular occasion?

With pursed lips she opened her small jewel case, considered its meager contents and shrugged.

If she couldn't cut Harry down to size on her own, no amount of sapphires and emeralds and diamonds—of which she had none in any case—would do the job for her. Better to be herself, possibly even a "self" that reminded him uncomfortably of the girl he had once taken jouncing across their adjoining estates on the pommel of his saddle.

"Harry, damn you—this is positively the *last* time," she muttered.

Then she paused at her dressing room door. Her

abigail raised snapping black eyes from the rent in the riding habit she was mending.

"I'm going back down, Hortense," Patsy whispered. "Miss Driscoll is asleep. Leave the poor thing be for a bit. She's had a *dreadful* morning. I should be returned soon, and then we shall see what we shall see."

"Poor little lady," Hortense agreed softly. "If she wakens, do you want me to have you alerted, miss?"

"Might be wise," Patsy agreed. "I leave it to your best judgment. Just don't let her out of these rooms. Sit on her, if you must. Miss Driscoll needs some time to regain her poise. I don't want her acting rashly, and left to her own devices—well, we've had drama enough for one morning."

With that she sped down the stairs once more, darting past the family parlor.

She wasn't ready to confront Lady Daphne or Louisa yet. While the morning's upheavals might have appeared to take forever, barely half an hour had passed since she and Elizabeth stood at the head of the stairs watching Harry arrive. The imparting of disaster could always wait. Her small feet twinkled down the last flight to the entry and along the hall to Rawdon's library. There she paused once more, waved the hovering footman away, settled her skirts, gained every inch she could from erect posture, steeled her features and knocked.

A sour-faced Giles eased the heavy oak door open, darting suspicious looks up and down the corridor and pulled her inside. She glanced about. The room, except for Giles, was empty.

"Where are they?" she inquired breathlessly.

"That blasted room by the front door. Leastways, Richard and Harry are. Rawdon's joined the ladies. Sally Jersey's come prying, tongue hanging out like a bitch in—Pardon! Forget I said that. Thank the Lord all was quiet when she arrived and I'd already dragged Harry back here, or we'd *really've* been in the suds."

"What're you doing here, then?"

"Least wanted all the way 'round. Richard insisted on private words with Harry. *Very* private. And, they don't trust me near Silence, for which I don't blame 'em. I'd *'silence'* her, given half the chance, for I've got it on good authority she's the one been spreading scurrilous tales about Miss Driscoll and the earl."

"Whatever do you mean, Giles?"

"You hadn't heard that part? Oh, yes," he expounded bitterly, dragging Patsy to a sofa by the window and forcing her to sit, then plunking himself down beside her, "all *sorts* of moonshine, like *she* was born on the wrong side of the blanket, and *he's* only marrying her because she's with child. Then there's the one about her disgracing herself at home—caught *in flagrante* with the local butcher's son, if you please! According to *that* one, they packed her off to London where nobody knows her in hopes she'd land a rich husband. Then there's the one says she's had a child out of wedlock her parents pretend is their own, a boy named Willie. Things like that. And then there's the one claims she's naught but a serving wench let in from the rain by some brainless lackey. According to that one, she knocked DeLacey over the head, dragged him into his bookroom, ripped her bodice, cried 'rape' and summoned the Watch—for all the good *that* would do her. But the Jersey woman didn't start 'em, for all she's been spreading 'em with the determination of a—never mind that, either!"

"Good heavens, what a farrago of nonsense! Willie's nine years old. Elizabeth'd've had to've been only ten when he was born."

"Be that as it may, there's plenty who believe it. And, that scene at the rout's been embroidered to a fare-thee-well. They have her half naked and ravished now, if she's not the one doing the ravishing."

"Ridiculous! Why, Lady Jersey herself saw nothing of the sort occurred."

"But, she'll remember it and tell it just the way she wants. No fun in telling the simple truth, y'know," he returned bitterly. "Truth is dull when compared to the scandalbroth she's been peddling from door to door. Of course, there's one tale does have a scrap of truth to it. Harry's idiot-cousin, Aloysius Beckenham? He's been spreading it about Miss Driscoll lost her virtue on the road to London."

"What?"

"Not the truth at all," Giles protested. "Don't look at me like that! Fact is, the Beckenham runt and Nigel Farquhar and some fat crony of theirs were on a repairing lease. Aloysius tipped 'em into a ditch, and they ended in a hedgerow tavern for dunno how long. Poor Miss Driscoll had the rotten luck to happen on the same place while they were there. Wasn't ravished at all—not that they didn't try. Jug-bitten, the lot of 'em. Chanced on the place myself, as luck would have it, and put a stop to it. Hate to think what might've happened otherwise.

"Gorgon'd thrown a shoe, you see, and it was raining and I needed shelter for the night for the both of us. Place was deserted when I fell asleep, and the next thing I know, there's Nigel and Aloysius and some nameless tub of lard trying to attack the poor girl. Darkened their daylights and sent her on her way. No idea who she was at the time, of course. Looked like a farmgirl, for heaven's sake! DeLacey knows all about it. *She* told him, not knowing it was she I was hunting all along. Twits me about it unmercifully, blast him. Had her right under my nose and didn't even know it."

"But why ever would he twist things so—"

"Didn't like having his daylights darkened, I suppose. Daren't come after me, so he goes after her, the bas— never mind that, but I've a good mind to call him out, *if* I can get him to meet me, that is.

"Then there's the dishonorable Nigel. Knew *him* at Eton, worse luck. A bleater if ever there was one. *He's* been bruiting it about the clubs Miss Driscoll's father is down on his luck. Supposedly lost the family fortune at the gaming tables. *What* gaming tables? The man *never* comes to London, so the story's patently ridiculous, but according to *that* one, the good doctor *sold* Miss Driscoll to the earl for a *chère amie*, and the earl's only just discovered she's of good family and is trying to put the best face possible on the situation. The rest of us're in on the conspiracy."

"So *that's* why you and the earl suddenly appeared on the doorstep."

"Laid Farquhar out, offered him satisfaction—the crawler declined in front of a roomful of witnesses at White's, so he's done for no matter *what* happens next— and then hot-footed it back to Rochedale House. *Something's* got to be done, and *quickly*. First task is to silence 'Silence,' and for that I'm least wanted. After that, we'll see. I just want to know who started it—that's all."

"Nigel Farquhar at White's, you say. Farquhar. I've heard that name before. Does he have a sister?"

"Yes, a pretty little thing, delicate-looking, very lady-like but not missish. Lots of golden curls. Not permitted to waltz yet, unfortunately."

"Wasn't she at Rochedale's rout? Not a word to say for herself? Trots about after a mother who dresses like a guy and stomps like a plowhorse?"

"That's her. Perfect description."

Patsy leaned back against the sofa, smiling smugly. "Look no further," she came close to chuckling. "Lady Daphne's the one to handle this part, I think, and she'll handle it beautifully. Stay out of it. You'd no more be able to rout the unprincipled hussy than you could rout Lady Jersey.''

"Not the little Farquhar chit," he protested in disbelief. "She's a babe barely out of the nursery. Sweetest thing I've ever seen.''

"Only indirectly. No, she's probably as innocent as she looks, but she's a confirmed prattlebox once she's away from her Mama's eagle eye.''

"Well then, who is it, Patsy?"

"Aren't you aware of the one lady among all the ladies of the ton, even if not the very *highest* ton, whom Millicent Farquhar most admires? Whom she copies slavishly whenever possible? Whom she positively *fawns* upon?''

Giles shook his head, frowning. "No," he said.

"For whom she would do *absolutely anything*?''

"Blast it, Patsy, who is it?" Giles growled.

"Guess!" she demanded.

"Good lord, I don't know," Giles protested. "I ain't much in the petticoat line, never have been. How should *I* know?''

"You haven't much imagination, have you, or very well developed powers of observation. Miss Driscoll's over-dressed, self-consequential cousin—*that's* who.''

"Sybilla Wainwright? Fustian! No member of a family'd do such a thing to another. Besides, she's *fast*. A girl can't behave as *she* does 'til after she's married and expect to be made welcome by those who count, but she don't seem to know it, or else she don't care. Got entry almost nowhere," he protested. "Nobody'd believe her.''

Patsy's expression soured as she regarded the young half-pay officer steadily. Slowly his eyes fell.

"Sybilla Wainwright," he said softly, ears red-tinged. "I know she don't care for Miss Driscoll particularly, but—yes, I can see it, now you grind my nose in it. She sets the two of *them* gabble-mongering, and sits back and laughs while they do her dirty work for her. Even Boney's Frogs weren't *that* devious, damn her to hell forever for the hellcat she is.''

"Well, perhaps not *forever*," Patsy protested, "but for a lengthy period of time at the very least. There we *do* agree. Not *all* the stories may be hers, but I'd wager almost anything she's at the bottom of some of them. Who else would know about Willie?''

Patsy almost felt sympathy for Harry Beckenham when she abandoned Giles for the small downstairs drawing room. One swift glance across the exquisite little room told her there was nothing she need say. The earl had done it all. Harry was as immobile as one of the sparkling marble busts adorning the pilastered niches. Still, she had her part to play—for her own sake, if not for Elizabeth's.

Ignoring Harry—an art at which she was becoming experienced—she darted to Richard DeLacey with every appearance of impetuosity, sinking to her knees before him and grasping his hands.

Then, with utmost simplicity and sincerity, she said, "You were a *fool*, my lord. *Why* did you not tell her the truth in the beginning?''

"You, too," he smiled, returning the slight pressure of her hands. "Would you believe the truth frightened me? That I feared she'd draw precisely the conclusion she *has* drawn? A fine irony, that.''

"Enjoy your irony all you wish, my lord. I find myself incapable of appreciating it, given Elizabeth is sobbing her heart out abovestairs. Of all the idiotish—"

"Have done, Miss Worth. My hide's already blistered. Giles waxed rather verbose on the subject. Lady Daphne has taken me to task—earlier, girl, *earlier*, before all this drama occurred—as well as Viscount Wainwright. Rather an eloquent man, when he wishes. As for Rawdon, he's ever had a scathing tongue once he warms to his subject. I'll redeem the error somehow, that I swear."

"You think so? Elizabeth is beyond reason. I wish you luck. You will need it." Then she rose gracefully to her feet, and turned to face the man frozen at DeLacey's side. *"You!"* she spat. "What are *you* still doing here?"

"Waiting to abase myself," Harry ground out.

"See you do it convincingly! If you don't, avoid Marleybourne. I'll see to it you're received nowhere, starting with my father's house. Harry, damn you, you're *impossible.*"

Then, with a swirl of skirts, she was gone.

"That girl loves you more than you deserve," the earl commented quietly after a moment.

"No more than I love her—I've come to understand that, if nothing else, over the last two weeks," Harry sighed, then, at the incredulous look on DeLacey's face, continued. "It crept up on me when my back was turned, I think, or else I've been refusing to recognize it for what it was. Maybe for months. Maybe for years. Hit me between the eyes like Jackson's right the other day."

"Then why in blazes d'you treat the poor thing as if she were your worst enemy? I've considered you a fool for years, but *this* is beyond belief."

"I'm a danger to her," Beckenham returned with a bitter twist to his lips.

"Frightened of parson's mousetrap, by damn," DeLacey snorted. Then he laughed good-humoredly. "I never thought I'd live to see the day when *anything* disconcerted you. But, hiding behind cryptic comments won't save your groats, my friend. Might as well make your peace with her, and turn it into a double ceremony in a couple weeks' time. Both Elizabeth and I'd be delighted, and Elizabeth would be grateful to have some of the attention diverted elsewhere. She and Miss Worth have become almost inseparable. They've much more in common than merely being from the country.''

"Minxes, both of them," Beckenham agreed with a slight sad smile. "No chance of boredom when they're about, I'll grant you that. And, I'll grant you I was a bastard to attempt what I attempted with your little 'angel.' You deserved better of me, even if she didn't. I *will* do my best to repair the damage, that I promise you."

"We've already been over that ground," Richard DeLacey protested uneasily. "No need to belabor the point." He'd said some rather harsh things when Harry finally sat up on Rawdon's library floor, hand gingerly exploring a very sore jaw. Some of them he almost regretted. Life hadn't been all that easy for the embittered Peninsular hero during the past few years. And, like it or not, Harry had believed he was protecting him. "You still haven't explained why you go out of your way to treat Miss Worth to massive doses of calculated incivility."

"Let's just say I consider it the wisest manner in which to proceed."

DeLacey turned slightly, amber eyes regarding his old friend with a combination of disgust, derision, and disdain.

"You'll have to do better than that, or I just might consider involving myself in your affairs with as much lack of principle, though far more commendable motives, as you have in mine."

"Dammit," Beckenham glared, "stay the hell out of matters that don't concern you!"

"Give me a good reason and I might consider it."

"I'm no green stripling just arrived on the town."

"Is that a threat, Harry?"

DeLacey's mock incredulity had precisely the effect he intended. The viscount surged to his feet, stormed about the room, glowering and muttering, only the string of curses intelligible. Then his shoulders sagged as if in defeat. He regained his seat, brows drawn down, gazed confusedly at his old friend.

"Richard, I suspect someone's after my hide," he said simply. "If I were to but smile in her direction, she'd be at risk. So, I daren't."

"What in blazes—"

"I've beaten off three bands of rowdies in the past week," the former major ground out, "each more persistent than the last. But, I've only a single arm. I'm more or less unscathed so far. That won't last, but I'll be *damned* if I'll cower here like some lily-livered park-saunterer, or scurry home to Marleybourne."

"You're serious?"

"I've never been more serious in my life, dammit! Someone's determined to see me planted and sprouting daisies."

"Perhaps you shouldn't go about alone so much," DeLacey suggested, eyes narrowing, "especially at night. You're known for haring off to God knows where solo whenever the mood strikes you. Makes you an easy target."

"I'll not hire some bully-boys to guard me, so don't even suggest it."

"I'm thinking more along the lines of some of Gentleman Jackson's cronies, or a few of the crew at Cribb's."

"No!" Beckenham snarled. No way would he hire a pack of former pugilists to dog his steps. He'd had enough of that once before.

"Tried Bow Street?"

"Nodcocks, all of 'em. No better'n the Watch. Besides, what could I tell 'em? That someone's taken

me in rather pointed dislike? They'd laugh in my face!
Aside from which, I'd sound like a puling idiot. Worst
of it is, I can't think of anyone whom I've antagonized
sufficiently to elicit such a response. I don't make a
habit of baiting cowards, and whoever's behind this,
they're cowards of the worst sort."

"You haven't been flashing the ready, have you?"

Harry snorted in disgust, shook his head. "I didn't
come on the town yesterday, ready prey for every Captain Sharp and ivory-turner on the prowl for fresh pick-
ings."

"Didn't say you had," DeLacey returned calmly, "but
we all make mistakes on occasion. Things like this don't
happen without a reason."

"Certainly there's a reason. Somebody doesn't like
me," Harry bit out, "and given their persistence, either
I hide or I ignore 'em. I choose to ignore 'em as best
I can, but any gamester, even the most amateur, is aware
of the law of averages. The next time, or the one after
that, and I'm done for, though you can rest assured I'll
take some of 'em with me. Even if it's nothing more
than your usual rowdies, I've run my course."

"For pity's sake, don't be such an idiot!"

"If I can't take care of myself, how can I take care of
anyone else?" Harry growled. "If little Patsy believes I
despise her, she'll cry a bit when it's over. A few flowers
on my grave, a few tears, and then she'll look about
her. Some young hunt master'll catch her eye, and she'll
settle down contentedly and produce a gross of children
to keep her occupied. And, I'll watch over her from
wherever I am and wish her well."

"And they call *me* a fool!"

"I'm no fool, Richard," Harry sighed, eyes bleak.
"I'm a pragmatist, just like that old reprobate, Voltaire.
Cogito, ergo sum. That *was* Voltaire, wasn't it? Or was it
Descartes? Doesn't matter. Somebody said it. *I think,*

therefore I am. I've been doing a damnable lot of thinking lately, Richard. I'm on someone's infernal list. So, *cogito.* But I'll be damned if I'll permit Patsy to be injured or worse while I'm cogitating."

"Have you discussed this with Giles or your brother-in-law?"

"What could they do? No, I'd be putting them at risk. Best to leave 'em out of it. I do have my sister to consider, you know, as well as Patsy. And then, there's Aunt Daffy. She's quite taken with our Giles, spent the days after Waterloo in a stew of anxiety until we learned he was safe. Wouldn't do to place either of 'em in danger, and calling for their assistance would do just that."

"You're a maudlin idiot, Harry. I think I liked you better the other way—despising all women and prickly as a hedgehog."

"Sorry about that."

"Sure it isn't just the usual combined with a run of bad luck? One arm," DeLacey said apologetically, "could be a considerable temptation to thieves. You know what cowards most stews toughs are."

"Could be," Harry sighed. "Either way, it doesn't make any difference. I'm not much use to myself, and I'm not much use to anyone else either. I learned that three years ago, and the lesson's been reinforced since. Doesn't show so clearly at Marleybourne, which is why I spend most of my time there, but I'm sick unto death of hiding away in the country. Better to get it over with and be done with it."

Patsy Worth avoided Lady Jersey and the family parlor with all the determination of a young woman who knew precisely where and when she should absent herself.

The powerful Almack's patroness did not approve of her—too *worthy* a country miss, and no antecedents *worth* mentioning, she had proclaimed publicly, laughing shrilly at her own cleverness.

The woman was forced to acknowledge her, of course, thanks to Rawdon and Louisa. She would even provide vouchers for the exclusive Wednesday evening assemblies at Almack's, the *sine qua non* of young girls of the ton on the catch for wealthy titled husbands of impeccable pedigree, should Patsy still be in Town when the time came. There were distinct advantages to being a friend of the Duchess of Rawdon. That didn't alter the fact that the woman would delight in humiliating or cutting Patsy if provided an opportunity. Patsy had no intention of providing it.

Now she sped back up the stairs and to her suite of rooms close by Rawdon and Louisa's apartments. She paused at her door, once more settling thoughts and skirts, then took a peek at Elizabeth.

The girl was still asleep. The more she rested the better, as far as Patsy was concerned. But, with the earl waiting impatiently below and Giles incarcerated in the library, companionless and bored, less was advisable, unfortunately. And then there was poor Harry, champing at the bit to get his embarrassing moment of apology and explanation over with, and Lady Jersey in the family parlor, sharpened claws extended, waiting to torment and rend given the slightest opportunity. So far the gossipy woman had only Sybilla Wainwright's inventions to bandy about. They would be easy enough to disprove. But, if the three men abandoned their retreats and word of the on-again, off-again betrothal leaked out, genuine scandal might be difficult to avoid.

The little whimper, the restless tossing decided her. "Elizabeth," she said softly, shaking the girl's shoulder. "Elizabeth, you're wanted below."

The tear-stained face that turned to gaze into hers would have broken her heart had she not been con-

vinced Lord DeLacey had a silken tongue, and Harry a
determined and guilty one. The sooner this was gotten
over, the better. So, instead of commiserating, she
smiled brightly.

"Time to be up and about, sleepy-head," she caroled
as if the morning's dramas had never occurred. "Your
dress is rumpled, and your eyes're red and your hair's
a mass of tangles, and the earl and Harry are waiting
for you."

"No." Elizabeth rolled over, determinedly turning
her back.

"So—you're a coward? I wouldn't have thought *that*
of you. What would your brothers say?"

"I don't care."

"Very intelligent. What d'you think Lady Daphne'd say?"

"I don't care! I want to go home."

"Well, and so you shall—once you've seen Lord DeLacey and Harry, and listened to what they have to say."

"If they're waiting for me, they'll have a long wait—
until hell freezes over."

"You know, you're not being very fair," Patsy said
with the slightest touch of calculated acid. "You con-
demn your fiancé on Harry's word, and then you won't
give either of them a chance to explain themselves."

Elizabeth's back remained determinedly intransigent.
Patsy shrugged.

"Besides, you're playing directly into your delightful
cousin's hands," she prodded, plunging the dagger a
bit deeper. "Won't *she* be ecstatic when you crawl back
to your aunt and uncle's house with your tail between
your legs! Within two seconds she'll be swooning on
Lord DeLacey's doorstep, a victim of the plague at the
very least. Within three she'll've so compromised him
he'll be forced to marry her or flee to the colonies."

"I'm sure she's welcome to him," Elizabeth mumbled, but her voice was slightly less certain.

"As for your family in Devon, *they'll* be proud as peacocks. Not every country miss gets to throw over an earl."

"They'll understand," Elizabeth protested, rolling over at last. "I *know* they will."

"Will they? Why did they insist you come to London for the Little Season in the first place? Well, *why?*"

"To see the sights."

"Ha!"

"All right—to acquire a husband. I don't think they want me at home anymore. *Nobody* wants me. It's all such a dreadful muddle."

"Now *there's* a foolish statement, if ever I heard one. Is that what they told you, or is it something you invented all on your own?"

"They insisted I come," Elizabeth sniffled, "and Mama made it most clear they were hoping I'd find a husband in London."

"Well, of *course* they were. Marriage *is* considered the happiest and most rewarding life for a woman these days, and the selection here just *has* to be better than in Saint Mary-Grafton. That doesn't mean they don't love you or miss you. They're thinking of *you*, you silly girl! Now, enough of this foolishness. Up you get. You look a positive fright."

Elizabeth sat, her chin set mulishly. "I'm going home," she insisted. "Don't you understand? Lord DeLacey's made a May Game of me. I won't permit that of *anyone.*"

But, Patsy Worth prevailed in the end, perhaps because Elizabeth, with the contrariness of youth, insisted she would not see Richard DeLacey or Harry merely to hear herself cajoled and contradicted. Or perhaps, despite the lost look lurking in her gray-blue eyes, she truly had no desire to ever encounter the earl again, and Patsy genuinely overcame her reluctance. In any event, her face was washed, her hair brushed and coiled, her dress quickly pressed, and she was escorted to the formal little room off the entry by a determined Patsy, her arm in a grip so firm it left marks for hours afterwards.

She was propelled across the threshold. Patsy glared at the two men, then firmly closed the door and turned to the footman dozing in a chair whose sloping seat was intended to keep him awake at his post. The man had tilted the thing on its hind legs to keep from sliding to the floor, and was contentedly snoring.

"Mason," she said softly, then, a bit more loudly, "Mason!"

The chair crashed down, short front legs striking the floor with a smart crack, propelling the delinquent footman to his feet at something close to a stumbling run. Patsy quickly jumped aside, waited for the discomfited man to right himself and straighten his livery. Then, giving him a sweetly innocent smile, she inquired as to whether Lady Jersey were still with the duchess and the dowager countess.

No, she was informed, Lady Jersey had departed some fifteen minutes earlier.

"How did she appear?" Patsy asked, ignoring the fact that the sleepy footman could have no notion of the precise length of time.

The flustered Mason cast his eyes at the ceiling, the walls, the floor—anywhere but at Patsy.

"I'm sure I don't know what you mean, miss," he returned stolidly.

"Of *course* you do, Mason. Did she appear pleased with herself?"

"I'm certain I couldn't say, miss."

"Fiddlesticks! *I'm* certain you could if you wished."

Mason continued to regard her with bland inscrutability. Patsy sighed.

"Oh, very well. What of Lady Connardsleigh and Miss Connardsleigh, then?" She did *not* want to appear on the scene without Elizabeth—the primary purpose of their call had been to meet the bride—but she might have no choice. The trouble was, she couldn't think of a single valid excuse for Elizabeth's continued absence. A torn hem didn't take *this* long to mend. "Are they with her grace?"

"Yes, miss, taking tea, I believe."

"Oh, bother! Is Lord Fortescue still in the library?"

Mason admitted as to how he wasn't certain of *that*, either. Patsy considered indulging in a bit of minor blackmail—sleeping at one's post was cause for dismissal—and discarded the idea. She strode determinedly down the corridor leading to the back of the house, rapped sharply on the library door. Once more Giles warily eased it open.

"All's clear," she dimpled at the concerned look on his face. "We can safely join Louisa and Lady Daphne now, but take heed: Miss Connardsleigh and her mother are still here. They must suspect *nothing* of all this."

"Lady Jersey gone?"

"I'm not certain in what state—Mason was *most* unforthcoming—but she's gone."

"Thank heavens! If I'd had to endure another minute of my own company, I'd've gone mad. Besides, I can count every knob of my backbone—from the front. Nothing to eat since breakfast, and that was hours ago. Think there's a chance Lady Louisa might be prevailed upon to ring for something more sustaining than the usual ratafia biscuits and seed cake?"

"Such as a side of beef and a venison haunch?"

"Well, perhaps a bit of game pie," he suggested hopefully, "or even some cheese and bread if there's nothing more substantial readily available."

"I think she *might* be convinced to take pity on you," Patsy twinkled, "if you ask her very nicely. Shall we go see?"

"How's Miss Driscoll?" he asked, casting an uneasy glance at the closed door as they passed the small downstairs drawing room.

"Melting, if Lord DeLacey's as adroit as I think he is, and Harry as contrite. No, you will *not* go in there and find out for yourself," she yelped, grabbing his arm as he turned toward the ornate door. "You'll wait just like the rest of us, and you won't start blurting out questions the moment they come into the parlor either."

"What d'you take me for?" Giles demanded with considerable pique. "I ain't a babe born this morning."

Behind the closed door, Harry had abased himself until he felt he could sink no lower, but it hadn't done a particle of good. Elizabeth Driscoll, features frozen in an expression of polite disinterest, sat primly erect in the same chair she had selected earlier, as if its stiff formality would give her added courage to refuse to listen to reason. At least Harry suspected that's why she'd chosen it.

"Damnation, Richard," he now protested, turning to his friend, "I don't know what else I can say!"

"Tell her the truth," DeLacey suggested with a tight smile, "the *whole* truth, not just the part you're comfortable with."

"I don't know what you mean. What 'whole truth?'"

DeLacey merely continued to look at him, brows rising. Harry turned toward the door, grumbling imprecations, started for it, stopped, turned back. "Even *you* don't know the whole of it," he muttered.

"Perhaps it's time I did."

Harry shuddered, stalked to the windows overlooking the square, staring blindly into the liquid fall sunshine. There were children playing in the little park, leaping about like a pack of hounds at the end of a successful run. Lord, how simple life was when you were a child! And then, you grew up.

"It's not you personally, Miss Driscoll," he ground out finally. "I wouldn't've wanted Richard to marry *any* female, not if he believed she'd show him one particle of loyalty. Not if he thought he cared for her. That's the quickest, easiest road to hell I know of. As for a petticoat chance-met on a battlefield? That's not a very high recommendation," he explained almost apologetically. "I'd've stopped the betrothal, if I could. Barring that, I *had* to stop the wedding. I was convinced you'd play him false as soon as you had the right to dip your fingers in his purse. You were following a pattern with which I'm all too familiar: wealthy, wounded officer, large family of dependents, and, if not precisely purse-pinched, certainly with shallow pockets."

Then he faced them, shoulders back, feet braced as if he were at attention, eyes focused on a point above their heads.

"In '09," he said tonelessly, "just after the Corunna retreat, I met a young lady. She was the daintiest, most elegant, loveliest, sweetest creature I'd ever seen, my own very special angel. I tumbled into love as only a young fool briefly home from the wars can do. By the time we were to return to the Peninsula, I'd convinced her to marry me. Our betrothal was to remain a secret until I returned permanently. At her father's insistence, I made a will in her favor, leaving her my personal fortune should I fall to the Frogs. Given my angel's willingness to wait for me, it was the least I could do.

"I was wounded at Salamanca in '12, invalided home, sold out. I then presented myself to the young lady, desirous of making our betrothal public and wedding her as soon as might be."

He turned his back on them, pacing the room restlessly, as if to escape from himself and his memories, empty sleeve swinging at his side. Elizabeth glanced at the earl. He shook his head. They waited. When the former major ceased his pacing, he was so close they could have touched him.

"Over the next weeks several attempts were made on my life." He sighed, looked directly at Elizabeth. "The Horse Guards became involved. It would appear her family considered me a form of fortune on the hoof, you see," he explained gently, "as the will still stood, and they were at low tide. And, I had most inconveniently survived. The evidence was there, but I refused to believe it.

"They were apprehended. I pleaded her case everywhere, making a thorough nuisance of myself. When all hope was lost, I begged her to marry me and let me accompany her into exile. My angel informed me she'd never intended to wed me. Only my pockets were of interest, you see—she was brutally frank about that—and marriage wasn't required for access to them. I was physically imperfect, and being perfect herself, she deserved perfection.

"And here you are, a country miss with seven brothers to settle? And Richard, so crippled he can barely get about when the weather's foul, but so very, *very* wealthy. What was I to think? If the sweetest girl in the world couldn't face being married to a maimed relic of the wars, how could you?"

"Lord Beckenham," Elizabeth broke in disjointedly, "I—"

"No—you needn't say a word. Just listen. When I finally accepted my angel was no such thing, I decided *all* women were untrustworthy because of the perfidy of one—a fool's conclusion, of course. You were quite right about that. I still felt the same way when Richard began his search for you. I don't now. This morning I cast aspersions on his motives for marrying you because *you'd* had the temerity to point out I wasn't quite as infallible as I thought myself, or quite as good a friend. I desired to revenge myself upon you, nothing more. And, I was in the habit of attempting to keep you apart.

"If you were foolish enough to believe me then, be wise enough to believe me now: Richard isn't trying to reward your father and he didn't fall in love with you a few days ago. He fell in love with you that night in Belgium and never forgot you. His Angel of La Haye Sainte, he called you. And, his description of you, his analysis of your character, were accurate in the extreme. If you do marry him, he'll be a lucky man."

Harry stood there, looking from the pale, horror-struck Elizabeth to his scowling friend. "I won't attempt to apologize for what I tried to do," he said, "for no apology is adequate. I hope, however, that you'll both find it in your hearts to forgive me."

Then he turned wearily and started for the door.

"Just a moment, Harry!"

DeLacey struggled to his feet, made his way to his friend, bad leg dragging noisily across the floor. He took Harry by the arm, as much for support as to lead him as far from Elizabeth as he could.

"These recent attempts on your life—could there be a connection?" DeLacey asked in low tones.

Harry shook his head. "Impossible. When I said they

were exiled, I meant it. They were transported to Australia. Rawdon receives regular reports on them.''

''When was the last?''

''You're actually serious, aren't you! A week ago, I believe. Ask him.''

''I'll do that. Do me a favor in turn,'' DeLacey prodded. ''Don't go about at night unless Giles or Rawdon are with you. And no more haring off on solitary rides in the country either. Has that will of yours been changed?''

''Damn it, Richard—''

''Please. We old soldiers need to survive so we can bore our grandchildren with tales of how it really was over there, and make sure the same thing never happens again. Too many didn't come home, Harry. We're the lucky ones, for all we aren't what we once were.''

Harry shrugged, gave a half-hearted nod. ''Not a word to Giles or Rawdon about my little problems, mind you,'' he cautioned uneasily. ''No matter what it is, I don't want them involved.''

''Not a word,'' DeLacey agreed.

They turned at the sound of soft footsteps. Elizabeth cocked her head, gazing questioningly from one to the other. Then, apparently satisfied, she slipped her hand in DeLacey's. He gave it a quick, hard squeeze.

''You can be rather eloquent when you choose, Lord Beckenham,'' she told Harry seriously. ''Have you considered taking your seat in parliament?''

''Not my style,'' he said gruffly.

''Consider it then, as the bar is deemed beneath a gentleman—which is a distinct pity. Should I ever be in need of defense, it's you I'd want to plead my case.'' She paused, glancing up first at her betrothed, then at Beckenham. ''You're such a good friend of Richard's,'' she said. ''Would I be totally hoydenish if I requested your permission to call you by name, my lord, and that you employ mine in turn?"

"Not at all."

"Good," she smiled. Then she stood on tiptoe, placed a feather-light kiss on the startled Beckenham's scarred cheek. "I think I'm going to like you a great deal, Harry," she whispered huskily. "A very great deal indeed. You *will* stand up for us when the time comes? And *sincerely* wish us joy?"

"If you will permit me the honor."

"It's yours. Just make an attempt to be a bit civil to poor Miss Worth, will you? She's done nothing to earn your dislike, and I should hate to see the pair of you coming to blows at the wedding breakfast. A hail of bride's cake would be most distressing to the other guests."

Then she turned to DeLacey. "Richard, I'm so *sorry*," she quavered. "I should've known better than to lose faith in you."

"So long as you never do it again," he said, pulling her into his arms.

Harry Beckenham slipped quietly from the room, closing the door behind him, accepted his hat and swordstick from the hovering Mason and went out into the sunny afternoon. He couldn't face anyone at that moment—not even himself.

Eleven

The Earl of Rochedale had just returned to his little bookroom after seeing Colonel Jason Ventriss of the Horse Guards to the head of the rotunda stairs.

He'd sunk into his chair, slapped his cane in its rack, and propped his throbbing leg on the padded stool he'd finally permitted Elizabeth to convince him might ease the ache when it rained, as on this bitter fall afternoon two days prior to the formal betrothal party he dreaded. He'd poured a liberal dollop of brandy in the glass at his elbow, downed it half from need, half from a sense of celebration.

He had only agreed not to discuss the matter of Harry's little troubles with Rawdon or Giles, after all—not Ventriss. So, the letter of his word had been kept, if not in the spirit Harry intended.

And a most fruitful discussion it had proved.

When pressed, the Horse Guards colonel grudgingly mentioned a ring of former troopers preying on maimed veterans as the possible culprits. The matter was being kept quiet for fear of terrifying the public while tarring the innocent with the same brush as the guilty. Destitute discharged troopers had enough problems without that. So far, none of the ring had been caught or even identified. With Beckenham as a possible known target, that might change.

A floating paddock, Ventriss called it, an invention of which he appeared particularly proud: a group of ordinary-appearing London types indistinguishable from the real thing, often because they *were* the real thing. They'd surround Harry, assuming different roles and disguises, prepared for anything. Harry, for the time at least, would be safe. If there was one thing Richard DeLacey wasn't about to permit, call him selfish if you will, it was being summoned from his honeymoon to attend Harry Beckenham's funeral.

Of course Ventriss had given it as his opinion that the matter was merely a series of unconnected happenstances, with the former major placing himself in harm's way with the pertinacity of the suicidal or the oblivious, and then drawing overly dramatic conclusions. That would have been his song no matter what his private thoughts. But, he *had* been disturbed. Of that DeLacey was convinced. And, at the news that apparently Harry's will had never been redrawn, his brows had soared.

Ventriss *was* going to take action, at least for a time, and see what eventuated. That was the essential.

The earl stretched out, nestling deeper into the comfortable, worn leather chair, the slightest of smiles playing around his lips.

And then of course there was little Miss Worth to consider, and Elizabeth's probable reaction should she ever learn the truth concerning the embattled pair and Harry's feelings for the girl. A Harry six feet beneath his Marleybourne estate would be no use in pleading his case then. How he'd justify calmly acceding to Harry's dictates in such a situation he had no idea—let alone how he'd justify it to himself.

No, what he'd just done might not be strictly

according to the codes of honor and gentlemanly behavior, but it had been eminently sensible. After all, there was no way he, crippled as he was, could tend to the matter directly. And if Harry'd given it a single moment's consideration, he'd've spotted the enormous chink in DeLacey's promise and understood precisely what he intended.

The earl had just decided once and for all that the slight twinge of guilt he felt—surely a phantom school-boy reaction to a schoolboy's code—was totally inappropriate to the circumstances. That was when the pounding came at the door of the main entry one floor below.

It wasn't a polite knock.

It wasn't even a determined summons.

It was a furious, ungoverned, demanding assault that echoed through the halls and up the stairs like a pronouncement of doom.

"What the devil?" DeLacey muttered, attempting to rise.

Then he sank back in disgust. The blasted leg was impossible. How he'd get through the betrothal party, let alone the wedding two weeks after that, he had no idea. Irritably he jerked at the tasseled bell-pull dangling beside his chair.

Suddenly the pounding ceased. Thank the Lord for small mercies—*someone* had seen fit to open the door. He jerked the rope again. From below rose a jumble of voices. The door to the bookroom burst open. A sturdy boy of about nine years stormed across the floor, skidded to a stop, glowering at the earl.

"I *demand* satisfaction," he piped, flinging a much-mended glove in DeLacey's face, "so *there!*"

"Hello, Willie," the earl returned with a relieved grin. "I'm delighted to meet you, too."

"How d'you know my name?"

"Because your sister's told me all about you. Frogs in the vicar's parlor, indeed! You and Stevie are a pair of hell-born babes if ever there were one," DeLacey chuckled, his tone taking any sting from his words. "How'd you find me?"

"Simple—the door was closed and there was a light under it."

"Aha! So the next time I wish to hide myself, I should leave the door open?"

"Wouldn't hurt. If a door's open, no one wonders what's inside. I learned that *years* ago. Why're you marrying Lizbeth?" Willie Driscoll demanded, getting down to essentials as rapidly as possible.

"Because I love her, and I can't live without her."

"Oh, yes, you could!"

"Well, I shouldn't *like* it," DeLacey explained. "That's much the same thing, when you're as old as I am."

Willie cocked his head in a gesture very familiar to the earl.

"Will you let her climb trees?" he demanded.

"If she wants to."

"Even if you can't?" the boy asked with a jaundiced glance at the earl's leg propped on its stool and the cane resting in the rack at the chair's side.

"What has that to say to anything?"

"And go fishing? Lizbeth's the best fisherman of any of us. It wouldn't be *fair* if you didn't let her."

"I fish occasionally myself," DeLacey smiled. "That's something I *can* do, at least from the bank, if I've a stool to sit on."

"Oh. But, Lizbeth's a *girl*," Willie objected doubtfully. "Our vicar says she hadn't ought to fish. *He* says it isn't *proper.*"

"I doubt *my* vicar'd object. His wife's an excellent fisherwoman."

From below came more sounds of heated debate,

the stentorian tones of DeLacey's very superior butler, Morton, rising above the others. Banks poked his head through the bookroom door.

"You be needing something, Colonel?" he asked.

"Sort out that *mêlée* downstairs, put Morton in his place if necessary, and see my future father-in-law and brothers up, if you will," DeLacey instructed with a grin. "We've been invaded, but the attacking force is *not* to be repulsed, Sergeant. It's to be accorded full military courtesies. A very friendly force, you understand—or soon to be one. Then we'll be needing lemonade, and biscuits of some sort, and—?"

The earl glanced inquiringly at Willie.

"Apples, and cheese and bread, and anything that's left over from breakfast and lunch and last night's dinner," Willie suggested. "None of that sticky sweet stuff girls like. *Real* food! We haven't eaten *forever,* and we're *hungry*—even Papa. We've been traveling like the wind. Had to, to get here so fast, but Papa was in a taking. So were the rest of us."

"You have your orders," DeLacey grinned at the twinkling former batman. "*Real* food, Banks. See to it."

"Please hurry," Willie called after the retreating sergeant. "I could eat a whole larder-full all by myself." He turned back to DeLacey. "You *really* an earl?"

"I'm afraid so."

"What's wrong with your leg?"

"It was injured—at Waterloo," DeLacey appended. Then, because more seemed required, "A gun carriage fell on it."

"Oh, I'm sorry," the boy said simply. "Does it hurt?"

"Sometimes."

"Papa says old wounds hurt when it rains. Does it hurt now?"

"A bit," DeLacey admitted.

"Lizbeth won't mind, you know," Willie told him

proudly, "about the cane or anything. She understands about things like that. *She* was at Waterloo, too."

"Yes, I know," DeLacey smiled. "It was she and your brother Jeremy who found me, and your Papa who saved my life."

"And your leg?"

"Yes, and my leg as well."

"So, you're *almost* a member of the family already?"

"Almost," DeLacey agreed, "so long as you don't mind."

"Oh, I don't mind, and Robert'll be glad 'cause he says you're like Horatio or those two Frenchies down in Spain back when the French weren't our enemies—leastways, I don't *think* they were—and Jeremy wants to know how to tie his neckcloth better, and I *suppose* you c'n teach him that, so *he'll* be glad, too. It's just that—"

There was the head again, cocking to the side, and the serious, considering look. DeLacey waited. Nothing came. That, given his experience, was unusual.

"Well, it's just that *what,*" he prompted.

"Well, Billa wrote Papa a letter, you see."

"Yes?"

"And she said you *had* to marry Lizbeth 'cause she tore her dress, but that you didn't like her at all. 'Course Billa's a *drefful* liar, and most times if she says something you c'n count on it's being just the opposite, but *Billa* said you *ruined* Lizbeth, and that *Lizbeth* trapped *you* into doing it. It sounds to me like the only thing got ruined was Lizbeth's dress. Why d'you have to marry Lizbeth just 'cause she tore her dress? I keep asking and *asking*, and *no one'll* 'xplain it to me."

"Willie!"

DeLacey's head spun toward the agonized bleat from the doorway. Good Lord—that had to be Jeremy. The collar points were even worse than Elizabeth had described, and the quizzing glass and fobs belonged at the bottom of the ocean. As for the neckcloth—well, only a schoolboy with delusions would dare call it a neckcloth. His work was cut out for him. Just behind the would-be dandy hovered a boy with brown hair on end, a look of awe on his candid features.

"Hello, Jeremy," DeLacey grinned, "Robert. Come on in and join us." Then, at the sight of the robust, gray-haired gentleman just beyond them flanked by two more boys, one who had to be Andrew, the other his constant shadow, Steven, Banks on their heels, he struggled to his feet. "Lord Driscoll," he said, limping painfully to the door, hand extended, cane forgotten. He wavered and the two older boys leapt to catch his arms and force him erect. "Must run in the family, this rescuing business," DeLacey muttered, flushing bitterly. Of all the times for the damned leg to give out on him!

Then he gently pulled his right arm from Robert's grasp, held his hand out again.

"I owe you everything, sir," he said, eyes looking directly into the stunned doctor's, "from my life to every hope of happiness for the rest of it. Come in please, and have a seat. I'm honored to have you in my home."

"I *told* you Billa lied!" Willie shouted triumphantly. "He's nice as he can stare, and he *is* an earl, and you saved him at Waterloo, and he *hasn't* made a May Game of Lizbeth! It's all just nasty old Billa making things up again. Banks, please *hurry*. We're starving, all of us, even if the others won't say so."

The confusion produced by the unanticipated arrival of Elizabeth's father and brothers was quickly sorted out—especially with a former officer and his batman setting their minds to the problem.

DeLacey's preference would have been to have the Driscolls stop with him.

He found the irrepressible Willie and the scholarly Robert a pure delight. Then there was the need to see to Jeremy's sartorial solecisms. Those three were the easiest to sort out from the troop, but young Steven and the older Andrew, an excellent country squire in the making if DeLacey had ever seen one, showed high promise of proving equally diverting. Certainly proposed excursions to the trout stream at Lacey Hall come summer left the lads with shining eyes. When Scotland and the possibility of seeking out salmon was hinted at, they metamorphosed from vocal enthusiasm to silent ecstasy. Lonely as a youth, always regretting he had no brothers or sisters, DeLacey suspected he would enjoy his sudden immersion into the boisterous life of his betrothed's family with all the enthusiasm of a schoolboy set free for the long vacation.

As for Baron Hawls, or Lord Driscoll, or however he preferred to style himself, the resemblance to both Lord and Lady Wainwright was clear. Not in looks, of course. Driscoll was tall and muscular, with the powerful physique of a man who spent most of his spare time in country pursuits and had to scramble to keep the pace of seven active sons. Wainwright, by contrast, was the typical London resident, sedentary except for the occasional stroll through Hyde Park, or the rare country weekend when he might throw a leg over the saddle if the day were particularly fine. The warmth and lack of pretension, however, were identical. DeLacey quickly came to the conclusion that he was not only fortunate in his betrothed. He was infinitely fortunate in her family.

To have them remain at Rochedale House, however, was impossible. Lady Lavinia, alerted by the officious Morton, made that clear within moments of their arrival, sweeping into the study uninvited, peering with disdain at the country doctor and the five sons who had accompanied him to London as her thin brows soared.

"Why are you receiving a sweep and his climbing boys, Richard?" she inquired sweetly, ignoring the fact that even Willie was too large to scramble through chimneys, and that there wasn't a speck of soot about them. "The dirty, smelly creatures will foul the entire house. Send them to the kitchens where they belong."

Then, without waiting for introductions or explanations, she swept from the room leaving a leaden silence behind her.

While DeLacey would have packed her off to Kent without a moment's compunction, that was no solution to the problem. Lady Daphne insisted the dowager countess must be present for both betrothal celebration and nuptials to carry the thing off with any hope of success. Little as he liked it, he knew she was right.

"My grandmother, the dowager countess," he muttered by way of explanation and apology, mortified beyond any mortification he would have dreamed possible. "A rather myopic old lady, on occasion. Please pardon her."

Willie cocked his head, looking from the closed door to the earl.

"Don't feel bad," the boy said with an innocent candor that made the earl want to offer him anything in the world his heart might desire, and his father and brothers to strangle him. "We got Billa. You got her. Doesn't mean we got to like 'em. We just got to live *around* 'em."

Then fortunately Banks arrived bearing a heavy tray and the agonizing moment was over.

DeLacey didn't bother to offer his own home as their base of operations. Instead, he scribbled a note and signaled Banks—the only messenger he trusted in the infernal barn of a place—in the confusion. After a low-voiced conference, Banks nodded and quietly slipped from the room.

Once creature needs had been seen to and some general discussion indulged in, Elizabeth's father requested private conversation with the earl. As he said, while Sybilla Wainwright's letter might not have been accurate as to details, or even as to the general sweep of events and the motivations of those caught up in them, there were a few things he wanted clear in his own mind before seeing his daughter.

Mindful of Wainwright's comments concerning the closeness of the family, and that he wanted every member of it, with the exception of Wainwright's daughter, to feel as if they'd known and trusted him their entire lives, DeLacey shook his head.

"Anything you wish to know, I will tell you, of course," he said, "but Elizabeth's brothers may have questions of their own as well. There is nothing you can ask me, sir, which you cannot ask me in front of them, and which I cannot answer in front of them. Elizabeth has told me of what she calls your family conferences. I suggest we be private among the seven of us, rather than as only two."

Driscoll's brows rose as a smile of approval broke on his face.

What followed was confused, often noisy, occasionally punctuated by brief uncomfortable silences. Questions flew at the earl from every corner, and if some were not precisely impertinent, they were at the very least distinctly pointed. Refreshingly—so far as DeLacey was concerned, accustomed as he was to the manner in which marriages were arranged among the ton, where finances rather than character and suitability was the great issue—not a one concerned his estates, his wealth, or any settlements he might be prepared to make. Still, there were moments when he wished he were facing Wellington rather than his future father-in-law and brothers.

Somehow Harry's role and the briefly broken betrothal came to light, greeted by furious scowls and Willie's stated intention to call the nasty man out.

The tale of Elizabeth's ruined dress, and precisely how and when that dress had come to be torn, left DeLacey with scorched ears and a fear all five boys intended to meet *him* on the field of honor.

The night in Brabant was examined until DeLacey realized he was remembering things even he had forgotten. Strangely, the boys accepted the reality of his having fallen in love with Elizabeth in those few pain-wracked moments as totally logical. Only the good doctor raised his brows and sighed.

The subsequent search for Elizabeth, with every league of Giles's travels recounted, called forth hearty laughter—a welcome relief given the seriousness of the rest. As Robert said, "You can't find Saint Mary-Grafton unless you know it exists and just where it is, and *then* sometimes you can't find it. If he'd come upon us, he'd've been so lost you'd *never've* seen him again."

His grandmother's objections to the alliance between the families were reviewed in excruciating detail, her point of view given not a little support by Driscoll as the boys squirmed silently, overcome with disgust that *anyone* would have the temerity to consider their Elizabeth "not good enough."

Dreading every word, DeLacey volunteered information regarding the campaign of lies being spread among the ton by the Farquhars, Aloysius Beckenham, and Lady Jersey and her cronies. One source had been identified and silenced, he said, refusing to name the guilty party, but there were others. It was all spite. ("Bet it was Billa," Willie muttered into the distressed silence.)

All would come right, the earl assured them, but there might be some rough spots at first. Indeed, there already had been. He wanted the doctor and his sons at least aware of the problem. Then, if faced with it, they would know how to proceed.

In the end all were satisfied.

The Duke of Rawdon and his lady descended in person close on the end of the extended family conference to overcome all objections and sweep the mildly protesting country doctor and his sons off to Grosvenor Square. Hotels, Louisa Debenham insisted, were nowhere near so comfortable as private homes. And, Rawdon tossed in with a grin at the five boys, nowhere near so suited to active young men, nor half so convenient for midnight raidings of the larder.

The earl leaned back in his chair with an exhausted sigh once they had departed, and closed his eyes. Life would never be dull or predictable again. Not in London. Not at Lacey Hall. Not anywhere. On balance, it was a wonderful prospect.

That evening proved DeLacey's assumptions correct. A family dinner at Rawdon House, followed by the rambunctious hilarity of parlor games, had left him more convinced than ever that he was not only the happiest, but the most fortunate of men.

"Two weeks and a day," he smiled down at Elizabeth after easing her away from the others, arm around her shoulders, as they waited for their carriages to be brought round. "Then, my sweet, no more of this incessant socializing, at least for a bit—that I swear. Did I tell you that you were particularly beautiful this evening? Like a glowing fire."

Not that this informal evening had been distasteful, DeLacey grudgingly admitted to himself, except for the total impossibility of having Elizabeth to himself. Far from it, if for no other reason than the delight she took in her family's arrival, and the news of her new sister's advent. Convinced no one could be watching amidst the scurrying for cloaks and the animated conversations, he planted a quick kiss on her upswept curls.

"Amelia Caroline," he whispered. "Who'd've thought it!"

"Mush!" a voice piped behind them.

"Oh, Lord!" DeLacey muttered. "Miniature dragons!"

"Willie—wherever did you pop up from?" Elizabeth gasped, flushing.

"Right behind you," the boy grinned, slipping around to confront them, thumbs hooked in the pockets of his diminutive waistcoat. "Is kissing Lizbeth something you like to do," he asked the earl, cocking his head, "or is it something you *must* do?"

"Willie!" Elizabeth protested, blushing even more furiously.

"Both," the earl grinned, winking at Willie. "They expect it, you see, once they're betrothed."

"Guess I'll never get married then," Willie muttered, wandering off in disgust to join Lord Fortescue and Lord Beckenham. *"Girls!"*

DeLacey smiled down at his betrothed, tilted her chin after first sweeping the entry with his eyes to make sure all her brothers were occupied, and deposited a second kiss on the tip of her nose.

"With him about, and if the others were the same, one wonders how there came to be so many of you," he whispered. "There are times when I feel those five pairs of eyes drilling me like bullets. Your father's not half so intimidating."

"At least they haven't mentioned, well, you know, what happened the night of our wager," Elizabeth whispered back.

"Your torn rags? Oh, yes, they have—this afternoon, right after they arrived. First order of business: Why, if a lady tears her gown, she must marry."

"They know about that?" Elizabeth gulped, blushing even more furiously.

DeLacey broke into a delighted roar of laughter. "Well," he choked, "it's only fair. After all, I know about the frogs in the vicar's parlor and Jeremy's attic dressing room and pot-metal quizzing glass. You'll notice they're perfect gentlemen, though. Not a one of 'em taxed you with it, not even Willie."

"Can't you be serious?"

"Around your family, my dear, it's most difficult," he protested, eyes smiling down at her, then scowled as Bartlet came bustling up to collect her charge, velvet evening cloak carefully draped over her arm. "We never seem to manage two minutes together without someone interrupting," he grumbled. "Once I get you to Lacey Hall, I'm going to lock the gates and throw away the key."

"Will you provide tents for the boys to sleep in by the high road come spring?" she grinned. "They're counting on the trout stream, you know."

"And Robert wants access to the library," DeLacey sighed as he took her cloak from Bartlet, propping his cane against a chair. "At least they'll all be in school for a bit, and as we'll be joining them for Christmas rather than their joining us, there'll be a temporary peaceful hiatus. Too late for the trout stream this year."

He settled the cloak around her shoulders and tied its ribbons snugly, if not stylishly, beneath her chin, hands lingering on her shoulders.

"Two weeks," he repeated, his heart in his eyes, "and one day."

She nodded, lips trembling, then slipped from his gentle grasp and swept a graceful curtsy. "Until tomorrow, my lord," she whispered, not quite daring to meet his eyes.

"And tomorrow, instead of the Park, we'll go by Rundle and Bridge's," he assured her, retrieving her hand and tucking it in his arm, then picking up his cane, "whether the weather's fair or foul. Amelia Caroline deserves the most beautiful porringer and mug we can find. And a coral for teething. And a silver frame for a miniature of her to grace your mother's dressing table. And then we'll stop by a toy shop, see about a rocking horse and some rag dolls and an elephant and—"

"Richard," Elizabeth protested, "you'll spoil her!"

"I intend to," he smiled into her eyes, "just as I intend to spoil you if you'll ever let me. Besides, soon I'll have an Amelia Caroline—or two or three or four—of my own, and I must learn how to go about it properly. Little girls are very special."

"What, no boys, Richard? No heir?"

"Eventually," he grinned, "but I'm *much* more interested in a diminutive Elizabeth than a diminutive Jeremy at the moment, or even a diminutive Willie. One of each of them is quite enough."

"You don't like the boys?" she inquired with a troubled frown. "I'd never've guessed it, you're so patient and open with them."

"I love them dearly, and that's on the basis of almost no acquaintance at all. They're positively wonderful, every last one of 'em, and I'm sure I'll like Charles and John every bit as much, and Amelia Caroline and your mother as well. There's no way I couldn't, and with Amelia we'll be on even footing, at least. It's just that it's you I adore, and I'm much more interested in having little facsimiles of my wonderful wife prattling at my knee than little facsimiles of myself, at least for a bit."

"You speak of the most improper things so openly," she blushed once more.

"Our children are *not* improper. I'll have you know ʸhey're the very souls of propriety, even if they haven't been born yet, or even—Well," he broke off hastily as Robert strode up, "their mother'll make 'em toe the mark, my love, just you wait and see. She's had lots of experience. Why, she'll probably even ride roughshod over *me*. Life under the cat's paw—that's what I'm doomed to. Not spoil Amelia Caroline? The very idea!"

"Certainly a delightful family," Rawdon commented to his wife as they prepared for bed after dismissing valet and dresser. "D'you think those lads are what Marcus will become in another few years?"

"With so many to choose from," Lady Louisa chuckled, "one or another of them must surely be close to the mark. Which do you favor?"

"Oh, Willie," he laughed. "Willie, without question, unless it might be Robert. A fine mind there. Jeremy reminds me too much of myself at the same age. But then, if I wanted to go fishing Stevie would be indispensable, and if I required information on the latest in farming techniques it would have to be Andrew. Perhaps we need a few more sons so that whatever I desire in the way of companionship will be ready to hand."

"I'm *so* glad we remained at home, and had Richard and Elizabeth join us," his wife grinned in response. "I haven't played at lottery tickets in eons!"

"Even Harry unbent a bit at the end," Rawdon chuckled. "The Driscolls are quite a breath of fresh air in our rather stilted London world. How d'you think this will all sort itself out? You've heard of yesterday's near-disaster, I suppose?"

"From Giles. From Patsy. From my dresser, who came running with the tale of Giles planting Harry a facer, as well as Miss Driscoll's tears in Patsy's sitting room. A pin cannot drop in this house without half the servants hearing it, and the other half hearing *of* it! Even from Harry," Louisa sighed from her dressing table. "A most contrite Harry. Only the principals have not come running to me begging advice. To tell you the truth, I've no idea. If only they could be left to themselves, there would be nothing to fear, but one never is, is one? I suspect we may be treated to more fireworks, and we may not be entirely happy with the resolution, whatever it may prove."

"At least the child has her family to support her, now."

"I dread the betrothal party," Louisa shuddered.

"Oh? I would've thought *that*, at least, was well in hand," Rawdon commented with raised brows from the window of the capacious dressing room they shared.

A man loitered against the fence surrounding the square's private gardens, hat pulled low, collar pulled high. Rawdon didn't like it. He didn't like it one bit more than he'd liked the persistent flower seller he'd spotted making her rounds earlier, or the drayer who'd spent an inordinate time gathering his spilled turnips and cabbages and potatoes after a minor mishap. With an impatient tug he closed the heavy velvet draperies, and turned back to his wife.

"Lady Daphne placed the arrangements in your capable hands when Richard's grandmother proved uncooperative, and I happen to know just how capable those hands are," he concluded as he unwound his neckcloth, then tossed it aside, still scowling.

"I've done what has been permitted," Louisa protested, unfastening the pearls at her ears, then loosening her thick mane of golden curls from the pins that held them upswept. "It's just not very much *has* been permitted."

"How so?"

"Oh, the invitations are sent, and the responses are arriving in droves—all acceptances, which would be *most* gratifying were it not so worrisome."

Rawdon glanced at his wife of three years and chuckled. Louisa, when she wished, could say things that weren't just puzzling. They were downright self-contradictory. It meant he often had to listen with extreme care. Otherwise he tended to discover while he *thought* he'd agreed to one thing, he'd *actually* agreed to something else entirely. The discrepancy could be rather disconcerting.

He walked over to her dressing table, unfastened the heavy rope of pearls at her neck, slid them in the velvet pouch lying before her, then seized her hands, trapping them in his own and pulling her around to face him.

"Louisa," he said with infinite patience and not a little humor, "I have yet to hear of an entertainment where the hostess—and that is what you are in this instance, as there is no other to take on the role—is desirous of her invitations being *refused.*"

She smiled at him, sea-green eyes sparkling as she realized what she had just said. Then her smile faded as a minute pucker appeared between her brows.

"It's not that, precisely, James," she explained as he sat on the wide bench beside her, "but I attempted to call on Lady Lavinia this morning to discuss my arrangements with Gunter's and the flower sellers and wine merchant. And yesterday, and the day before that. Lady Lavinia was never at home to me. Neither, if you'll credit it, was the housekeeper. And it's *there* the rout is to be held, for pity's sake. They *need* to know what's to be. I've no idea what the dowager countess is about, but you may be certain it's nothing pleasant. You may also be certain it's nothing to her credit. She's taken poor Miss Driscoll in determined dislike, you see.

"And then, there've been too *many* acceptances. It's

unnatural. The only refusals have been from those who must be invited for courtesy's sake, but never go anywhere—people like Edmund Brassthwaite and his wife."

"You've warned Richard?"

"There was no need. He arrived just as I was being refused the door this morning. I thought he'd dismiss the butler on the spot. Indeed, I rather wish he had. The man is insufferably insolent, and totally fearless with it."

"Have you consulted your aunt?" he inquired after a moment's thought. "She and the dowager countess've been bosom bows for more generations than I can number."

"She's tried calling, as well. 'Lady Lavinia is indisposed' is all any of us hears since the night of that dreadful rout. If Harry is impossible, I don't know *what* to call *her*. They were actually spreading straw before the place as I left this afternoon. If *something* doesn't give way, I fear disaster.

"And, it's not just Lady DeLacey. Patsy tells me Elizabeth has been cut, or as close to it as makes no difference, each time the earl has taken her for a drive in the Park. I observed much the same thing the two evenings I chaperoned the girls. And then there was Sally Jersey today, implying all sorts of filth, and with her ears flapping as rapidly as her tongue and twice as avidly.

"And why aren't the Driscolls staying at Rochedale House? Not that I mind having them stop here, for I don't, and we've plenty of room, but so does Richard. It makes no sense, no sense at all—that great barn of a place with all those bedchambers going begging, and Miss Driscoll *his* fiancée, and he daren't ask her family to stay because of his grandmother! If things continue in this manner, I have serious doubts of there ever *being* a wedding. The old besom will prevent it somehow, and little Miss Driscoll and Richard will *both* be broken-hearted, and there'll be nothing any of us can do to rectify matters. Why Aunt Daphne is so fond of the woman I'll *never* understand."

"Habit, perhaps. Lady DeLacey and your aunt are part of each other's youth. That means a great deal once one reaches a certain age. They'll sort it out somehow," Rawdon consoled her. "Richard's a very determined man when he wishes. How d'you think matters are progressing between Patsy and your brother?" he asked in an attempt to put the uneasy topic behind them. "Any hope there?"

Louisa chuckled, and shook her head, instantly diverted. "Harry's silent around her now, rather than insulting. That's progress, I suppose. And he watches her when he thinks he's unobserved, and with *such* a look in his eyes—as if he were gazing into his own grave. Truthfully, I understand neither of them any better than I understand the fortitude and patience Richard shows his grandmother. We've always joked about Aunt Daphne's little schemes, but *she* has never attempted to make our lives more difficult. Quite the opposite," she dimpled at him.

Before retiring for the night, Rawdon extinguished the candles in the dressing room as was his custom. Then, uncharacteristically, he ushered his wife into their bedchamber, telling her he would join her in a bit. Then he closed the door on her and strode to the large double windows at the front of the house, eased the draperies slightly apart, peering into the night.

The Watch had just passed, calling the hour and assuring those in the stately houses lining the square that all was well in this city of London in the fall of 1816. Rawdon wasn't so certain.

The loiterer had decamped, but at the far end of the roadway fronting his residence a hackney lingered. It might have been the weather that caused the jarvey to pull his hat down and his collar up, but the rain had ceased and there was no wind. Besides, what business had a hackney at that hour in that place?

The duke ignored the sodden beau—a Corinthian, given his shorn locks, hatless and with cloak flung back from his shoulders—who staggered from railing to railing, warbling tearfully of love eternally lost. Such sights and sounds were all too common.

With a grunt of disgust Rawdon dropped the drapery in place and went to join his wife. In the morning, besides seeing to the entertainment of his unexpected guests, there were a few calls he intended to pay, starting with Jason Ventriss of the Horse Guards.

Twelve

The last of the straw was gone from the courtyard and drive of Rochedale House.

The hatchment, brought down from the attics by a furtive Thatcher, had never been mounted over the door. "Well, *someone* is forever dying among our connections, and I meant to honor them," Lady Lavinia protested when Richard, alerted by the repulsive Banks, descended on her rooms in a fury the day before. "Indeed, as I am feeling so unwell myself, I thought it best to see if it required refurbishment in case of sudden need."

Richard had been so pettish and unreasonable as to destroy the thing.

Then he had been so uncivil as to demand she behave herself—As if *anything* the Dowager Countess of Rochedale might do could be out of the way!—and stalked from the room snarling that if she did not have a care she would find herself *not* at the Dower House in Kent, but in the hold of a ship bound for the Antipodes. Lady Lavinia had smiled sweetly, in no way deterred. There was more than one fletch to her arrow, and more than one arrow to her quiver.

Now, on this morning of the day preceding the rout intended to celebrate the Earl of Rochedale's betrothal, she dressed with care in a gown of utmost elegance and simplicity. The high ruched collar hid the crêped depredations of age. The silken skirts swept in shimmering ebony folds from the slightly raised waist, banded in black velvet and touched by sparkling jet— not quite in the modern style, not quite in the ancient, but rather a compendium of the two, lending Lady Lavinia a timeless dignity that was totally idiosyncratic and intrinsically overpowering.

She contemplated herself with satisfaction in the tall pier glass set in the corner of her dressing chamber. Black was so delightfully intimidating. And, so eminently practical, for—as she had informed her grandson— *someone* among the extended Rochedale connections *was* forever dying.

"I'll do, don't you think?"

"You'll more than do, my lady." Thatcher twitched a fold, settled a hem. "You are perfection itself. The rubies?"

"I think not," the dowager countess decided after a moment's consideration. *"That* point has already been made. The betrothal ring, if you will retrieve it? And the smaller emerald tiara. It has something of the look of a crown."

Thatcher passed into her mistress's sitting room, and went to the larger of the ornate ebony chairs flanking the fireplace. With infinite care she released the left jeweled eye from the dragon's head forming part of the back, slipped a piece of chipped green glass in its place. Then, with a sigh of self-congratulation—the unde-tected hiding place was her suggestion—Thatcher returned to her mistress.

Moments later Lady Lavinia swept down the marble staircase to the great domed receiving area, past a gawking Banks, and into the cavernous state drawing room, followed by the complacent Thatcher. Banks watched, eyes narrowing, then peeped through the closing door. His eyes widened. He stood silently for a moment, frowning, then turned and rapidly mounted the stairs to the east wing, either ignored or unnoticed by Lady Lavinia.

A double brace of muscular footmen in gray and silver livery awaited her in uneasy discomfort. Meticulously powdered wigs framed features that were at once hard and sly. Heavy shoulders strained at the seams of ornate frogged coats. Priceless silver lace frothed over chests more accustomed to coarse woolen shirts and leather jerkins. Broad feet in tight pumps shifted in a delicate dance to relieve severely pinched toes.

"*She* will be arriving in a matter of minutes," Thatcher cautioned, eyes flicking over the carefully designed setting to make certain everything was in place.

The opposing marble-faced fireplaces were devoid of fire, the draperies left drawn. A stand of thick candles flickered in the gloom where an oaken chair in the Roman style stood on a small platform. A Persian carpet in the intricate *mille fleures* design, its jeweled tones glowing like an ancient tapestry, hid the scuffed surface. The delicate Queen Anne table beside the chair held a decanter of Spanish sherry, a single Waterford glass, and a dish of ratafia biscuits. The rest of the furnishings had been pushed against the walls.

They had discussed how this scene was to be played, she and the dowager countess, delving into tomes pilfered from the library to ferret out the trappings of medieval majesty. Trumpets and heralds had been out of the question. So was a sea of courtiers. Understated though they considered their creation, it did contain the essential elements. The great chasm between country upstart and titled lady would be noted.

"You and you," the dowager countess commanded, "there and there," pointing to positions flanking the farther fireplace where the footmen would be little more than menacing hulks. "While *she* is here you will not so much as breathe—unless I signal you to seize and gag her. That is only a last resort, remember." They had rehearsed it five times. If the men got it wrong, they were even greater dolts than she thought. "You and you, by the door," she instructed the other pair with a regal wave. "When Morton scratches you will open to him. When I dismiss the chit you will *not* open for her, but you *will* permit her to pass. Beyond that, you will do absolutely nothing."

Then, ignoring them, Lady Lavinia posed herself in the chair, the great Rochedale betrothal emerald flashing balefully in the meager light, the delicate emerald tiara twinkling like a coronet among her silver curls. Thatcher stooped to arrange the train they had added only that morning, sending it to flow across the dais to the floor below.

The awaited scratch came. Lady Lavinia nodded. The pair of footmen at the far end of the room grasped the gleaming handles, jerked the doors open, one yelping as the door's edge caught his aching instep. Morton stood framed in the entrance, padded chest thrown impressively forward, padded shoulders drawn impressively back, padded calves unfortunately slipping. Elizabeth peeked around him and stifled a giggle.

What was the old lady intending *this* time? She'd only caught a glimpse of this room when the housekeeper conducted her on a tour that amounted to little more than a lower servant's introduction to her duties two days before. Then it had been bright, sunny, rather cheerful despite its overstated formality. Now it was dark as a tomb and twice as chill, resembling nothing so much as a quickly contrived stage setting for the amateur production of some horrific melodrama complete with clanking chains, howling ghosts and leering villain.

"The Driscoll person, your ladyship," Morton intoned, bowing.

Lady DeLacey signaled Elizabeth to approach. With a resigned sigh, the girl marched forward. Behind her the doors crashed shut.

"Good morning, Lady DeLacey," she said brightly.

Whatever the old besom intended, it wouldn't work. She might be reluctant to engage the dowager countess in endless skirmishes, but neither would she be forever saying aye-and-amen to whatever the woman placed in her dish. Besides, since Papa and the boys arrived, she was no longer alone. It was a reassuring thought.

"I hope I find you recovered from you recent indispositions," the girl now said politely, dipping a perfect curtsy.

Lady Lavinia's hand sprang up.

"That is quite far enough, Driscoll," she said.

Elizabeth halted. "You wished me to call?"

"We summoned you into our presence," Lady Lavinia corrected tartly. "There is a considerable difference. One does not *invite* the lower orders."

"Well, ma'am, I've answered your *summons*. What may I do for you, other than suggest the curtains be opened? Such darkness is *not* good for the eyesight."

"Insufferable chit," hissed Thatcher. "Kneel to your betters!"

"I think not," Elizabeth returned pleasantly, "for I see none here who *are* my betters. Now, as my calling on you at this early hour has caused considerable inconvenience to Lord and Lady Wainwright, and Papa and the boys await me at the Duke of Rawdon's, could you please tell me the reason for my visit?"

"It won't do," Lady Lavinia almost spat, sending the girl a scathing look.

"What won't do? This darkness? I quite agree. If you would be so kind as to open the draperies," Elizabeth said, turning to the footmen by the door, "Lady DeLacey and I would be—"

"Silence!" Lady Lavinia roared, then glanced about her in consternation, as if uncertain it was indeed she who had spoken in such an uncouth manner. "You are above yourself, hussy," she continued with more moderation, if no less venom, attempting to bring the interview back to where she intended it should be. "We have summoned you in order to convince you of your folly in attempting to entrap our grandson. You *shall not* succeed, you know. Your sort never does in the end."

She flirted with her ring-burdened hand, watching narrowly to see if the girl noticed it. Then, "Wine, Thatcher," she snapped. Truly, the chit was *most* uncooperative. A good thing she had planned for such a contingency.

"Thank you for your hospitable offer," Elizabeth smiled demurely, "but I do not customarily indulge in spirituous refreshments at this early hour—or, indeed, at any hour, except under exceptional circumstances. Tea would be delightful, however, if you would be so kind? And, if you would request that a chair be found for me, I would appreciate that also. I suspect there are some about, and I feel rather like a stake planted to scare away the crows, standing here like this."

Thatcher made a great show of pouring the sherry, of standing so the little rustic could see there was but a single glass, and that one *not* intended for her. Lady Lavinia made a great show of glancing about the room in boredom, of yawning and covering her mouth so the famous betrothal emerald of the Rochedales was displayed to perfection. Thatcher almost sank to her knees to present the glass of sherry to her ladyship.

Elizabeth held her peace, observing the little panto-mime with the first stirrings of irritation. The charade pained her *not* because she didn't understand it, but because she understood it too well.

How in heaven's name was she supposed to share a roof with this old woman? She couldn't be constantly running to Richard. Old habits of deference would always outweigh the new. He might take her part, at least at first, but he wouldn't be pleased about it, and *she* would be blamed for not keeping the peace. The business about a man forsaking his parents and cleaving only to his wife was all fine and well, but it didn't work that way. Look at John. At least they all loved Clarissa dearly for his sake as well as her own. Where there was active dislike and resentment? And she would be living under Lady Lavinia's nose! Live under her thumb she would not.

Lady Lavinia continued to ignore Elizabeth's presence.

She daintily sipped the wine, commenting on its superior bouquet.

She daintily nibbled at a biscuit, commenting on its superior richness.

She yawned delicately once more, and commented unfavorably upon the inferior manners of vulgar country rustics, then commented favorably upon the superiority of a certain Lady Serena Duchesne, daughter of a duke, whom she intended to introduce to her grandson's notice the next evening.

Elizabeth's unease gave way to disgust. She shrugged.

"Enjoy your sherry, my lady," she said, spun upon her heel and started for the doors.

"Stop!" The dowager countess's voice was not loud

this time, but it carried well, generations, as she was fond of saying, of dowager countesses at her back. "You have *not* been granted permission to withdraw."

Slowly Elizabeth turned.

"You know, Lady DeLacey," she commented from just within the doors, "I find London customs *fascinating.* In Saint Mary-Grafton it would be considered the height of ill-breeding to invite a person into one's home, then ignore her while taking refreshments and carrying on a conversation with another intended to wound one's guest. Of course, we rustics have not the advantage of such high-born ladies as yourself to show us how to go on. Is it any wonder country girls are considered ill-mannered once we quit our native villages? Let me see if I correctly comprehend polite behavior among the ton. First, one must be insulting as possible. Second, one must—"

"Silence!"

It was the roar again. Lady Lavinia blushed. *No one* had *ever* caused her to raise her voice before, not even Wharton at his worst. Truly, the chit was totally lacking in proper feeling. Skin like a rhinoceros. That, or the setting they had contrived was not so perfect as they thought. Why, it was almost as if the little rustic were in charge of the encounter—and *laughing* at *her* in addition, which was intolerable.

Lady Lavinia indulged in a rapid mental review of the jewels at her disposal, the carriages, the country houses, the estates major and minor, the neat little house on Laura Place in Bath where she repaired to recruit her forces at the end of each Season. She catalogued plate, paintings, china services, wine cellars, crystal, wardrobe, and bibelots. The exercise had the desired calming effect.

"I have summoned you here to speak with you concerning your family," she continued with sudden sweetness, setting her sherry aside. "You have, I believe, seven brothers?"

"Yes, I do," Elizabeth responded, startled by the seeming inconsistency in Lady Lavinia's manner. "John and Charles and Robert and—"

"I am totally uninterested in their names," Lady Lavinia snapped. "Their mere existence within a single family is an affront to the sensibilities of any lady of refinement."

"Is *that* what you are?" Then, quickly, before her ladyship could interrupt, "I am afraid I find it impossible to apologize for their presence on this earth, Lady DeLacey, no matter how greatly your sensibilities may be affected."

"Curb your impertinent tongue, girl!" Then, with menacing softness, she said, "You *are* moderately fond of them, I suppose?"

"Extremely fond."

"The eldest, I believe, has established a practice of medicine in Shropshire. And, is but recently wed? And, his wife expects a child?"

"Your information is astonishingly accurate."

"Noble patrons would be of great use to such an individual, I should think."

"They would indeed."

"And, contrarily, a word dropped here and there by those same noble patrons might cause him a certain degree of embarrassment, wouldn't you say? Even eventuate in his finding himself penniless upon the high road, child and wife trudging at his heels? Rochedale," Lady Lavinia continued with almost placid indifference, convinced she was now in control, "has a *sizable* estate in Shropshire. Should it become known that the sister of the sawbones peddling his services in the vicinity had the temerity to attempt to entrap—well, you do take my meaning, do you not?"

"Quite clearly, your ladyship," Elizabeth seethed.

"And Devonshire," Lady Lavinia continued, watching Elizabeth closely from the corner of her eye. "I have a considerable acquaintance in Devonshire, as well. A not unpleasant place, if one wishes to rusticate. And then, there is Cambridge. The Rochedale name is not unknown to the dons of Cambridge, nor to the masters of Winchester."

The words hung in the air, totally innocuous, totally damning.

She smiled in satisfaction as the girl's posture stiffened. She understood. Oh, she understood! Such a lovely notion it had been. And, so successful! A good thing the little adventuress had no idea she had never seen Shropshire or Devon, had no acquaintance there. And Richard had attended Harrow and Oxford, not Winchester and Cambridge.

"Consider my words carefully," Lady Lavinia resumed almost genially. "My influence is extensive. On the other hand, if you inform the earl that you have mistaken your feelings, I might find it in my heart to mention this eldest brother of yours quite favorably to my Shropshire acquaintance."

"Why, you dreadful old—"

"*As well* as your father in Devonshire to my acquaintance *there*, again most favorably. Or, possibly otherwise. My course would depend upon yours. *Naturally* I would recompense you for the time you have wasted in London. An hundred pounds, shall we say, and the wardrobe you have acquired? Perhaps an extra bonnet or two. Bonnets are *so* useful when one desires to captivate a gentleman. Oh, and that ridiculous copy of the Rochedale betrothal ring. It is really valueless, you know, being a mere *simulacrum*. The stones are *quite* inferior, but you should be able to sell it and add another few pounds to the hundred I offer."

"You are all kindness, Lady DeLacey."

"So I have always been told. I am willing to defray the expenses of your journey home, and send an abigail to accompany you as well. Your father's expenses, and those of your brothers, are naturally their own."

"Naturally," Elizabeth choked out.

"Once in your own country, you should have no trouble snaring some bucolic squire's sprig and regulating your situation," Lady Lavinia continued in a tone that was almost conciliatory. "I doubt the scandalous stories about you circulating in Town will reach so far, though even *that* is possible if you prove unreasonable. However, I am convinced you shall not. So much is at stake, you understand—for both of us. A cheerful country squire would be much more in keeping with your station and interests. Local assemblies, parish concerns, the occasional tea at a neighboring great house when the family are in residence and feeling of a particularly democratic turn—much more pleasant for you, believe me."

"I believe *you* may believe what you say, my lady. That does not necessarily render your opinions valid."

"Oh, they are valid. You will *never* be accepted here, for *I* will never acknowledge you. Only misery and mortification await you unless you heed them."

"I had not heard you had been elevated to the throne, my lady. Perhaps your sponsorship is not so essential as you imagine," Elizabeth broke in, horrified at her own rudeness, but driven beyond what she could bear.

"The sponsorship of the Dowager Countess of Rochedale? Not essential? You misguided little adventuress," Lady Lavinia spat with a combination of contempt and disgust. "He may wed and bed you, but without *my* nod you will bring Rochedale nothing but humiliation. Acquire some wisdom and look to your family's interests."

"There is no need. You are most generous, Lady

DeLacey, but I fear I must decline any assistance to my father and brothers.''

"Don't be a fool, girl! At least this way you would depart with something to show for your efforts.''

"I hardly think so.''

"Oh, you shall! Because—*believe me in this*—depart you will, and as unwed as you arrived.''

Lady DeLacey raised her hand. The footmen flanking the far fireplace started forward, shoulders bunching. From without came sounds of violent altercation. The doors crashed open.

The Earl of Rochedale stood there, flushed and disheveled, the heavy stubble of a dark beard gracing his jaw, a brocaded banyan hastily thrown over his nightshirt and pantaloons, his cane gripped in his white-knuckled hand. Banks bulked behind him, an anxiously hovering Morton wringing his hands just beyond. More than calves had now slipped. Chest was at mid-belly. Shoulders sagged dispiritedly. Absent wig revealed a bald pate and thinning gray fringe.

"Richard!" Elizabeth breathed. "Thank heavens! Where *have* you been?''

"Asleep, my love. My leg was troubling me, and I took an over-large dose of laudanum last night. Banks had the devil's own time rousing me. Must be gallons of coffee about me, inside or out.''

He held out his free arm. With a whimper Elizabeth took refuge there, bonnet crushed against his chest.

"No more of this foolishness, darling—I promise you that," he whispered. "She's over-reached herself this time. Bear up now, there's my angel. Only a little bit more to be gotten through, and we're home free.''

Then, with slow and awesome deliberateness, the earl raised his head and turned to his grandmother.

"In what sort of charade are you indulging yourself this morning, Grandmama?" he inquired mildly, then jerked his head at Banks. "Open the draperies," he snapped. "Let in some air and douse those candles. They look like they belong in some demented monk's cell. Who'd you acquire them from, Grandmama? Some ecclesiastical purveyor? Or, was it a hungry curate?"

Lady Lavinia watched in horror as her carefully constructed setting shrank to a tawdry and rather pathetic attempt to impress. Why, the *mille fleures* carpet didn't even cover the dais. Never had she so badly miscalculated—*never*—not even when she agreed to wed Wharton. And the miserable train was coming loose from its hasty basting, and there was a crumb stuck in her throat.

The earl surveyed the room as Banks extinguished the last of the candles. Damn! Four footmen, and he didn't recognize a one. The two easing their way toward the pair by the door didn't even appear to have proper livery.

Then he took a second look.

"What the devil?" he muttered. Then it was all he could do to keep from laughing, at least at first. "Who in blazes are these brutes?" he shot at his grandmother.

"Part of your staff," she coughed.

"They are? You're certain? I'm amazed! The bread lines must be shrinking, for they look like they belong in Seven Dials," he said, referring to one of the viler London slums. Then he spun on them, all the Earls of Rochedale forgotten, military commander springing to the fore. "Get the hell out of my house!" he barked. "Every last one of you! You were promised remuneration?"

"Old mort said a Yellow Boy each, yer wership, oncet 'er's put on t'coach good 'n' proper," the least disreputable mumbled, jerking a clean (if broken-nailed) thumb at the shrinking Elizabeth, "be the little tart willin' er not. An' these 'ere togs ter sell."

"A shilling each, Banks," DeLacey snapped, "to

encourage them from the premises, and burn the livery." He turned back to the four toughs, now gathered in an uneasy clump by the door. "If I *ever* see your ugly faces near my home," he said with a quiet menace more intimidating than any roar could have been, "or in the vicinity of this young lady, I shall call in Bow Street. I'm positive they'd find you of interest."

"We was h'only ter be 'er *h'escort*," the talkative one protested. *"H'onerst,* yer wership!"

"Get 'em out, Banks," DeLacey spat. "Now!" Then his head dipped to Elizabeth, arm tightening around her shoulders. "You're all right, sweet? They didn't touch you?"

"No," she whispered, "I'm fine, now you're here."

"What has my blasted grandmother been up to this time? The truth, now. I've endured her games all my life. I'll know the difference."

She gave a delicate shudder, thinking of the "escort" she might have had were Banks not so persistent in his guarding of Richard's interests. Then, with the memory of countless hours spent instructing small boys in the art of the fly rod—far more useful a reminder than bibelots or estates—she gave herself a quick shake and pulled away from the earl, settled her sadly crushed bonnet more precisely, and smiled. Perhaps, just perhaps there was a way to handle this damnable situation, turn it to her advantage, gain the dowager countess's respect and gratitude at least, and make all come right.

"Why, we were merely having a pleasant cose," she protested. "You *did* know I was to call this morning, Richard—I *know* you did. Everything was quite as it should be between a prospective grandmama-in-law and granddaughter-in-law."

"Was it, indeed!" he snorted.

"We merely discussed family matters," she insisted innocently, raising guileless eyes to his, "and how Lady

DeLacey might be of assistance to Papa and my brothers. And, naturally, to me. The draperies were drawn because poor Lady DeLacey suffers from the headache, but did not wish to disappoint me by canceling our visit. As for the rather unusual footmen, they were newly hired. Lady DeLacey has been terrified by reports of a resurgence of the Mohocks. She hired one pair for her protection, the other for mine. *Such* a kind gesture."

"And tonight I shall dance the jig at Almack's," her fiancé retorted, "out of season and garbed as a Sepoy. It won't fadge, my dear. I've never known you to speak in such *clipped* phrases. Barely one breath would get one through 'em. Who d'you think my parents were, a pair of cabbages? I want the truth, which I can guess only too easily."

"We were merely conversing, Richard." She laid a restraining hand on the threadbare sleeve of his old banyan. "Lady DeLacey had just offered to be of assistance to my father and brothers by means of her acquaintance in Devon and Shropshire."

"My grandmother *has* no acquaintance there."

"Those who spend the Season in Town often pass the period between Seasons elsewhere," Elizabeth asserted with a certainty she did not feel. "Ask Thatcher, if you don't believe me. Truly—that's all of which we spoke that's of interest to anyone."

"Thatcher will say anything Grandmama tells her to. I hope you haven't descended to the same state of awe-struck servility?"

"Hardly," Elizabeth twinkled. "You know me better than that, I think, my lord?" she inquired with deliberate provocation.

"Richard, my love, *Richard*," he protested with a sharp glance. "How many times must I tell you? My name is *Richard*."

"Richard," she acquiesced, smiling winsomely. "And now, have you broken your fast? Neither Lady DeLacey nor I have done so. I'm convinced that's why she suffers from the headache, and *I* am *famished*. Do you think we might perhaps repair to a cozier spot and indulge ourselves in gammon and kidneys and muffins and chocolate and—"

"Good Lord, girl! D'you intend to eat me out of house and home before we're even wed?"

"If I don't, I shall *perish* of starvation. You don't want that, do you? Richard," she said with utmost seriousness, "I'm utterly *gut-foundered*. An' if you refuse to feed me in the next instant, I shall go into a decline, or faint, or do something equally repulsive and missish. Banks," she said, turning to the just-returned batman, "could you procure his lordship a neckcloth and coat? There's no sense in his climbing all the way up to his chambers, and then all the way down again."

"Sir?" Banks shot inquiringly at his employer.

"Go ahead, Banks," DeLacey said with an exaggerated sigh. "See how I'm already under the cat's paw? What a life she'll lead the pair of us! Set out whatever is needed to make me presentable. I'll meet you in upstairs in a moment."

"Indeed you will *not*, Richard. Bring what is needed to the bookroom, Banks," Elizabeth countermanded. "That will do for the moment, but is there not some suitable room on this level that might be converted to your use, Richard? Why no one has ever thought to make things more convenient for you I shall *never* understand."

"I'm not often in Town, sweet. It never seemed worth the bother."

"*That* will change," Elizabeth said firmly throwing a challenging glance at Lady DeLacey, "no matter how rare your visits. The bookroom, Banks. Wait for him there, Richard. Your grandmama and I shall join you for breakfast presently.''

Elizabeth waited until the doors had closed behind her future husband. Then she turned to the old lady still posed in the Roman chair.

''Well,'' she said, ''do we cry peace? Or, is it to be Donnybrook Fair between us, with Richard the greatest sufferer? The choice is yours.''

''You believe your officious interference has humbled me?'' Lady Lavinia snorted. ''Think again, girl! My offer stands. Consider it carefully.''

''Donnybrook, then,'' Elizabeth said softly. ''I have seven brothers who have taught me to fight cleanly and fairly. I wonder if the same can be said of you, my lady?''

She swept a curtsy as graceful as it was unexpected, and was gone.

''Lady Jersey,'' Thatcher suggested. ''A word in her ear should turn the trick.''

Lady DeLacey nodded, eyes narrowing. ''I'll send her a note. That interfering little rustic *shall not* usurp my position. Serena Duchesne it must be. If getting an heir requires a sturdy farmgirl with broad hips on one side and the Duchesne woman wearing pillows for nine months on the other, it won't be the first time it's been done.''

Thirteen

All was confusion at the Wainwright residence on Portman Square on this afternoon hours before the great betrothal party in honor of the Earl of Rochedale and his intended bride. Great-Aunt Delphinia Witherspoon of the cheese-paring ways and hundreds of cats had just pulled up, dilapidated coach bucking like a North Sea scow, team of job horses snorting through foam-flecked nostrils. Outriders clogged the road, their heavy armament giving them the air of Spanish banditos. Gawking crossing sweeps pointed and laughed, their ribald comments fortunately incomprehensible to the emaciated old lady and her equally emaciated companion as they descended to the cobbled pavement and glared about them.

A baggage wagon piled high with everything from bed and chairs and dressing table to sheets, bed hangings, twelve baskets of favored felines and numerous trunks and bundles, lumbered into view at the far end of the square. A strolling dandy paused to observe the show, quizzing glass rising to penciled brow, smirk ornamenting supercilious features, walking stick at the precise angle from which to discourage stray dogs and impertinent children.

Both ladies were garbed in rusty black, their coal-scuttle bonnets limp, their travel cloaks whipping about their ankles in the stiff breeze. Shawls and reticules and walking sticks and parcels and umbrellas depended from shoulders and arms and wrists and hands like so many oddly shaped chandeliers. Above them patchy clouds scudded across a sky of such a sharp blue one would have thought it an unusually fine winter day. Crisp brown leaves eddied across the pavement in dancing whorls like children at a harvest festival. Tree branches snapped and bent with a singing sound. There was a distinct bite to the air, a hint of the coming descent into the tag end of the year.

Miss Delphinia Witherspoon, spinster, sniffed. She scowled. She viewed Portman Square and the small brick town house tucked between a pair of more substantial residences with utmost distaste.

"Damnable place!" she snapped. "Unhealthy. Dirty. Ugly. *Pheh!* Always knew t'would be. Didn't need to see it t'know that. Billings," to her companion, "fetch someone!" Then, as the poor woman struggled to divest herself of the shawls and scarves tangled in her skirts, "Go knock, devil take you, Billings," poking her in the shoulders with a walking stick she had somehow freed from the rest of her impedimenta. "Bloody, bleeding place. Bad as I expected. Worse! Doesn't anyone answer doors in this monkey's-arse city? Deaf and blind, the lot of 'em. Well, what're *you* starin' at?" to the smirking dandy, shaking her stick. "Never seen a female before? Demmed man-milliner!"

The dandy tried contempt, found hers by far the greater, and scuttled down the pavement. From the drawing room window, Viscount Wainwright gazed down and blanched.

"Oh, Lord deliver us," he muttered, and made for the stairs and his wife's chambers at as close to a dead run as he could manage. *"Mehitabelle,"* he whimpered, crashing through the door and nearly knocking Bartlet off her feet, *"she's here!"*

"That's nice," Lady Wainwright murmured absently as she reviewed the guest list one last time. "Tea, perhaps. And biscuits. It's incredible, Woodruff: not one refusal. Even Mrs. Drummond-Burrell has accepted. Thank heavens Lady Cheltenham suggested the celebrations be conducted at Rochedale's mansion, for otherwise—"

"Mehitabelle! It's Great-Aunt Witherspoon!"

"How lovely." And then, with a sudden horrified flinch as her head snapped up, *"Whom* did you say?"

Viscount Wainwright stared back at his wife, as close to tears as a grown man is permitted to come, the picture of abject terror.

"But, that's impossible," she protested. "Surely you're mistaken. She *never* leaves Staffordshire. That was the basis on which I accepted your proposals, my dear. *You* assured me the old harridan would never descend upon us, and *I* agreed to wed you."

"She's here," he said with all the simplicity of a hangman inquiring as to whether the rope were comfortably adjusted. "On the stoop. In fact, she's probably in the entry by now, God help us."

From below, uncounted cats yowled counterpoint to an elderly crackling voice, each demanding instant attention to needs specified and unspecified. The lower tones of Cochrane at first flowed like a soothing river beneath the chaos. Then the dam was breached, and the flood crashed upon them.

"But, how?" Lady Mehitabelle pleaded over the rumpus. "And why *now*? Oh, Woodruff, whatever shall we *do*? There's only the one guest chamber. We *can't* fob her off, and we *can't* put Elizabeth with Sybilla, and we *can't* put Great-Aunt Witherspoon in the attics as we did

Elizabeth and the boys after Waterloo. And, what of this evening? I realize she's only the most *distant* sort of connection to Samuel and the children, but I suppose we *must* offer her the opportunity to attend the festivities." Then the true horror of the situation descended upon the poor lady. *"How long will she stay?"*

"How should *I* know?" Lord Wainwright quavered. "She's never gone *anywhere* before. Not *ever.*"

From below came a sudden roar. *"Woodruff! Meribelle! Attend me on the instant!"*

Just down the corridor, Sybilla Wainwright smiled with immense satisfaction. She disordered her curls, scrubbed every trace of rouge from her cheeks and dusted them with finest rice powder. Then she opened the tiny pot of scraped onion she had purloined from the kitchens earlier that day. She inhaled deeply, shuddered, choked, then dipped a finger in the liquid mass and dabbed it beneath her eyes.

Almost blinded, tears streaming down her face, she bolted from her room, sped past the open door to her parents' apartments and down the stairs.

"Dearest Aunt Witherspoon," she sobbed, tears almost genuine the pain from the onion fumes was so great, throwing herself to her knees before what she assumed to be her father's elderly relation. *"Oh, thank heavens you've come to set things to rights!"*

"Miss Wainwright!" Cochrane protested in horrified accents, setting aside the muddle of scarves and shawls heaped in his arms, "do permit me to assist you."

It was at precisely this inauspicious moment, with Sybilla kneeling before the family butler, a pair of footmen struggling to carry an ancient oversized wooden trunk up the undersized stairs, two grooms staggering under disassembled parts belonging to a bed of royal proportions, Lord Wainwright cowering at his wife's door and twenty-four cats scrambling up and over and down draperies and curtains, that Lady Daphne Cheltenham and Elizabeth Driscoll entered the little house, laden with parcels containing the last minute essentials to complete Elizabeth's toilette of the evening.

The cats, with concerted howls, gave chase up the stairs, tearing past Wainwright and down the short hall. Sybilla "swooned." Miss Pugh appeared at the top of the stairs, brandishing an umbrella and shrieking that the house was being overrun by wild animals. The footmen with the trunk wavered as the umbrella seemed about to poke out their eyes, lost their grip, and trunk and footmen crashed into grooms and bed pieces. The trunk split open, spewing coverlets, shifts, stays, petticoats, pillows, medicaments, and a sack of withered apples across the landing and down the stairs.

"Demmed arse-heads!" roared the salty Miss Witherspoon. "I was bloody-well *born* in that bed, and I bloody-well intend to *die* in it! What're your brains made of, chicken dung? I'll skewer your privates for breakfast if you've put a dent on it, an' I'll hack 'em off first—with a rusty blade!"

"Great-Aunt Delphinia," Wainwright bleated, scuttling to the landing where he became inextricably entangled in pillows, apples, and coverlets, "welcome to London."

"Horse-piss!" the old woman retorted. "Y'ain't glad t'see me, so don't pretend y'are. *You,*" to Cochrane, "I'll have the best room. If that's *his,*" indicating the viscount, "move him out. Put 'im in the attics.

"Now, what's this nonsense about some vicar's byblow snaffling Sybilla's intended? *And* the younger by a pair o' years. Never heard o' such a thing! Eldest *always* marries first. Rack 'er up an' give me a dirk, an' I'll show you justice, I will! Pair o' tit-suckin' milk-sops—that's what you an' that Mayflower of yours are. Can't even see to your own gel's welfare."

Above, Lady Wainwright pulled the covers over her head, moaned, and did her very best to faint as Lord Wainwright beat a hasty retreat to the top of the stairs.

Lady Daphne, accustomed to taking charge in the worst as well as the best of circumstances, for once in her life found herself at *point-non-plus*. With a resigned sigh she retreated to a safe corner from which to observe the chaos and thank her guardian angel she neither had now, nor ever *had* had, a Great-Aunt Witherspoon.

Elizabeth, her identity revealed, found her shoulders painfully assaulted with a walking stick as hordes of cats reappeared, streaking down the stairs, skittering across the highly polished hall floor, attacking arms and necks, biting toes and fingers and ears. Human howls joined feline.

Sybilla remained picturesquely collapsed, peeping at the disaster through her lashes with a slight smug smile until she realized no one was paying her the least mind. Incensed, she moaned in full voice. Great-Aunt Witherspoon turned her attentions and her stick upon Sybilla, prodding her sharply about the ribs and posterior while thundering she wasn't about to save the groats of any devil's dung so missish as to playact at fainting. Imogene Pugh tore past Lord Wainwright and descended the stairs in awkward leaps, hissing in her turn that no old harridan was going to assault her dear, poor, injured Miss Sybilla. With furled umbrella *en forte*, she engaged the enemy, parrying the walking stick with agility if not grace and form, and scoring not a few hits. Billings cheered on the one she must, and privately prayed for the success of the other.

At a harassed wave from Cochrane, footmen and grooms scrambled about trying to play least in sight, avoid the fracas, and whisk the detritus of trunk and bed abovestairs. Through all this Viscount Wainwright remained petrified, eyes staring from their sockets, heart pounding. But, at the sudden crashes that told of his *own* bed being disassembled and the sight of his *own* bed hangings and favorite chair being unceremoniously carted toward the attic stairs, he gave a wordless roar.

Startled heads spun. Disbelieving eyes flew upward. Beneath her coverlets, Lady Wainwright quaked and quivered and wondered if it were possible to summon a constable even if the unwanted intruder were one's very own husband's great-aunt.

Wainwright straightened his cravat and his shoulders, commanded his heart to return where it belonged, and descended in the sudden silence. A man could be pushed *too far*—even a peace-loving man such as he.

"Miss Pugh, please go to Lady Wainwright and assure her that all is in hand. I shall join her shortly," he commanded in his new tone. "Cochrane, have Miss Witherspoon and her companion shown into the drawing room, and procure them refreshment." Then he turned and, essaying his new tone yet again, called up the stairs, "Hawks, Winters! Leave my bedchamber be! *And*, every *other* room in this house! Take Miss Witherspoon's furnishings to the attics. Leave her personal effects in the corridor for the moment. After that, we'll see.

"How come you and Miss Billings to be here?" he continued, turning back to his great-aunt.

"Well! A fine welcome *this* is, you ape-faced monkey-bait!"

"You've not answered my question."

Sybilla eased behind Miss Pugh, settling her skirts and patting her curls.

"Yer gel wrote me," Miss Witherspoon roared. "Told me a fine tale, she did, 'bout how you permitted that hoor's get," pointing at Elizabeth, who had retreated to a safer location next to Lady Daphne, "t'nab her intended. Came t'sort things out."

"The only sorting out needed here," Lord Wain-wright retorted, "is a sorting out of my daughter. She invited you?"

"Invited, *ha!* Didn't need to. Read her letter—more curlicues to it than Fat Old Harry had doxies—an' packed m'trunks. If I'd waited for my vinegar-faced, mule-arsed sod of a nephew to invite me, I'd've been waiting 'til his balls shriveled. And I don't want tea," she shouted after Cochrane's retreating back as a footman attempted to bow her toward the drawing room. "Dog-piss, that's all it is. Rots the tubes. Get me a bottle o' port. The good stuff mind you—not the swill m'nephew serves to guests."

And then somehow the entry was disencumbered of all save Lord Wainwright, Elizabeth, Lady Daphne, and Sybilla. It seemed *very* empty.

"If you will pardon me, ladies," he said to the former with a tight smile, "this won't take but a moment. Sybilla, the library. Now!"

"I must see to Great-Aunt Witherspoon," she protested, turning to mount the pair of steps to the drawing room.

"Think again, my dear. I suggest you join me immediately," her father countered, "unless you wish to depart for Staffordshire in the morning with Great-Aunt Witherspoon."

"Oh, now Papa," Sybilla pouted, gliding back to her father and patting his cheek. "You *know* you don't mean that. Banish your darling Sybilla? Come now!"

She dimpled. She fluttered her lashes. She glanced about her as if abashed, swaying her skirts. She glanced at her father, and knew a moment's uncertainty.

"Why, Papa dearest, there's *nothing* you can have to say to *me,*" she protested, fluttering hand flying to palpitating bosom. "*None* of this is *my* responsibility. T'wasn't

I insisted Cousin Elizabeth come to Town for the Little Season. T'wasn't *I* insisted she attend the Rochedale rout, and ruin us all. Mama *knew* of my interest in his lordship, and *still* she persisted. If you must affix blame, affix it where it belongs—upon your own shoulders and hers.''

Lord Wainwright folded his arms, staring at his daughter from what felt like an enormous height.

"Given that I was receiving no support whatsoever from those whose *duty* it was to see to my welfare, what was I to do, dearest Papa," she begged tremulously, a tear glistening in her eye. She laid her head on his shoulder, glancing up at him through moist lashes. Drat! The usual ploys didn't seem to be having the least effect. "You and sweetest Mama had cast me aside. You had *abandoned* me. You had left me without recourse! You cannot *imagine* my lonely hours of anguish.

"Besides, *someone* must see to dear Great-Aunt Witherspoon's comfort," she added with a toss of her curls at total variance with her winsomely cajoling manner of moments before, starting once more for the drawing room. "As you and Mama have more important matters demanding your attention, *I* shall—"

She was halted in mid-sentence and mid-stride by her father's hand on her arm. He said nothing further, merely escorted her firmly toward his library.

"Well!" Lady Daphne sighed, *"That* was an interesting few moments. My dear, I suggest you stop with *me* for the rest of your time in London. No-no," she smiled, as Elizabeth opened her mouth to protest the imposition, "your aunt and uncle have enough on their plates already, and while I know Louisa would dearly love to have you, she and Rawdon have as much as they can handle between Miss Worth and Harry Beckenham. And then there are your dear brothers and father. Thank heavens Richard saw fit to suggest they visit the Royal Menagerie today under Giles's escort. Rather the inventive commander, Richard, when he so desires.

"Besides, I've wanted you with me from the beginning, but couldn't see how to manage it without giving offense to your aunt and uncle. *This* way, I shall appear to be doing everyone a kindness, while the only one I'm doing it for is myself."

In less than an hour Elizabeth's belongings had been packed and transported to Lady Daphne's elegant little townhouse, her presence swept clean from the equally Lilliputian but far less elegant Wainwright home.

Lady Wainwright's tears when her niece kissed her a fond and grateful good-bye-and-thank-you-see-you-this-evening were quite genuine. So was her uncle's warm hug and insistence that she would always be welcome in their home—always! Sybilla, by contrast, was notable for her absence, just as on the day of Elizabeth's arrival. That young lady had barricaded herself in the drawing room with Great-Aunt Witherspoon. The two were in low-voiced conference concerning how best to remedy such an untenable situation as a country nobody acquiring a title while a diamond of the ton languished unaffianced and—worse yet—currently unsought.

Not that Miss Delphinia Witherspoon considered marriage a state to be desired by a woman of intelligence. Far from it! Men were sods—every last one of 'em. Dirty, filthy things, untrustworthy devil's spawn that they were. But, if marriage was what Sybilla wanted, marriage was what she'd have. And, if the Earl of Rochedale were her chosen partner in that degrading exercise, then Rochedale would be hers. The ends were not in question—only the means to achieve them.

Miss Pugh, discovering a kindred spirit in the abused

Billings, scurried her off to her nook of an attic bed-room, there to partake of lukewarm tea—so much bet-ter for the digestion than hot—and soda biscuits, and to share tales of unreasonable employers and unforth-coming relatives.

After the cacophonies of the Wainwright household, the serenity of Lady Daphne's establishment was a relief to the dazed Elizabeth.

Too much had happened too quickly from the moment the farmer's gig deposited her on her uncle's doorstep. Now there seemed time to breathe, to gather her forces before facing what she knew would prove to be an ordeal that evening. Between Lady DeLacey and Miss Witherspoon (who had stuck her head out the drawing room door to announce her intention of attending the betrothal rout no matter who proclaimed the contrary), and the certain presence of such luminar-ies as Lady Jersey and Mrs. Drummond-Burrell (who, by her very bearing and cold arrogance, defined the term "high-stickler"), disaster would be but a breath away the entire evening.

Lady Daphne instructed an upstairs maid to see to the unpacking of Elizabeth's effects and the pressing of the exquisite silver and white gown touched with deepest blue intended for that evening's festivities. Then she penned a pair of notes, informing Louisa and Richard DeLacey of Elizabeth's change of domicile. It was with a sense of relief that she at last retreated to the cozy little rose-tinted parlor at the back of the house, ensconced herself among multitudes of plump pillows on her favorite chaise-lounge, kicked off her half-boots, wiggled her toes, and requested tea and ratafia biscuits for them both.

"No need to start your preparations *just* yet," she twinkled at Elizabeth as soon as the order was given. "Too much prinking results in a lacquered look which

I *do not* want you to have. Better a curl or two out of place, and the appearance of naturalness."

The parlor door flew open before the words were fairly said. The maid quivered there, a mass of palest blue and white dripping over her arm, her eyes flashing.

"We have a minor problem, milady," she said indignantly. Then, looking with pity at the puzzled Elizabeth, "Well, perhaps not quite so minor."

The beautiful gown of silver-shot spider gauze and ice-blue silk was unwearable.

Somehow, during the period between the day when it was delivered and the evening of the great festivity, it had changed sizes, the seams taken in and trimmed so that not even a wraith could have worn it. The same was true of every other suitable gown in Elizabeth's not extensive wardrobe, the whole rapidly examined by the maid as soon as Elizabeth's effects were installed in the same sunny room overlooking the street that had been Louisa's during her eventful Season.

"It's the dreadful waste I mind most," Elizabeth fumed as Lady Daphne inspected the damage after they had gone upstairs, "and, the beautiful sapphires Richard gave me only this morning to wear with it. They made my eyes seem almost blue." Then she shrugged, refusing to permit the tears that brimmed to spill over. "Ah, well," she said, "as Sybilla kept insisting, there was no sense in trying to turn a sow's ear into a silk purse. I'll wear my old fawn muslin. It'll do well enough."

Lady Daphne glanced from the hacked seams and clumsily set stitches to her young charge while the little maid sniffed in sympathy. Had the situation not been dire, she would have been tempted to chuckle. And *this* was the young country miss who had so vigorously resisted the least elegance of style and trim?

"Over my dead body," the diminutive Lady Cheltenham proclaimed vigorously. "Your delightful cousin's work, of course. And you're ready to give her the victory? Where's your backbone, child?''

Then, with a martial gleam in her eye, she summoned Holfers. The tall, angular dresser had an unparalleled way with a needle, and a sense of style that surpassed even Lady Daphne's own—not that she would ever have admitted it. But, whenever disaster—such as a few unwanted pounds acquired over the Yuletide—struck, Holfers inevitably solved the problem with the least fuss and greatest invention possible, though also with the most reproving looks. They were to be at Rochedale House within three hours for a family dinner of state magnificence. With extreme economy of motion and word, Lady Daphne apprised Holfers of the challenge.

The dresser glanced at the dress, then at the defiant Elizabeth.

"Done you a right nasty turn, hasn't she?" was her only comment. She, too, was finding it hard not to chuckle. The little country mouse had definitely been turned into something which, if not quite a sleek social lioness, was a far cry from the *démodé* fawn muslin trimmed with frayed brown ribbons the girl had just retrieved from the large armoire in the corner, and was on the point of handing the maid with instructions to press it. The angular dresser cocked her head, then smiled. "My lady has no great love for the new silk hangings in the drawing room, has she?"

"None whatsoever," Lady Daphne agreed, blithely consigning draperies it had taken her months to decide upon to the past. Someday she'd again find bolts of almost diaphanous Chinese silk in just that perfect shade of emerald that hid elusive hints of blue in its folds—though when or where she'd not the least notion. "What d'you have in mind?"

"It can't be a *gown* in the usual sense," Holfers cautioned, "for there simply isn't time. It shall have to be built upon Miss Driscoll. One wearing—that's all it will be good for, and," turning to Elizabeth, "you'll have to hold yourself *very* still and erect at all times, Miss Driscoll, with absolutely *none* of your customary twitching. But, with a bit of draping here, a bit of pinning and stitching there, we shall contrive."

It was definitely the royal "we."

And, contrive Holfers did, with every maid in the house plying a needle and Matthew and William, Lady Daphne's stalwart London-bred footmen, running errands to flower stalls and the closest featherer's. Two girls were even set to pulling threads in interlocking patterns to create an unusual matching shawl of the emerald silk. The style that emerged under Holfers's direction was indefinable: a trace of exotic Indian sari perhaps, a touch of dignified Roman toga, a smattering of naughty French *Directoire*, all combined with that certain *je ne sais quoi* that was Holfers's genius.

The ruined gown had been customary perfection—the elegant ensemble of a young girl of birth and breeding about to enter upon womanhood, the charms that enchanted her husband-to-be only hinted. This was other, entirely other. Every head would turn, every woman in attendance be wracked with jealousy. Thanks to Sybilla's sabotage, Lady Daphne's goal to transform Elizabeth into an Original was achieved at last.

Its simplicity was stark: brilliant emerald silk swirled over the barely glimpsed white satin of a hastily-converted peignoir of Lady Daphne's. Miniature cream roses set among miniature feather leaves of deep gold and emerald-green were sprinkled through Elizabeth's hair, and graced her wrist in a golden filigree tuzzy-muzzy fastened with green and gold silk ribbons. The gown's hue echoed the enormous Rochedale betrothal emerald which had at last been wrested from Lady Lavinia's possession by her grandson the morning before, its sparkle almost as brilliant as that in Elizabeth's eyes. The color and fabric were totally improper for an unwed girl in her first Season, but absolutely perfect for Elizabeth. As a bow to Rochedale tradition, they were a masterpiece.

"Oh!" was all the country girl could find to say when she was at last permitted to view herself in the tall glass in Lady Daphne's dressing room. *"Oh . . ."*

Her almost-black locks swirled around her delicate skull like the waves of a midnight ocean. The close-fitting bodice was bound at the front, and yet the skirts at the back appeared to fall from the shoulder as if they were a regal train. The customary tiny puffed sleeves had been daringly dispensed with, golden kid gloves soaring to far above the girl's elbows. Tiny deep-green sandals with golden ties peeped beneath the hem.

"Holfers," she choked, "I don't know what to say," as tears filled her eyes.

"Well, don't turn into a watering-pot," the starched-up dresser retorted tartly. "Won't do to have red-rimmed eyes. They'll clash with the green and ruin all our hard work. Best thanks you can give is to look that vixen of a cousin of yours in the eye and watch her shrivel. A pity about the sapphires, but I'm sure his lordship will understand. They simply won't do with this thing we've contrived."

While Miss Sybilla Wainwright did not precisely shrivel when Lady Daphne and Elizabeth entered the state drawing room of Rochedale House only slightly past the appointed hour, she did waver.

Sybilla sported a new gown of stylish cut and plunging décolletage, its gold satin underdress covered by an overdress of deepest gold-shot garnet spider gauze embroidered with golden roses. A wreath of gilded roses

sprinkled with *faux* garnets and gilt beads and twined
with garnet ribbons peeked from among her curls, garnet and gold plumes soaring above. Gilt and spangled
garnet fan, deeply fringed shawl of garnet-embroidered
gold silk, gold-beaded reticule, garnet parure purloined
from her mother's jewel box—each individually was of
the utmost elegance. Indeed, except for the colors and
neckline, her toilette was almost identical to that originally intended for her cousin.

The change in color and neckline, however, and the
addition of plumes and an excess of jewels, had made
for a drastic change in the character of the ensemble.
Now it resembled nothing so much as a costume
intended for a performance at Astley's Amphitheater.

And Elizabeth? Beside her fresh, glowing elegance,
Sybilla's flamboyance became tawdry indeed.

Lady Daphne shot a triumphant glance at her old
friend the dowager countess. Lady Lavinia sniffed and
turned her head, ignoring the new arrivals beyond a
loud comment concerning the discourtesy of lateness
as Willie, ever irrepressible, darted up to his sister. Then
he took a second look, and his eyes widened.

"*Garn!*" he said. "If you ain't become grand, Lizbeth!"

"I'm just your same old sister," she twinkled, then at
the boy's look of distressed awe sank to her knees and
gathered him in her arms, ignoring the pricking of
countless tiny pins. "It's just the gown," she said consol-
ingly, giving him a hug and a kiss. "I haven't changed
one whit underneath, and I never shall. Look at *you*,
fine as sixpence and twice as bright! Yet you're still my
dearest Willie, aren't you?"

Lady Lavinia shot *her* triumphant glance at Lady
Daphne. Lady Daphne merely smiled as DeLacey, with
a hasty apology to Lord Wainwright and Ned Connardsleigh, limped over to his betrothed, his cane striking

the floor sharply. He held out his hand. She placed hers in it, rising lightly to her feet. Then, hand still in his, she swept him a deep curtsy.

"My Lord DeLacey," she said.

"Miss Driscoll," he whispered with an answering bow, his eyes glowing their own private message, "I *told* you you were beautiful."

"*Mush!*" proclaimed Willie of the sharp ears. "Don't go all milk-n-treacle—*please!* This is *supposed* to be a party, and we're *supposed* to have fun—least that's what the duke said—and nobody'll have any fun if you're going to be like *that.*"

Elizabeth and the Earl of Rochedale obligingly stopped being "like that," though the earl tucked her hand in the crook of his arm and refused to release her from his side. If his grandmother was infuriated by his rearrangement of the table seating—though this dinner before the rout had been intended for family and closest friends only, she had interpreted this to mean she could invite whomever she pleased, and had requested the presence of Lady Serena Duchesne—*that* was the old lady's concern.

The dinner passed, if not in precisely the jollity Willie anticipated, at least with a minimum of contretemps.

Miss Witherspoon *did* comment loudly on Elizabeth's slight figure and the probability such a titless, scrawny plucked chicken would never be capable of producing the Rochedale heir. She also, quite loudly and with considerable anatomical detail, extolled the attributes of her great-nephew's daughter as a brood mare, to the immense gratification of that young lady and the equally immense mortification of her parents.

If the rest of his guests chuckled, the earl retained his poise and his bride-to-be her *sang-froid.*

Lady Lavinia *did* ostensibly ignore each and every one of the Wainwright and Driscoll contingents, passing her

time in commenting to Lady Serena on the magnificence of DeLacey's various estates and his right to aspire
to the hand of even a *duke's* eldest daughter. She also
managed to comment upon children—especially dirty,
nasty, loud young ruffians—not belonging in polite
company; upon country upstarts; upon vulgar mushrooms; upon the illustrious Rochedale ancestry—there
was royalty there, if only French, and only on the wrong
side of the blanket—in the loudest possible tones.

Lady Serena Duchesne, in her turn, spoke equally
loudly at the bloodlines of her dogs, their diets, their
idiosyncrasies, their illnesses, the excitement of their
birthings and the agonies of their deaths, employing a
fidelity to anatomical detail that garnered an approving
nod from Miss Witherspoon. If Lady Lavinia found her
conversation lacking, her assertive voice unappealing,
her *démodé* yellow satin gown with its tarnished gold
beading hideous, and her perfume (a heavy mixture of
musk and attar of roses) unsettling, she gave no indication of it.

And if, in her turn, Lady Serena found the dowager
countess a self-consequential, acid-tongued, encroach-
ing cipher of little intellect and less grace, and toadying
into the bargain, there was no indication of that either.
Her eyes did dart to one or another of the Driscoll
boys with considerable amusement on occasion, but her
glances were so fleeting no one noticed them. So were
the considering looks with which she observed the
young ladies and gentlemen present. That her responses
to Lady Lavinia when that lady was holding forth on
one topic or another were rather abstracted, that her
attention might perhaps be elsewhere, never occurred
to her fellow guests, let alone to her hostess.

Lucinda Connardsleigh, in Town to take part in the
coming wedding, oblivious to the undercurrents and
thrilled at the prospect of being a bridesmaid, prattled

happily with Elizabeth's brothers of watercolors and Greek ruins and the breeding of horses. As for her parents and great-grandmother and the rest of the company, they watched and listened with no little amusement as Sybilla Wainwright desperately attempted to set up flirts with first the indifferent earl, then the unresponsive Harry and finally the highly embarrassed Giles, cut her cousins and Patsy Worth at every opportunity, and sprinkled her conversation with so many French phrases that she became totally incomprehensible.

At the head of the table, with the Duchess of Rawdon on his one side and his bride-to-be on the other, DeLacey determinedly ignored his grandmother at the foot and exerted himself to play the welcoming host.

There had been no further discussion of the scene in the state drawing room the morning before. The carpet, the candles, the livery had all been disposed of, the descriptions of the four ruffians sent round to Bow Street, and—after some consideration—to Jason Ventriss of the Horse Guards. That should be the end of it. In two weeks' time he and Elizabeth would be gone, and Lady Lavinia could play any games she desired so long as they impinged on neither his wife's comfort, nor his own.

At last, at a signal from his grandmother, the ladies retired leaving the gentlemen to their port and brandy and cigarillos. And, then began perhaps the longest, the most miserable night of Elizabeth's existence.

The caterers from Gunter's had spread their magnificence upon trestle tables in the ballroom, complete with intricate cherubbed champagne fountains and fanciful ice sculptures of Love the Supplicant and Love the Conqueror.

Sumptuous arrangements of flowers and forests of potted palms were as lavish as on the night when Elizabeth rescued the earl. Sparkling crystal chandeliers again shattered the light into thousands of rainbows. The same dais (with the three others that matched it) employed by Lady Lavinia the morning before as an emblem of the semidivine right of interfering grand-mothers to arrange their feckless grandsons' lives to their liking was now banked with flowers, and held the small orchestra providing music for the evening. Marble floors gleamed. Candles glowed. The air was redolent with the heady scent of roses. Everything was as perfect and as ostentatious as wealth could make it.

The gentlemen joined them in minutes. The first guests would be arriving at any moment. Private guards waited below to sort out the anticipated crush of car-riages. Extra footmen waited at the bottom of the rotunda stairs to see to capes and cloaks and hats and canes. More footmen lined the stairways. Eros stood poised on his marble toe in the embrasure between the flights, ready to send his darts flying at the unwary. The flambeaux were lit by the door, the canopy erected, the red carpet laid from the imposing marble portico down the outside steps and across the paved courtyard to where the carriages would deposit their aristocratic pas-sengers. No lady would soil dainty hem or delicate slip-pers that night.

The earl signaled the orchestra to begin and accepted a glass of champagne from a bowing lackey. The spar-kling strains of a Mozart *divertimento* echoed across the high ceilings and through the empty reception area. It danced between marble pillars and played among gilded carvings. It whispered among palm fronds and roses, and stirred the draperies, and circled the great stained-glass dome.

They waited.

Mozart became Handel.

And they waited.

Handel gave way to Monteverdi.

And, still they waited.

Monteverdi yielded pride of place to Haydn.

Lady Lavinia avoided Lady Daphne's accusing eye and made much of Serena Duchesne. Sybilla smirked. *Plan B* (Great-Aunt Witherspoon) might not have succeeded, and *Plan A* (the letter to Devonshire) definitely had not, but it seemed *Plan C* was all she could have desired. Millicent Farquhar was truly the most *useful* acquaintance. That she was giving herself far too much credit, that her *Plan C* had been Lady Lavinia's *First Scheme* she had no notion, nor would she have particularly cared.

Mortified, certain what was occurring, Elizabeth had but a single desire—to take French leave of the palatial residence of the Earls of Rochedale and never see London again. Instead she held her head high, ignoring the pins that pricked if she moved too precipitously, and chattered with determined gaiety as she clutched DeLacey's arm.

An hour passed and part of another. The hired orchestra, its repertoire exhausted, once again assaulted Mozart.

"Good heavens," Lucinda asked in an undertone of her great-grandmother, "don't they know anything else?"

"I doubt they've ever needed to," Lady Charlotte whispered back. "Normally one can't hear a thing at these do's, and the guests are forever changing in any case."

Willie and Steven, exhausted by their day's excursion to the Royal Menagerie, found the little settee in DeLacey's study, curled up and went to sleep.

Lucinda, increasingly puzzled by the strange celebration, did her best to entertain Robert and Andrew and Jeremy, occasionally throwing anxious glances in her parents' direction. Finally, when the three boys wandered off to help themselves to more punch and lobster patties, she sped to where the young half-pay lieutenant with ginger hair and sidewhiskers and the customarily bubbling Miss Worth were conversing in low voices.

"Please," she said haltingly when they turned to her, "what should I do? Miss Driscoll looks ready to bolt, and I've an inclination much in the same direction myself. This is the most *uncomfortable* evening I've spent in my life, and while my life may not have been a *long* one, if you knew the boarding school I attended for some years in Yorkshire, you'd know what an indictment *that* is. Misery was a way of life there."

"Can't none of us bolt," Giles returned from his considerable height, glancing down at the slender, flaxen-haired girl. "Leastways, perhaps *you* can, if you can convince your parents. I'm *staying* here, for my sins—guest of DeLacey's."

"I didn't say I was going to bolt," Lucinda protested with pardonable pique. "I only said I'd *like* to. It's Miss Driscoll I'm concerned for."

She glanced across the cavernous reception area to where her great-grandmother stood beside Elizabeth Driscoll and the earl. The quickly contrived emerald silk evening gown (concerning whose origins Miss Driscoll had confided the amusing details to Lucinda and Patsy in quick whispers just before the gentlemen joined them) was showing the first signs of becoming drawing room draperies once more. Worse yet, there was a determined gaiety about the trio. Just so had her great-grandmother always been at the end of the holidays when she was about to return to Yorkshire. And, just so had she always responded—as if the world were not rapidly coming to an end.

"What is happening?" she begged. "Why is no one here? Have they mistaken the date? If you'll only tell me, perhaps I shall know what to do."

"Ain't nothing any of us can do," Giles informed her

sourly. "Lady DeLacey and Sybilla Wainwright, between 'em, have played their tricks, and they've succeeded."

"Miss Driscoll is being *cut,*" Patsy Worth explained at the young girl's blank look. "So is the earl."

"Cut? But why? I know I've only just met them, but they're so nice. From what little I know, that's only done to positively *awful* people."

"Nice has nothing to do with it," Giles expanded the explanation. "Miss Driscoll ain't the daughter of a duke, and her father ain't wealthy, so the old bes— never mind that, but Richard's grandmother don't want him to marry her, and the witch in red wanted him for herself. They've spread some nasty tales about Miss Driscoll and the earl. The tales stuck, for all they're a passel of lies."

"How perfectly dreadful!" Lucinda frowned, then looked back up at the young half-pay lieutenant. "Precisely how d'you cut someone? I know the term, but I've never seen it done before."

"Look about you," Patsy gestured bitterly. "There should be *hundreds* thronging these rooms. We are a party of precisely twenty-four. That's how it's done."

"Isn't there any other way?"

"Well, you can always walk up to someone you know, look 'em straight in the eye while pretending you don't see 'em, and turn your back," Giles explained. "Saw it done, once. Thought the poor sod—pardon that— would perish on the spot! Not that he didn't deserve it, but that's not a tale for your ears."

"I see. Thank you."

Lucinda turned to survey the room. "I imagine," she said consideringly, "if one were actually to speak to someone with whom the individual to be cut were conversing, it would be more pointed yet. Well, all games may be played by more than one."

"T'isn't a game," Giles cautioned her. "Behave yourself, brat! Things are bad enough as they are."

"Naturally," Lucinda agreed, sweeping Patsy and Giles a demure curtsy, then gazing at them through innocent ice-blue eyes. "I *always* behave myself. Thank you so much for explaining something I did not entirely understand, not being *quite* out yet, though I suppose this celebration would have served as well as any as my introduction to the ton had matters proceeded as they ought.

"Certainly I must be out Saturday fortnight, mustn't I? Otherwise I could *never* participate in a London wedding. That's what Mama said and Papa concurred. Indeed, it almost made him refuse his permission, but Great-Grandmama was most insistent, and Lady Daphne's letter most persuasive, thank goodness. Being neither quite one thing nor quite the other is *infinitely* discomfiting, and I don't *feel* as if I belong in the schoolroom anymore, for all I'm only fifteen. Perhaps that's because I was forced to survive Miss Broward's. Adversity can mature one rather rapidly, you know.

"Lady DeLacey appears to be the ultimate in highsticklers, does she not?" she inquired of the rather distraught Giles.

Then she began an aimless wandering that took her past her mother, seated beside Lady Wainwright's cumbersome Bath chair. The two ladies were determinedly comparing housekeeping problems. She paused for a moment, giving every appearance of bored attention.

Her path then left her hovering briefly on the outskirts of a vigorous discussion concerning farming methods between her father and the Duke of Rawdon (who both cited practical experience) and Viscount Wainwright (spouting theory with the single-mindedness of the informed non-participant). Next she ambled past Lady Cheltenham (whom she positively *adored*), the duchess (whom she found delightful, if slightly intimidating because of her high rank) and Miss Witherspoon (whom, to her shame, she found wonderfully amusing), favoring them with an innocent smile.

That took her close enough to the refreshment tables to procure a cup of punch.

She glanced back at the lieutenant and Miss Worth. They had resumed their conference. Lord Beckenham was across the way, apparently trapped by Miss Wainwright. Nothing could be better.

She continued her promenade, pausing before Lady DeLacey and Lady Serena Duchesne, staring her hostess straight in the eye until that lady noticed her presence with an arctic sniff while Lady Serena's eyes sparkled with an appreciative glint.

"How kind of you to bring me some punch," Lady DeLacey condescended, reaching for the cup. "Perhaps you would be so kind as to procure some for Lady Serena, as well? We are both parched."

Lucinda turned her back without so much as the flicker of an eyelid and continued on her way, cup firmly in hand. So *that* was how it was done. The old besom—she knew *precisely* the word the peppery lieutenant had choked off in mid-syllable—had actually *spluttered*. How utterly delightful. It worked!

With a slight mysterious smile, she continued across the echoing reception area, passing the Driscoll boys with a nod, making her way past her great-grandmother, the earl, and his betrothed. She favored the latter with a conspiratorial smile and kept on her way, the slightest sway to her skirts.

"Oh, *dear*," Lady Charlotte muttered, "I dislike that look. What now?"

From below came sounds of arrival.

Lucinda approached Sybilla Wainwright and the desperately bored Lord Beckenham with a decided skip in her step. Then she shrieked. The cup of punch inundated the pulchritudinous Miss Wainwright. Lucinda ended up clinging to the viscount.

"Oh my lord, I'm so *desperately* sorry!" she gasped. "I tripped. Have I spilled my punch all over you? I'm such a clumsy ninny! Here, let me get the drips."

Heads spun as she pulled a lacy scrap of nothing from her reticule and began dabbing at Beckenham's severe evening wear—as free of punch as her own very girlish blush muslin.

"You jade!" Sybilla Wainwright screeched. "You despicable little bumpkin! You've *ruined* my new gown!"

It was at precisely this moment Lady Jersey reached the head of the stairs, the sole member of the ton—with the exception of Lady Serena Duchesne and the other dinner guests—to attend the betrothal celebration of the Earl of Rochedale and Miss Elizabeth Mary Driscoll of Saint Mary-Grafton, Devonshire.

Fourteen

Sally Jersey lingered, sipping champagne, nibbling at lobster patties and accepting one of Gunter's famous ices, all keen observation. Her brittle, artificial laughter crackled above the quiet voices, her sly questions as barbed as ever, her escort—the foppish scion of a prominent political family—giggling rather soddenly at her side.

The earl stayed by her elbow, on the alert for insults or innuendoes—of which there were many. Arch commentary on the presence of Lady Serena and a possible interesting announcement had the earl fuming. Lady Jersey's raised eyebrows, her initial silent inspection, her condescending "Oh, yes," when presented with Elizabeth's father and brothers were galling enough. Her slow turning of her back upon Samuel Driscoll when he was in mid-sentence was worse.

The woman's total disregard of Elizabeth's presence—except when she ordered the earl's betrothed to fetch her more champagne without quite seeing her, just as any lady of breeding and refinement never "saw" a member of the lower orders—thrust that young lady into angry, mortified silence and put the earl in such a rage that he had difficulty concealing it. Her moments spent complimenting Lady Lavinia on her perspicacity in ferreting out unpleasant truths regarding undesirables but lately come upon the Town, and placing the information where it would do most good, only confirmed what the earl, despite his personal wishes, had accepted two days before.

In a corner Lucinda huddled with her amused father and reproachful mother. Patsy and Giles joined the family group, Giles casting looks of fury at Lucinda that caused her first to gaze at him disdainfully, then lift her chin and turn her back. Patsy told him to behave himself. Outraged and unrepentant, he took Lucinda aside and treated her to a dressing down that had much of Wellington to it, and very little of the rather endearing young man he customarily was, reducing Lucinda to white-faced tears.

As for Lady Jersey's amused minutes spent in Miss Witherspoon's tart company, a swiftly returned Sybilla hissed and poked at her parents and pleaded the old lady's extravagances be curbed, but there was nothing to be done. Lady Jersey was gathering enough fodder for a year's entertainment. For the first time, Sybilla wondered if summoning her old champion had been the wisest course.

At last Lady Jersey made her departure, coming as close as she could to ignoring the Driscoll pollution and the presence of Louisa Debenham—never a favorite of hers, no matter how much she doted on the duke—and quite "oblivious" to Lucinda's halting apologies for lack of decorum.

As if at a pre-arranged signal, Lady Jersey's departure broke up the uncomfortable gathering. The hour was excessively late. It was clear no others would appear.

As his betrothed and her family and their few guests were summoning their carriages, the earl apologetically requested Rawdon and Lady Daphne to await him in his little bookroom. He saw the Wainwrights, the Connardsleighs, the Driscoll family and Louisa Debenham (who would deposit Elizabeth at Lady Daphne's door) across the cold reception area. He ordered the state rooms stripped of their burdens of flowers and refreshments, the detritus sent to the usual hospitals and charitable institutions. Then he turned to the duke's daughter in her assertive gold-trimmed yellow satin and topazes, still being made much of by his triumphant grandmother.

"Lady Serena," he smiled with as much courtesy as determination, "before she left Miss Driscoll asked me to join her thanks to mine for honoring us with your presence this evening. Your attendance was greatly appreciated."

"Lord! Glad to come. M'father said it'd be quite the thing, you know, after he and your grandma spoke. So," Lady Serena shrugged, "I said I would. Nothing more important to do at the moment. Puggsy won't whelp for another week. Did I tell you about Puggsy? Suffers from the mange. Weakens her, you know. Nasty thing, mange. New litter coming on—not much help. Offered one t'your grandma. Said she'd like it. Pup, not the mange."

DeLacey's brows soared as he glanced at Lady Lavinia. His grandmother almost, but not quite, shrugged. She detested dogs, but was a consummate politician when it suited her purpose.

"Delightful for her, I'm certain," he murmured soothingly. "Most gracious of you. However, I'm positive you're anxious for your pets."

"My dearest little Poopikins," Lady Serena agreed. "Puggsy, I mean, who's my sweetest woozy, and the rest—not your grandma. Wouldn't presume to call your grandma *little*. Definitely not the woozy-Poopikins type. But, we'll deal together, the lot of us. Told your grandma so. Intelligent woman, for all her airs. Haven't made your offer yet, by the bye. Best get it over with. I accept. Understand about your bit of country fluff. Don't stand there puffing like a grampus! I won't interfere—my word on it."

The earl blanched, then reddened alarmingly. An older man would have been suspected of teetering on the verge of an apoplectic fit.

"Slight problem there," he choked, throwing a fulminating glance at his grandmother. "Already betrothed to Miss Driscoll, you see. Reason for this do. Can't break it off. Not the act of a gentleman."

Dear Lord, he was already speaking like her! If a few seconds could do that to a man, what would happen over a lifetime didn't bear contemplation.

"So that's how it is." Lady Serena looked him up and down without a tinge of regret. "All a hum?"

"Afraid so."

"Should've known. Not the marrying sort myself, but the Pater seemed to like the notion, so I thought, why not? Generally accommodate him if it ain't too inconvenient. No hard feelings?"

"Of course not. Honor would've been mine, had the thing been possible."

"Cry *pax*, then," she said, extending a surprisingly elegant hand. "Friends're much more comfortable than husbands."

"*Pax* indeed, and friends," he agreed, giving her strong, slender fingers a firm shake, then taking her arm once more, attempted to ease her toward the stairs.

"Your grandma can still have a pup, if she wants one," Lady Serena condescended, standing her ground. "Your country girl as well, if she's a mind to. Looked the gentle sort, but firm. Be good to the pup. Should've known. Y'don't look at her like she was fluff. There's a difference. Family's here, too. Not at all the thing—t'have the family of *fluff* about.''

"Both ladies would be most grateful, I'm sure." Certainly Elizabeth would. The slightest show of friendliness had the poor girl melting with gratitude these days. As for his grandmother, it would be excellent retribution for placing him in such a horrendous position.

"What about the Wiltfork female? Woman that age needs an interest."

"Miss Witherspoon? Cats," he cautioned. "*Hundreds* of 'em."

"Lord! *That* wouldn't do. Nasty creatures, cats."

"Indeed they are," the earl, who had never held an opinion regarding the matter one way or the other, agreed. "Wouldn't do at all. Dogs'd suffer. Totally unfair to 'em. Speaking of your dogs, poor things've had to do without you for hours. Must be pining. Permit me," guiding her to the head of the stairs leading to the entrance rotunda.

"They c'n wait a few minutes more. Bit of a bother over your country gel, y'know," she said, looking the earl in the eye. "Heard all about it. You began like an idiot, and went on like a fool. Bound to set people's backs up. Tonight's perfect proof, if you need any. Sweet gel, of course. Brothers seem jolly sorts, too. If I c'n help, glad to. Call tomorrow, discuss what's to be done."

"Very kind of you."

"Not kind. Just never have liked that Jersey woman. Mean look about her eyes sometimes, like a bitch you can't trust with her pups. Had one like that once. Had to put her down. Bad strain. Destroyed the pups as well. Only thing t'do."

"How unfortunate for you," the earl murmured distractedly.

A quick signal to the hovering Banks brought his man

to his side, and as Lady Serena Duchesne resumed her monologue concerning one Puggsy's Bloom Eternal and her problems with mange, now to the batman, he watched the single-minded (if generous-hearted and socially powerful) duke's daughter ushered down the stairs, handed her moth-eaten fur cloak, and firmly but gently eased from the premises, still expounding on proper diets and the efficacy of coal tar and herbal washes. What England permitted her eccentrics!

Then he turned back to his grandmother. She was already ascending the stairs to the west wing, moving with a precipitousness that had more of hasty retreat than strategic withdrawal to it.

"Grandmama," he called softly, "please be so kind as to give me a few moments of your time."

"I'm an old woman and rather frail, and I'm *tired*, Richard," Lady Lavinia protested, inserting a delicate quaver to her voice and a tremor to her step as she continued up the stairs. "All those woozies. I couldn't keep them straight. *Mange*, for pity's sake! *Most* fatiguing, but I had to make the effort for your sake, you know. *Anything* for my darling grandson. Quite a superior woman, Lady Serena. Excellent bloodlines. If you wish to see me, you can do so in the morning."

Again DeLacey nodded to Banks. Again Banks performed the actions the earl's leg, throbbing with the insistence of a thousand drummers on parade, did not permit him. Lady Lavinia had a choice: to indulge in a wrestling match with an inferior (most degrading) or to accede to her grandson's request (most disturbing). Disturbing was bad enough. Degrading she simply would not endure. She shrugged off the despised Banks's hand and returned to the reception area, a rather petulant, sour expression on her strong features.

"The ladies' retiring room, I think," the earl instructed Banks.

They made a strange procession—the elderly dowager countess, the former batman and the earl—as they crossed the highly polished black marble floor while temporarily hired flunkies bowed themselves out of their path. No sooner had the door been firmly closed behind the earl and his grandmother than she spun on him, head high.

"Now, Richard," she cautioned, ignoring the dainty room with its cherubbed ceiling and garlanded walls and superabundance of gilded mirrors, "before you say a word, I want one thing understood: What I've done, I've done for you. Tonight should have taught you an important lesson. *Like to like.* The ton will accept nothing less. *I* shall accept nothing less. Lady Serena is in every way superior to that—"

"Then you, *and* the ton, may go hang, Grandmama."

"I will not have such words used to me in my home."

"This is not your home," he returned gently. "It is mine, which I have permitted you to occupy. *Your* home is the Dower House at Lacebrough."

"Now, Richard, don't be difficult. Rochedale House has *always* been my home."

"You attempted to make it so, at least. Unfortunately, you've now made it impossible for yourself to remain. Tomorrow morning you shall depart for Kent with Thatcher, and any of the present staff whom you wish to retain in your employ. I'll want a list within the hour. The rest will be dismissed."

"You wouldn't dare," the dowager countess spat drawing herself up, putative exhaustion forgotten. "I ruined that little adventuress, and I'll ruin *you* if I must, but—"

"At ten o'clock the traveling coach will be at the front

door," DeLacey went on implacably. "At half past the
hour it will pull away with you and Thatcher. If necessary, I shall have you placed in it forcibly. Your personal
effects will follow later, but I'll take the rubies now."

"No!"

"Immediately, Grandmama," he insisted, limping
over to her and holding out his hand.

"I could break you in two," she snarled with contempt. "Why, you're not even *half* a man! You're nothing but a pathetic cripple."

"The rubies, madam," he returned coldly, blanching.

"You think these are the real ones? Ha! Fooled you,"
she grinned maliciously. "I had 'em copied years ago,
you idiot, while Wharton was still drooling his way from
mistress to mistress, squandering every penny he could
lay his hands on and demanding *my* jewels to deck his
trollops when the dibs weren't in tune—which was
often, let me tell you. You'll never get the real rubies,
I promise you that! No one will. They're *mine.* I earned
'em a hundred times over, what with one thing and
another."

He sighed, and turned toward the door as the old
lady watched him in fury.

"I did not want it to come to this," he said dully,
"but if Elizabeth did not understand Lady Jersey's little
barbs and insufferable behavior, and the source of them,
or what you had planned the other morning, or how
this evening's debacle came about, I do. You've run
your course. Now, it's time for you to depart. Do it with
grace or not as you wish. I will not have my wife forced
to contend with your games."

"This is *my* home, and *no one else's,*" Lady Lavinia
hissed after him. "Wharton built it out here to hide me
from the ton, but I showed him! I turned it into a palace.
I made it a venue to which his beloved ton thronged. At
first they were curious. What had the little cit's daughter

done with the place? They expected to titter. Instead, they began to regard me with respect."

"The truth of the matter is, there were no properties closer to Town of sufficient size to hold what you demanded, Grandmama," the earl said tiredly, turning to face her. "The place was built with your money, at your demand, precisely to your specifications. Oh, yes— I know it all. Grandfather told Father just before he died. He didn't want you able to fabricate more legends, such as the one you're regaling me with now. And, Father told me before I left for the Peninsula. We both knew I might not return, but we also knew he might not still be here if I did. Unhappy men rarely reach the full span of their lives. He didn't want me able to be hoodwinked anymore than his father had him."

"Then you know the place is *mine*. Accept that, or you'll live to regret it!"

"My only regret is that it's taken us Rochedales so long to show you the door. You made a misery of all our lives, including Grandfather's. Why d'you think he sought companionship elsewhere?"

"The man was nothing but a filthy, buggering sodomite!"

"A lie, Grandmama, like all your other lies. You took everything he offered, and gave him nothing in return, not even faithfulness which, given his patience with you, you owed him at the very least. Now, it ends."

"It will *never* end—not so long as there's breath in my body."

"Are you willing to undo the damage you've caused?"

"Damage? What damage," she hurled at him. "I've merely protected my own. I shall do so until the day I die."

DeLacey opened the door. "See her ladyship to her rooms, and see she stays there," he tiredly instructed his waiting batman. "No one's to go in or out. Have the traveling coach ordered for ten o'clock. Lady DeLacey finds, between the demands of the Little Season and our recent family excitements, that a repairing lease is in order. She departs for Kent in the morning. Baggage wagons and servants will follow. We're making a clean sweep, Banks. By tomorrow night you won't recognize this barracks.''

Then, leaning heavily on his cane, he made his way across the marbled hall to his little bookroom. A fire had been lit, branches of candles set about. Lady Daphne and Rawdon awaited him, companionably discussing a pot of tea and a platter of cakes left over from the calamitous betrothal celebration. With a grunt DeLacey eased himself into his chair beside the fire, lifted his aching leg onto Elizabeth's hassock, and stuck his cane in its rack.

"You said I should leave my grandmother to you," he reproached Lady Daphne. "The result has been unmitigated disaster—not that I blame you. I blame myself. I should've known. She refused to accept the possibility of Elizabeth's existence before I found her. Once Elizabeth's reality was proved, she did the next best thing: She attempted to make her cease to exist in the only world which matters to her.''

"After that first night, I was never able to speak with her," Lady Daphne excused herself tiredly. "That dreadful butler of yours showed me the door each time I called.''

"I know, and I apologize. He'll be gone tomorrow."

"You intend a change in staff so close to the wedding?" Lady Daphne asked in surprise. "Is that wise? Lavinia is most pleased with them all.''

"There won't be a one of the insufferable lot left by tomorrow night with the exception of my man. *He's* never been part of that horde of starched-up sycophantic incompetents. Why, I've never been able to get a one of 'em to so much as lay a fire. Banks has to see to all my needs."

He turned to Rawdon. This part, at least, was less painful to discuss. "I may be calling on you and Louisa for some assistance," he said. "I'll do my best to replace 'em in time and have everything prepared, but knowing there's a competent force at my back ready to ride to the rescue if necessary will make my mind easier."

"Why don't I summon the staff down from Rawdonmere," the duke suggested. "They'd be more than up to the task, and Sturgess could round you up a competent set of servants in days. The two groups could work together through the wedding, then yours take over."

"Not wise," Lady Daphne countered. "It's mandatory to placate Lavinia and bring her to reason. Dismiss the staff she's spent considerable effort collecting, and of which she's extremely proud, and you'll risk—"

"She'll be gone by noon tomorrow," DeLacey threw in coldly. "*No one*, and that includes my grandmother, will *ever* be permitted to treat my wife with the contempt and lack of consideration and respect she's demonstrated toward Elizabeth."

"Don't be pompous, Richard. What she did is perfectly understandable. Lavinia's survived more than you'll ever appreciate—how I'll never know."

"More to the point, we survived *her* and her games. To you they may have been amusing. For those of us in this house they made life a living hell. My patience has run out. *Someone* should've packed her off long ago. If they had, we wouldn't be faced with the current problem, but she had us all totally cowed, even my grandfather."

"You're *banishing* her?"

"To Kent," DeLacey ground out, "for as long as it takes her to learn that she is not at the center of the universe, nor does she order its running."

"A major error. You just don't understand Lavinia, that's all. She's the dearest, kindest, sweetest—"

"Precisely how would you characterize what she has attempted to do to the young lady I intend to marry? And you don't know the half of it. Tonight was minor."

"You don't understand," Lady Daphne protested helplessly.

"That's generally the plaint of youth to age," DeLacey retorted. "In any case, the matter is moot. She leaves tomorrow. We have far more important matters to discuss than my insufferable grandmother's likes and dislikes."

He sighed at the indignant look shot him by Lady Daphne. "I suppose you want to try what you can do," he said with resignation.

"If you have no objection, my lord," Lady Daphne returned with biting irony.

"None whatsoever. Unfortunately, I'm afraid you'll find it won't do a particle of good. You know the way. Jamie, if you'd be so kind as to give me ink and paper," he requested, gesturing toward the small writing table set in the corner, "I'll pen a note for—oh, damnation! Banks can't read. Perhaps you'd best accompany Lady Daphne. My leg simply isn't up to all those stairs at the moment. Tell Banks she's to be admitted, but if he lets another solitary soul in those rooms, including yourself, I'll have his head on a pike."

They were back before DeLacey had time to more than take a few sips of the brandy he was pouring as they left the little bookroom. He glanced at Rawdon, brows rising. Rawdon shook his head and returned to his seat as Lady Daphne, face ashen, took refuge by the windows well away from the two men as she surreptitiously retrieved a lace handkerchief from her reticule and dabbed at her eyes.

"Give her a moment," Rawdon murmured. "It's

rather difficult to change one's long-held opinions at any age. At hers? Immensely so."

"What happened?"

"Your sainted grandmother informed my wife's aunt—through the door—that her beloved Archie didn't expire at Newmarket as she believed. He expired in this house, in *her* arms, while indulging in spirited exercise."

"I see. Think there's any truth to it?"

"Not a particle, but either way Lady Daphne's rather had the pins pulled out."

"She's over-wrought," Lady Daphne countered tremulously from the windows, "that's all. You've hurt her, Richard, and she's striking out in the only way she knows at the most convenient targets."

"What about the hurting *she's* been doing? I offered her an option: to repair the damage. She as much as laughed in my face. Were you aware she tried to buy Elizabeth off? And, when that didn't work, she attempted to blackmail her, using threats against my new family? That, had I not entered on the scene, she had a gang of toughs prepared to rush Elizabeth out of London to God knows what sort of destination? And, beneath it all ran her scurrilous tales concerning the Driscolls, should all else fail. Blast it, Lady Daphne, how much should I accept before calling a halt? Where is deference to that woman's crotchets permitted to end, and concern for my own happiness to begin?"

"I cannot believe Lavinia would—"

"If you wish, I'll call in Banks. He'll confirm the whole thing, including the ridiculous setting she created in an effort to intimidate Elizabeth. Turned the state drawing room into a parody of some medieval throne room.

"No—the Wainwright chit's efforts would have been laughable, had *Grandmama* not done her worst. And, my grandmother would've been suspect alone. Her games when my father first married are still a matter of minor scandalous speculation, I understand, though I've never known the whole of it. Individually, neither had a chance of success. United they became invincible, especially with young Farquhar and Aloysius Beckenham at the Wainwright chit's beck.

"I'm not certain if Harry mixed himself up in it or not," DeLacey continued, turning to Rawdon, "beyond that one incident with Elizabeth at your home. I don't *want* to know. If he did and I learned of it, I'd be forced to call him out. I'm content to believe he involved himself in other ways, but not in the spreading of scurrilous lies, no matter *what* the truth may be. Please, Jamie—make sure he understands that."

Rawdon nodded, concerned eyes flicking from the restive Lady Daphne to the insistent earl. Slowly, with dragging feet, Lady Daphne turned from the window and resumed her place on the little settee.

"I'm all right, truly I am," she said with the slightest of sniffs. "You're both absolutely correct: Elizabeth is the one who matters at the moment. Oh, Jamie was reading me verse, chapter, and book as we came down the stairs. I'll see what I can do about Lavinia tomorrow."

"Best you understand: I'm going to marry Elizabeth, no matter what anyone says, in precisely two weeks' time," DeLacey insisted with a tone so flat there was no doubting his determination. "The ceremony, as originally announced, will be held at Saint George's, with wedding breakfast to follow here. I don't give a damn whether my grandmother's in attendance or not. If she is, it'll be on my terms.

"Now," he sighed, "what do we do to lessen the damage? How serious is it? How long will it take to overcome? Whose aid do we enlist? Is my chosen wife to be treated to the same insult the day of her wedding she was accorded tonight, or will they come fawning about her in droves? I don't know which possibility sickens me more, but I *am* a realist. It'll be the one or the other.''

Tongues wagged the next morning in the stately homes of Mayfair. Carefully pressed copies of the *Post* and the *Gazette* languished unread as whispered scandal combined deliciously with wigs and coffee and chocolate. The *truly* important news of the day had occurred neither around conference table nor on battlefield. It did not spring from the Americas or the Indies or the Houses of Parliament or the counting houses close by London's docks. It had not crossed the Channel from France or Germany.

No—it was quite indigenous and, beyond those select few known as the beau monde, was of absolutely no interest to anyone.

Titillated lords and ladies smirked in satisfaction. Had everyone heard? The Connardsleigh chit had ruined herself, and she not even truly out of the schoolroom yet! Lady Jersey had seen it all, and "Silent" as ever, spread the tale of youthful disgrace with a scalpelled tongue well suited to the task. As for the set-down accorded the bold Devonshire adventuress who attempted to hoodwink the ton and marry an earl, *that* had succeeded to perfection. Each lady of the polite world was privately convinced her own absence had done the trick while generously according a modicum of credit to others.

Beyond Lady Serena, only Sally Jersey among all those who accepted invitations to the fête had breached the invisible barricades, but as she said, *someone* had had to attend in order to see precisely how the little *déclassée* reacted when she understood her insolent game was

over. Unfortunately, there had been merely dignified
courtesy on the part of both earl and betrothed, no
matter how severe the provocation—a totally unnote-
worthy occurrence.

That part Sally Jersey did not relate.

Undesirous of spreading complete fabrications—she
had her reputation as the ton's premier gatherer and
disseminator of news to consider, after all—she con-
tented herself with looking mysterious and smiling sig-
nificantly. When pressed for details of more interest
than empty rooms and melting ice sculptures, her denial
of drama was so weak as to imply drama had occurred
in abundance.

Left to its own imaginings, the tonnish world speedily
manufactured tales of faints and hysterics, of earl abased
and dowager countess triumphant, of mushroom contemptuously shown the door as duke's daughter clung
to chastened earl's arm, smiling upon him beatifically.
That it was all as much a farrago of nonsense as the tales
that had caused them to turn their backs on Elizabeth in
the first place concerned them not a whit. Only Lady
Jersey's sly suggestion that the adventuress's gown bore
more than passing resemblance to Lady Cheltenham's
much admired emerald-green drawing room draperies
had the weight of truth on its side.

Printers scrambled to create broadsides. Cruikshank
swiftly executed an acid portrayal of a scrawny young
farmwoman swathed in green portières being run out
of town on a drapery rod. By midday, the Prince Regent
himself, delighting in gossip as he did, was aware the ton
had once more defended itself against the incursions of
the unanointed, and was safe from pollution.

In her bedchamber at Lady Daphne's, Elizabeth
paced the floor, turned, paced again as the sun climbed
the sky, hovered at its zenith, and began the descent
toward night. Dry-eyed, she considered the past days

and contemplated a bleak future in which the Earl of Rochedale played no part. One thing was clear: not only his grandmother found her unacceptable. Even his slightest acquaintance considered her beneath contempt. Confused and bitter—for news of the malicious untruths spread among the ton thanks to Sybilla Wainwright and Lavinia DeLacey had been kept from her—she reached the only possible conclusion. There were two Englands. She belonged to the wrong one.

Patsy Worth and Lady Louisa arrived, huddling in conference with Lady Daphne in the rosy back parlor, and departed.

Samuel Driscoll and the earl came, both silent, both with features so care-worn, so exhausted as to arouse concern in the others.

Giles Fortescue, red-faced and sputtering, pounded at Elizabeth's door, begging her to pay the polite world no mind, choking out the history of his sister and Harry Beckenham to demonstrate how conscienceless those of rank and position could be, unaware she had already heard the tale from one of the principals. He bullied. He implored. He ran the full course from impassioned rant to humble supplication, persisting until Lady Daphne persuaded him away for the sake of a little quiet.

A grim-faced Lord Wainwright appeared as his brother-in-law was leaving. Sybilla, he informed them, would depart on the morrow with Miss Witherspoon for an extended visit, indeed might take up semi-permanent residence in Staffordshire. The mortification of what his daughter had caused, her total lack of compunction, her insistence the earl might still be hers if only she received a little assistance from those who owed it to her, had finally pushed him beyond his limit. If there was anything—*anything*—he or his wife could do, Lady Daphne need only ask.

Lady Serena Duchesne descended on them carrying a pup in a basket, offering support for them all and the pup as a distraction for the reclusive Elizabeth. She intended, she informed them, to pay a few morning calls and see what she could do once her carriage had been noted at Lady Daphne's door by enough fools the tale would spread.

Harry Beckenham outlasted them all, stubbornly refusing to be dislodged until the hour was so advanced there was no way he could reasonably remain.

Lady Charlotte Connardsleigh arrived in early afternoon, determined to settle in and defy the world. Lady Daphne accepted her presence with a sigh of relief. Untouched trays, locked doors, and resolute silences were too close a reminder of the days when Louisa and Rawdon were at odds. A companion of her own age who saw things more or less as she did was a godsend. They quietly agreed that Lady Charlotte, slightly removed as she was from the center of controversy, would attempt to deal with the eremetic and recalcitrant miss while Lady Daphne handled all others.

As for the Dowager Countess of Rochedale, she remained in seclusion in her luxurious apartments at Rochedale House, her departure postponed by one day to allow for the packing of clothing and personal effects. That one concession Lady Daphne had wrung from the earl the night before, but no others. Her own early call to see Lady Lavinia, as with every other call she had made upon her old friend since the first Rochedale rout, was refused. This time, however, it was an understanding and apologetic Banks who courteously turned her away rather than the supercilious Morton.

That night, as Elizabeth stared across the city from her window, the revelries were gayer than customary. The ton celebrated its triumph, laughed and gossiped, and never paused to wonder if that triumph were honorable or even just.

The next morning Elizabeth scrubbed her wan face 'til it glowed, donned her shapeless gray stuff gown, brushed the bedraggled curls from her hair, plaiting and twisting it into its old clumsy knot at the base of her neck. Then, head high, she unlocked her door and descended the stairs. A concerned Lady Daphne glanced up as she entered the little breakfast parlor, signaled for Hoskins and William to leave them in private. Elizabeth watched their departure, understanding it only too well, and smiled.

"I'm famished!" she said. "I hope you don't mind if I consume enough for ten?"

"Of course not," Lady Daphne smiled in encouragement, privately deploring Charlotte Connardsleigh's tendency to be a slug-a-bed, "but why ever are you wearing that dreadful rag? Surely *something* escaped your cousin's depredations."

"I didn't bother to look," Elizabeth told her hostess from the sideboard, piling her plate high with kidneys, kippers, gammon, and scrambled eggs. She cocked her head, added stewed mushrooms, two muffins, a spoonful of plum compote, a slice of cold pigeon pie and some clotted cream. "This was handy, unscathed, and appropriate." She turned with a sunny smile and seated herself. "Those other things don't really belong to me," she explained. "They belong to someone else entirely, and I've decided to stop attempting to be that person. It doesn't work—for a mouse to don a peacock's feathers."

"What a *ridiculous* statement. You're not a mouse!"

"The next closest thing," Elizabeth insisted. "I'm from Devonshire, you see, where we're not accustomed to the grandnesses of London. We're rather simpler,

both as to how we live and what we expect of ourselves
and others.''

Then she tucked in with a will that left Lady Daphne
confused.

Misses thwarted in love—which Elizabeth gave every
indication of considering herself, given her determined
isolation of the day before and the hideous garment
she had elected to wear this morning—didn't consume
everything in sight with the enthusiasm of a farmer just
in from the fields. Neither did their faces glow with
health nor their eyes sparkle with humor. Either the
little sparrow was unaffected by recent disasters, or she
didn't comprehend them. *That* Lady Daphne was
unable to believe. Yet, the ghastly betrothal emerald of
the Rochedales remained in place, a good sign if ever
there were one.

She seriously considered requesting Lady Charlotte's
presence, decided she could handle matters for the
moment, and turned back to the morning post since
her young guest appeared to have nothing of greater
import on her mind than consuming as much food as
possible as rapidly as possible.

"D'you think the earl would be so gracious as to call
if I asked him to?" Elizabeth inquired when finally her
plate was empty.

"He spent most of the day here yesterday," Lady
Daphne replied absently, glancing up from a letter
from an old schoolmate in Scotland. Her rotund and
rather dull son, Lord Harald Donclennon of the re-
mote estates and clumsy habits, had just been presented with an heir by his equally clumsy and rotund
wife, which clearly called for a silver porringer and
mug. She would see to it later. "Yes, I rather imagine
he would." *Really*—the girl was most unsettling. Why
couldn't she behave as girls in distress were supposed

to behave? Tears would be much more the thing, and much more manageable.

"Good, for I need to speak with his lordship briefly." Elizabeth popped up from the table and returned to the sideboard as Lady Daphne followed her progress with troubled eyes. "I'll send him a note then, with your permission? And, another to my father. I need to see *him* as well, and as soon as possible."

"Yes, of course." *Oh dear*, Lady Daphne thought to herself, *his lordship*. That didn't bode well, ring or no ring. Was this how it took some? Eating until one would think—well, where the child found room she would never know. Of course, the little fool hadn't consumed a scrap yesterday. "What are your plans for today, my dear?"

"Why, the same as they've ever been," Elizabeth returned innocently, neglecting to specify the precise meaning of her words. She frowned at the platters and dishes set over warming flames, then with a shrug proceeded to refill her plate with the same items she had selected before. "Your cook truly has an excellent way with kidneys. I've never had them prepared precisely this way before—larded and wrapped in gammon and then grilled. D'you think I might have the method, or is it a secret?"

"She soaks them in milk and sherry first, I believe, with crushed juniper berries and mashed prunes, and then peppers them heavily—a favorite of my late husband's. There's no more to it than that. What d'you intend to say to Richard?"

"I intend to tell him the truth."

"Which truth?"

"Mine," Elizabeth said. Then, at the doubtful look on Lady Daphne's kind face, "The only one there is. He needs to hear it from me this time."

* * *

While Elizabeth was consuming her over-sized breakfast and pretending to a cheerfulness she was far from feeling, a very different scene was taking place at Rochedale House.

Heavily veiled as if in mourning, swathed in multitudes of shawls and cloaks, the dowager countess swept down the stairs to the great entry rotunda she had created to celebrate the return of her grandson to an active life within the ton and provide a proper setting for his marriage to a suitable young woman of her own choosing. She refused assistance with a determination that spoke of courage in the face of adversity, of pride in the face of calamity. Head high, she moved forward with a steady inexorability that had about it something of Joan mounting to the stake, of Michael facing the dragon, of Napoleon departing for Saint Helena.

Behind her came Thatcher, jewel case clutched possessively to her bosom, her figure equally burdened with veils and shawls and capes, her step firm.

Behind them streamed an army of footmen and maids and hastily hired carters and removers, struggling under the burdens of portmanteaux and trunks, shifting packing crates and massive pieces of furniture, among them the pair of ebony chairs that lately graced Lady Lavinia's sitting room.

"Let her take anything she wants," the earl instructed Banks with supreme indifference the evening before when he returned from Lady Daphne's little house to find his protective manservant almost dancing on the balls of his feet with indignation at what he had observed being stripped from the mansion. "Just keep her out of my bedchamber and the bookroom. Beyond those, she's welcome to anything that takes her fancy. It's only going to the Dower House."

If Lady Lavinia's taste ran to priceless paintings and exquisite furnishings, to collections of jade and porcelain and antique enamels and jeweled bibelots, if not a quarter of what was being prepared for transport would fit in the relatively modest Dower House, it concerned DeLacey not in the least. She would realize her error. If she didn't, they were, after all, only objects, and would be recoverable in time.

Now, at the sound of his grandmother's name being spoken beyond his bookroom, he limped into the echoing reception area and across the highly polished marble floor to the head of the stairs.

"Lady DeLacey," he called.

Two heads spun. He knew which belonged to his grandmother only because Thatcher carried the jewel case.

"Please understand, Grandmama," he said, "the decision to depart is yours."

Both women turned their backs and continued silently across the giant rotunda, through the soaring portico, and disappeared from view.

"Well, that's that," he muttered, standing there a moment. "I tried. The good Lord knows, I *tried.*"

Then with a sigh of resignation, he tapped his way back across the gleaming expanse of marble, closeted himself in his little bookroom, and poured himself a generous portion of brandy. If the leg had been torture the past few days, now it was hell. Nothing seemed to touch its assertive agony.

Beyond him the procession of servants and temporary hirelings continued, each bearing his or her burden to the removal wagons waiting below. Slowly the wagons filled and pulled out, each in its turn. And the servants, each in their turn, collected small bundles and heavy purses awaiting them at the delivery entrance at the rear of the great house, and departed in the last five wagons.

Only then, on toward noon, did the lumbering ancient traveling coach of the Earls of Rochedale, insisted upon by Lady Lavinia as the only dignified sort of conveyance in which to be transported from one place to another, pull slowly from the entrance and make a single majestic circuit of the small lozenge-shaped park beyond the gates. Then it vanished from sight, taking the London road. Behind it, it left a shell— a great marble and stone and plaster barn stripped of its greatest treasures, and empty of all inhabitants save a former batman and his crippled former officer, and a young half-pay lieutenant.

Some few minutes after the last of the impressive *cortège* pulled out, two elderly housemaids garbed in funereal black stole down the servants' stairs from the empty west wing in which Lady DeLacey had had her apartments. They descended to the abandoned kitchens and passed through a side entrance into the service lane, locking the door behind them, then followed the lane lounging the brick wall to a side street. There, unobserved, they mounted into a waiting hackney. The jarvey cracked his whip. The spavined horse lumbered forward at a slow walk, dragging his creaking burden behind him, and disappeared into the busy London-bound traffic.

It was Banks who first smelled smoke ten minutes later—an acrid, nagging annoyance that brought on his old Peninsular cough and made him frown in puzzlement. Then, with a sudden widening of his eyes, he understood.

He frantically roused Giles Fortescue, who was snoring off an intemperate evening at White's. Between

them they managed to carry the heavily slumbering earl
to the safety of the extensive rear grounds. And, with the
assistance of servants from the neighboring residences,
they salvaged most of the items from the earl's bookroom. Even the furnishings of the earl's bedchamber,
located in the opposite wing from that in which Lady
Lavinia had made her home, were rescued. Of the rest,
by nightfall, nothing remained.

Subscription to fire companies was a necessary precau-
tion, but gave little security against the evils of private
disaster so far from Town in this year of 1816. The
devouring flames had been held temporarily at bay,
permitting rescue of personal mementos. That in itself
was a considerable achievement given the distance from
the Thames—the only reliable source of water following
a long summer other than an ornamental basin in the
gardens behind the house—and the fact that low wells
and leather buckets passed by human chains had had
to be replied upon. The second floor of the west wing
was engulfed within twenty minutes of the fire's start,
the central section and east wing not long thereafter.

The stunned and disoriented earl, awakened by
repeated slaps and dousings of water, at first watched
the conflagration from relative safety at the back of his
gardens as clothing, bed hangings, and books piled up
around him. Finally, in disgust, he turned to the scurrying Banks, who was attempting to direct the hopeless
battle.

"Let it burn," the earl said flatly. "It's never been a
happy house. Tell the men to see to the safety of the
neighboring places and the stables, but that's all."

Then, in a carriage sent by Rawdon, who had seen
the smoke rising from the direction of Hammersmith
and arrived quickly on the scene, he set out for Grosvenor Square as Banks directed the duke's men in load-
ing the salvaged items into hastily procured wagons.

Fifteen

How Elizabeth got through the first part of that day she was never to remember with any certainty.

The morning passed in a haze of numb determination. Her eyes registered things they did not quite comprehend. Her ears heard words which were sounds only, and not a means of communication between sentient beings—even her own words. Nothing mattered but Richard DeLacey and what she knew she must do for both their sakes. Until he arrived she was trapped in a featureless place where the world was neither quite one thing nor quite the other, just as she was not quite one thing or the other. That only he could set her free was axiomatic, but that freedom? Oh, how she dreaded it.

If only he would come. If only it were over, the irremediable step taken, and the anticipation of pain transformed into the pain itself, a thing to be endured and survived.

There were flashes: her father's face, concerned and frowning, Willie and Robert at his side as he left to arrange transport to Devonshire on the morrow; Lady Daphne, forever pouring tea; little Lucinda Connardsleigh, come so early they were still at breakfast, accom-

panied only by her abigail and intent on begging
forgiveness for the scene she had caused in her effort
to avenge Elizabeth. The child's misery was so palpable
that Elizabeth roused to it, offering comfort where she
could find none for herself.

There were Patsy Worth and Lady Louisa, claiming
the entire incident would be forgotten in days, or as
soon as Sally Jersey found a new *on dit* or *crim. con.* to
occupy her inquisitive nature and insinuating tongue.

And, there was Harry Beckenham, perhaps the closest
of Richard's friends, pleading his case, certain he knew
what was about to happen and absolutely correct in his
assessment—not that Elizabeth did more than smile
politely and hold her own counsel.

Through it all ran the calming tones of Lady Daphne
and her old friend, Lady Charlotte Connardsleigh,
totally powerless to avert disaster if only they knew it,
for disaster had already occurred. All that remained was
its acknowledgment.

Still, once Harry departed, a look of sour dissatisfac-
tion marring his features and extremely puzzled by Elizabeth's cryptic reassurances concerning Lady DeLacey's
lack of malice and her own culpability, the doughty
old lady threw Lady Daphne a cautionary look, hustled
Elizabeth into the back parlor and rang for still more
tea. It seemed, Elizabeth thought, they would float away
on a sea of the stuff before the day ended.

"Now," Lady Charlotte demanded as soon as the door
closed behind Hoskins, "of precisely what are you guilty,
child?"

"Of acting hastily in a confusing situation I could not
control, and which I did not understand," Elizabeth
shrugged defiantly.

"There's no dishonor in that."

"Of being swept along by events."

"That happens to the best of us, especially when we're

young and—if you will pardon the expression—struck by the *coup de foudre* of first love. Lightning bolts can be *most* disconcerting."

"Love had nothing to do with it," Elizabeth countered, not quite meeting Lady Charlotte's wise old eyes as she wandered the room restlessly. She paused by the dainty escritoire, toying with an ornate paper knife reposing on a stack of invitations. "I saw a title and a fortune and a great mansion and tremendous advantage to my family, and I grasped what was offered."

"Oh, you did, did you? How extremely interesting. I was not there, child, but dear Daphne has been *most* colorful in her descriptions."

"No, you don't understand. Mama and Papa sent me to London to catch a husband," she explained, a touch of genuine pain in her voice.

"That's the general purpose of the Season," Lady Charlotte replied with a decided twinkle. "Nothing out of the way in *that.*"

Elizabeth turned away from the overly perspicacious old lady and moved to the windows giving on the little garden at the back of the house.

Truly, this was much more difficult than she'd anticipated. The tale, when she'd woven it over yesterday's despairing hours, had appeared so reasonable because so very close to the truth. That was what John always said—that if one must fabricate something, one should tailor it as close to reality as possible—not that he recommended the exercise. Now it seemed a heap of nonsense, even before she'd well begun.

Absently she fingered the tasseled passementerie loops holding the lighter curtains back. A stiff breeze stirred the dead leaves around the tiny fountain at the rear of the garden, sending them to dance and scurry like playful kittens. It was a pretty little place, that pocket garden tucked away from the noises and busyness of

Town, even now with almost nothing blooming, hinting as it did of country peace. Lady Daphne called it her home wood, and laughed. Country-bred she might have been, but Elizabeth could not imagine the elegant little lady anywhere but in Mayfair and its environs.

And, she? She belonged only in Saint Mary-Grafton and nowhere else.

Her eyes lifted unconsciously to the freedom of the sky, leaving the sooty walls and roofs of London behind. Then she stiffened.

"Dear heaven," she murmured. To the west a leaden smudge of black lay across the sky as if a pot of ink had been spilled over cotton wadding. "There's a fire. It must be a monstrous one."

"There are *always* fires in London," Lady Charlotte retorted even as she came to take a peek. "A good thing, too, so long as no one's injured or killed. Clears way for more modern buildings. You stray from the subject, child. My, it does seem to be a big one!"

She frowned, watching. Even in full day, the under-belly of the smoke seemed tinged by flickers of sullen reddish orange. A big one indeed. But, fortunately, at some distance. There was not the least tang of smoke, nor had there been sounds of a fire protection company rattling through the streets. Whatever was burning, it must be providing quite a show for those closer by.

Lady Charlotte turned from the window, sought a comfortable chair beside the glowing grate and indi-cated the matching chair across from her.

"Still, it's no concern of ours," she smiled. How *obvi-ous* young people could be with their distractions and obfuscations. "You were explaining how you came to accept Richard DeLacey," Lady Charlotte prodded. "I'm afraid *that's* of much more interest to me than any fire, no matter how large. It was all very sudden—a matter of moments, I've been given to understand."

"Precisely," Elizabeth agreed from the window, still watching the smoke. "It seemed at first I'd done quite well for myself. I never saw the man behind the estates and the great wealth until just these last days, it happened so quickly. And, of course he seemed to offer the solution to all my problems, but that was an illusion. Such easy solutions always are."

"Richard DeLacey appears to me the answer to any reasonable maiden's prayers. You have a rather skewed vision of the world, child."

"No individual can ever be the answer to another's troubles," Elizabeth insisted. "Solutions come from within—not without. Upon more careful consideration, I find we should not suit. I'm the country sort, and prefer simplicity in all things. He's an earl, with all that entails. He has no place in my world, and I have none in his. I'm merely a bit of unfinished business left over from the wars, and a rather unimportant one at that.

"In the end, he would find himself ashamed of his bumpkin wife," she continued, descending into the truth at the derisive look in the canny old lady's eyes, "and longing for his grandmother's approval far more than for any companionship I might offer. I would be packed off to one of his remoter estates, and he would return to his interests and friends in Town. They would pardon his brief aberration, and we should become mere distant acquaintances. I could not bear that. The prospect of a marriage of convenience makes my blood run cold. Even my parents would not expect it of me. Far better to end it now. There'll be less pain for both of us, and far less humiliation. But, men are dreamers. He won't accept that's even remotely possible—not until it happens. So, I'll tell him the other, which he *will* accept."

"So *that's* how you intend to play it," Lady Charlotte

said with the hint of a chuckle. "And over the years I've been according honors for occasional insanity to Ned, to Lord Beckenham, even to dear Daphne."

Elizabeth turned from the windows, gazing reproachfully at the old lady, head high.

"*You*, however, will take the prize, I believe," Lady Charlotte continued tartly. "Make certain you don't gaze at Richard DeLacey with those doe's eyes of yours, however, or he won't believe a word you say."

"No, it's the truth, unfortunately—to my shame," Elizabeth confessed in a sad little voice. "I'm not very proud of myself, and deeply concerned over any distress or embarrassment I may have caused Lord DeLacey, but we should *not* suit."

"You know, I'm not a bad judge of character. In your case, however, perhaps I was. I didn't take you for a jellyfish."

"I'm not," Elizabeth protested with a touch of her old fire. "It's merely that I'm a realist. Papa and Mama raised us all to be."

"I call it spinelessness. Oh, I understand it well enough. Lavinia DeLacey is as hard as untanned leather and twice as tough, but she should be well on her way to Kent by now, and likely to remain there for some time, if not permanently. I never *have* understood what Daphne sees in the woman, but there, that's none of my concern. We all have our blind spots, and they're not to be criticized for we'd be rather dull and predictable without 'em. Just see to it *yours* don't cause you a lifetime of regret and misery."

"I don't *like* it here," Elizabeth insisted, "and I refuse to cater to the vagaries and frivolities of Town life. Like it or not, *this* is Richard's world. I have no desire to become part of it, and should I attempt the thing I'd make a dreadful mull of it."

"The imbroglio of the other night is not as serious as you believe, my dear. A little backbone will see you through."

"No," Elizabeth said sadly, "it's over. I haven't the stomach for it, call me a coward if you will. I could not bear to see Richard come to despise me, and that's what would happen. The Lady Lavinias of this world always win in the end—she was correct in that. Since Richard would never accept the truth, I'll give him a tale he *can* accept: that I mistook my feelings, and find we should not suit. We'll both be happier—or, at least, less unhappy—in the end."

"Foolish beyond permission!"

It was upon these words that a smoke-stained, soot-begrimed Giles burst into the room.

"Dear heaven—what's to do?" Lady Charlotte gasped, whirling on the young man as Elizabeth, after one stunned glance, pressed back against the wall, trembling so violently she could barely stand, her eyes wide with dread. "Where've you come from? Not Rawdon's, certainly! Nor my grandson's. It's the wrong direction, for pity's sake! Tell me it's not my grandson's. Lucinda and the babies—"

"No-no, nothing like that," Giles panted, coughed violently, turned to Elizabeth. "Miss Driscoll," he said, fire-blistered hands held out, "I'm sorry. We did the best we could, but—"

"Dear God," she whispered, the color draining from her face, *"Richard?"*

"Bit green about the gills and his leg aches like he's been on a forced march, but he's fine. Coming to see you soon's he c'n clean himself up a bit, and your father's had a look at him.

"Reason I rushed over—wanted you to know the facts first off. No, it's just, well, Rochedale House?" Giles hesitated, then shrugged. Sometimes there weren't any gentle ways or words. Best get it out before they imagined worse than was. "There *ain't* a Rochedale House, not any more, or at least not so's you'd notice."

"Is *that* all! Well, it's bad enough, I suppose," Lady Charlotte admitted as Elizabeth gripped the back of the closest chair. "We saw smoke to the west, but never gave it a thought. What happened?"

"You don't want to know," Giles said flatly, then frowned, considering. "Well, maybe you do," he admitted. "Leastways, I ain't certain. None of us is. DeLacey's not saying a word, but Banks and me, we've got our own ideas. Old besom cleaned the place out yesterday and today, you see. Not much of real value left but the books, and we managed to save most of those."

"Lavinia DeLacey?"

"Oh, she's long gone. Left on toward noon in some lumbering affair of a coach, heading in to Town. So're all those thick-headed servants of hers—gone, I mean. Wasn't a soul about the place but DeLacey, Banks, and me."

"You're certain?"

"Banks watched her go, all got up like some foreign royalty trying to pass unnoticed. Veils, scarves, that sort of thing."

Lady Daphne bustled in, alerted by Hoskins to the arrival of a guest, took one look at the smoke-stained Giles, and sank into a chair.

"What now?" she asked leadenly. And then, at Giles's accusatory silence, "She did it. Dear heaven—she did it! She said she'd bring the walls down about Richard's ears, but I thought she meant it *metaphorically*, the way that silly French king did. It never occurred to me to *warn* anyone."

"Good thing Banks was on the *qui vive*, then," Giles threw at his old friend and mentress reproachfully as he sank into a chair without waiting for invitation, hands dangling between his knees. "DeLacey and me, we was both sleeping. We think he'd taken laudanum, or else something'd been added to his brandy. *Still* a bit fuddled. Can't get a sensible word out of him, mostly. Keeps mumbling about justice and retribution and the sins of the fathers and too many generations, and *laughing.* As for me, didn't need anything. Made rather a late night of it yesterday, or an early morning today, take your pick. White's, with some choice spirits. Ended up playing whist with old Maitland until all hours. Not as dull as you'd think. Hadn't been for *him*—Banks, not Maitland—we'd both be cinders by now."

"Why?" Elizabeth whispered in horror. "Lady Lavinia loved that horrible place. Indeed, I suspect she's the only one who did. Richard certainly detested it. Nothing but bad memories, he said. *If* she did it, *why* did she?"

"You've been rather holding yourself aloof from matters, ain't you," Giles shot back with a touch of contempt. "Well, DeLacey chased her from the place. Packed her off to Kent for an indefinite stay, though my guess is she'll never turn up. Banks's already sent a messenger to inquire. Doesn't dare do more without orders from Richard, and he's not thinking too clearly at the moment. We'll check sailings later, but my guess is she's already on her way to France or Italy, or some such place. If the dibs're in tune, one can manage most anything, and *her* dibs were singing like canaries."

"But, why did he send her away?"

"You little fool!" Giles exploded. "Because he *loves* you, that's why! Because *he* wouldn't stand for her nonsense, and he wasn't about to force *you* to, either. And *you* go about playing tragedy miss behind locked doors, and sending trays back to the kitchens untouched, and refusing to so much as speak with him. You don't deserve him, and that's a fact. Sat here all day yesterday, and never said a word. Just sat there with that same look he had after Quatre Bras. Was there *ever* such a dimwitted girl?"

"That still doesn't explain her burning the place down," Elizabeth protested with a furious blush. "You're far off the mark there. It *must* have been an accident. A neglected fire that spat over the grate. A candle left burning. Something of that sort."

"Started in her apartments. Banks and me could tell that much," Giles said with an air of finality. "Carpet charred in a straight line right down the corridor. Didn't catch there at once, for a miracle, though the rooms did. Lamp oil, is my guess. Must've been sodden with it. Solid wall of flame and smoke by the time we got there. Of course the other's a good story to spread about. There'll be enough comment as it is."

"No, Giles has the right of it," Lady Daphne countered numbly, hardly realizing what she was saying. "Lavinia swore she'd permit no other woman to be mistress of the place—certainly not a country upstart. It's rather like that dreadful custom they have in India, tossing widows on their husbands' funeral pyres. Oh, poor, darling Richard! With all the rest he's had to bear, this is too much."

"I don't think so," Giles said with a charged glance at Elizabeth, "not if *somebody* doesn't go making bad worse. He seemed glad, almost as if she'd done him a favor. Told us to let it burn, and then sat there watching it go up with a little smile on his face."

"Dear heaven—at least the place could've been used as an orphanage or a hospital. Such wanton destruction is unconscionable," Elizabeth broke in.

"Precisely the point," Giles said, now watching Lady Daphne uneasily. "The old besom *had* no conscience."

"And such a use as you suggest?" Lady Charlotte smiled bitterly. "Don't be foolish, child. She'd've prevented that at any cost."

"The worst of it is," Giles hesitated, still watching Lady Daphne, "Banks and me, we rather suspect she didn't care if Richard went up with the place or not. *Or* any of the rest of us."

"One did not cross Lavinia lightly," Lady Daphne agreed in a hollow tone.

Elizabeth looked from one to the other, pulling herself from what threatened to become a brown study. She could still see the pall of smoke from where she stood, almost smell it. And then she realized she *could* smell it. Giles had brought the stench of the senseless conflagration into the room with him.

"Let me see those hands," she sighed. "They look nasty. Does Cook have any remedies below?"

"Oh, dear me, yes!" Lady Daphne leapt from her chair in a flurry of lavender skirts and flowing lace. "Whatever is the matter with me? Giles, you poor boy, you came here directly, didn't you?"

"Ain't a boy," Giles protested, reddening to match his hair, "even if I act like one on occasion."

"Of *course* you're not," Lady Daphne agreed. "Not since Waterloo. Oh, yes, Richard's told me, and so has Rawdon, but I keep *forgetting!* Forgive me, won't you? I'm just a silly old fool!"

And then, without the least fuss, Lady Daphne burst into the first tears anyone there could recall having seen her shed.

As the wind died, the pall of smoke Elizabeth had observed from Lady Daphne's parlor window hung over the ruins of the great Palladian mansion of the Rochedales like a shroud sheltering broken dreams from prying eyes. There was, to all intents and purposes, nothing left. Embers still glowed among the ashes. Red eyes gleamed on blackened beams and skittered along shat-

tered timbers, their tiny squares like so many rubies and
garnets set in a dancing jeweled mosaic on an ebony
ground. The walls steamed and crackled, shimmering
in the great heat. Smoke twined from the debris, seeking
the freedom of the sky. Occasional flames flared
upward, sending sparks flying and setting more flames
to spurt for a bit, but for the most part it was over.

The mass shifted and collapsed on itself from time
to time, rumbling in exhausted menace. There was a
constant noise to it all, even now, that had nothing to
do with the human, nor even the natural. The house,
or what was left of it, spoke. It complained, groaning
out its death throes and screeching its torment. It hissed
and spat like an assaulted feline. Then it would settle
a bit lower as some supporting beam or floor gave way,
more of the detritus tumbling into cellars and under-
ground passageways.

The stench was incredible—an amalgam of smoke
and rot, as if the earth had opened up to spew its bowels
into the air.

The heat of the conflagration had been so intense
courtyard cobbles had cracked, and great gaps showed
in what walls still stood sentinel like rotten teeth, bastions of invincibility or else spared by sheer luck. The
statue of Eros that had graced the entry rotunda lay
broken on the steps, never again to send his mischievous
darts winging. The trees and shrubs closest to the house
were scorched, blackened, their leaves shriveled or
gone. Only the stables and carriage house, tucked in a
far corner of the property, had escaped.

And yet the great wall surrounding the copious acres
stood as if nothing had changed, gates flung wide to
welcome guests who would never call again.

And the gardens patterned on the stiff formality of
Versailles remained, topiaries and mazes and geometric
flower beds untouched except for their dusting of gray-

black ash and cinders, like so many funeral offerings for the dead house. Classical statuary in the Roman style marched along the broad graveled alleys, aloof and uncaring, smut-laden Sabine captured by dusky soldier and Minerva, gray-caped, standing in judgment unaffected. So, briefly, must Pompeii have appeared, until the fall of ash buried it. Broad marble steps below the terrace swept down to the long rectangular *basin* from which much of the water to fight the flames had been taken, the urns lining them still sporting their colorful array of geraniums and dripping vines.

Beyond the gates a steady procession of carriages passed, the horses slowed to a walk, as those who withheld their presence two nights before came to gawp and comment, and thank heaven such a blaze as this must have been had not occurred closer to Town, or the wind been from a more dangerous direction. And yet, the crowds were democratic, for London's more common citizenry joined in the steady procession, so curricle followed drayer's cart and gig rolled after landaulet. Rude stuff gowns bowed to silk and velvet, cloth caps were tipped to elegant beavers and bonnets, and all the conversation was of but a single topic.

Speculation, as is generally the case following such extravagant disasters, was rife. Rumor took wing, flitting from carriage to carriage, so here one heard a tale of servant carelessness, there the whisper of a mindless distant cousin sequestered in the attics and an overturned lamp, still further along the suggestion the French had come seeking vengeance for the earl's triumphs in the Peninsula and outside Brussels.

And, the breaths of potential fresh scandal insinuated themselves into the susurrus to tingles of excitement and shudders of vicarious horror: Where was Lady Lavinia DeLacey? What part had she played in all this? Her hatred of the Driscoll miss and her determination that the nuptials would never take place were well known.

One would have expected to find her sobbing before the ruin like Mary at the foot of the cross.

There had been strange tales circulated on occasion, barely rustling through the drawing rooms and clubs, hinted at in only the most hushed of tones and given expression with only the most indirect of euphemisms. Hadn't there been an unwanted betrothal once before? And, hadn't the girl been found floating in the ornamental water still reflecting the sky behind the smoking ruin? Accident had been the conclusion then. And hadn't there been another who simply vanished? A generation back, all that was. Memories were vague. Still, there had been *something*.

Far down the Thames, past the Woolwich docks and on toward Gravesend, a windowless wooden warehouse stood slightly separated from its brethren, its doors thrown wide. Before it waited an endless line of wagons. Into the single-storied building a procession of carters and drayers and former footmen and maidservants marched as if in a victory procession. Crates and barrels and enormous boxes were matched against a long inventory, each item ticked off by a hollow-chested, narrow-shouldered individual with wispy gray hair plastered across a shining pink skull, then carefully stacked against the walls. Paintings and furniture protected by tarpaulins were assembled in the center. Slowly the building filled. When at last the final wagon was emptied, the unimpressive, spindle-shanked man locked the doors, chortled, conferred briefly with a private guard, then made his way back to London to await instructions.

In quite the opposite direction, near by the little town of Weymouth directly across from the Channel Islands of Alderney, Guernsey, Jersey, and Sark, a fishing smack accustomed to running contraband during the late wars set out to cross the sparkling wave-tossed water. Her sails were trimmed to make the most of the stiff onshore breeze. She tacked, skimming and darting, climbing the foam-crested waves and plunging into their troughs with the gay abandon of one set free. It must be assumed the smack's captain understood he was again running contraband, though his sole cargo consisted of two elderly ladies garbed in rude servants' togs, but who had arrived at his door in a light hired chaise drawn by a spanking team of lathered sixteen-mile-an-hour tits.

Did he believe them to be servants? Doubtful. The offered payment had been generous indeed and his silence, should anyone come inquiring after them, demanded as part of the bargain.

Sixteen

The consternation caused by the unusual event of Daphne Cheltenham succumbing to tears was efficiently seen to by Lady Charlotte, who whisked her old friend from the room with a stern admonition to Elizabeth and Giles to remain precisely where they were. Hoskins appeared at the open door, and was sent to inquire of Cook what remedies were readily at hand for burns while Giles disgustedly protested the fuss. Moments later Cook herself braved the little parlor toting salves, a basin of water, and clean cloths.

"No gabble from you, young fella-me-lad," she said sternly, plunking the heavy tray on the handiest table and pointing Giles to a chair beside it. "Set yerself down, button yer mummer, and let's glim them dabblers."

Given that Cook, at close to sixteen stone, far out-weighed the young man, besides topping him by a good inch, Giles meekly subsided and extended his abused hands, which he interpreted as obeying Cook's rather obscure orders. Apparently the interpretation was close enough. She nodded for Elizabeth to proceed, arms akimbo, blocking the doorway, a stern presence that cautioned Giles he had best submit without complaint, or deal with an extremely robust arm.

"They're not as bad as they look," Elizabeth murmured after careful examination, "though I'll wager they hurt like the very devil at the moment. This'll sting a bit, but the most important thing is they be *very* clean."

Then, as Giles grimaced but manfully held his peace, she immersed his scorched, reddened hands in the water and began to move them about gently.

"I'll need more water. Ewers of it," she tossed over her shoulder at Cook. "Lukewarm, not hot. And then ice. And salt and vinegar—preferably clear, if you have any. And plain soap. Dissolve some in another basin. I'll need that next. And more towels and bandaging. Gauze is best, but soft cotton or linen'll do if you've nothing better. What's in that salve," pointing to a small jar of unguent.

"Aloysius. Heathen concoction. Come from Afrik," Cook shrugged. "Used it on me dabblers a mort o' times."

"Aloe? Perfect! Most people don't understand its finer properties."

And then, with absolutely no thought to her surroundings, Elizabeth went to work with a single-mindedness that proved her very much her father's daughter. It was upon this scene the Earl of Rochedale came some forty-five minutes later, just as Elizabeth was fastening the second bandage. He stood at the door, smiling slightly, as he watched.

"Told you she was an angel," he murmured as Giles, sensing movement, glanced up. Then, more loudly, "Maybe *now* you'll believe your elders, you young make-bait. She didn't exist, indeed! What the *devil* did you think you were doing, going into that blasted inferno after *things*? *Nothing* was worth the risks you and Banks and the rest took. If I hadn't been half over the windmill, I'd've had the sense to stop you at once."

"Oh, hush, Richard," Elizabeth muttered absently as Giles squirmed. "Don't natter so." Then she dropped Giles's hand with a thud and whirled, staring in disbelief at the earl. "What're *you* doing here," she almost wailed. "You belong in bed after an experience like that, or resting at the very least."

Then she was across the room, throwing her arms around DeLacey and clinging to him for dear life, fine resolutions of self-sacrifice temporarily forgotten, face buried against his shoulder as she sobbed out her terror and thankfulness and despair.

DeLacey smiled with satisfaction as his free arm found her shoulders. He jerked his head at the door, indicating Giles was not particularly wanted or needed. With a distinctly flushed countenance, Giles eased himself past the couple and out into the little entry hall. He plunked himself on a chair beside a small marquetry chest, and cast an imploring glance at the returned Hoskins. Cook, with a minatory look at the pair of them, stomped toward the green baize door leading to the nether regions.

"D'you think I might have some brandy," Giles requested plaintively. "And a bite to eat? I've had nothing since last night, and my guts're echoing like a cave. Nobody seems to want me about at the moment, but they're sure to change their minds once they come to their senses, so I daren't leave and *these,*" indicating his bandaged hands, "are throbbing like a pair of trip-hammers, besides which it ain't been exactly a *restful* day so far, if you catch my meaning? And if somebody could give the boy I got walking Gorgon a shilling or two, and take her round to the stables, I'd appreciate it. Old girl's had a rough time of it, just like the rest of us."

DeLacey risked releasing Elizabeth briefly, reached behind him, and closed the door on Hoskins's soothing murmur.

"No tears, now," he said huskily. "The blasted place isn't worth it."

"I don't care about *that,*" Elizabeth hiccoughed, gave an immense shudder and pulled away, blushing and straightening her skirts. "How kind of you to call so soon following such a terrible personal disaster, my lord," she sniffed, not quite meeting his amused eyes as she surreptitiously wiped away the tears, her back to him. "Quite unnecessary, of course, but *most* courteous. Lady Daphne and Lady Charlotte will be delighted to see you. They've been extremely concerned regarding your safety."

"And you haven't, I suppose?"

"Well, *naturally* I—that is, anyone would!" She sidled her way toward the door. "If you'll excuse me, I shall inform them of your arrival."

"Oh, Hoskins'll see to that," he countered casually, playing a shifting game of position with her. "He's most efficient. No need to trouble yourself. Recovered from your megrims of yesterday? I'm glad. Turning tragic miss isn't your style at all."

"I don't know what you mean, my lord," she said, now quickly easing to the right. He followed her.

" 'My lord,' is it? What happened to 'Richard?' "

She darted to the left. Again he followed, blocking her path.

"Quite inappropriate," she protested, turning away in defeat—Really, this dodging first to one side and then to the other was *most* undignified!—as she tugged determinedly at the heavy emerald. It seemed caught on her knuckle.

"Is it really, minx? I had no notion. Partake of a substantial breakfast this morning? I understand you had nothing yesterday. You must've been perishing of hunger. That might explain your current temper. Incipient starvation does strange things to the intellect, even the female intellect."

Her back to him, she continued to struggle with the recalcitrant ring, not trusting herself to say more than she was absolutely forced to say.

"Cat got your tongue?" he chuckled. "I've never known you to be at a loss for words before."

"I take it there's nothing left of Rochedale House," she tried.

"Not much," he agreed. "Both wings're shells, and the central section is rather less than that. They rescued our settee, though."

"I'm so sorry, my lord." Then, with a touch of real concern, "And your leg?"

"How totally improper! You're not even supposed to be aware I've got any," he grinned, "let alone mention their existence—though how one's supposed to get around without 'em I've no notion."

"Please, my lord—"

"Your father gave it a thorough examination," he said more seriously. "No problems there. Come spring, he thinks something might be possible with a bit of surgery. We'll discuss the matter with him later, decide if it's worth the aggravation. And, he recommends Italy for the winter, or possibly some little place on the south coast of France if the Frogs continue behaving themselves. No jouncing over rough roads, though. We'd go by ship, and I'd be cabin-bound, but it seems an excellent idea for all of that, especially if you'll keep me company. How're you bearing up?"

"I? Why, I'm blooming," she said with a light artificial laugh. "Why ever shouldn't I be?"

"Oh, I don't know. Perhaps your determined withdrawal from the world yesterday? Perhaps that ridiculous dress today. Perhaps the copious waterfall you treated my neckcloth to a moment ago. Perhaps the way you're torturing your finger in an attempt to disembarrass it of its burden. That horrible barn didn't matter in the least, you know—not like the Hall would've." He took a determined step into the room. "I presume Giles informed you my grandmother's departed."

"Yes, indeed, my lord. There was no need for such extreme measures."

"I don't expect to disagree with you overly much as time progresses," he said seriously, "but there you're quite out. There was every need. I should've realized the imperative days—if not months—ago, but occasionally old habits linger past their time."

"No-no, my lord. The wrong person left London this morning. If only you'd not been so precipitate—a *very* bad habit of yours—I would've been gone, and all once more as it should be. I've given the matter of our betrothal serious consideration," she managed.

"Oh, have you? So have I. Two weeks more is *much* too long, don't you think?"

"Indeed I do, my lord, as it is quite evident we should not suit," she ground out. Lord—would the damnable thing never come off? "An hour would've been excessive, before the thing was called off."

"You think we should not suit? How interesting. Would you mind explaining your reasoning?"

She could hear the laughter in his voice, level as it was. She held her tongue.

"I was thinking we should suit *very* well—precisely the same opinion I have held for eighteen long and lonely months," he countered. "Of course, I'm not known as a hereian-and-thereian. And, I was thinking that this coming Wednesday would suit us both very well as a wedding day, as holding an overblown celebratory breakfast at Rochedale House is now quite out of the question."

At last the dratted ring popped from her finger, leaving behind a most sorely abused digit and a skinned knuckle. She clutched the ring in her fist, faced him determinedly.

"My lord, there can be no question of *any* wedding

breakfast being held *anywhere*. You have mistaken your feelings, as have I. We both became enmeshed in a situation we neither comprehended nor could control. Had no one broken in on us that night, I would have vanished onto a balcony or down a hall or through some hidden servants' entrance. You would have returned to your guests with no one the wiser. We should never have seen each other again."

"You expect me to forget La Haye Sainte?"

"Not at all if you don't wish to, but it was truly meaningless."

"Meaningless?" he almost shouted, the first trace of concern clouding his amber eyes. "My God, girl—you saved my life."

"That *was* important," she agreed, "but really, my lord, I played only a very minor role. You've made me into something which I'm not at all. If anyone deserves your gratitude, it's Papa and the boys."

"Unfortunately, I'm not in love with them. Besides, what has gratitude to do with anything?"

"It's at the heart of our misunderstanding, I imagine."

"Misunderstanding? You forget the matter of our little wager," he protested. She wasn't running on as she usually did. He didn't like that. He didn't like it one bit. *"I won,"* he stressed.

"You were foxed, Lord DeLacey," she returned with cold calm. "That's the only possible explanation for your subsequent reprehensible behavior *or* your mad wager. I demand you release me from our ridiculous betrothal."

"Ridiculous, is it? So—you don't consider debts of honor serious matters? What would Brother John say?"

"He'd say there was no 'honor' involved," she retorted. "Men in their cups must be forgiven their aberrations."

"Is that what it was? D'you truly believe that's what it was?"

He felt ready to explode, to tear her limb from limb in an effort to pound a little sense into her. Then he thought of the slight trembling body clinging desperately to his moments before, and almost smiled.

"Got to you, did they?" he inquired sarcastically. Sweet words never did seem to work with his little prattlebox. "I thought you had more bottom."

"I've all the bottom in the world!"

"Do you? Then kiss me farewell, sweet, before I let you pass, and we'll cry quits."

"N-no," she protested, backing further away. "That's hardly necessary. It's not even proper, as we're no longer to be wed."

"Since when were either of us ever proper? Besides, I've yet to release you from our betrothal," he laughed. And then, at the terrified look in her eyes, "My dear, I would *never* cause you pain. Don't you understand that, at least?"

"I only understand I do not belong here," she protested defiantly.

"Is *that* why you chose to wear that hideous rag? I thought I told you it wouldn't do, not even for the country. Not even in *Devonshire*, as I'm sure your mother attempted to inform you time out of mind," he added more gently, advancing on her, cane tapping relentlessly against the floor. "I'd've thought Lady Daphne or your good aunt destroyed the cursed thing days ago. Why did you *really* wear it?"

"It's *me*. It's the only me which exists. It's the only *me* which matters. If *it's* not good enough, then *I'm* not good enough."

"So that explains the hair, as well. I liked it much better the other way, you know. *Much* more becoming."

"Your preferences do not concern me, my lord."

"They don't? And I was so full of myself as to believe they did."

"Well, now you are disabused."

"Oh, no—merely *abused. And* rejected. *And* belittled." With each statement he was another step closer. "*And* derided. *And* denied. *And* rendered despicable in my own sight. Is that what you intend?"

"No, my lord. Merely that you admit our entanglement was no more than that—an entanglement from which we are both much better freed."

Elizabeth found herself trapped against the table where she had cleaned and bandaged Giles's burns, hand plunging accidentally into a bowl of dirty tepid water. She leapt—quite inadvertently—in DeLacey's direction. Ever one to seize the moment, he caught her, tossing his cane aside and proceeding to kiss her most thoroughly, praying his leg would hold. It did, for a miracle, and then he forgot about it entirely.

"Foolish little angel," he murmured into her hair, "promise me you'll *never* wear that dreadful gray gown again, but that you'll keep it always? I want to be able to show it to our grandchildren so they'll understand love has nothing to do with externals."

"What grandchildren?"

"The ones we'll be acquiring in thirty years or so," he said, and kissed her.

"Your grandmother—"

"Is gone," he insisted, and kissed her.

"But Lady DeLacey—"

"You will be the only Lady DeLacey who matters," he assured her, kissing her again.

"But the ton—" she struggled on with the determination of the truly honorable.

"Are idiots," he informed her, and kissed her yet again, "suitable only to be ignored, as I'm sure everyone has attempted to inform you. Besides, your brothers are counting on our excellent trout stream. How can you contemplate disappointing such sweet lads?''

"But one doesn't wed merely to provide one's brothers with fishing privileges," she protested waterily, more than half prepared to be convinced she was indeed being the ninny he—and almost everyone else—believed her.

"Of course not. Trout streams for brothers or fishing for salmon in Scotland, are merely side issues. One marries for many reasons. The best is if one has no choice whatsoever if one wishes to avoid permanent misery."

"Is that what it would be? Permanent misery? For you as well?''

"Most definitely, my sweet little goose. And, I do *not* deserve such a fate. I'm much too nice of a fellow. Anyone will tell you that."

He pulled back a moment, gazing tenderly at the curly dark head pressed against his shoulder, the face tucked so he couldn't see it.

"But, you will be *cut,*" she protested. "We *both* will! *And* our children."

"Not by anyone who matters," he smiled, "and not for very long, if at all. Now—have you more questions," returning to his previous delightful occupation, "or will you accept your destiny? I *do not* approve of those who attempt to deny their vowels, and while I do not precisely hold yours, I *do* have your given word," punctiliously punctuating each question and statement, each phrase and partial phrase with a kiss, traveling smooth cheek and soft lips and warm curving neck with the avidity of an intrepid explorer—which, indeed, he was. "Besides which, it is not the thing at all to attempt to break the same betrothal twice. Much worse than springing from Saint Mary-Grafton, or being incapable of a simper or an attitude."

"It's not *right,*" she protested when at last given the

opportunity. "I don't *belong* here. I never will. That's very clear."

"Wednesday," he said, "at the hour of half past eleven, at Saint George's. I will *not* give you time to attempt to cry off again. But *not* in that gray monstrosity."

Like any young lady—or military commander—who has done his or her best to avoid defeat, Elizabeth fought a courageous rear-guard action by proclaiming a suitable gown was not to be procured in the time allotted, to which Rochedale responded she could come naked to the nuptials as far as he was concerned, so long as she came. A soft giggle set this improper statement in its proper perspective.

Capitulation, given victory would have been bitter indeed, was quite rapid. Negotiations for a peaceful settlement—Thursday rather than Wednesday—had just been concluded, the overly large Rochedale emerald located in the water basin and returned to Elizabeth's reddened finger and the earl's cane retrieved, when the door to the little parlor burst open.

Lady Serena Duchesne regarded the rumpled pair with satisfaction.

"Thought you'd more to you than a military reputation," Lady Serena complimented the flushing earl as she deposited a fat Chinese pug on the carpet. "Glad to see it!" The pug squatted. Lady Serena patted its head. "Good Poopikins," she said. Then, "Puggsy," she explained. "Really too near her time t'leave behind. Didn't think you'd mind. *Always* coddle breeding bitches, y'know. Take a lesson, DeLacey. From the look of you, you'll need it."

The earl choked, bowed, and straightened his moist neckcloth. Elizabeth curtseyed, and saw to her distinctly less severe hairstyle in as surreptitious a fashion as she could.

"*Never* believe what's occurred," Lady Serena declared with immense satisfaction, glancing about the room and selecting the chaise-longue as the coziest spot for Puggsy. "Fire you had? Rochedale House destroyed? Perfect! Still smoldering, by the bye. Probably will for days. Went to see. Curious—always am.

"Great loss, of course, but not an *insurmountable* one. Location's the thing. Sound head, your grandfather. Country air. Very healthy—for dogs *and* for children.

"Thing is to rebuild, but to a modern style. Much more comfortable. Palladian monstrosity if ever there was one—the old Rochedale House. Designed for the Mediterranean climate. Imposing, but impossible to heat. All the crack when it was built, of course. Lots of fools back then. Lots of fools about most any time, come to that. Slaves to modality, most of 'em.

"Thing is, got 'em all clattering their jaws," the eccentric duke's daughter rattled on, charitably giving the couple a chance to restore their equanimity as she settled herself beside the wheezing pug. "Latest? Lady DeLacey tried to kill the lot of us. Had it straight from the Jersey herself."

DeLacey whirled on her, scowling furiously, as Lady Daphne and Lady Charlotte and Giles slipped back into the room.

"I will *not* have a personal misfortune transformed into a Bartholomew Fair," DeLacey growled. "My grandmother's on a repairing lease to Kent after suffering a bout of ill-health, and there's an end to it."

"That where she's gone? Interesting. Must've been someone else I saw heading for the road to Winchester, then. Besides, I don't see as you've much say in the matter," Lady Serena protested. "They'll think what they want. They always do."

"That's true enough, Richard," Giles agreed, a balloon of brandy held rather tenuously between barely exposed fingertips. "*This* time there might be an advantage to it. Rather ironic, that would be—burning down the place making all come right in the end. Tidy. What is it exactly they're saying?" he asked, turning back to the strapping Lady Serena after throwing a quick glance at the two older ladies.

"You don't mind?" she said, glancing doubtfully at the earl, her manner subtly altered. "They truly will say and believe what they wish, and there's not a thing you can do about it, you know. It's a way of life with them."

"Might as well hear the worst of it," he conceded in disgust.

Lady Serena sighed, and her aspect changed again, almost as if she were slipping between the characters of two people. The dog snorted. She gave a tight little smile.

"They're claiming the fire started two nights ago," she explained, almost the Lady Serena they knew. "Smoldered in the attics 'til today. Not a parcel of truth to it, but it serves the purpose. *She's* the villain of the piece now—all sorts of gossip coming to light there—and *you're* the heroine," Lady Serena declared in triumph, turning to Elizabeth. "Pulled his lordship from the flames. Thursday? I'll be there, but you'd best have bandages on your hands. Sticklers for detail, the ton.

"Don't look at me like that," she laughed at Elizabeth's consternated glance, now firmly in control of herself. "Thing about me and his lordship? All a hum. Knew it from the start. Just wanted t'see if he was man enough to own it. Otherwise, he wouldn't've deserved you. No backbone, y'see. Men *need* a backbone. So do females, for that matter. Rather dull without 'em. Point is, never would've married him, even if he'd've had me. My apologies, DeLacey, but there it is: I'm not the marrying sort.

"But you and I, Miss Driscoll—*we* must be bosom bows by nightfall. That'll put the crowning touch to it.

And the Connardsleigh chit. Got her below. Re-establish you both at the same time. Efficient. Laid the ground-work yesterday. Bunch o' fools, the ton. Believe what they're told t'believe. Hint here, suggestion there—works most times. You'll learn. To your detriment before. To your advantage now. All depends on who's doing the hinting, and what the hints are.

"So, upstairs you go! Carriage dress—that's the ticket. Something smart. Borrowed the Pater's barouche. Got the calash down so we'll be seen. We're taking the Park by storm, Miss Driscoll. In ten minutes, mind," she cautioned. "And, bandage those hands."

Take the Park by storm they did, though a stubborn Elizabeth dispensed with unneeded bandages.

At Lady Serena's raised brows she merely smiled, saying she was who she was, and part of what she *wasn't* was pretending to be anything else. DeLacey confirmed this with a grin as he indicated the shabby gray dress peeping from the long deep rose pelisse provided by Holfers from Lady Daphne's extensive wardrobe.

The hour was perfect, the Park already filled to over-flowing with the witty and the not-so-witty, the elegant and the overblown.

Heads whirled. Eyes spun in their aristocratic sockets. Carriages actually halted as stunned matrons rapped parasol handles on coachman's backs and gazed in per-plexed confusion at duke's and country sawbone's daughters and schoolroom miss companionably making much of a pug that coughed and scratched and prevari-cated, and ultimately allowed as how it *might* accept a smidgen of stewed cock's comb *en gelée* or a trifle of goose heart braised in wine and garnished with truffles if the tidbit were presented in a crystal dish set upon an embroidered linen *serviette*—all of which Lady Serena had available in the capacious inner pockets of her mustard frieze cloak and the basket at her feet.

The drive through the Park was long, though hardly tedious. There were times when Lucinda and Elizabeth wished they'd refused the forceful Lady Serena's commands. Blushing became an almost permanent state. But, it appeared to work.

At first the trio was greeted by perfunctory nods, and those nods sent exclusively in the redoubtable Lady Serena's direction. But, by definition Lady Serena—being a duke's daughter—was neither abrupt nor rude nor outré, nor occasionally given to consorting with those who were beneath notice. She was merely an eccentric maiden lady of great personal wealth, rather unusual habits, and idiosyncratic speech. Her umbrella of protection sheltered those in her company, so that distant acknowledgments began to be accorded Lucinda and even Elizabeth, accompanied by not a few impertinently curious stares.

Then Mrs. Drummond-Burrell, who was sharing her carriage with the almost equally self-important Princess de Lieven, wife of the Russian ambassador, paused in her stately circuit and inclined her head.

"Lady Serena, always a pleasure," she intoned, eyes darting from the duke's daughter to her companions as the dark-haired princess pretended boredom, observant eyes almost hidden beneath lowered lids. "You'll be so kind as to pay your charming father my respects, naturally. Tell his grace to call on me. No need to wait for one of my at-homes. Always glad to receive him."

"Rather busy, the Pater," Lady Serena returned, "but I'll see what I c'n do. Nice of you to think of him. Doesn't go about much though, you know. No liking for the social round. Waste of time, he says."

Mrs. Drummond-Burrell's eyes narrowed, seeking insult. She found it, glossed over it as mere abruptness of speech, raised her nose higher, and gazed down its considerable length at Lady Serena's companions.

"Miss Driscoll, isn't it?" she announced after due

consideration. "Quite recovered from your late indisposition, I see." She leaned forward, nose twitching. Elizabeth inclined her head. "And, what is the latest news concerning Rochedale House? Is it a complete loss, as I have been told, or was anything able to be saved? I haven't been past myself, you understand, not being prey to common curiosity."

"Not much left," Lady Serena informed their inquisitress when it became clear Elizabeth did not intend to respond. "Stopped by earlier."

"Ah—you have been in communication with his lordship, then, Lady Serena?" the Burrell inquired with a hungry, insinuating cast in her eyes.

"Miss Driscoll has," Lady Serena corrected, enjoying herself hugely. "Or rather, he's been in communication with *her. Close* communication."

"Ah?" Mrs. Drummond-Burrell's eyes shifted coldly to Elizabeth. "His lordship is uninjured?"

Lady Serena gave Elizabeth a swift poke with her elbow.

"Oh, yes, madam," Elizabeth returned as Lucinda stifled a giggle. "Lord DeLacey is in the best of health despite the tragedy."

"And the betrothal remains, ah, in place?"

"Wouldn't have it any other way," Lady Serena interjected quickly before the words trembling on Elizabeth's lips could be uttered. "Never any question. Rather forceful, DeLacey, when he wants."

"But I understood from Lady Lavinia DeLacey that *you*, Lady Serena, were to—"

Lady Serena guffawed. "Took you in too, did she?" the duke's daughter grinned. "A passel of nonsense. Wouldn't have him if he asked. Why, he's almost a member of the infantry, compared to me. Pleasant acquaintance, but—"

"I see. Pity. Plans to rebuild?" Again the untitled but

distinctly aristocratic nose twitched, very much in the manner of that of a hound on the scent.

"Advised him to. Excellent location."

"Oh, hardly that," Mrs. Drummond-Burrell demurred with another sniff. "Hammersmith? Not the thing at all. Mercantile pollution in the environs, and lamentably bucolic. One of the established squares of Mayfair would be *much* more in keeping with DeLacey's position. Sell the other place, or put in housing for the middling sort. Doctors and solicitors and such. Lease the places out. Excellent investment. Tell his lordship I said so," she instructed Elizabeth firmly, rapping on her coachman's back with the handle of her parasol. "Rebuild in Hammersmith? Out of the question, now the place's burned down. Highly inconvenient paying calls all the way out there. Proceed," she commanded in her stentorian voice.

"Healthy, though," Lady Serena called after Mrs. Drummond-Burrell's retreating carriage. "Country's always healthier than Town. 'Course, he'll do precisely as he wishes. Always does."

"Oh, dear—d'you think I shall *ever* accustom myself to people like that?" Lucinda inquired innocently of Lady Serena, eyes following Mrs. Drummond-Burrell's stately progress. "She's so *very* rude, and yet Mama says she's the very highest ton."

"Don't need to accustom yourself," Lady Serena laughed. "Toad-eat is all. Simper and blush, and all that nonsense—leastways 'til you're leg-shackled. Can't abide doing it, m'self. Never could. One of the reasons I never took. But, you're right—she's all the crack, p'rhaps because she scares 'em all half to death, p'rhaps in spite of it. Me, I never pay her any mind. Being a duke's daughter can be useful."

From that moment their progress through the Park was one of triumph indeed.

Sally Jersey condescended to bow and even exchange a few words of encouragement concerning the loss of Rochedale House while inquiring as to when and where the nuptials and following celebrations would be held given that day's great tragedy. What courage—going forward as planned, and even holding the ceremony sooner than the announcement originally specified. And, did they have any notion as to where she might reach her dearest friend, Lady DeLacey? She did so want to send her a note of commiseration concerning the loss of her favorite residence.

Elizabeth suggested the Dower House in Kent as the likeliest spot.

Petite Emily Cowper offered the services of her quite exclusive modiste should Elizabeth find herself in need of more than could be readily procured from Madame de Métrise in so few days' time.

Lady Sefton waved regally, and extended an invitation to her next musical evening—to be held on the Wednesday—were his lordship in need of a bit of diversion to distract him from the day's unfortunate events. She'd send cards 'round. Of course everyone knew Miss Driscoll was staying with Lady Cheltenham, but where was Lord DeLacey stopping now he was homeless? With the Duke of Rawdon until the wedding in three days' time? Well, *naturally* she would invite their graces as well, and Baron Hawls, should he be so inclined, though she didn't quite believe all those little boys she'd heard mention of would enjoy such an evening, and might do better remaining at Rawdon House. Active boys and music did *not* mix well.

Mothers made certain to present their fluttering daughters to the soon-to-be countess, anxious for invitations to prospective balls and routs and fêtes, wherever they might be held. These young ladies simpered and dimpled and curtseyed or bowed on cue, every bit as

anxious to partake of future treats as their mothers were
for them.

Young Corinthians and fops and dandies on the strut,
and rather more undistinguished young men of the less
easily identifiable but perhaps steadier sort, tipped hats
and bowed and proffered courteous greetings and carefully phrased compliments, eyeing the not-quite-out
Lucinda with interest.

Elizabeth was established as a lovely and unpreten-
tious country original from one of the best old families—the Hawls of Hawlsey Manor in Suffolk, matrons
whispered behind gloved hands, and her mother the
granddaughter of an earl. And so dreadfully abused by
that horrid old harridan, Lavinia DeLacey. They'd
always known something wasn't quite right there, but
she'd been so powerful they hadn't quite dared say so.
As for the Wainwright chit, everyone knew what *she* was!
And the little Farquhar girl? Oh, she was a wet-goose
if ever there were one, gobbling up gossip and then
spreading it with the air of one starved for excitement.
The tales about the Earl of Rochedale's fiancée must've
been spiteful fabrications after all—a disappointment,
perhaps, but then the fire and Lavinia DeLacey's banish-
ment were *far* more interesting.

As for Miss Lucinda Connardsleigh, she was a sweet
young thing. Father a war hero of some sort before he
sold out—not that that counted for much these days.
But, he was a crony of Rawdon's. The child just might
take in a few years despite that outlandish fly-away hair
and overly slender figure. The matter of her disrespectful behavior the night of the failed betrothal celebration
had to have been exaggerated. Grandmother was Lady
Charlotte Connardsleigh, after all. And, her father had
a tidy little property in Kent. Rather an agricultural
experimenter along the lines of Townshend or Russell,
though nothing quite so extensive, naturally.

And, added mothers with unwed sons, the girl would come into a tidy sum on her marriage or her majority, whichever came first. *Extremely* well-dowered as well, if the *on dits* were to be believed. Well worth cultivating, though it was early days yet.

"Can it be so easy?" Elizabeth demanded as they exited the Park gates at last. "It all seems a bit anticlimactic, somehow. Why, yesterday not a one of those people would have deigned to notice my existence."

"Fickle, that's the ton," Lady Serena smiled, nodding. "Told you so earlier. Burning of Rochedale House's *much* more interesting than a broken betrothal. And then, most of 'em never liked Lavinia DeLacey to begin with. Scared to death of her. Like me a sight more. *I'm* not the least intimidating, you see. So, I spread a few tales of my own. Rather good at it when the need arises. Important thing is, now *you'll* control the invitation lists to Rochedale House. They'll come fawning it in droves, for that's what matters to 'em, no matter whether you build in Mayfair or Hammersmith."

"I've been foolish, haven't I," Elizabeth admitted in a small voice.

"Infinitely. See you learn a little wisdom. There'll be babes depending on you in a bit. Hate to see you make a mull of their lives the way you almost did of your own."

"But, they *cut* Miss Driscoll," Lucinda protested. "Are we supposed to pretend that never happened?"

"That's what they'll do—that, or claim it was all a misunderstanding. Wisest thing all around: *Least said, soonest mended.*"

Well satisfied with herself, Lady Serena deposited both girls at Lady Daphne's door and drove off into the lingering sunset. It had been, she decided, a worthwhile rescue exercise, and wondered when her next opportunity to play social Samaritan would come. Life was occasionally rather dull.

* * *

Elizabeth made no further attempts to play the self-sacrificing jilt.

The Rochedale-Driscoll nuptials were held on the Thursday specified by the earl at the hour of half past eleven, and the bells of Saint George's pealed with all the joy of which they were capable.

The bride, in rose silk and blond lace and carrying a simple nosegay of cream and pink roses, was almost beautiful, and as radiant as a bride ought to be. The groom was tall and proud, his limp in no way marring the joyously triumphant glow in his eyes, and if he was not precisely handsome, he was something better—a gentleman of strength and character.

Groomsman and bridesmaids performed their functions with aplomb, and not the slightest altercation. The bride's exuberant brothers were unaccustomedly still for the few short minutes their sister stood at the altar, awed by the church, the ceremony, the fact that they were acquiring such a very desirable brother. It wasn't just the trout stream made him so, as Willie whispered to Stevie behind a slightly grubby hand. When Richard DeLacey's mouth smiled, his eyes smiled as well, just like their father's and Uncle Woodruff's, and everyone knew what jolly sorts *they* were.

It was, all agreed who were fortunate enough to attend the ceremony at Saint George's and the wedding breakfast that followed at Rawdon House, perhaps not the most *fashionable* of weddings—not with all those little boys dashing about and treading on toes—but the deep love glowing in the eyes of the Earl of Rochedale and his new countess made it one of the loveliest.

If Patsy Worth shed a quiet tear of envy among all those of joy, few there would have blamed her. And, if Harry Beckenham had all he could do to keep from throwing caution to the winds, circling his country neighbor's daughter with his arm and declaring his love, that was his private anguish. Somehow he would find those who silently dogged his steps, put an end to the farce, and seize life with both hands—or, at least *one*, but in such a firm grip he'd never let it go.

And so the former colonel found his angel of La Haye Sainte, and captured her and made her his own, for not all the barbed tongues of the ton nor all the machinations of a determined old lady and a spiteful young woman were sufficient to keep them apart. If their early course had been rougher than the usual, their later was perhaps slightly more smooth, if only by contrast. Certainly their joy, their delight in each other, waxed rather than waned as the years sped past.

And Lavinia DeLacey? Reports were heard, on occasion, of a lady who greatly resembled her living in luxurious seclusion in a villa in the Roman *campagna*. Sometimes she was purportedly glimpsed in Paris or Florence, in Saint Petersburg, even in Philadelphia in the former colonies. No one ever troubled to confirm or disprove the reports. They didn't seem particularly important, somehow.

* * *

A French and English tutor when she's not writing, Monique Ellis lives in Arizona with her artist husband. She loves to hear from readers, and can be reached at P.O. Box 24398, Tempe, AZ 85285-4398.